BREAKAWAY

KINDLE ALEXANDER

Edited by Jae Ashley
Edited by Jamie Keeler Piatt
Cover art by Reese Dante https:// reesedante.com
Cover content is for illustrative purposes only. Any person depicted in the content is a model.

ISBN Print: 978-1-941450-35-2
ISBN ebook: 978-1-941450-34-5

AUTHOR'S NOTE

Creative license was taken with this story.
It's a work of fiction.

AUTHOR'S NOTE

Creative license was taken with this story.
It's a work of fiction.

DEDICATION

Kindle, you're forever in our hearts.

Perry, you're missed every day.

Daddy, I love you.

CHAPTER 1

June

"I think I got it," Ducky yelled over the mind-jarring, ear-bleeding volume of Denzel Curry's insane cover of "Bulls on Parade." Even though Dallas Reigns only stood a few feet away from his youngest brother, he had to concentrate on each word spoken to ensure he'd heard correctly. Since there was no way to be certain, and turning down the music was never an option, Dallas moved closer to where his software-manipulating brother sat working.

Ducky's head bobbed in a controlled head-banging motion, keeping time with the angry rapper and the menacing sounds of the electric guitar. Ducky liked it loud. Usually the rap-metal music played on a loop in his headphones, but not today.

Ducky had mad skill behind the computer screen. Dallas was convinced his little brother had never come across a code he couldn't understand or eventually break. The gibberish filling the monitor was as rhythmic to Ducky as the music he listened to. Even though he created greatness by manipulating the digital language, it was the process to that greatness that left something to be desired. Dallas bent over Ducky's shoulder. He stayed far enough out of reach to avoid any potential head-butting. Ducky sang along with the fiercely polemical lyrics as if they rang true to the very meaning of his soul.

"Try it!" Ducky called out.

"Now?" Dallas questioned, yelling into the sudden silence when the song abruptly came to an end. He and Ducky both lifted their gazes to the ceiling at the loud banging from the apartment above. Dallas's cell phone alarm chimed. If their neighbors were already home and his alarm was going off, it meant he only had an hour or so before his shift at Total Elite Gym began. "Text Donny."

Hurriedly, Dallas took his seat on the wired stationary bicycle facing the equally circuited wall mirror turned into a monitor and began to pedal. He pushed the power button on the gaming controller that had been rewired and duct-taped to the handlebars. With each turn of the pedal, his hopes and dreams began to materialize. Their hastily crafted logo appeared in the center of the mirror. A grin pulled at his lips at the next sound.

"Hello, Dallas, would you like to begin a live or pre-recorded class?" The electronic greeting used his profile name, welcoming him to the session.

Dallas used the buttons on the game controller to accept the invitation. Since this was all coming together right in the moment, their business had no previously recorded classes available. In the next few seconds, his single image in the mirror became two, splitting the screen with another administrative profile. At the top was Donny, their oldest brother. Dallas's profile shifted to the bottom. Donny's Texas-size grin matched Dallas's.

"This is sick! You did it, Duck." Donny's pedaling came to a stop and his image began to fade, requiring him to continuously turn the wheel to stay connected.

"It's a work in progress," Ducky admitted, coming to stand right beside Dallas, his image now in the mirror with theirs.

"It'll work out. I need to get all these wires figured out, but we're getting there," Donny added.

"Hey." Donny's wife Cari came into view on top of Donny's image. A first, having all three on the same screen.

Ducky's excitement couldn't be contained. He jumped up, giving an all-air fist pump. "I told you I could do it!"

"Yeah, you did." Dallas pushed another button as the stats of each member appeared in the upper right corner of the mirror. The mini leaderboard was designed to be an instructor's tool, listing every member's placement once the classes began.

The next button on the controller cleared all the statistical information from the mirror, leaving behind their images on the split screen. In theory, the mirror could hold up to two hundred profiles with specific stats, allowing the instructor to assist those members who might fall behind or need encouragement to help finish the session. All members would have the ability to set their profiles to either public or private, giving the rider a choice on how much information they wanted to share with the world.

Dallas sat back on the seat, letting his arms dangle by his sides, keeping his feet moving in slow motion to keep everyone together. The impromptu Thanksgiving table brainstorming was somehow coming to fruition right before their eyes. Yes, they had a ways to go, but apparently, if a person had luck, talent, and time on their hands, dreams did come true. They were living theirs right now.

"We could eventually sell the mirrors," Ducky said excitedly.

"Absolutely. Then we could sell bikes, row machines, interactive exercise mats," Cari added, saying all the things Dallas had been too afraid to speak aloud.

"Right now, let's just focus on the original plan," Donny cut in. He always had a way of making sure their excitement remained tamed.

Their original idea had been a simple device that turned any stationary bicycle into a social exercise machine. Its name: BikeBro.

"Did you get my text?" Donny pointed to a device, the size of a small streaming box, sitting between the two handles, duct-taped to the center of the bar.

"Is that an Amazon TV box?" Dallas asked.

"Yeah. I used the components. I'm connected through Bluetooth and can see everything perfectly. I taped my cell phone to the handlebar. It tracks my heart rate and motion spin. Ducky and I can work tomorrow on building a prototype to incorporate it all into one device."

Donny was an ex-military computer hardware specialist who came home to a job in the IT department at a local hospital. It was where he'd met Cari. Though Donny's six-foot height towered over her five foot nothing, she fit her husband perfectly.

"And I can see you great by the way, very clear." Cari gave him a bright smile.

Dallas took a closer look at her setup. She had the same style black box strapped to her cycle.

"Cari, you're signed in through the social network. Did it open properly?" he asked, continuing to slowly pedal.

"Yeah, it's a tedious sign-in process while on the bike," Cari answered, pushing herself back on the seat, mirroring Dallas's stance, pedaling just enough to stay connected.

"I gotta work on that too." Ducky turned back to his computer, clearly done with the excitement of the moment. After sitting behind the dual monitors on his desk, he reached for his noise canceling headphones, ready to drown them all out. "And also work on the interface. We gotta look like we know what we're doing so y'all can find investors."

Dallas's cell phone alarm rang again. Shit, he had forty-five minutes to get through forty minutes of rush hour traffic. "I gotta go. Keep working and text me how it's going."

"Recruit us an instructor," Cari called out. "See if Skye's still interested."

"Set up a meeting with the gym's owners. We need investors," Donny called out.

Dallas agreed both were needed. He had no choice but to leave the bike, waving at his brother and sister in-law as the images faded from the screen.

Their need for cash was a growing problem. Ducky hadn't worked in four months. Dallas had to dig into his savings each month to pay Ducky's portion of the bills while his brother dedicated more than full-time hours to making their dream come true.

Ducky moved one headphone off his ear and turned to look at Dallas over his shoulder. "I was thinking the mirror doesn't necessarily have to be a new mirror/monitor from us. We could create an overlay film that can cling or hook on to any mirror. It would stick with the theme of BikeBro. The customer can use what they already own at home to get a professional workout."

"Sounds reasonable. Whichever's cheapest to produce," Dallas said, grabbing a couple bottles of water from the refrigerator and placing them in his backpack. "I've got room on some credit cards and a new client starting at the gym who plans to train four days a week. Work on the best option for the mirror and check out Donny's box. See if it's truly as usable as it looks."

"If we have to go to the bank for money, would I have to wear a suit? You know I don't like dressing up. The clothes never fit right."

Dallas had to mash his lips together to keep from laughing out loud as he slung his backpack over his shoulder. There was no world where he would ever put his younger brother in front of any financial investor. Ducky was barely fit company for Dallas, and they were related.

"Lock the door after I leave," Dallas instructed and pointed to the ceiling. "And keep the noise down. She called in a complaint last night."

"My bad," Ducky said, distracted, clearly not caring in the least.

Dallas rolled his shoulders, loosening the tension that had started collecting there anytime they talked about finances. Surely something as simple as money wouldn't stand in their way.

CHAPTER 2

March, nine months later

"They fuckin' turned us down again," Donny snarled angrily as he crossed the threshold into Dallas's small apartment. Dallas followed, the heavy weight of continued rejection slowed his step and had his mood plunging. A pent-up sigh escaped. Dallas poked a finger in the tight knot of his one and only silk necktie, heading into the living room, staring at the back of Ducky's earphone-covered head.

"He didn't hear you," Dallas drawled, looking back over his shoulder to see Donny throwing open the refrigerator door with more force than necessary. The few condiment bottles in the side trays of the door clacked together. His older brother grabbed a coconut water with the same aggression.

"What the hell's wrong with this country? We have a great product. It could turn the fucking physical fitness industry on its ass. We need cash and can't get it because we don't have any cash. It's an absurd process." Donny only took a break from his rant to gulp down several swallows of the water as he leaned his ass against the edge of the counter, his shoulders slumped in clear defeat.

Dallas agreed and had agreed with each of the twelve times they'd had this same conversation after being turned down for a loan. Every refusal incited this same aggravation, making it harder and harder to remain positive and stay the course.

Dallas tugged his tie free and absently tossed it on the coffee table, heading for the old thrift-store sofa that had seen better days long before he got it. God, he sure could use some extra cash right now. They all could. This little venture desperately needed to get off the ground. He barely got the small irritating button at his neck free before dropping down on the soft cushion, his own dejection showing in his landing.

"American dream my ass," Donny muttered loudly.

Dallas and Ducky's two-bedroom apartment was so small Donny only had to turn to the side to be seen from every angle of the living room.

"What the fuck are we gonna do? This is costing more money than we have. Cari and I are gonna have to move in here if we keep going like we are."

Finances. Fuck, they stressed Dallas the hell out. Donny had no idea the debt he had hanging over his head. He had tens of thousands of dollars in school loans for an education he didn't use and half a dozen maxed-out credit cards. Dallas's stomach churned as he leaned forward, dropping his elbows to his knees, hanging his head. He stared down at the ugly woven rug, a prized dumpster-dive find, at his feet. Between his debt, his job at the gym, and being the main trainer to their nine-hundred strong user-base, Dallas was growing frazzled and exhausted.

The BikeBro social platform had really taken off among their daily users. Ducky maintained an enormous workload as the sole webmaster of the site. The local buzz about their company had already increased membership even before Ducky had the bright idea of taking all this to YouTube. Dallas and their second trainer, Skye, had started doing cycling videos to help drum up new sales and give them a much-needed revenue source from YouTube's advertising. They were selling about fifteen BikeBro boxes a day. Why didn't any of the financial institutions see their value?

On top of everything else, Dallas had no idea how the hell they were going to manage the newly arriving inventory of a thousand boxes being stored inside this tiny apartment, waiting to be shipped out. How would it all fit?

"We're making a little money off YouTube," Ducky said absently, his fingers never leaving the game controls on the keyboard. "Did you tell the bank that?"

"Apparently, we're not making enough to make a difference," Dallas explained patiently, watching the frustration build on Donny's face. His hot-headed brother stared at the back of Ducky's head, raising his eyebrows.

"Then we've got to go corporate." The doom and gloom in Ducky's voice sounded resigned. Dallas gave a quiet huff, knowing his baby brother resisted the establishment on every level.

Donny gave an irate shake of the head, tossing out an affronted sweep of the arm in Ducky's direction in a serious *what the fuck* gesture. Donny and Ducky had an almost ten-year age gap between them. Donny was thirty-two to Ducky's twenty-three. Dallas, at twenty-seven, sat in the middle. He always played the intermediary between his siblings. If he were being truthful, that was getting exhausting too.

"That's what we've been trying to do, Duck," Dallas said before Donny could say anything else and make this whole day worse by picking a fight with Ducky. "My credit cards are maxed out. So are Donny's. We're at the end. We're running out of options." Dallas turned to Donny, changing course in the discussion, hoping to draw his attention. "Maybe we need to sell the concept now that we've got it started."

"This is our dream." Donny's tone was clipped and sharp, showing no give for the idea building inside Dallas. "We can't sell right now. Look what's happening. People like this idea. It's working. Dad said he'd get a second mortgage."

"And then what?" Dallas asked. They'd blown through thousands and thousands of dollars to get to this point. Their parents had made a kind offer, but it would not be near enough cash to float them through the next year.

"I play *League of Legends* with Chad Reeves," Ducky said. "His father's interested, so I sent him a box." Ducky's fingers never stopped moving over the keyboard, his gaze trained on the death and destruction currently playing out on the screen. He never looked away.

"What the hell is he talking about?" Donny barked when Ducky didn't elaborate. Donny angrily chucked the empty coconut water carton across the kitchen in the general direction of the trash can. He missed the opening by about a foot. Of course, Donny didn't go after it, making Dallas's inner clean freak go instantly nuts. As Donny stalked to the living room, Dallas had no choice but to rise and pick up the discarded trash.

He liked his shit organized and a thousand BikeBro boxes were going to be an organizational nightmare...

"Hey!" Ducky yelled.

Dallas was still bent over the discarded water container on his floor but turned his head to see Donny towering above Ducky, intimidating him. Hushed sounds of music came from the headphones in Donny's hand.

"What're you talking about, dumbass?" Donny demanded, angrily.

Ducky pivoted around, outrage clearly etched on his features.

He made a grab for his headphones. Donny dodged the move, taking several steps backward, lifting the headphones high in the air out of Ducky's grasp. Those headphones weren't wireless. As Donny darted backward, the attached keyboard went flying in the air, slamming Ducky in the back of the head.

"Stop! You're tearing up my stuff. Give me my headphones!" Ducky kept his cool long enough to disconnect the wire from the keyboard to protect his other expensive electronics from Donny's intended destruction.

Ducky had to know Donny wouldn't give easily. Donny bolted backward into the kitchen, Ducky right on his tail. It wouldn't be the first time for Donny to douse Ducky's equipment under a stream of water in a burst of out-of-control anger.

"Ducky, who's this guy you're talking about?" Dallas intervened, inserting himself between the brothers to stop Donny from moving closer to the sink.

"You're gonna break 'em." Ducky growled and ignored Dallas altogether. He made another grab at Donny's arm who moved this way and that to keep the headphones from Ducky's reach. "Don't hold 'em like that. You're gonna break 'em, and we don't have the money to replace 'em."

"Douche, who did you send the box to?" Donny bellowed.

"The guy that used to own Secret. His son. I told y'all about him." Ducky's heated frustration built as he squared off with both Dallas and Donny.

"No, you fuckin' didn't." Donny's unyielding tone sounded icy sharp over Dallas's shoulder.

Dallas had to defuse the battle as understanding seeped through all the haze of anger swirling around them. "Wait! You know the guy who owns Secret?" he asked his little brother.

Ducky tossed his hands in the air, rolling his eyes as if Dallas were a simpleton. "Noo-wa! I never said I knew him. I know his son…" The bluster suddenly left Ducky who stood in the middle of the kitchen, looking confused. "I'm pretty sure I told you about him. Y'all never listen to me."

"No, you didn't fuckin' tell us anything," Donny yelled again. "You know we've been beating our fuckin' heads together trying to find money, and you have a lead like Secret in your back pocket?"

"Okay. Okay! Wait!" Dallas finally raised his voice. They had much bigger, more important questions that needed answers. Dallas towered over both Donny and Ducky. He easily plucked the headphones from Donny's outstretched hand before his brother damaged them any further. "When did you send him a box, Ducky? Has he had time to receive it?"

"Chad's been taking our classes," Ducky explained, all his attention on the headphones as he carefully took them from Dallas. He inspected each side for damage as he turned away, walking back into the living room toward his desk. "He thinks we need more classes, but I told him we're a start-up and there would be more. He wants to see the mirror—"

"Oh. My. God. He's taking classes and you didn't tell us? We talked about this! We can single people out, work with them directly. Dammit!" Donny's hands flew in the air before they fisted, his biceps bulging. Donny's glacial gaze sharpened as he stared at the back of Ducky's head. Luckily, Donny took several steps backward instead of going forward, controlling himself so Dallas didn't have to. "He's a moron."

"I am not, and I told you!" They had to get past this point to develop some sort of functioning game plan on how best to proceed. Dallas rolled his shoulders to release some of his irritation. He pointed a finger at Donny, instructing him to cool off, then he went for his youngest brother.

"Ducky, focus for me. Now tell us again about Chad's father. Is there a way we can talk to him ourselves?" he asked, allowing a bit of hope to soften his inquiry.

Ducky took his seat and put his headphones back on his head, adjusting the fit. "Chad told me his dad's signing on for classes tonight. He wants to see how it works."

"Ducky!" Donny exploded, stalking toward them in attack mode. Frustration and rage clearly guided his steps. Dallas instantly intervened. Using brute strength, he put both palms on Donny's broad chest to keep him from advancing on Ducky as he got right in his brother's face.

"Calm the fuck down. And think. This is big," Dallas said. Ducky seemed oblivious to their fight, making a show of putting his equipment back together in exactly the right spots. "It's *Secret*! We need to get every one of our members to sign on tonight. We need to do a contest or something on the social site, get all the members active and participating."

Seconds ticked by before understanding sank in, but Donny's scowl finally transitioned into a grin. Dallas's mind raced at the possibility as his heartbeat drummed wildly against his rib cage, sending adrenaline rushing through his veins. It wasn't too late. This could be the answer to all their problems.

"I'll call in late and reschedule my clients, but I think Skye should lead the class tonight. I'll sign on in my second account as a cyclist. I can build a decent speed to give our members something to compete against," Dallas said, thinking out loud.

"You're a dipshit." Donny reached around Dallas to swat at the back of Ducky's head, dislodging the headphones again. The petty move was designed to give him the last word. Donny had always been an asshole.

Dallas turned a pleading gaze to Ducky, willing him not to throw another fit.

"I'll call in late to work too, and I'll go home right now to put the whole site on blast. Talk to Skye. Tell her to wear the new workout gear. I know it's early, but maybe we should debut the leaderboard tonight," Donny said.

"Sounds great. This is big." Dallas's grin grew as hope filled his heart. Donny must have felt it too because he drew Dallas into a tight bear hug. Ducky deserved all the praise for this one.

Tonight might just be the big break they'd been waiting for.

The overhead lighting in Greer Lockhart's uptown Dallas, Texas, office suddenly brightened, taking his concentration and focused gaze up to the ceiling then over to the floor length windows overlooking a patch of winter-dried grass. The dark gray sky caught him off guard. He wasn't prepared for dusk to already be settling over the hustle and bustle of his busy day. Still in doubt of the time, Greer lifted his cell phone, verifying the hour. Five thirty in the afternoon. Where had the day gone?

Probably the same place the week had gone. Time always flew in the wild chess game of his life. Greer shoved back from his office chair while reaching for his mouse to put his desktop to sleep. He grabbed the small remote control next to his keyboard and pointed it at the panel of television monitors attached to the wall across from his desk.

Now that the stock market had closed, all six screens were focused on a spirited volley, rehashing the volatility of any given security during the day's trading. He never had the volume high, just loud enough to drown out anything other than the numbers constantly running through his head. To Greer, they were like an orchestra playing the finest symphony. He loved everything about the chatter of the stock exchange.

A quiet knock on his open door drew his mind away from his inner musings. He cast a glance over his shoulder as he took his suit coat off the hook behind his desk. "You asked me to remind you it's five thirty."

"The days fly," he said by way of acknowledgement, not as any sort of conversation starter.

He shrugged on his suit jacket as his assistant, Kailey, stepped fully inside his office. She was a sassy woman who always dressed sharply and stood ready to give him a hard time. She crossed her arms, the pointy fingernails of one hand drumming on her bicep. They were freshly polished in the same color as her shoes. Every day she coordinated her fingernail color to match something in her ensemble. All the time it must take to accomplish that seemed exhausting to Greer.

Kailey was also married to his best friend and silent business partner, Beau Harris. They were newlyweds. Deeply, if not a bit sickly, in love.

"Are you signing on to BikeBro tonight?" she asked.

"I am. Skye texted, asking me to." Greer barely spared a glance in her direction as he made sure his collar lay down correctly.

"Good. They're all excited. They're doing their first site-wide competition. They're giving away big prizes—a year's free membership." Kailey waggled her perfectly plucked brows as if that were a huge incentive.

Skye had become Kailey's best friend. She was also Greer's personal trainer and latest "maybe" sexual interest. It had been a while since he'd been interested in a woman. So long in fact that he thought he had tipped the Kinsey scale all the way over to gay man. Skye drew him in with her tight athletic body, long dark hair, and even longer legs. Her thick black eyeliner—man, he had a thing for eyeliner—had captured his attention.

They had been dancing around one another for a while now. Skye claimed to have a strong moral compass. She wanted to get to know him before taking things to the next level. Greer didn't doubt her sincerity, but he wasn't looking for long-term anything. He only wanted to fuck her. The idea of having to date someone just to get inside their pants seemed its own kind of tedious hell, and that was probably why he preferred men in the first place. Men never had a three-date requirement for sex—at least none he'd met. Hell, opening the front door could be foreplay enough for the men in his life.

In January, right after meeting the captivating Skye, Greer had allowed her to talk him into giving each of his thirty employees a BikeBro box for a New Year's health and fitness challenge. All came with the added expense of a year's membership to the company's social networking site. Greer had ponied up the cash, bought the boxes, and yet still hadn't been able to talk Skye over to his way of thinking.

Honestly, it hadn't taken him too much longer to learn Skye was better friendship material than anything more. He just liked to watch her dance around his audacious prodding.

"Tell the staff, if they win tonight, those are my winnings," he teased, reaching for his cell phone.

"BikeBro has a new leaderboard they're debuting tonight," she said as he walked toward her.

"Woohoo." He feigned excitement.

Her brows shot up, playing along as if he hadn't just been patronizing. "The second and third place prizes are a personal training session with Skye."

"That's second and third prizes? She's expensive." Greer stopped in front of Kailey, extending a hand to encourage her out the door before him.

"She just increased her hourly fee. I can't afford her," Kailey quipped. He might have bought into her little white lie if he didn't know Beau's extensive net worth.

Besides, she had a regular joke she teased him with, something she'd done for years now. A joke well played and growing old by Greer's estimation.

"Don't say it," he warned. Greer took her elbow to move her through the doorway, and followed her out, closing the door behind him.

"If I got a raise…" she continued happily as if he hadn't warned her. Her grin mocked him as she watched him pass by.

"You're the worst assistant in the world. Why would I give you a raise? I feel like you should pay me for letting you work here," he interrupted her. He'd used those same words at least once a day for the last four years. If she could tease him, he could certainly dish it right back, tenfold.

"It's not my fault you literally have nothing for me to do," she answered defensively.

Luckily, she couldn't see his giant grin. He slowed, letting her catch up as he walked toward the center stairwell, leading to the first floor of his refurbished two-story Victorian style home. The very place he now called an office.

"I remembered to remind you of the time so I'm not the worst ever."

"And what else did you do today?" They took each step down in unison, approaching her workspace in the center of the entryway foyer. Her personal laptop sat on the reception desk, blocking her company workstation. Last year, Greer had blocked all access to social media sites and YouTube on company computers. The current political climate had too much controversy that distracted his staff. Work production had dropped by a third. Everyone but Kailey seemed willing to follow his simple rules.

"Well, Kate and Meghan are rumored to have been fighting over Charlotte's tights. Meghan wanted Charlotte to wear them at her wedding, and Kate didn't think those were a good choice for her little one. Tights are difficult for children, so she probably made the right decision."

Greer blinked, processing her words. He had no idea who those women were and wasn't entirely certain if Kailey had pulled his leg or not. "I have no idea what you're talking about."

"The royal family, Greer." Kailey's hand flew out and her eyes grew wide as she took the last step down, staring at him in complete disbelief. "You need to pay attention to the world. No wonder you don't have anyone important in your life. How do you not know who Kate and Meghan are?"

Kailey was insane. How Greer had been talked into hiring his younger sister was beyond him. A headache threatened to form.

He could feel the slight throbbing starting to take hold. "You know I should fire you, right? You sit in the middle of the office. Everyone has to see you breaking all our company policies."

Just like every time he suggested Kailey find new employment, she scoffed at him. "But you won't. Who are you going to hire to sit here all day and do nothing because you handle your whole life yourself? Beau takes his silent partner status too seriously. There's nothing for me to do. Hang on. I'll walk out with you."

Greer didn't wait for her. He kept heading for the front door, even picking up his pace a little. As the founder and CEO of EnviroCapital, Greer had gone to great lengths to make his own offices as eco-friendly as he could. His reputation depended on his success and looking successful seemed a false sense of security to his investors, the people who trusted him with their money.

He loved the open layout of this remodeled two-story, which he'd had gutted and rebuilt into a sustainable office setting. The newly decorated interior added a splash of color with all the living plants both inside and out. The modern furnishings were a sharp contrast to the older feel of the Victorian's exterior. Everyone who worked for him had a collaborative working u-shaped pod lining the interior walls. They maximized the limited space while promoting a fresh progressive synergy required of his staff. He hired the best of the best and gave them the tools needed to make his venture capital firm one of the most successful in the country.

Greer powered through the front door, hearing Kailey's high heels clicking on the polished floor behind him. The fragrant scent of winter honeysuckle wafted through the air, hinting at their landscaper's latest addition to the flower beds circling the building.

Where his sister shined was in her ability to schmooze his clients. Both men and women alike seemed drawn to Kailey. She regularly served as his dinner companion with little to no complaint, so he relented and slowed his steps, letting her catch up.

"So don't be mad."

Greer cocked a brow, refusing to look back. "If it's about dating, I don't want to talk about it."

"No, I saw the plans for the green community in Seattle."

Stunned, Greer stopped in his tracks. Kailey bumped into him from behind. Those architectural concepts were locked away securely on his private server. Only he and Beau had access. Greer dropped his head between his shoulder blades and closed his eyes. Either Beau had given her his access codes, or more likely, she'd gone snooping and found them on her own.

"Kailey."

"*Kailey*," she mimicked his disgusted tone as she came around to stand in front of him.

"What about it?" The damage was done. Another thing he had to let roll off his shoulders as he mentally set a reminder to change the password to the server. Greer started again toward his car. "It's not the first time we've invested in a living building. It's been done many times."

"It's the first time it's been done in the United States on that scale," she countered, smartly.

"Not really…" he said, knowing it was a lie.

The project was important to Greer. He had dreamed of such a community for more years than he could count. The plans included a sustainable community with retail, event centers, schools, and homes. The monumental undertaking had the very real possibility of going grossly over budget and still failing altogether.

"I think you should have another set of eyes look over the latest architectural plans before you sign off on them. I'm not sure it can be done for the money you've allocated…"

She voiced his biggest fear. He couldn't decide if he wanted to punch himself in the face or throat-punch his sister for her interference.

"Kailey, listen to me. I don't want you in my personal

accounts. You're not to open my email or go through my things. I've told you this over and over." He slapped his hand down on the hood of his sports car. His stare sharpened and stayed on his sister as he fought the frustration. His glare usually intimidated anyone who dared cross him, but not his sister. She ignored him completely.

"You're missing the point, Greer. We're too far away to keep a proper eye on the construction. If you're going to insist on moving forward with this project, either move it here to Dallas or plan to travel there frequently. It's only going to come together properly if you and your forceful attitude keep everyone accountable, every day." She used her pointer finger to circle around his face and where he'd slapped the car as her example.

What the hell did Kailey even know about such things? Truly, the amount of time she spent worrying about her fingernails spoke volumes to how little she had ever cared about what happened around her. Greer shook his head, staring at her as if she were mentally deranged. "I'm not a general contractor. I'm the money man. And you need to stop worrying about my money. I know what I'm doing."

He reached over, yanking the door open on the only frivolous purchase he'd ever made in his life, his BMW i8.

"Stop, Greer. I've been watching you since the minute you saved your first sea turtle from the plastic netting when you were eleven years old. If you'll think about it, you'll see what I said makes sense." She placed her hip against the side of his car, crossing her arms as if he wasn't about to take the wheel and drive away. "You can relocate to Seattle. You've done this venture capital thing. You have a ton of money. You move billions of dollars of other people's money around every year. It's time to take the next step. Go build those sustainable communities all across the United States. That's where your heart is. Not here, doing this."

Greer pointed a finger in Kailey's face, turning dead serious. "You have no idea what you're talking about, and I better not catch you ever repeating those words to another living soul. You'll ruin everything with those loose lips of yours. Now step away from my car. I've got to go."

He dropped down in the driver's seat and pushed the button to start the engine that delivered a satisfying roar.

"I don't know why I try to help you. You're too pigheaded—" Kailey was starting in on her frustrating lecture, so he shut the door in her face and put the vehicle in reverse. He never looked at her as he backed out of his designated parking space. She'd get over the brush off, she always did.

CHAPTER 3

The sudden hammering of Dallas's racing heart had him halting in midmotion of hooking his leg over the seat of his stationary bike. What if this was it? What if they had it wrong? The chaos running rampant through his head made him retreat, stepping back a few feet to put some distance between him and the bike. His heart threatened to pound straight out of his chest.

Dallas had to get a hold of himself.

Hell, he had to catch his breath before he passed the fuck out. He had to somehow shake off the fear of everything that could go wrong. If he didn't, he would most certainly crash and burn tonight. Fail in what might be the most important night of his life. This could change their future. Tonight, could be the start of something big for all of them.

Dallas looked down at his sweaty, shaking palms before he

clenched his fists tightly.

He forced a deep cleansing breath to settle his addled nerves.

With a dramatic flair, he gave an exaggerated shoulder shimmy to loosen his tight muscles and to shake off any bad juju before rolling his eyes at his own superstitious actions. Whether it would make a difference in the whole scheme of things wasn't certain, but the silliness somehow settled him by a fraction of an inch. The magnitude of how badly he wanted BikeBro to succeed took his constant state of low-level anxiety and sent it skyrocketing into the stratosphere.

Dallas knew their reality. The understanding had been dancing around the edges of his thoughts all afternoon. They were at their end. If this didn't work, they'd have to put their baby on the auction block, selling to the highest bidder. They had no other choice.

The deep sadness at the idea of losing their company came second only to the fear of not finding a buyer willing to pay them enough to cover their enormous debt. He saw nothing more than complete financial ruin in his life.

Maybe he should go back to teaching and let Ducky and Donny handle BikeBro. It would give them more cash to funnel into their business. He had a good list of clients at the gym. The two jobs might help save their small company…

"Calm your ass down and get on the bike," Dallas said aloud, forcing his head back into the moment. "Focus. You're not losing anything. It's fucking Secret. This is the break we needed."

"What?" Donny asked by way of a bark. Dallas looked over to see his brother's image in the prototype mirror now affixed to his bedroom wall, one of the now four full length mirrors ready to manufacture if they did in fact find an investor.

Shit. He'd forgotten about how Ducky's latest upgrade had them automatically connected to one another anytime the mirror was powered on. "Ignore me." Dallas pushed his uncertainty away.

Donny was the focused and driven one, determined in everything he did. Ducky was always a tad bit weird and misunderstood. Dallas had his feet firmly planted on the ground. He understood the importance of a balanced life while fading into the background, going unnoticed as much as possible.

He craved peace, which somehow landed him in the middle of many arguments between the people he loved as he tried to calm everyone down. He'd learned long ago to never let his true feelings be known, because they didn't really matter. He doubted anyone in his life understood the anxiety he lived under every single day.

"Focus, Dallas." Donny's unyielding tone pierced the silence. "You must be your best tonight. No room for failure. Head in the game. This is everything." His brother's intended pep-talk fell flat with the aggression lacing his tone.

"He knows that." Ducky's image appeared in the mirror, splitting the screen, one image on top of the other. His youngest brother looked concerned.

Ducky's image left the screen, causing Donny to toss his hands in the air. "Why did you leave your computer? What the hell's going on with you two? We have five minutes before Skye goes live."

"Ignore him, Dallas," Ducky said from down the hall. Seconds later, Ducky appeared in his bedroom doorway, crossing his arms over his chest. He looked worried. "You're on a new profile. Your personal information isn't connected, and you're locked to private. I tested it myself. No one can see you have the same background as your training videos, and I added an avatar. The new emojis are ready to launch after the session is over. We're good. I promise."

"Thanks, Ducky. You've done a really good job on everything," Dallas said, taking another deep breath, looking over at his twin mattress pushed against the wall so the room looked more like an exercise room than a bedroom. Dallas worked to emotionally slip back behind his long-established walls to keep himself hidden. He went back to the bike and mounted the seat. "I'm good. I promise. Go get ready."

"Okay." Ducky nodded one time before leaving him. His brother only had about ten steps to take to be back in front of his computer.

Skye's image split the mirror. She slowly pedaled her bike, looking perfect in their extremely limited work-out merchandise. Adding Skye to their team had turned out to be a hugely successful decision. She had a natural ability to draw people to her. She was pretty with a fun personality and an encouraging way about her. Under her tutelage, and with enough hard work, anyone's physical fitness challenges could be conquered. Men and women alike were drawn to her sweet way of getting the best out of people.

"Three minutes," she said with a giant grin. "We're gonna do great tonight."

"Keep it comfortable, but clutch," Donny instructed.

"Of course. Ducky explained the new leaderboard. I'm just waiting to begin." Skye's bright smile spread, and she clapped her hands together in anticipation.

Since their four mirrors were designed as trainer mirrors, Skye had access to the information of every biker who signed on. She could see their profile names and statistical information. With tonight's upgrades to the social site, the participants should now be able to show themselves to the rest of the class if they chose to.

They had so many plans.

Please let this work out.

"Just be yourself and you got this," Dallas encouraged, his true worries completely hidden from the others now.

The timer alarm buzzed at the one-minute mark.

"Remember, my goal's to be the leader in the class. Push everyone to try and beat me until about the two-minute mark, then I'll back off. Let the others win," Dallas explained as if Skye didn't already know the plan.

"Your profile name says Biker101. I'll call attention to you." Skye stretched, extending her body, pushing her arms in the air before she lowered into position.

"Perfect. Donny, you're Chaos89," Ducky added. "He's gonna stick to the moderate level cyclists."

"Forty-five seconds. Ducky, you ready?" Skye asked.

"Yup." The simple confident word made Dallas smile.

"Then let's go." Skye pedaled with a little more strength. She had ten seconds before her image went live to all the cyclists. "We got this. And I want a raise."

"You'll be director of programs," Donny said.

"Hey, that's my position," Dallas called out at the perfect diversion to get his head in the game.

"Then come get me," Skye teased, giving him a wink.

She went live. The leaderboard showed almost five hundred bikers queued and ready to begin. He watched the participant numbers increase by the second.

Dallas tuned everything else out and got in the zone, following Skye's directions.

"Omigod, why're you doing this, Greer?" Kailey whined via the Zoom call she initiated ten or so minutes before the cycling class began. Greer paid her no attention as he ignored both the sweat pooling on his brow, dripping to his handlebars, and the acute burn seizing every muscle in his body.

When Greer added this interactive exercise box to his daily exercise regime, he had very little faith in the workout it would provide. Man, he'd been wrong.

They were thirty-five minutes into their forty-five-minute hard-core workout session with five minutes left to go before the cooldown phase. Greer's muscles were on fire and hurt like he had never experienced in his life. Buckets of body sweat soaked his clothing and dripped to the tile floor below. The very essence of his competitive soul had exploded to new heights and refused to allow him to take second place in this competition.

"He's got that look, babe," Beau's deep voice muttered.

Kailey and Beau, both lightweights by Greer's estimation, had already thrown in the towel. Beau lasted a good twenty-five minutes before ducking out. Wimps.

Greer continued to ignore them both and did what he did best, pushed himself harder.

Four minutes to go.

He closed his eyes and panted, trying to fill his oxygen-deprived lungs as every muscle began its own form of mutiny.

"He's got something to prove," Beau explained.

"This isn't about showing-up for Skye," Kailey reflected, of course way off the mark.

"No. No person causes that look. He's jonesing for the win," Beau psychoanalyzed. If Greer's eyes weren't stinging from the deluge of sweat that dripped down his forehead, he might attempt to roll his eyes at his best friend and remind Beau that he was a surgeon, not a psychiatrist.

"Win what?" Kailey didn't understand that sometimes just being number one in a hard-fought battle was enough to justify the sacrifice.

"Winning period, baby. Three minutes, buddy. You got this," Beau encouraged.

Greer's sweat-soaked focus willed the leaderboard to inch his score upward, knowing he was completely maxed out. His last-ditch effort was all he had to give as deep disdain swirled through his gut over Biker101. He hissed, "*Fuck!*"

"He's good." Greer instinctively knew Kailey's praise wasn't directed at him.

"Biker101's killing it," Beau added.

Both of his cheerleaders would get a good talking to once he found enough oxygen to breathe properly again.

Something deep inside Greer recognized this wasn't going to happen for him. Desire to win hadn't been enough. No doubt, he'd given his all. A second later, Biker 101's name blinked on the leaderboard and dropped three positions. Greer's breath heaved. His thighs finally surpassing the pain, going into a blissful state of numbness as his profile name moved to the number one position.

Biker 101's name blinked again, dropping three more positions. His current rank, number six.

Motherfucker! He hadn't bested Biker101. The fucker had quit on him.

"*No!*" Greer shouted, giving a throaty grunt, pushing back on the seat to a sitting position. *No!* The class timer buzzed loudly, ending the competition.

"You won, Greer! I didn't see that coming at all," Kailey cheered.

"Right?" Beau agreed.

"Whoa. We did it. Great job everyone!" Even Skye sounded out of breath, and she always seemed to have endless energy. "Let's take it down a notch. Congratulate our winners. You guys worked me hard tonight."

Greer saw nothing but his nemesis, Biker 101, dropping through the ranks until he came in close to the bottom.

Whoever the hell Biker101 was, he threw the damn race.

"Wild_Rider," Skye said, seeming to look straight through the monitor at him. "Great job! Shoot me an email, and I'll get your membership comped."

"Why isn't Greer saying anything?" Kailey asked Beau.

Being robbed the satisfaction of a true win ate at him. The fucker had given up too early. Why? That shit just pissed him off.

"Buddy?" Beau asked.

Greer absently tossed a glance away from the leaderboard to see Beau still sitting on his bike slowly turning the pedals and Kailey laying spread across her bedspread as if the ten minutes she'd logged were too exhausting for anything more than rest.

"Those seats hurt my butt." Years of Greer picking at his sister had Kailey knowing exactly what he meant by the weakling glance he gave her.

Greer reached for the small hand towel he'd placed nearby. The deeply unsatisfying win sent his mood into a maddening downward spiral. He swiped the towel over his face then over his wet hair as he said, "Beau, your wife's broken into our private server. Keep a better eye on her for me."

"Greer! I can't believe you told him," Kailey screeched, sitting straight up in all her outrage. "You've literally had the same three passwords your whole damn life."

"Alexa, turn off my Zoom call." The screen darkened, ending their session. Greer then pushed the power button on the BikeBro box securely clamped to his handlebars. The screen on his mounted pad went instantly dark.

He was left completely disheartened after a grueling workout and started to edge off the bike's seat. First, he needed to gain feeling in the lower half of his body then find a way to blow off some of his pent-up steam. He was truly angry to his core. A win wasn't a win if it was handed to you.

Something deep inside instantly rejected his plans to meet up with Skye tonight. He didn't allow himself to dig too deep as to why he wanted to cancel, mainly because he didn't really care. It seemed his infatuation with his personal trainer had run its course.

Besides, he had more pressing goals. He needed a cold glass of ice water. After that...well, he saw shots of something alcohol-related in his near future. Then he probably needed to find a willing sex partner on Scruff to relieve him of this sudden aggression from the stupid cycling class. His swipe-right needed to be strong and fit to do all the heavy lifting during sex. There was no way his thighs were going to participate. He saw rebellion in their future.

Fuck, he was pissed off.

Greer started for his personal bathroom, needing a shower, appreciative that his legs held him upright. A dissatisfying black hole grew in his chest, darkening his mood with each step he took. How could he be this frustrated after such a hard workout? Because the fucking win didn't matter when the person turned tail and ran.

His cell phone rattled from its charging station on the nightstand. He slowed, looking down at the small screen. Skye's name appeared. He let it ring as he headed for the shower.

CHAPTER 4

"What the fuck was that?" Dallas asked, slowly pedaling his bike, out of breath and dripping with sweat. He reached for his water bottle, resisting the urge to dump it over his head.

"He's one of our corporate clients," Ducky called out from the living room, creating an earsplitting echo of feedback from the mirror. He must have heard it too. His voice lowered, now only talking through the mirror. "My bad. He's the one that bought all those boxes in January for his staff. He paid for all their membership fees in advance for the whole year. Remember him?"

"Yeah, yeah, I remember him. He's a badass," Donny said, nodding at the memory. His focused gaze landed on Dallas, giving him a critical eye as he looked him up and down. "You gotta be as exhausted as you look."

"My legs are jelly." Dallas registered the uncontrollable quiver in his thigh muscles. He spent hours a day working out. How was he already feeling this level of soreness?

"Wild_Rider's competitive as hell. When he gets something in his head, he's a force. Nothing gets in his way." Skye gave a quick shake of her head, her ponytail bouncing as she grinned at some unknown thought. "Greer doubled the pace of the second and third riders. I've never seen him work this hard. He acts like our training sessions are brutal. I knew he lied. I bet he went nuts when you pulled back. He would never consider this a win."

"Well, don't tell him who Biker101 is. We could use his excitement," Donny said. The cell phone clamped to his brother's arm rang. He paused for the briefest of seconds, staring off in the distance. "It's Cari. I'm gonna talk to her. She's upset she couldn't get out of work." Donny didn't wait for a response. His section in the mirror darkened, increasing the size of both Ducky and Skye's images.

"I promise I won't tell him. Greer's been pushing to hook up. I think it might be time. He made the whole session better. He's super gorgeous too. He looks like a Ken doll." Her grin spread when she looked directly at Dallas and added, "But watching Dallas work so hard to keep that number one spot might've made my whole life better." Skye could say whatever she wanted. Dallas knew when he stepped off this bike he'd most likely fall to the ground. What an unexpectedly intense workout.

"Wild_Rider came close to kicking his butt, and Dallas spends hours a day working out." Dallas's inner motivating voice really appreciated Ducky's commentary much more than Skye's. Ducky sounded in awe compared to Skye's clearly teasing tone. "Chad's calling!"

"So soon? No way!" Skye jumped off her bike and yelled to the mirror, "I'm coming over."

"Dallas, go in there right now." Donny's voice startled him. He'd thought his brother had ended the session. Clearly, Donny had found a new function in their equipment if he could stay connected through audio only. "Don't leave this to Ducky."

He had no idea how effective he would be at talking business with anyone right now. He needed recovery time after such a devastating workout.

It didn't really matter. Today had taught him that Ducky was the mastermind behind most of their accomplishments. His younger brother managed all their growth through social media while he continued to fine-tune BikeBro's programming and edit every one of their YouTube videos. More importantly, Ducky had created their company-saving financial opportunity. Ducky wasn't near as inept as Donny always implied.

Dallas resisted the urge to put Donny on blast. He'd pick his time to defend their younger brother. "I'll call you when we hang up."

Now all he had to do was get off the bike. Dallas carefully lowered a foot to the floor, encouraged when it held some of his body weight. "Dallas! His father wants to talk to you."

Oh hell, he wasn't ready.

Dallas took his water bottle, tossing back his head to squirt a good mouthful of water inside then hooked his other leg over the bike. The few steps he took toward the living room were shaky, but he found his land legs as he went over the essential talking points in his head.

What were their goals?

Going nationwide.

Get the mirror patented.

Cash. They needed revenue. The most important part to all this.

When he turned the corner into the living room, his apartment door flew open. Skye lived in their complex, two buildings over. Ducky's dual monitors were filled with Dylan Reeves and Tristan Wilder on one side. They were local celebrities in the DFW area, he'd know their faces anywhere. The other monitor showed a younger version of Dylan, chatting quietly with Ducky.

Dallas grabbed a towel off a folded stack of clean laundry sitting on the countertop and ran it over his face and short wet hair.

"I told them you were the lead rider and exhausted," Ducky said, eagerly looking over his shoulder at Dallas. Ducky pushed out an old office chair, another dumpster-dive treasure they'd found last year. Skye grabbed a chair from the kitchen table and came toward them.

"Who was number two? You two had a strong competition going," Dylan asked, looking directly at Dallas.

"He's a corporate account of ours with a wild competitive streak," Skye answered for him. She lifted a hand and waved at all three men. "I'm Skye. I work for them."

"I was watching the active members and the chatter going on. Even those not participating were absorbed in watching you two through the leaderboard. It was a great class," Tristan complimented. If his and Dylan's rumpled, sweat-soaked appearance was any indicator, they too had been active members of the class.

"I'm Dylan Reeves, by the way. This is my husband, Tristan. My son Chad's on the feed too."

"Hey," Chad said, lifting his chin in greeting.

Dallas again ran the towel over his wet head and squirted a small amount of water inside his dry mouth, thankful his breathing had returned to normal even as his heart thumped excitedly in his chest.

"I'm Duncan, but everyone calls me Ducky. This is my brother, Dallas, and Skye. You met her. She's like a sister to us. She's an instructor and a personal trainer like Dallas," Ducky explained. "We call our instructors trainers. You know, it makes us different that way."

Skye's brows rose as she glanced at Dallas, her surprise clear.

Ducky rarely spoke to people, and even less when Skye was around.

"Chad's told us you're a small start-up out of Dallas. That's Secret's hometown. I started Secret in my home office in North Dallas when the kids were young," Dylan reflected. "Looking back, those were some really incredible years as I destroyed our savings and maxed out every credit card I could get my hands on." Dylan's musings had just given BikeBro validity as a business by describing the exact desperation of their current situation.

Hope prevailed. How long had it been since Dallas had been hopeful?

"That's how I started Wilder too," Tristan added. "My parents took out a second mortgage on their home. I was fifteen years old at the time. They really took a chance on me." Wilder was the most used search engine in the world. A few years ago, Wilder had purchased Secret to become the leader in social media platforms. Together, they had veered off into interactive technologies, making another name for themselves in artificial intelligence.

To know neither would be here today if it weren't for a savings account and second mortgage blew his mind. Dallas sat up a little straighter out of respect for who sat across the screen from him. "That's pretty much where we are. Ducky's responsible for the technology development. He's got a real knack for it. He also monitors the social media site to make sure everyone's following the rules. Our older brother, Donny, handles the design and production. I'm running the classes with Skye. We've also started a YouTube channel. We currently have a nice number of orders on back list, waiting for the boxes to arrive any day now. Our supplier is a small company in West Texas."

"This was all Dallas's idea," Ducky added proudly, looking over at him. "He taught physical education at an elementary school in Grand Prairie where we grew up. He became a personal trainer. They both are." He hooked his thumb over his shoulder toward Skye. "I think I might've said that."

"Chad told us you have more than just the BikeBro box. That the social network went live a few months ago and tonight was the introduction to the new leaderboard. I like how participants can go live and stay shadowed as they ride. Privacy's important. It was surprising how personal the class felt. That's hard to do while you're alone in your house with just a monitor," Dylan said, turning serious.

"That's Ducky's vision and Skye's ability. She can pull the most out of the participants. She's great," Dallas explained, letting the praise be placed where it should.

"I need some time, but I'm coming to Dallas at the end of the week for about a week," Dylan said, and Tristan looked at him like he'd lost his mind.

"I thought it was a turnaround trip," Tristan said.

"It was, but things changed." Dylan looked at his son who had remained quiet for much of the call. "Chad's having a ceremony and celebration. He's passed his golf pro test. We're so proud of him."

Tristan completely ignored them, staring at Dylan with a clear *what the hell* look. Whatever the problem, he didn't appear to be on the same page as Dylan and didn't plan to ever be there by the look of things. Tristan's brows finally slid together, and he pushed back in his seat, crossing his arms over his chest, moving away from the screen. Was he…pouting?

"That's a hard test. Congratulations," Dallas said, ignoring Tristan like everyone else seemed to be doing. Dallas had trained several golfers preparing for the brutal ability test. Many never scored high enough to make the move into professional. Chad's was a sizable accomplishment.

"Thanks. I want to invest in this, Dad. I think it's a good idea. Ducky was telling me they have an interactive mirror. They already have a prototype, and they're working on something that can affix to an existing mirror. That's their thing. They want to eventually sell equipment, but right now their focus is on turning any piece of exercise equipment into a trainer by using their boxes. Isn't that right, Ducky?" Chad waited for Ducky's confirmation. When he nodded, Chad said the words Dallas wanted desperately to hear. "What's it gonna take to get in on this? I have a small trust fund."

Dylan barked out a hearty laugh, drawing every eye his direction. "You don't have a trust fund."

"Well, I should have one. I want to invest in this. What's it take?" Chad pressed, staring at Ducky, staying focused on the answer.

Skye chuckled at the exchange, causing Dallas to join in too, especially when Ducky's head jerked around toward Dallas, giving his best *deer in the headlights* look.

"Don't answer that," Dylan said, his face moving closer to the screen. "Let's all get together and talk later this week. I'll have my assistant reach out to set a time. My schedule should be relatively open. This is mainly a family visit." Dylan still seemed oblivious to the sulking Tristan, who remained tight-lipped.

"We'll work around your schedule, for sure. Thank you," Dallas said.

"Good job tonight. I look forward to talking to you soon." Dylan smiled and lifted a hand, giving a small wave.

Skye's excitement could barely be contained. She gave a little bounce in her seat. Dallas had worked hard to hold it together, be a professional, even as hope built at record speed as their future began to brighten. Ducky even broke character and extended a hand for a high five.

Dylan chuckled after watching them and turned his bright smile toward Tristan who wasn't giving in to the excitement of the moment.

"Babe, really? Five days?"

"Maybe longer, Tristan," Dylan said. He turned away from the camera, facing fully toward Tristan. "You know Chloe's trying her first case. Cate has her runway show. I need to be there."

"I agree," Tristan said, as if everything Dylan said was obvious. "But they're my kids too. Let me change my schedule. I need to be there. You know I don't sleep well with you gone."

"Tristan, you can't postpone the Zurich project." Dylan tossed out a hand toward Chad. "They know you would be there if you could."

Ducky waved at Chad and reached over to push end to the video call. Both screens went blank. No one moved from their small cluster next to Ducky's desk. It took several seconds of utter quietness, with the three of them looking at one another in disbelief, before anyone spoke.

"Say something," Ducky said. When they didn't, Ducky misinterpreted their silence. "I thought it sounded like a personal deal that we shouldn't be listening to, so I ended the call."

"No, that was good of you. The rest, well, I'm afraid to say anything out loud. I don't want to jinx it," Dallas said. His brain felt almost numb with hopefulness. "We can't celebrate yet. We don't know what they're planning to offer. We need to manage our expectations."

"But what if they want to invest?" Skye asked, her lip pushing between her teeth at the prospect.

"Or they might want to buy us out, and we're not ready to let go," he countered, playing devil's advocate even as his heart clung to Skye's far better idea.

"You're right. Let's not do this, but our little company had a great night!" Skye said, crossing one of her long legs over the other. "And let's put out into the world what we want to happen. What is that exactly?"

"Serious capital," Dallas started, using his fingers as a ticker.

"And connections," Ducky said. Dallas lifted a second and third finger, when Ducky added, "We have to get material costs lowered. We need to make more money off each box, right?"

"Completely, right." Dallas tossed out a fist bump to Ducky. He'd truly broken so many of his internal barriers tonight. "You're the man, bro."

Ducky beamed, causing Skye's grin to widen and throw out her own fist bump. Ducky happily obliged. "I think we need to celebrate our successful day and worry about tomorrow, tomorrow." She jumped up, happy with her idea. "I'm gonna cancel my plans. Let's go out. Dinner and dancing, and Ducky, you're coming with us."

"I don't know," Ducky hedged. Dallas could almost see his brother pulling back into himself, trying to hide from a world he truly didn't understand. Ducky gave a hard shake of the head and started to turn away, reaching for his headphones.

"I do know. We're going out at least for dinner." Dallas pushed the button to turn off Ducky's CPU and got the anticipated outrage.

Skye only laughed and headed for the door. "I can start teaching two classes every night. I think we need more variety. Are y'all good with that?"

"Sure," Dallas said, stretching out his body as he got to his feet. "I think it's a great idea. I'm teaching about three classes a day, but those are daytime hours. We need more evening classes."

"Give me thirty minutes. You're driving. I'm drinking," she said and left their apartment, door swinging closed behind her.

Dallas decided right then this would be an Uber night. They all needed a drink to celebrate. Maybe Donny could meet them.

"Dallas, I don't want to go. We don't really have the money…" Ducky started. The squeak of Ducky's chair, and the stomp following him made Dallas's grin grow. Ducky always backed out of anything going-out related. He should let his brother celebrate however he saw fit, but not tonight.

"Go with us for dinner then you can come home if you want. We need to celebrate you, bro. You did this. Go shower first. I'm calling Donny."

Ducky still hesitated. Dallas had to push his brother by the arm into their shared bathroom before going for his cell phone.

CHAPTER 5

No doubt with as badly as his body already hurt, Greer would seriously regret this workout in the morning. His legs ached as he padded across the room, running his fingers through his freshly dried hair. The blond strands were cut and styled in such a way they easily fell into place—good thing, because his biceps burned from the force he'd used to grip those handlebars.

Greer perused the clothing he'd laid across his mattress. They were designed to impress. The slacks and dress shirt he chose to wear tonight complimented his naturally tanned skin tone and were tailor-made to fit his body like a glove. He wasn't entirely sure the quivering in his quads wouldn't be seen under such a snug fit.

As he reached for a pair of underwear inside the dresser drawer, his cell phone rang again. He almost didn't answer, maybe his silence would be enough to imply he and Skye should change their plans to another day. Since it actually hurt to lift his foot into the leg hole of the underwear, and that was technically her fault, he tossed the black briefs on the bed and went for the phone.

Skye's name appeared on the screen, just as he'd expected. Greer answered after a swipe and a heavy sigh. "Your BikeBro tried to kill me."

Her singsong laughter indicated she knew exactly what he was talking about. "I saw your truth tonight, Mr. Lockhart. You're super competitive. You made the whole class more enjoyable. The battle was fierce and fun. Congratulations on the year's membership."

He instantly sensed the mockery in her sweet tone. How could he blame her?

"Donate my winnings to someone else," he grumbled and looked at the time. He wasn't in the mood to sit and make small talk tonight. He needed alcohol, popular music that he didn't even know was popular, and maybe a tranquilizer. A horse tranquilizer to allow him to sleep until his muscles fully recovered. "I'm backing out tonight."

"Good, because I'm calling to ask for a raincheck. We're having an impromptu celebration. I know it's late notice."

Greer narrowed his eyes and stared unseeing across his bedroom. Something told him he and Skye were more alike than he realized. She most likely spent time with him for the same reasons he spent time with her: the sheer boredom of life.

Could that be the true meaning behind a choice to marry? Holy hell, he'd spent years contemplating why the people in his life married and divorced then married again. He gave a silent, humorless huff. Marriage had to be a response to boredom, not love at all. Something to spice up life for however long it lasted. Huh.

"Are you there?"

"I am. Call me later." He dismissed his musings and fought a yawn. Now his brain hurt as badly as his body.

Technically, he could stay in tonight. He wasn't the young buck he pretended to be.

Oh fuck no! He wasn't having those recurring thoughts tonight.

His thirty-year-old old-man status had officially grabbed him by the balls and squeezed the shit out of his youth. Greer went for the bed, gathered his clothes hangers, deciding on a soft pair of jeans for whatever the night might hold. And going out was exactly what a youthful person would do.

"We're good, right?" Skye's tone had changed, more speculative than sweet. Something he'd never heard before. He carefully hung his clothes back in place before reaching for a folded pair of jeans and a soft, well-used SMU sweatshirt.

"We're good. I should cancel tomorrow morning's session. My body already hurts from the crazy man I became in your class. We'll catch up later this week." Hopefully, he'd eased any worry she had. "You did great tonight. You're a natural instructor. I got a great workout. I need to go."

"You were pretty amazing."

"I don't know about that, but I had fun. Call me." Greer disconnected the call, tossing his phone on the mattress and sat on the edge, carefully pulling his underwear up his sore legs.

Nothing more than the sheer force of his will had him contemplating his changing plans for the night. He could swing by M Street Bar for a couple of hours. It was casual and within walking distance of his home. Maybe his old college buddy, Mac, was working tonight. If he got lucky, he could talk Mac into making him one of those Mac Special Burgers that were no longer on the menu. His stomach let out an approving loud rumble. Surely, he had burned the five hundred calories that burger would cost him.

Before committing to wearing real pants, Greer picked his cell phone up again and dialed Mac.

"Hey. You know it's dinner rush," Mac said in a hurried greeting after the fourth ring.

"I'm on my way." Food became the most urgent motivator pushing him out the door tonight.

"See you then, buddy."

Greer hung up the phone. With a little more pep in his aching step, Greer finished dressing, wondering what level of laziness it would be for him to Uber the two blocks to the bar instead of walking.

Several relaxing hours later, Greer leaned his back against the edge of the bar, elbows anchored behind him as he contemplated the effects of all the alcohol he'd consumed. The low-key music selected from a nearby jukebox played a happy little ditty about a sawed-off shotgun. No, that didn't sound quite right. Maybe he wasn't hearing the lyrics correctly.

"How you doin', buddy?" Mac asked from behind the bar.

Greer looked over his shoulder, the swing of his head causing a bit of double vision. His content grin was instant. The easy joy in his heart wasn't surprising. Alcohol generally made him a happy drunk, or so he'd been told.

"I'm good. It's been a good night. I could use another." Greer nodded toward the empty cocktail glass sitting on the bar beside him. He swiveled back around, staring out at the grill turned sport's bar in the late hour. Groups of different people gathered around the assorted pool tables. Others played rounds of darts. Some had spent hours at the various video game consoles lining the interior wall. "You do a good business here."

"You should know, silent partner," Mac said proudly.

He cocked his head back toward Mac. His body followed more slowly as the barstool rotated under his butt, turning Greer in Mac's direction. "Not silent if you say it out loud."

43

A cocktail glass with clear liquid was pushed forward. Mac filled another glass with something similar and lifted it toward Greer for a toast. "The plans to expand are finished. Five restaurants by the end of the year. Six more next year. Two in the Austin area. Thank you for hooking me up with investors. I wouldn't have dreamed it possible."

Greer gave a nod and a wink that seemed to take total concentration and use of his whole face to accomplish. He lifted his glass, meeting Mac's halfway with a little more force than intended for a simple toast. "It's nothing more than knowing the right people. You're a good risk. We're all going to make some money."

He took a big, hearty gulp and paused. The taste confused him. After swishing the liquid around his mouth, he swallowed, shoving the glass back toward Mac. "What the hell? Water? That's your idea of a celebratory toast? I'm pretty sure you just jinxed yourself with that fucked-up move."

"You've had enough. You're drunk. It's close to midnight, my friend. Tomorrow's gonna be hell. Go home," Mac said and lifted his hand, calling someone's attention as he nodded toward Greer.

"It's that late?" Greer looked around for a clock, surprised to see it was in fact midnight. He instantly sobered, reaching for his cell phone. Dammit, he had hoped for a Scruff date. Man, he could use some forceful sex tonight. Someone to grab him by the hair and own his ass. His dick pulsed its approval of the mental image conjuring in his head. It had been far too long.

Mac's hand covered his phone screen, drawing his attention up. "I'll get you home."

"I might not be going home. It's Scruff."

Mac's hand clamped down, but Greer pulled the phone free, concentrating on the suddenly complicated workings of the dating app. He had to admit the double vision made things a little harder than they needed to be, so he closed one eye to help. Voila! Like magic, it all came together.

"I thought there was some chick you were chasing," Mac said, easily plucking the cell phone from Greer's hand, and turned it to look at the screen.

"Nah, not anymore." Greer stood, extending his upper body and hand across the bar, reaching for his cell. Mac effortlessly dodged his attempt, using his thumb to push the sidebar button to darken the screen.

"Go home, Greer." Mac kept the phone just out of his reach. "Marisol, take Greer home for me."

Mac was being a jerk. He handed Greer's cell across the bar to Mac's long-time employee and right-hand woman. Greer lost sight of the phone as he reached for his wallet, thumbing through the cash. "You know you don't pay, you bastard. You worked that stipulation into our contract."

Yep, that was right. He did do that. Greer's grin split his lips, remembering the brilliance of that last-minute addition. He still put twenty dollars on the bar top. "I'm leaving a tip."

"I was your waiter, drunk ass," Mac barked then tightly wound the hand towel in his hands, popping Greer directly on his fingers when he reached to take the cash back. Greer's outrage was immediate when the sudden sting spread across his knuckles. After years of practice, Mac's snap had pinpoint accuracy.

"That fucking hurts! No wonder I had such bad service with your grizzly ass hovering so close. I was barely able to eat." He managed to get the twenty back inside his wallet and pulled out a single dollar bill, making a show of leaving it on the bar top.

"It was a wonder you didn't choke to death the way you inhaled that food." Mac laughed.

Greer paid Mac no mind. He pushed off his stool and tried to tuck his wallet inside his back pocket. The unexpected towel pop hitting his ass had a sharper bite this time.

He shifted his balance, trying to get away from another strike. Greer shot Mac the middle finger, at least he hoped he had, and got a booming round of laughter that brought joy to Greer's heart.

And with that, his evening here was done. He grabbed his jacket, slid it on, and walked toward the front doors in an awfully crooked straight line. No matter how he tried, he couldn't quite navigate his steps. He kept veering off to the right as he went.

"Come on, Marisol," Greer called out, trying to encourage Marisol to follow him out.

"Right here, boss," she said, directly behind him. She was so close her breath tickled the back of his neck.

Marisol had been barely sixteen years old when Mac first hired her to bus tables. He and Mac had been straight out of college—new Southern Methodist University graduates—when Mac decided to open the bar. Greer had watched Marisol grow into a smart, accomplished young woman. She seemed to always be indifferent to her surroundings. He respected that about her. A trait he mimicked often.

"I can get home," he said, turning to push the door open with his ass.

"Mac wants me to drive you. Here, take your phone," she said, stepping past him, extending the cell phone as she went. The fresh, cool March air helped clear Greer's foggy head enough to have him looking across the street at the quiet darkness of his neighborhood. The bright lights of the restaurants and other businesses lined this side of the street.

He had two blocks to walk. The liquor had helped dull some of the muscle pain. He could make it home, no problem.

"I got it," he tried again, following behind Marisol at a slower pace. "Besides, now that I got my phone, I bet I can find someone to meet me there. Make sure I get inside safely." In his inebriated state, Greer thought that was the funniest thing he'd ever said. He had to hold his side, laughing even as Marisol pointed him to the passenger side of Mac's brand-new car. Her stone face never cracked under all his good jokes.

"The last time you walked home, I believe you were robbed.

Isn't that right?" The automatic locks released as she stared at him over the top of the car.

Exasperated, Greer threw his hands in the air. That was the disadvantage of having lived in the same area most of his life. Those well-established roots made sure all the people in his life never let him forget any of his transgressions. "That was years ago. I was dumb to take the shortcut. I've walked home a hundred times since then with no incident."

"What happened to Skye? I thought she was going to settle you down." Marisol's perfectly arched brow lifted as she opened the driver's side door.

Greer gave a dramatic roll of his eyes and followed her lead, opening the passenger side door. "That ship's sailed. We've always been better friends than anything else." He placed both hands on the top of the shiny red sports car, leaning forward, asking a heartfelt honest question. "Do you think I'm getting old?"

Marisol busted out with a loud cackle and dropped down into the driver's seat. His eyes narrowed. Finally, he got a laugh out of her, but he didn't know why. It took a second more before he lowered himself into the car and shut the door behind him. "You know, I was serious out there."

"We all gotta grow up some time," she said, pressing the ignition. The rumble of the engine vibrated the seat. "I heard you were Wild_Rider."

Yup, his whole world was way too connected. He dropped his head back on the headrest, took a deep whiff of the new-car leather smell, and swiveled to look her way. "I kicked ass."

"Like a man possessed," she said as if that wasn't a good thing. She tossed her long dark hair over her shoulder as she looked over at him. "What the hell, Greer, I could have used the year's membership."

"Then I'll transfer my prize to you. I already paid for mine." He nodded as if that solved every problem in the world. Mac's new car was more luxury than flash. The seats were comfortable, lulling him into closing his eyes. The spinning started, but not too terrible. Maybe even a little calming for his always active brain. "So," he paused. "The BikeBro is a big deal?"

"Yeah," Marisol replied. "Especially around here, but Skye says they're starting to break into Houston and Austin. I like it. Less money than the gym." She pulled them out of the parking spot and drove slowly through the lot. If she went a certain way down an alley, they'd end at the beginning of his street. "I heard Secret's taken an interest in them."

"Hmmm." News to him. That Secret/Wilder combination could really help the BikeBro's social site. Dylan had money to spend. Tristan, of course, had more. He couldn't remember hearing any whispering of BikeBro looking for investors.

Wait, no. He needed answers to something far more important. "Do you know Biker101?" His head never left the relaxing headrest, but he opened his eyes and rolled her way again.

"I don't know. It's hard to know who's who because literally no one uses their own name," she said, taking the corner onto his street a little too quickly. His stomach roiled as he reached for the dashboard to help keep himself in place. "They have an interactive mirror coming that'll work directly with the box. It sounds really sick."

"I haven't heard that either." Greer closed his eyes, lulled by the sultry tone of Marisol's voice and the silence inside the car. He gave a big jaw-cracking yawn. "I'm slipping fast."

"Then yes, you are getting old," Marisol teased.

The perceived insult snapped his eyes open. She smiled again for the second time in five minutes. That had to be some sort of record. He hoped he remembered the momentous occasion tomorrow.

"I'm thirty years old. I'll take mature, but not old," he explained, indignantly.

She laughed straight out at his outrageous explanation, and

barely had the car stopped in front of his house before he shoved open his door, stepping out into the brisk night air. He made a show of wrapping his jacket around him as he bent his head back into the car.

"You know, I used to like you." He hurriedly slammed the car door to stop her from getting the last word.

Greer started around the hood to hear Marisol's window lowering. She cackled with laughter. He liked the sound. Halfway up the walkway to his front door, he heard, "Love you, Greer."

He shot her the finger then a smile over his shoulder.

She stayed until he made it inside the house. He gave another giant yawn. Maybe he was a little old. Greer abandoned his Scruff plans. He needed to be in the office early tomorrow anyway.

CHAPTER 6

Five days later

Ducky had managed to hold his excitement until a few steps outside the rotunda of Secret's Dallas high rise. "I can't believe Tristan Wilder offered me a job."

His little brother was enthralled by the tour of Secret's floor after floor of data centers. Donny had doubted the wisdom of bringing Ducky along with them today. What a mistake that would have been to leave him behind. Their rage-against-the-machine brother spiritedly spoke Dylan's and Tristan's language just like Dallas had hoped.

"You aren't leaving us," Dallas said. Ducky had turned the unexpected offer down on the spot, but Dallas liked seeing Ducky proud of himself, and it had been quite a surprise for all of them.

"So, what do y'all think?" Donny asked, the last one through the revolving door. Dallas looked up at the bright sunny sky, letting the warmth of the early spring sun bathe his skin.

Dallas didn't want to add negativity. They'd had a great meeting, but the cash they had hoped to receive had never fully materialized.

"Having our social site as an app of Secret's will give us a better interface, and we get to keep all our privacy and company focus and policies in place. Just the use of their servers alone could change things. We could never afford something like that up there." Ducky pointed to the building where the data centers were housed as they started for the parking lot across the street. "Another positive thing, users can access their Secret profiles to access our network. So, less logins and hassle for our customers. I can't see any reason not to join forces. They said they wouldn't charge us anything for three years. We'll know by then if we can make it work."

"I'd hoped they wanted to invest cash," Donny said his piece, ignoring Ducky altogether. He spoke Dallas's truth aloud, making the weight of their load feel a little heavier than before. Why did no one want to invest money in them? BikeBro was growing into a substantial business.

Dallas grabbed the back of Ducky's suit collar to keep him from stepping off the curb into oncoming traffic. His brother was too excited to pay attention to something as trivial as traffic lights and street signs.

"Tristan offered a lot of money to buy our company. That has to mean they see value," Ducky said.

True. Tristan's reasons for wanting to buy over investing were solid. He had the procedures in place to move the product forward. The three of them, and their lack of knowledge in just about everything other than running classes and the social site, would be a hindrance he didn't have time for. Dallas couldn't fault the logic. As far as the business went, they did have a steep learning curve to overcome; he saw it in them every day.

"Hey, guys!"

The three turned in unison to see Dylan jogging toward them, his hand raised, trying to gain their attention.

"I'm glad you didn't get too far. I was inspired by you three. I want you to give me a couple of days. Let me run your business through the investment groups I'm involved with. If I can't find anyone interested, let me see how much money I can come up with. I think the box is a good way to get people moving from home. I like adding the *getting fit* concept to the Secret brand. And that mirror of yours is going to change things in the physical fitness industry."

After hearing those words, the heaviness in Dallas's heart instantly lifted. An ease he hadn't felt in months made him smile and quickly prompted him to extend his hand to shake Dylan's. "Thank you, sir. BikeBro has been our whole world for a long time now."

Dylan continued shaking all their hands, grinning or maybe laughing at each of them in their enthusiasm. "There's something else. I want my branding team at Wilder to get a hold of your logo and polish it up. I took a look at your YouTube channel, and I'd like to see if we can do some brainstorming together to come up with a name for your company that will encompass all your different products and services. You're more than a stationary bike streaming box. You have the social site and the mirror. You're fully integrated and interactive."

"It took us days to agree on the name BikeBro," Ducky said, sounding disappointed. "But most people don't know we're brothers and that's why the name fits us. I guess we can change it though."

"If you don't like what the branding team comes up with, there's no harm, and I'll instruct them to work closely with the three of you to keep your vision. Sound good?" Dylan added.

"Yep." Ducky nodded his head vigorously. Apparently past

any concern for the name change. Any hope of taming Ducky's thick, longish locks broke when the ends sprang outward, bouncing back into his regular chaotic look.

"Yes, sir," Donny answered with his military tone lacing each syllable. Dallas could almost hear the back of Donny's dress shoes snapping together.

"So, I'll be back in touch." Dylan walked backward toward the building, adding, "Dallas, I'll call you, correct?"

"Yes, that's fine." Both men nodded in agreement. Dylan turned away and took off jogging back to the building.

As all three of them stood there staring at the retreating Dylan, Dallas decided right then and there that the highs and lows of owning his own business were more stressful than monitoring a gym full of hyperactive, obstinate first graders.

"I'm not gonna lie, I left our meeting disappointed," Donny muttered as he watched Dylan disappear back inside the building. "We didn't get the cash we needed."

"Do you think he can get it?" Dallas asked, afraid to hope, but doing just that.

"I don't know, but this was the best meeting we've had. Their advice is incredible. I've got my work cut out for me," Donny said. He turned away and started back for the street corner.

"The most important thing to me is their concern regarding the lack of classes. We've gotta increase the class loads. Maybe I can get someone other than Skye in the evenings. Do you think adding an additional two classes a day will help for now?" Dallas swiveled on his feet, following behind Donny.

"Cari said she'll teach a class at night if she gets moved to days. She should know soon," Donny said absently.

Cari teaching an evening class would help. "I don't really need to sleep. I can add some overnight classes to get more recordings. We need more content for YouTube anyway. Maybe we can upload two videos a week," Dallas said.

Ducky gave a sudden burst of laughter straight out loud at his serious contemplation. "You only sleep about five hours a night."

Dallas cast a glance over his shoulder. Where he and Donny had turned strategic, Ducky's casual gait and bright smile suggested his little brother was relishing his achievement.

The signal changed, and they stepped off the curb together.

"I gotta get back to the hospital."

"No matter what, our business had a good day," Ducky said.

Dallas slapped Donny's outstretched hand, nodding his agreement. Ducky had already veered off, heading in the direction of Dallas's car when Donny called out, "Ducky, call Dad and tell him Wilder offered you a job."

Their father lived by a strict set of rules. So did Donny for that matter. Dallas couldn't count the times their dad had gotten onto Ducky and pushed him out the door to play outside, but he had to remember to tell Ducky not to mention the job offer. As much as his father wanted his boys to work a nine-to-five job, he'd never approve of Dylan and Tristan's relationship and what that might mean about the Wilder, Inc. company values. Hell, Dallas was surprised Donny had handled it all so well.

CHAPTER 7

Greer sat on his bike with the remote control in hand, pedaling. His heavy breathing slowly returned to normal. This damn cycle class had become addicting. It weirdly met all his requirements for a good workout: intense, unforgiving, and competitive. Who would have thought riding a stationary bike could be so cathartic?

He lifted the remote control and pointed it to the icon at the bottom of his monitor, switching from class mode to the BikeBro social network. Since his obsessive competitive streak currently was laser focused on beating Biker101, he searched for the person behind the profile to see if anything had changed.

He found the user, but the profile was still shadowed in lockdown private mode. Only a few details were available for public view—Biker101's stats being one of them. Honestly, Greer liked the privacy feature the site gave its clients. It was a good safety measure to keep the pervs away. But damn, he wanted to know more about Biker101.

His aggravation at the whole thing was more emotional than sensible and one hundred percent self-centered. Greer's obsessive side demanded he learn more about the user. The person behind Biker101 had whirled around inside his thoughts for the last five days. Early on, he'd decided that if he had a say in who the person was behind the Biker101 account, he wanted them to be a younger man, built like a powerhouse, with thick thunderous thighs.

Greer closed his eyes, thinking about those fictional muscular legs wrapping around his waist, controlling his every move as he worked the guy's ass over. Biker101 would most definitely be a versatile power-bottom. He also really liked the idea of a strong jawline and thick full lips, maybe a light dusting of a beard. Just throwing it out there.

"Augh," Greer rolled his eyes at his impromptu fantasy.

The self-mockery didn't slow his newest obsession. Greer's dick grew tight as he thought about the fictitious man. It wasn't the first time he'd had these thoughts; the image of the guy took shape in his head. His mouth watered with the anticipation of licking down 101's defined stomach muscles...

Maybe he was becoming addicted to sex.

Greer barked out a laugh and clicked off the screen. Surely a person had to *have* sex more than once or twice a month before worrying about that.

Maybe that was his true problem. His diagnosis should be an under-sexed man, fixated on a fictional cyclist.

He stepped off the bike, proud his wobbly legs were growing stronger when he didn't crumple to the ground. He could feel the increase in his entire body's core strength with as many miles as he'd logged on this stationary bike in the last several days. Skye was an excellent trainer. As Greer started toward his bath to shower, the doorbell rang causing him to look over at the Echo to check the time. Damn. Apparently, he had dawdled too long.

Instead of going for the shower he needed more than anything, Greer changed course and headed for the front door. He had met Vance a few months ago. When the guy had randomly texted tonight, it seemed like divine intervention. Vance was tall, slender, and wore his sun-kissed light brown hair long. He looked very much like a displaced surfer—lost and trying to find his next wave.

Greer opened the front door to find Vance with a giant grin on his face. He stepped back, inviting the guy in with the sweep of his arm. "I'm running late. I just finished a workout and need to shower." He cocked his head toward his guest room right off the entryway. "Join me, or give me five minutes, it's up to you. If you wait, get a drink." Greer cocked his head in the other direction toward his loaded bar right off the kitchen.

The sweat still cooling on his skin encouraged Greer to head for the bathroom in the guest room. Either choice Vance made was fine, but a little shower play wouldn't be a bad thing. The guest room was really his designated sex room, equipped with lube, condoms, soaps, towels, assorted toys, everything needed to have a good time. He dropped his shorts, kicking them aside as he pulled his sweat-soaked tank top off, tossing the shirt toward his bedroom further down the hall.

"Fuck, Greer. Your ass is perfect." Vance's husky words were followed by heavy footsteps thudding toward him. This would be his preference too. He ran his fingers through his thick hair, making sure it wasn't standing on end before looking over his shoulder. Vance shed his clothes as he drew closer. The guy played the exact way Greer liked.

Greer barely had the shower faucet on before strong, calloused palms slid around his waist. "We need to do this more often. You're hot as fuck."

"Exactly my thoughts," Greer cooed.

Greer had no idea how Vance had talked him into catching an UberPool to Club Indigo. It was late and Greer clearly hadn't been thinking properly when Vance invited him to go.

Of course, he'd been to the dance club many times over the years. Club Indigo was a staple attraction of downtown Dallas nightlife. The place wasn't all that exclusive, but it was expensive...

With that thought, it had just occurred to him that his job tonight was to cover the costs. Probably the reason Vance had suggested he tag along in the first place. Everything made better sense now, except for the body pressed snugly against his side inside the crowded compact car's backseat. If he'd had any idea that UberPool meant splitting the cost with people going his same direction, he would have most certainly declined.

Lesson learned.

This had to be what sardines felt like packed inside their can. No wonder the little fish smelled so bad.

Vance had somehow managed his way into the front seat of the vehicle. The fucker. The car stopped at the curb in front of the club and Greer pulled at the door handle. The door didn't budge. He tried again. What the hell?

Unexpectedly, his date tugged open his door from the outside. "I see that look in your eyes." Vance's smug laugh didn't hinder Greer's growing bad mood one bit.

Once out of the can and on his feet, Greer made a show of swiping at his clothing like a third grader to rid himself of the imaginary cooties he'd acquired from riding with the other passengers.

"We could have brought my car."

"Quit being a snob," Vance replied.

Greer's grin begrudgingly slid in place as the car drove away. Vance's comment was way off the mark. Now, Greer was calculating how much this night was going to cost him and how long he had to stay before he could duck out without looking like an old fuddy-duddy. "You think you know me?"

"My ass does." The quip worked to ease his building bad attitude. So did the little flip Vance gave to his hair as he turned with swagger and started toward the front doors.

Vance wasn't the only one with a tender ass.

Greer shook his head at all the arrogance strutting toward the front doors and let the muted beat of the music pick up his spirits. Vance's spectacular bubble butt bounced to the thump of the electronic dance tune, and of course, Greer followed.

"I'm only staying for about an hour." Greer grabbed the door, giving Vance a little shove to get him moving faster. The volume of the dance music increased, making it almost impossible to hear. Vance twerked against his ass as Greer paid their entrance fees.

Once inside, Greer glanced around. The club had been remodeled, allowing for more room to roam. People gathered in small clusters around booth-style seating, which edged the length of the interior walls. The center of the club incorporated a large dance floor. Lights flashed in time to the beat of the music, allowing enough light to easily find one of the three large bars in each corner. Round high-top tables were sprinkled all around the room. He got why the place was so packed on a weeknight. Both young and old seemed happy to be hanging out, mingling through the club. Club Indigo had a draw for everyone.

"I'm gonna dance. Go to that bar and tell Sam I'm on your tab." Vance pointed to the bar in the closest corner. Without another word, Vance took off, bounding toward the dance floor as Greer pulled his wallet free and dug for his credit card.

Greer worked his way through the crowd. About midway to the bar, a Daft Punk mix began playing overhead, sending the crowd into a screaming excited frenzy. With the way everyone reacted, he wasn't sure the club even needed the dance floor. Everyone began dancing where they stood. Greer ricocheted off writhing bodies, enjoying the brushes and touches as he went. The energy of the crowd ran through him, until he moved along with the others as he made the final steps to the bar.

"Are you Sam?" Greer called to the distracted bartender. He cast a glance up, but his hands never stopped working, filling orders behind the bar.

"Yup, do I know you?"

"Vance said to let you know he's on my tab." Greer waved his credit card in the air. The bartender laughed and nodded, reaching out to take the card, probably not the first time he'd heard those directives where Vance was concerned.

"Greer? What're you doing here?" Skye pressed against his back as she shoved herself between him and the guy beside him. She was just slight enough and pretty enough not to piss the other guy off as he was forced to make room for her.

"I'm asking myself the same question," he yelled back. "What're you doing here?"

"What do y'all want to drink?" Sam called out, gaining their attention again.

"Grey Goose on the rocks." He looked down at the cash in Skye's outstretched hand. "Who're you here with?"

"We have a table over there," she pointed absently over her shoulder. "The gym. Come join us. There's room."

He nodded. It might be better than standing alone, looking for a dance partner. "Tell him what you want to drink."

Skye ordered two cocktails and a beer and tried to put her money on the bar top. He pushed it back at her and leaned in to be better heard. "Put them on my tab."

"You don't have to, Greer." Her dark wide-eye stare showed she was clearly into her drinks this evening, already a little tipsy.

"Is Kailey here?" he asked.

The tempo of the music increased. The walls started thumping. He bent to lower his ear to hear her better. Skye still had to lean in, lift on her tiptoes and yell. "No, Kailey couldn't come. I'm here with some of the guys and Stacy from the gym. It's the owner's birthday. What're you doing here?"

"I'm not a hundred percent sure. It just happened," he explained vaguely, grinning at her confused look. Their drinks came, drawing her attention back to the bar, keeping him from having to say anything more. Skye reached for two of the glasses while he grabbed his and the other one, lifting them high in the air to avoid spilling them as they pushed their way through the throng of revelers. Luckily, her table was close by and did appear to have room for him.

"Hey, everyone! This is Greer. I found him at the bar. He's a member of the gym." Skye handed off one of her drinks before taking the one in Greer's hand and giving it to another guy. Luckily the popular, blaring song came to an end while ushering in another that wasn't quite as loud.

"Yeah, man, I've seen you around. Join us." One of the trainer's reached out to slap his hand in greeting.

"That's Tank," she said then pointed to the equally bulked-up bodybuilder beside him. "Jorge's the owner."

Greer nodded in his direction. Those two stood to the side of one table.

"You've been coming to the gym awhile now," Jorge said.

"I have. It's a good place to work out." Greer nodded, following Skye's finger as she ticked off the other men and the woman sitting on the booth behind the table. "That's Jon, Stacy, and on the far end, that's Dallas. He's had a little too much to drink."

Greer gave a chin lift to each of them. When his gaze landed on the last guy, the breath froze in his lungs. *Holy hell!* Sin personified. Dallas was gorgeous, and Greer couldn't stop staring. His heart leapt against his ribs. Every fiber of his being homed in on the relaxed man paying zero attention to him. Even seated, Greer could see Dallas was tall, maybe the tallest one among them all…and dark, not devilish, more Mediterranean with thick, rich chestnut hair and a nice, smooth complexion.

The loud clatter of dishes pulled Greer from his lustful stupor as his surroundings came back into focus. Greer lifted his drink to his lips as he turned back to Jorge in an attempt to hold his shit together and remember his manners.

"Happy birthday!" He hoped he sounded sincere as he glanced toward the handsome man again.

Full lips and a strong chiseled jaw—damn, he liked a good strong jaw. Spellbound, Greer watched in slow motion as Dallas's long dark eyelashes swept down then up again as he blinked. Every part of that man embedded himself inside Greer's very soul. He wanted to introduce himself to Dallas in so many ways.

Greer's dick grew rigid even though he'd been completely sated earlier.

Dallas was built but not with excessive muscle like Tank or Jorge. He was perfectly proportioned. More than anything, he wished he could see the exact color of Dallas's eyes.

Greer's heart hadn't slowed. In fact, it had sped up the more he watched the dark-haired beauty until the damned organ hammered in his chest, his pulse tripping as he took a deep breath, absorbing such a visceral reaction to another human being. Everything about Dallas's look just did it for Greer. The club and their surroundings only settled back around Greer when Skye ran her hand the length of his forearm, drawing his attention down to her.

"It's like pulling teeth to get these men to dance with me."

"Right!" Stacy yelled, elbowing Dallas in the ribs.

The guy turned back toward the group, looking down at Stacy then around as if he had completely tuned them out. "What?"

"You won't dance with me." Stacy's accusation sent worry surging through Greer that Dallas might have a girlfriend, but Dallas's humorless laugh eased his fear. Dallas stretched his long arms along the back of the booth, before letting a yawn free. His legs remained crossed at the ankle, showing no desire to fulfill her request.

"We didn't want to tell you, but you step on all our feet." Dallas's deep, rich tenor caressed Greer's unruly heart, giving a gentle squeeze. Dallas gave a single affirmative nod, driving the joke home until another quick jab of her elbow had him doubling over in laughter.

When Dallas lifted his head, Greer finally got his wish. For the briefest of moments, Dallas's stunning emerald-green eyes focused directly on him. The jewel-toned gaze touched places inside Greer he didn't know existed. For one or maybe two extraordinary seconds, the music faded, and darkness crept around the edges of his vision as everything disappeared except the one holding his undivided attention. His heart was fully ensnared by a single look.

He blinked once, then twice, trying to dismiss the hypnotic grip with which Dallas held him. His breath held in apprehension as he absorbed the high voltage currents of electricity arcing between them.

Dallas blinked, giving Greer the chance he needed to step back, to remove himself from the onslaught of sensations bombarding him. What the hell had just happened?

Stacy playfully slapped Dallas's arm before getting to her feet. "I do not. Come dance with me." Stacy whined as she took Dallas's drink from his hand and placed it on the table before reaching out to pull him up. "You can't get out of it. Come on."

Dallas moved with the grace of a panther, powerful and elegant as he rose to his feet. Everything about Dallas screamed forbidden even as every desire Greer ever had coiled tight in his gut, fanning his need to claim Dallas. Helpless to do anything other than track each step the gorgeous guy took toward the dance floor.

Once again, the earth shifted under Greer's feet. He knew what he needed to do. He wasn't about to let this opportunity pass.

"Dance with me," Greer said to Skye. His gaze remained fixed on Dallas's sculpted body as he spoke.

Greer only looked away long enough to place his glass on the table then took Skye's from her hand when she didn't move fast enough for his liking.

"These good here?" he asked Jorge and pointed to the drinks at the edge of the table, but didn't wait for an answer, sliding an arm around Skye's waist before practically dragging her with him. Dallas pushed his way into the crowd, his towering height the only way Greer had to keep an eye on the gorgeous man.

He started moving, paying little attention to the music or Skye who tugged him down by the arm to yell in his ear. "What's going on with you, Greer Lockhart?"

"What's Dallas's story?" he asked, deliberately avoiding her question. A second or two passed as Skye's pretty face contorted into a confused grimace before she stopped moving—not that she'd done much dancing to begin with—and stared him straight in the eyes.

"What?" Skye asked, confused.

His three-word sentence hadn't been complicated, so he waited for her to figure it out.

"I didn't see that question coming."

Greer continued swaying to the music, guiding his palms down to each of her hips, encouraging her to move along with him.

"He's not gay."

How had that answered his question? He gave a simple shake of his head. "I keep telling you and Kailey, everybody's a little gay. So, what's his deal?"

"No, he's not gay." Skye bit her lip and cut a worried gaze back toward Dallas. She had that protective mama bear look. Greer eagerly followed her line of sight. The warmth that seeped into his skin stunned him silent. A rare occurrence indeed. Dallas was enchanting in the silliest of ways because he absolutely couldn't dance at all, but he sure tried. Greer's genuine grin was immediate as he watched the dark-haired temptation move. Dallas had no shame in his game. This time Skye's cool palms landed on his flushed cheeks, snapping his attention back down to her. She gripped his shirt, tugging him closer to be clearly heard.

"He's a real good guy. We went to high school together. He's not married, but he's not gay. And he's one of my dearest friends. Like a true best friend since second grade."

He lifted his brow, encouraging her to say more as he began rolling his body with hers.

"He's got two brothers. He graduated from UTA. He was an elementary school PE teacher, but started working at the gym as a personal trainer. He works nights and has done really well there."

Now, they were getting somewhere. "Who's he dating?"

Skye's brows plunged into a hard V. He took her silence to mean she couldn't remember the last time he'd dated. A guy like Dallas would be sought out by women…and men, for that matter. Greer hoped there may be some sort of promiscuous curiosity on Dallas's part for no other reason than he really wanted it to be that way.

"He's busy with BikeBro. He doesn't have time for anything more."

Greer's smirk turned her confusion to irritation. But her statement made him curious. "Does he work for the company?"

Both her hands landed on his chest, and she started pushing him off the dance floor, not caring who she ran into as they went. "Greer, he started BikeBro with his brothers."

Once they were off to the side, her palms captured his cheeks, more forcefully this time. She drew him down to where their faces were only inches apart. Her gaze was guarded as she stared him straight in the eyes.

"Listen to me. He's not gay or bisexual. That's not going to change, doesn't matter how good-looking you are. Dallas had a long-time girlfriend in college. They dated until a couple of years ago. She took a job in Atlanta. He didn't want to leave his family. He's a good guy. Real down to earth. A sweet man who doesn't play your kind of games."

Greer nodded, hoping to indicate he'd heard every one of her cautionary words. "Okay, how old is he?"

She threw her hands in the air. "You didn't hear a word I said, did you? He's like a brother to me, Greer. He's not your type." Skye rolled her eyes at his raised brow. He waited for an answer. She finally gave. "He's twenty-seven. He helps anyone in need. He volunteers for things all the time, and when I plan to settle down, I'm marrying him. He would be a great husband and father. He's a genuinely good man." She tossed out her hands and gave him a clear, see-I-told-you-so look.

Pfft, like her reply answered anything. "Then can I have a crack at him before you two get married?" He flashed her his most charming grin.

She didn't find him funny at all. Her stern finger pointed in his face. "You're a player, Greer. A handsome one, and a fun one, but still a player. Seducing Dallas just to add another notch on your bedpost isn't right."

"Huh," he said and took her arm. The immediate connection he'd had to Dallas wouldn't allow for games, but he wasn't near ready to share what had just happened to him. Instead, he hid behind his charming, playful grin. "Let's move closer."

CHAPTER 8

Stacy lifted her long hair off her neck while Dallas danced to the beat of the music, swinging his hips, throwing his arms around, laughing, having fun, and encouraging Stacy to keep moving. For someone who whined about wanting to be out on the dance floor, she sure didn't ever want to stay out there too long.

"You're having a good time?" she yelled.

"I'm relaxed and drunk," he yelled back as a "Get Ur Freak On" mix began to play. Dallas instantly emulated Missy Elliott's famous dance moves, at least as best as he remembered.

Sweat trickled down the side of his face, and he struggled to determine his exact level of inebriation. He suspected complete intoxication hid somewhere in the wings, ready to attack after all the free drinks he'd somehow scored.

Dallas had forgotten how much he liked to dance. His

workload didn't allow for too many nights off. Since the gym had closed to celebrate Jorge's birthday, and Tank, the assistant manager, turned the party into a required meeting, Dallas had been forced to come along, and was happy to be there.

"You don't usually drink that much," Stacy called out, letting her hair fall down her back and raising her hands in the air as she danced up against him, motioning him lower. He bent his head as instructed. "Are you sure you're not using me to avoid Skye's client?"

Dallas knew exactly who Stacy referred to. It was growing late, the club's patrons were down by half, and from the gym only he, Stacy, Skye, and Greer were still there. With such a bold lack of manners, Greer had stared openly at him for the last hour. Dallas suspected everybody in the bar knew exactly who held Greer's undivided attention, but it hadn't bothered Dallas in the least.

"Maybe he's staring at you," Dallas quipped to Stacy's upturned face.

She barked out a laugh at him. "If he stared at me like that, we'd already be gone! He's my kind of sexy."

Dallas chuckled at the audacity as Stacy shuffled away, leaving him to dance alone as she retreated to the table. Stacy was right, Greer oozed sexy. The guy could have anyone inside this bar.

By Dallas's best estimate, it made Greer harmless and barking up the wrong tree, probably on purpose for how many eyes were on Greer, watching him watch Dallas.

And you've watched him like he's watched you.

He'd really grown to dislike the side of his brain that never allowed him to walk away from the truth.

Questioning his own sexuality had been a small blip in the story of his life. His truthful side rolled its eyes at such a generic way of describing how he'd let a dude kiss him at his first junior high boy/girl party. At the time, Dallas hadn't been questioning anything. He had wanted that kiss as bad as he'd ever wanted anything in his life. But the hell that had rained down on him afterward had been enough to never bark up that tree again.

The beat of the mix intensified as the movement of the crowd surrounded him. Thankfully, it took his thoughts away as he sang the words and changed his steps.

"You can dance." The warm breath hitting the back of his neck made him jerk his head over his shoulder. Goose bumps sprang up underneath his knit long-sleeve pullover. Even under the haze of so much alcohol, his body tightened, tensing under the assessment of those amber eyes. Greer danced with another guy directly behind Dallas.

Yeah. Greer had that deadly combination of handsome as hell and sexy as sin. Dallas might just have a dream or two about Greer under the guise of sleep. He was too nice-looking for his own good. He had player written all over him.

Dallas sucked his lip between his teeth and held the other man's gaze.

He could play on me, teach me a thing or two.

Skye popped up from out of nowhere. Within seconds, the four of them were dancing together. The sultry sound of a "Blinding Lights" mix began to play, slowing the group down, but lost none of the engaging vibe. Dallas moved freely, bringing forward every remembered step from his youth. He grinned happily and executed a partial spin, watching in slow motion the way the crowd bobbed along with him.

Dallas circled back around, with a shake of his hips. This time Greer was the only one there, closing the distance on him. Greer's style mimicked Dallas's, and he let the moment between them happen. He and Greer moved together, Greer anticipating each bump and thrust as if they'd been dancing together forever. Maybe Greer had the same junior high school dance training as Dallas. He burst out with a laugh and didn't back away as Greer took his levity as an invitation, coming forward, brushing against his chest.

The music changed again. A reggae tune had Greer circling a strong arm around Dallas's waist, drawing him flush against his body. Greer was a bold one. It felt good, dancing like this with him. Their bodies pressed tightly together. They slowed as Dallas stared straight into Greer's hypnotic gaze, losing himself in their depths.

Greer was tall, maybe only an inch or two shorter than Dallas and had a hard, muscular build. The twinkle in Greer's eyes took on a challenging glint as his grip tightened and his hips rolled forward. A rock-hard erection ground against him. Dallas's breath hitched as Greer scanned his face. The intuitive man grinned, deducing exactly what Dallas tried to hide. What a fucking turn-on.

A tingle slid along Dallas's heated skin as his heartstrings tugged at something unknown. The strict discipline he held over his body's sexual responses began to crumble. Dallas tensed, his body growing hard and hot all over.

Greer leaned in, the exotic dark spice of his cologne aroused Dallas's senses. His eyelids slid closed as Greer spoke a little above a whisper against his ear. "Don't close up on me. Go with it. It's hot as hell watching you dance."

His seducer's strong palms blazed a heated trail down Dallas's sides, gripping him by the waist. In an unexpected move, Greer sent Dallas's head reeling when he twisted Dallas around and hauled him back against his chest. Dallas's body fit snuggly along Greer's as if he were made for this man. The crease of his ass rested perfectly against Greer's groin. Those strong arms wrapped tightly around his stomach, holding Dallas securely in place. There was no denying Greer's intentions with the guy's hard cock nestled firmly into Dallas's ass.

Dallas didn't make any move to dissuade the blond either. Staying just like that, lost in the feel of the moment, they danced together once again.

Oh hell, his defenses were nothing but dust the second Greer thrust his hips into him. The erotic move ignited every cell in his body, setting him aflame from within. Dallas closed his eyes, willing himself to remember every synchronized dip and roll they made. He wished he hadn't had so much to drink. But then again, he wouldn't be wedged against another man on the dance floor if he weren't intoxicated. The feel of Greer's heated body moving with his, the scent of his cologne, the hard evidence of need cradling his ass, it all vanquished Dallas's inhibitions.

Man, he liked that cologne. There was an odd relaxing comfort in their embrace too. Something dreamlike and surreal that eased his burdens if for nothing more than the few minutes of this song. Dallas relaxed back, letting Greer guide their movements. The man eagerly took charge, tightening his hold, drawing Dallas head to toe against his body.

"You're beautiful," Greer purred against his ear.

"Thank you. And you're gorgeous… but I'm not gay," he said with a bit of slur, angling his chin to look back over his shoulder. The music softened, the song a slow one, easier on the ears. The guy rocking them together skimmed his fingers under the hem of Dallas's pullover. Greer's fingertips skated along his bare skin, sending an involuntary quiver over each of his stomach muscles.

"You sure about that? Not everything has to have a label," Greer cooed enticingly, against his ear. Greer's quick puff of breath sent uncontrollable shivers racing down Dallas's spine. His eyes closed of their own accord. Dallas allowed himself to just feel every one of the forbidden sensations firing his body up.

If things were different, this could have been his life.

But they weren't different.

"Yeah," Dallas finally managed to say and opened his eyes, the words leaving a bitter taste on his tongue. Reality crashed down around them.

The man.

The music.

The cluster of people.

All the eyes watching him and Greer dancing together.

Dallas's stomach churned. *Fuck.*

He pushed away from Greer and stumbled toward the bathroom, holding his mouth, willing himself to hold back the pending purge. He made it as far as the hall where a line formed outside the restrooms. The rancid burn raced up his throat. *Shit.* Dallas had no choice but to rip the top off the trashcan and empty his stomach inside.

"I'll get him," Greer said to the angry manager who had homed in on Dallas, making a beeline straight toward Dallas. Drunks throwing up in garbage cans weren't a good look for his business. Greer grabbed a stack of napkins, never breaking stride, trying to get to Dallas first. "Can you get us a glass of water and settle my tab?"

"Sure. Get him outside. There's a door to the right."

Greer followed the line of the manager's arm to the exit door nearby. Greer nodded and went to Dallas, resting his hand on his back as he shoved the napkins into Dallas's line of sight.

"Ugh. I'm sorry," Dallas croaked, still bent over the can.

"No need. Get everything out because they're kicking us out. The door's behind us," Greer explained, stepping a foot or two away as Dallas started to rise.

"I'm sorry," Dallas repeated, wiping the napkins over his mouth. The horror of the moment showed on his wary face.

"Here's some water. And here's your tab and card. You two need to leave." The manager extended a small black tray to Greer. Dallas took the glass, but hesitated, looking skeptically at the contents inside. Greer quickly added a tip to his bill and signed his name. He took his card then grabbed Dallas's arm, pulling him out the side door marked Emergency.

The cool, crisp fresh air sent a chill racing over Greer's heated skin. Dallas seemed oblivious to the bite in the air and went for the bench right outside the door, a streetlight nearby.

"I'm sorry for all that," Dallas said again. He finally manned up, taking a drink, swishing the water around his mouth. He leaned away from Greer, over the side of the bench, spitting the water out on a small patch of grass. Greer eyed Dallas closely before he took the seat opposite him, staying as far away as he could, just in case Dallas wasn't finished.

"You don't have to be sorry. I've had a better night tonight than I've had in a long time." Which was oddly true.

Dallas cocked his head, looking at Greer as if he were the craziest man in the world. His forearm came up, wiping across his lips. "You're a strange dude then."

Greer burst out laughing, nodding his agreement. "Hear that a lot." After a minute more, Greer reached for his cell phone to text Skye that they had been thrown outside. After he stopped typing, he lifted the phone to let Dallas see. "I texted Skye."

"Good. I need to go home." Dallas started to rise as if he planned to leave right then. Greer placed a firm hand on his shoulder, keeping him seated.

"She said you two are riding together, and she'll be out in a few minutes. She's met someone."

"Of course, she has." Dallas's tone had Greer cutting his gaze over and laughing at the clear exasperation. "When's there not some guy dragging after her?"

"I guess you're right. I think she has a trail of us waggling along behind her," Greer said. Dallas leaned back on the bench, looking up at the night's sky. Whatever he saw caused him to release a deep sigh.

Seconds later, Dallas's head pivoted toward him. "I thought you were into guys?"

"I am." Greer nodded, letting himself watch Dallas's intriguing face as he tried to sort that answer out.

"So you're bi?" he asked, studying Greer as if he were some sort of complicated puzzle.

"I'm not into labels," Greer explained honestly.

"I'm straight," Dallas blurted as if Greer had asked. Then nodded to drive his truth home. He looked down at the glass in his hand and took another drink of the water, this time swallowing. Dallas seemed to call it a win when the water stayed down and placed the glass at his feet.

"You keep saying you're straight." Greer's hand still rested on Dallas's shoulder. He gave a gentle squeeze before running his palm across Dallas's shoulder and neck with a slow, purposeful caress. He skimmed his fingers over the tight ridges and cords of muscle that had imprinted themselves on Greer's chest when they danced. "You own BikeBro?"

Dallas's serious look morphed into something humorous. His smile brought an involuntary grin to Greer, and he had no idea why. "If by own you mean financially extended beyond anything I'll ever be able to pay back, then yeah, I own it."

The revealing words shouldn't have held such a teasing tone. Greer's brows lowered, replaying the words over in his head to find how he'd misinterpreted the explanation. Dallas dropped his head back against the concrete wall of the building behind him and closed his eyes, the smile still on his face.

Greer let his hand trail down Dallas's large bicep. This might be a first. He couldn't remember ever feeling such a draw to another before. A possessiveness ran through him—certainly uncharacteristic of him—but it didn't change things. As much as he liked Dallas's eyes on him, this allowed Greer the chance to study Dallas without looking like such a creeper. From this angle, Dallas's hair looked more auburn than brown, and his masculine face, with its hard edges and soft, smooth skin might be the most alluring he'd ever seen.

"I've been taking classes on BikeBro this week. It's a great workout." Maybe the only thing that could have taken his mind off Dallas was Biker101. He had his chance to find out who was behind the account. The ethics of taking advantage of a drunk guy aside, Greer seriously wanted to know who'd beat him. "I won the challenge last week. Biker101 was hard to beat. Actually impossible, which is hard for me to say. Do you know that user?"

"He's crazy competitive too." A huge grin spread across Dallas's face, but otherwise he didn't move a single muscle or say another word.

Well, at least now he knew Biker101 was a guy. Greer's image of the fictional biker became a little more solid with the discovery.

"Tell me his name," Greer coaxed.

Dallas opened one eye, peering at Greer for several long seconds. His voice was low, the slur more pronounced when he said, "I can't say."

Which meant Dallas knew the answer. Greer opened his mouth, pressing his advantage.

Skye came around the corner. "There you two are."

Dallas closed his eye.

"Yep, your guy here got us kicked out," Greer said, and Dallas's head swiveled toward Skye.

"I did. I need to go home. I'm fading fast. Ready?" Dallas asked.

Skye nodded in Dallas's direction. "He's not gonna be able to make it to the front, is he?" Both Dallas and Greer gave firm shakes of the head, causing Greer to laugh out loud at the solemness on Dallas's face. "Let me get an Uber to pull around here." Skye worked her phone as Dallas tried to rise, only to misjudge every movement, ultimately falling back down on the bench again.

"I'll help you get him home," Greer said, reaching for Dallas to help get him on his feet. A set of headlights rounded the corner of the building, heading toward them.

"It's the opposite direction from you. He lives in my complex," Skye explained, raising a hand for the car as if the three of them alone on this side of the building weren't enough of a clue for the driver. When the car stopped and information exchanged, Skye took Dallas's other side and walked him to the backseat. Greer held most of Dallas's body weight as the guy teetered. Dallas provided absolutely no help. No way could Skye handle him alone once they got to their destination.

"You need my help," Greer said, placing a hand on Dallas's head as he guided him down into the backseat, carefully tucking him inside the car. "You can't manage him on your own." Greer stuck his head inside to speak to the driver. "If I ride with them, can you switch this to my account and get me home? I live close to Baylor on the M streets."

"Sure thing. Not a problem."

Greer shut Dallas inside and motioned for Skye to follow him to the other side.

"This feels like a lot," she said, scooting across the back seat. He followed her in. It did kind of feel like a lot, and weird for him too. It was the strange connection he couldn't define, but it didn't seem to matter either.

CHAPTER 9

Was every ride service this uncomfortable?

Greer lived his life as a normal, everyday kind of guy, but he was certain this was the last time he'd ever Uber anywhere again. The small backseat of the compact car provided little comfort for any of the three passengers nor did it block the snores ripping from Dallas's apparently serious sinus problem. Within three seconds, Skye shoved a couple of breath mints into Dallas's mouth and forced him awake long enough to focus on chewing. Skye's mother hen nature, where she was everyone's cheerleader in life, had seemingly found its end while sitting next to Dallas and his vomit breath.

Dallas and Skye lived on the outer edge of Grand Prairie, Texas. The town wasn't foreign to Greer. He'd heard of the place many times throughout his life, mainly due to the numerous tornado warnings that targeted the path down the I-20 corridor. Greer had grown up in Southlake, north of Fort Worth. He'd never ventured much farther south than downtown Dallas.

From the stories he'd heard about the southern half of the DFW area, he had expected the worst. All that manifested on their late-night jaunt was wide-open star-filled skies that cast shadows over what appeared to be rolling hills as they drove down the crowded highway.

"If you take this exit, you can drop us off at the back of the complex. The code is one-zero-one. Our buildings are to the right of the gate there." She pointed the driver to the off-ramp and down the service road, giving him Dallas's building and apartment number.

"Let's get you home first. It's dark out here," Greer suggested.

Skye looked at him then out the window before shaking her head. "We live close…"

"I know you. If we take him home first, you'll try to say you got it, then take off for your place in the dark." Greer leaned forward to speak directly to the driver. "Take her to her apartment first." He used his no-nonsense tone when he looked back at Skye. "Tell him where you live."

The car came to a rolling stop, the driver's gaze flitting to the rearview mirror, waiting for her answer. It took a second or two before Skye finally gave in and pointed the driver two buildings over.

Once there, Greer opened his door, stepping far enough out of the way to allow Skye easy access to scoot across the seat. He knocked on the driver's side window, motioning for him to roll his window down. Greer bent, speaking to the driver, but staring at Dallas who lay sprawled out, his head back against the seat with his mouth gaping open, oblivious to the world around him. "I'm going to make sure she gets in okay. I'll be back."

He got a wary nod from the driver who looked out at the night, turning his head this way and that to scan his surroundings.

The driver appeared as freaked out by the complete darkness as Greer was. He shut the back door and heard the locks initiate. Skye seemed oblivious to either the driver's or Greer's reservations. She was already striding toward her apartment.

"I have a roommate," she said over her shoulder as he jogged to catch up. "I'll be fine."

"They're not out here with us right now," Greer said and followed her up the steps to the second floor. His BikeBro overworked thigh muscles resisted, burning with each step up he took.

"I do this all the time. Every day in fact." Skye bounded happily upward, taking two steps at a time, her jaunty climb clearly mocking his weary muscles. He didn't even care. He was more amazed at how her legs didn't ache as badly as his. "It's not a bad neighborhood. I love it here."

"I'm making sure you get inside safely. It's the gentlemanly thing," he replied sarcastically and attempted to roll his eyes as he concentrated on his steps. "I wasn't raised by Neanderthals."

They stayed silent for the length of those steps until Skye slowed at the top and looked back at him reflectively. A seriousness came over her. Her gaze scanned the length of his face, assessing him. "I saw Dallas dancing with you."

At this angle, they were very close to the same height. The darkness did little to hide her concern. The uncertainty in her gaze spoke to his newfound, odd sense of unrest. The rawness of the possessiveness he'd developed for the passed-out man in the car seemed better left unspoken, making Greer do what he always did: hide behind something cheeky, keeping his true feelings buried as deep as they would go.

"I told you that no one's a hundred percent straight."

She nodded, laughing softly, most likely not to wake her neighbors. She started for her apartment door, keeping her steps slow and her voice a little above a whisper. "He's a real good guy, Greer. Like it's surprising how good he consistently is. He's great with children. The senior aerobics class at the gym loves him. He's fostered animals. He loves his family. They're all very close. His dedication to his youngest brother is probably the only reason Ducky functions normally in the real world." Skye stopped at her door, digging the key from her back pocket, then looked Greer directly in his eyes. "He's a real good man."

He nodded even as he had a hard time connecting with the deeds of such a saintly human being. If he were being honest with himself—and that was a rare occurrence indeed—Dallas sounded much like the kind of man Greer had always wanted to be. His damn innate arrogance and self-centeredness hadn't allowed him to believe all those good qualities truly existed in a person.

Skye pushed the key inside the lock and twisted the doorknob. The door unlatched and opened an inch or two. Her concern kept her from going inside. He plastered on his best grin and bowed his head just to keep some levity between them.

"Consider me warned."

"So you're going to chase after him?" Skye asked, pushing the door open wider.

Greer nodded slowly, not at all certain he planned to pursue. Whatever had happened in the club between them, all the draw pulling him to Dallas, made him restless and uneasy.

Besides, it seemed sleazy to think of sex with someone so close to being the next messiah. Greer reached out for the door, pushing it farther open to encourage Skye inside.

"Remember, no means no, mister." Her fingernail poked him in the chest. "And not tonight. He's drunk."

"I can be a gentleman." Greer furrowed his brow. She nodded once before closing the door. Once the lock clicked in place, he started down the stairs. The Uber's red brake lights illuminated his path.

Greer crawled in the backseat beside Dallas who looked as if he hadn't moved an inch since he'd left. The smiles just kept coming as Dallas let out another long loud snore.

"He's loud," the driver said as the vehicle started forward. Skye hadn't exaggerated, Dallas's apartment was truly only two buildings over. When the driver stopped, they both tried to look out the windows to see the numbers on the doors.

"Let me go check which one is his." Greer jumped out, jogged to the first door in the building, pleased Dallas's place was the closest to the parking lot. He went back, rounding the trunk to Dallas's side of the vehicle. He carefully opened the door, thrusting a hand out to keep Dallas from tumbling forward. "Okay, big guy. Time to wake up."

He couldn't help but feel the strength of Dallas's strong body as his hand roamed over Dallas's defined chest, jostling him a few times. When he didn't wake, Greer lifted his palm to Dallas's cheek. The soft whiskers of more than a five o'clock shadow had Greer sweeping the pad of his thumb up to the soft, bare skin of Dallas's cheek. The simple, intimate touch sent tingles shooting across Greer's body, rippling over his heart.

No doubt, Greer was drawn to Dallas. Everything about these unplanned touches had affected him in the most primal way. Instead of dwelling on the instant quickening of his heartbeat or the rapid puffs of his breath, Greer slapped Dallas gently a couple of times on the cheek. The guy barely moved. Then only to get more comfortable.

"Sometimes it helps to pull 'em out of the car." The driver's voice helped stabilize the suddenly unsteady ground beneath Greer's feet, reminding him they weren't alone. He ducked his head back inside the vehicle, judging the sincerity of such a suggestion. "Be careful, sometimes they just fall to the ground."

Great advice.

With an open palm and a little more force, Greer tapped Dallas on his cheek. Dallas's red-rimmed gaze met his as if nothing more than a gnat had bothered him awake.

Dallas's brows slid into a hard V, looking as if he tried to work something out in his head. "I thought I was going home."

"You are." Greer stepped back, letting Dallas see his building. "Come on. I'll get you to your apartment."

"Okay." Dallas gave a slight single nod and didn't move another muscle. His eyes closed.

"All right, we'll do this the hard way." Greer pulled Dallas's arm while moving one of his legs out of the vehicle. Luckily before he tried to lift this hunk of a man to his feet, Dallas jolted awake again, getting himself awkwardly out of the car.

"Where are we?" Dallas tilted his head, the dawning answer appearing in his eyes. He looked over at Greer then back at the car, placing a hand there to steady himself. "Why're you here?"

"I'm the designated," Greer answered, mesmerized again by the set of beautiful green eyes. How did Greer continually lose focus every time Dallas's direct gaze landed on him? This time it wasn't a stealing of his breath like before, but something deeper, more foreign. For a man who controlled everything in his life, Greer could only describe the emotion rolling through him as a giving. A giving of what? He had no idea.

Dallas's thick, dark eyelashes swept down. They stayed there for a second or two longer than they should. He swayed on his feet, and Greer caught him, jarring Dallas awake again.

"I'm not a big drinker."

"We'll get you to your apartment," Greer whispered, circling an arm around his waist, drawing him closer to his side.

Their closeness had Dallas glancing down at him, a weird expression crossing his face. Dallas's tongue darted out between his lips and stayed stuck out as he mouthed, "What's in my mouth?"

Greer couldn't help the chuckle as Dallas lifted a hand, trying to knock away the offending taste. "It's a breath mint Skye gave you."

At first, Dallas didn't seem to believe Greer until an understanding changed the harsh look on his face. "Mint. Yeah."

"Come on, big guy." As much as Greer enjoyed this unguarded exchange, Dallas was getting heavy. Greer started them toward the apartment. The arm around Greer's shoulders moved, hooking around his neck, drawing him closer to Dallas at a much more awkward angle.

Under the dark skies, Greer leaned Dallas against the exterior wall of his apartment to help hold him up. The happy drunk's head hit the bricks where his hooded gaze took his fill of Greer. His stare traveled the length of Greer's face, lingering on his lips before lifting to his eyes. The direct, unabashed stare remained trained on him.

Dallas's fingertip lifted to Greer's lower lip, swiping across the length. It might as well have been Dallas's hand caressing his cock with all the need it provoked.

Something instinctual made Greer release his hold and lean in flush against Dallas's long body, saying his truth. "I had an unexpectedly good time tonight. I'd kiss you goodnight, but, well…" Greer gave a wince, thinking about how they ended their time together at the club. "I think a kiss on the cheek will have to suffice tonight though."

Greer didn't allow himself to overthink. He leaned forward to press his lips against the whiskered skin right above Dallas's strong jaw. He stayed there, skimming his nose up, breathing Dallas in, taking the hints of a citrusy cologne and slightly musky man deep into his soul. Greer's hand traveled to Dallas's bicep, memorizing the feel of the bulge as he moved his mouth higher, to nip at Dallas's earlobe.

Dallas gave the slightest groan as he turned his head, his mouth pressing against Greer's neck. Oh fuck, Greer's body ignited as he closed his eyes, memorizing the feel of those perfect lips touching his skin. "Someday, I'll be inside you. You can count on that."

Greer drew back to look into Dallas's eyes as the apartment door opened, light flooding the small porch. A younger man stepped outside. Greer jumped backward, holding Dallas against the wall by way of one hand pressed to his chest. The guy looked curiously at him, not in a jealous or surprised way. "Skye called and told me you were bringing him home."

He nodded against the most intense disappointment he might have ever felt in his life. Who was this guy? Greer tried to cover his knee-jerk reactions and finally just stuck out a hand, hoping to hide the fact that he'd just been pressed from head to toe against Dallas's inviting body. The guy looked at Greer's offering for several seconds before he reached out and took the handshake. "I did… Yeah. I'm Greer Lockhart."

"You're the guy who bought all those boxes." Greer lifted his brows at the response, wondering how he knew such a thing off the top of his head. "You were fun to watch the other night. Let me help get him inside." Greer automatically moved out of the way. When the guy gathered Dallas in his arms, he looked casually over his shoulder. "He doesn't drink that much. I'm Ducky, his brother."

Hearing the word *brother* flooded him with an immediate feeling of relief.

As Ducky shifted Dallas and absorbed his weight, Greer watched Ducky melt underneath the bulk of Dallas's body. They both headed for the concrete, and Greer reached out to help hoist Dallas off Ducky.

"Let me."

Together they pushed Dallas back against the wall. Greer leaned in to haul Dallas over his shoulder in a fireman's carry. As he absorbed Dallas's weight, Greer blew out a quick breath and groaned. He was relieved his knees didn't buckle under the weight.

"Where to?"

"His room's this way." Ducky led the way through a tiny apartment. A computer desk and sofa took up most of the living room. There were no pictures on the walls, but hundreds and hundreds of stacked BikeBro cardboard boxes taking every available space.

Greer followed Ducky down a hall to an open bedroom filled with electronics, many wires of different colors and sizes, and an expensive stationary bike. A twin mattress had been pushed against the far interior wall and looked like an afterthought. The open closet door overflowed with all the things the bedroom couldn't hold.

"Dallas is a neat freak. This is hard on him," Ducky said, moving blankets back for Greer to place Dallas on the bed. Ducky helped. They narrowly avoided bumping Dallas's head against the wall. The bed wasn't long or wide enough to hold Dallas's height or bulk. Ducky pulled off Dallas's shoes. "He's real stressed. He needed a night out. He used to go out all the time."

"He'll probably regret it in the morning." Greer took a careful step back so as not to disrupt any of the wiring to the stationary bike where apparently the magic of BikeBro came to life. He tucked his fingers in his jean's pockets, watching as Ducky tossed Dallas's shoes toward the closet. He followed the path of the shoes as they went, one skidding farther than the other. If Dallas were in fact a clean freak, that would drive him nuts in the morning.

"Is this where he teaches classes?" Greer asked, motioning with his chin toward the rest of the room.

"Yeah."

Greer turned for a closer look around the room. The bike took most of the space. The backdrop consisted of another wall stacked with more cardboard boxes, their logo facing a mirror across the room.

"I guess I haven't taken one of his classes," Greer said absently, realizing he hadn't ever searched for an instructor other than Skye.

"He does day classes and works at the gym at night," Ducky explained, starting out of the bedroom. "Skye works five nights a week, but she's adding classes. They've been best friends since…

well, most of my life. She's like a sister."

Greer turned off the lights as the pieces to the Dallas puzzle slowly revealed themselves. He glanced back at the sleeping man, wondering if there were any secrets he kept from his family. Maybe the thought was way off base, maybe it was nothing more than his own hopeful need. One thing was certain, the more he found out about Dallas, the stronger the attraction grew.

"Get him a glass of water and Advil. He'll need it in the morning. Tell him I'll be in touch."

CHAPTER 10

A firm jostle startled him from the tight grip of sleep.

"Dallas, wake up."

Something wasn't right. Dallas reluctantly turned his head and forced his eyes open to a fuzzy image of his brother, Ducky, standing over him. Sharp pain pierced his skull, blurring his vision even more. He had no choice but to close his eyes. At the same time, the rancid taste in his mouth had him struggling to get out of bed to go brush his teeth. Ducky's hand gripped his bicep, helping to lift him.

"You've got thirty minutes before you sign on this morning. Do you want me to post an old class?"

"What time is it?" Dallas's tongue felt like it had grown ten times its size. His throat was dry, and his voice cracked as he spoke. He fell back on his mattress. This time, he threw an arm over his eyes to shield them from the brightness in the room. The pain in his head intensified with every second that passed, making him forget about the foulness in his mouth.

"Eight thirty. I've been tryin' to wake you up for a half hour. If you think the class needs to be live, I can try to be the trainer if you want."

The hazy image of Ducky, his primarily sedentary brother, leading a class of well-trained athletes sat inside his brain long enough for him to attempt a smile. The grin hurt his face, and he stopped that nonsense immediately.

"What happened last night?" he asked, remembering the bar and free drinks being placed in front of him. Why did he get free drinks?

"I don't know. A customer of ours brought you home. You passed out on me. There would've been no way to get you inside without him."

Dallas let those words gently roll around in his head.

He'd been sucking down mixed drinks and dancing, both opposite his normal behavior.

Rewinding to a little earlier, he remembered Skye urging him to relax and have a good time on the way to the club. She promised to get them home safely.

Then Stacy had wanted to dance. Dallas's eyes opened to Ducky still standing over him as he remembered the crazy attractive blond guy who'd shown up to their party with an unlimited drink budget.

Greer Lockhart.

A man as sexy on the dance floor as off.

A tempting promise in his amber eyes.

He knew the stare well because he'd felt it. Every time he'd turned Greer's direction, that devastating stare had been aimed his way.

How the fuck did desire stir within him even under all this

pain?

The tight clamp Dallas kept on his emotions gave a hard push back at the physical betrayal of his looming arousal. He'd fought the battle over his body's natural erotic response to the same sex. Dallas had learned to tamp down his urges, bury them so deep that he could almost pretend the feelings weren't even there.

His anxiety threatened to skyrocket. He took a deep breath to hopefully calm the racing of his heart.

No wonder he'd drunk so much last night. Greer's attention had been unwavering and utterly seducing. Dallas's body warmed and tingled all over, even as his gut churned with the worry of what that meant. He needed to stop this before it went too far.

Until now, Dallas had thought he'd learned to manage his sexual orientation issues at the age of fourteen. His parents had tackled his curiosities head on with daily bible studies, a pastor who counseled him several times a week, and strict pray-the-gay-away summer camps. The consequences of his feelings, deemed unnatural, had been beat into him over and over for years.

Where had all this newfound guy-wanting come from? Guilt rushed through him. The weight of his inner struggle was too much to bear.

"Augh." Dallas groaned as the anxiety spiked and his head throbbed. He sat on the edge of his bed, his feet planted firmly on the cold faux hardwood floor. His stomach roiled, making all the heavy thoughts from seconds ago fade. He doubled over, his arms hugging his waist as he fought the bile rising in the back of his throat.

"You smell awful. Skye said you threw up at the bar. I'm not sure you're gonna be allowed back."

Dallas figured Ducky added the last thought as opinion more than fact, but he was right in one thing: he felt like he smelled—awful.

"Here, take this." Ducky's palm appeared in his line of sight. He had Advil in one hand and a real Dr. Pepper can in the other.

"Greer said water, but I think the carbonation and sugar will help you more right now. Then drink the water."

Dallas saw the water bottle on the little table he used as a nightstand. Out of desperation, he took the can of soda, popped the top, and downed the Advil before taking a big swig of the sweet fizzy drink.

He did have a momentary reprieve from the pain as his body absorbed the soda. Then he reached for the water, forcing a large portion down.

"Do you want me to cancel the class?" Ducky asked.

"No." His denial surprised him. He'd been thinking Ducky should cancel his entire day. But he had to go on as if none of this had ever happened. He knew the drill. Moving forward with his values intact would get him back on track. This was a blip in time, a simple attraction he'd get over, nothing more. "Let me take a shower and I'll get on."

Dallas stood slowly, feeling a little lightheaded and a lot bad.

Push through.

Mind over matter.

BikeBro.

What if Secret's investors logged on today?

Okay, a sliver of motivation returned. Dallas pushed himself off the bed and wobbled toward the bathroom. "Can you bring me another water bottle and maybe some crackers or toast?"

"You don't eat bread," Ducky reminded him.

"I don't drink soda either." Dallas hoped those words came off as sarcasm, but the concern in Ducky's gaze, and on his troubled face, showed he'd missed the mark. As he passed his brother, Dallas clamped a hand on Ducky's shoulder. "I'm gonna be fine. It was just one night. Don't worry about me."

Without missing a beat, Ducky moved out from under Dallas's hold, and loped off toward the kitchen. "If I don't take care of you, no one else will. Including you."

Most likely the truest words Ducky had ever said, but not a subject he wanted to broach right now, or ever really. Dallas shut the bathroom door behind him.

"Dry toast, if that's okay. I'll make it fast," Ducky yelled.

A loud banging on the ceiling startled him, making him wince. Dallas lifted his eyes to the thudding coming from above.

"Sorry!" Ducky shouted to their upstairs neighbor.

Dallas refused anymore thought as he flipped on the shower's faucet and stripped out of last night's clothes.

Greer tossed the keys in the tray, pulling at the knot of his silk tie. He never missed a stride as he headed toward his workout room. He had approximately three minutes to change and climb on the bike to begin his first spin class with Dallas as his instructor.

He didn't let himself consider how rarely he left the office during working hours for any personal reason or how Dallas had a starring role in the loop playing inside his overactive head since leaving that tiny apartment early this morning.

Greer quickly stripped out of his clothes, hastily laying each article of clothing over a side chair, hoping to keep them from wrinkling. He grabbed a pair of cycle shorts, shoving one leg then the other through the holes while pushing his black sock-covered feet into his cycle shoes before mounting his bike.

With a quick press of his finger, he pushed the BikeBro power button and used the controls to select the current class. Seconds later, Dallas appeared, and Greer's heart jolted, instantly connecting to the trainer on the other side of the screen. Greer sat upright, slowly peddling with his arms hanging loosely by his side, drinking in everything about his instructor.

It seemed Dallas's big, powerful body spoke directly to Greer's overzealous cock. A guy like Dallas could easily give as good as he got. Greer's toes curled at the mental image of

Dallas tossing him on the bed, forcefully dominating him. What a fucking turn-on.

Lost in the mental image, Greer didn't immediately jump in when Dallas began the class. Instead, he kept spinning the wheels, watching Dallas bend over his bike and close his eyes. Skye started her classes on the floor, but Dallas was already mounted and ready to go. He saw the tired look on Dallas's face. The fine lines etched around his eyes and the firm set of his jaw and mouth. Dallas had to have a hangover, probably severe if he was in fact a non-drinker. He gave Dallas big kudos for manning up and teaching through the pain.

Dallas earned more of his respect with how he kept it together as he gave his verbal instruction. His eyes opened. They were red-rimmed and carried the weight of the world in their depths. They tugged at something unknown inside Greer. Something Greer had never felt for another human being before. An inherent need to wipe away Dallas's pain.

Dallas shifted from the warm-up into the workout. As if Dallas felt their binding connection, he lifted his eyes to the camera, staring directly at him. "We have a new rider in the class. Wild_Rider, pick up the pace. Join us."

The deep rich timber of Dallas's voice made Greer's lips curve into a grin, and he did slowly start to pedal a little faster. He didn't know what had pushed him home or even onto this bike. He certainly hadn't intended to get in a full workout this morning. He had things to do, but he leaned down, hands gripping the handlebars, and pumped his legs. His gaze never left the screen as he matched the pace.

"You know who Wild_Rider is, right?" Ducky asked, his fingers flying over his keyboard as he craned his neck, splitting his attention between the activity on his monitor, with one earphone dislodged to the side of his head. Dallas, who stood at the kitchen sink, forced another glass of water down.

"He's the guy who rode me into the ground the other night, right?" Dallas's body hurt. Something had to give before he tried to tackle his next class. Dallas reached for the Advil bottle, dumping a couple more tablets into his palm, wishing Ducky didn't feel chatty right now. His ass hit the counter as he tossed the pills into the back of his mouth.

"He's also the guy who brought you home last night."

Dallas stopped in midmotion of taking a drink, the pills already sliding to the back of his throat. He nearly choked when he tried to swallow and speak at the same time. "What?"

The information caused his head to pound as his pulse picked up, his blood double-timing through his veins.

"He brought you and Skye home. He's the one who got you to the door. He had to dump you over his shoulder because I couldn't carry you in…"

Those details were completely nonexistent from his memory. Something in the back of Dallas's head had a fuzzy recollection of sitting on a bench outside the club, and Greer asking about Biker101. Had he said he was Wild_Rider?

Oh holy hell. How did the nightmare keep getting worse?

Dallas crossed his arms over his churning stomach.

"He's interested in Skye, right?" Dallas asked lamely, trying to throw Ducky off from this weird reaction Dallas had every time the subject of Greer came up.

"Not with what I saw," Ducky said cheekily, turning his full attention back to his monitor. Ducky pushed his headphones to cover his ears again. Dallas only stared at the back of his brother's head, processing that cryptic remark. What had Greer done last night? Worse, what had his brother seen?

"Ducky, what's that mean?"

His brother didn't respond, already lost to his cyber world.

Did it even matter?

What about his company? How did his behavior last night affect their company?

Fuck. Dallas pushed off the countertop and went to the office chair beside his brother. He took the seat, letting the natural tilt cradle his body's weight. Ducky cast a glance his way, his fingers racing over the keyboard. With a jerk of his head, Ducky somehow managed to move one of the headphones off one ear again.

"What? I'm playing." Ducky nodded toward the game as if Dallas couldn't see for himself.

"What did you mean when you said, '*not with what I saw*'?" Dallas's leg started to bounce, his anxiety building.

"It's no big deal. I won't tell Dad." The unguarded words caused the air to suction from the room, stealing the oxygen from his lungs. Dallas's heart stuttered then slammed against his rib cage. His mouth gaped open, but his brain function ceased, causing no words to form at the implication of his father's involvement.

"What's that mean, Duck?" He intended his voice to be hard and forceful to gain all of his brother's attention. Instead, the words came out breathy, weak, and needy. His gaze penetrated Ducky. His internal fear had him drawing in on himself as understanding formed. Whatever Ducky saw made him lift his fingers off the keyboard resulting in instant death and destruction for the characters on the screen.

"The guy was all over you last night. When I looked out the window to make sure it was you, your hand was on his face. You looked happy. I didn't know if I should interrupt." Ducky's words rang with truth and held no shame or condemnation. His brother simply blinked as he laid out the facts for Dallas. He wished he felt the same way. His brain went numb as his body heated, absorbing the magnitude of his utter humiliation. Heat flushed his face.

Time stood still as they stared at one another.

"He was all over you, whispering in your ear. It seemed like you were into it too. I was glad you were happy. You deserve to be hap—"

"Stop." Dallas's calloused hands reached up to cover his face. The images Ducky described flooded through his head. He'd been attracted to Greer.

No, not attracted. Impressed with how well the guy was put together.

Fuck that. What a lie. Greer was drop-dead gorgeous.

Dallas had been spellbound by Greer.

No. *No.* He had worked hard to be the person his parents wanted him to be.

"Dammit."

"Dallas, I won't say anything to anyone, especially not to Dad or Donny. I promise," Ducky said, leaning toward Dallas, his hand squeezing his forearm.

His father would be livid and mortified. If anyone ever found out…no one could ever know. Dallas steeled his spine, pulled his shit together, and looked directly into Ducky's wide eyes. "What you think you saw was just drunk bullshit. We were both drunk. It wasn't real."

Ducky nodded until his nod transitioned into a head shake of *no.* "Greer wasn't drunk, but he was real nice. He seems like the kind of guy we thought he was when he bought all his employees a box—"

Dallas cut Ducky off. "Just stop, okay?" His heart threatened to drop out of his chest.

A clammy sweat broke out across his body. Anger made him bolt out of the chair, declaring what he desperately wanted to be the truth. "I'm not into dudes, Duncan. Nothing was going to happen. And for God's sake, don't ever say anything to Dad or Mom or Donny. Their bullshit caused me lots of unnecessary pain. It wasn't fair or right."

The long-buried wounds rose to the surface. The torture of the mental and physical beatings he'd taken at his father's hand as he'd tried to beat the gay out of him had pain slashing across his heart. He remembered the feeling of being so alone.

He refused to be that scared boy again, but damn, it was hard.

"Dallas, I would never say anything. I don't care. You need to be you. You're worthy and valued for being who you are, just like you tell me." Ducky's games were forgotten as he pushed his chair back, away from Dallas, giving him room. "I will always have your back. You know that, right?"

Tears threatened to fall. Dallas's blinding anger wouldn't allow him to rationalize Ducky's truth. He flipped around and left his brother sitting there before he said anything hurtful. Dallas slammed his bedroom door and dropped his ass on the side of the bed. His head fell into his hands. He was so confused and frustrated at the way things were. What would his father say?

He'd worked hard to keep tight control on himself. How could he have let his guard down now?

Watching in the rearview mirror, Greer backed out of his driveway, absently pushing the button to lower the garage door as his cell phone rang. He slowed at the end of his driveway, working the gearshift while glancing at the caller ID on his dash. He didn't recognize the local number but felt like living on the edge. He answered blindly through Bluetooth. "Greer Lockhart."

"Hey, it's Dylan Reeves. You got a minute?"

Talk about an unexpected blast from the past. "I haven't talked to you in a couple of years, then I hear your name twice in less than twenty-four hours. Of course I have time," he said.

"Good. I wanted to cut through the assistant game and schedule some time with you in the next day or two. I have something I want you to see." Intrigued, Greer shifted into neutral and pressed his foot fully on the brake, staying at the end of the driveway, letting his car idle. He reached for his cell phone to pull up his calendar.

"Sure. What're we talking about?" Greer flipped through his screens, searching for his calendar app.

"I've come across an investment opportunity that I want to put in front of you. It's a local business called BikeBro. Have you heard of 'em?"

Greer barely got the app open when he forgot about his cell phone altogether and stared out his front windshield. This was all too big of a coincidence.

"I have. I just had a workout with them less than fifteen minutes ago. I met one of the owners last night," he explained and looked around his car, waiting for the Punk'd guys to pop out. When they didn't, he added, "What're you suggesting?"

"Well, I'm not a hundred percent sure. You and I need a face to face. I'm interested in investing in them, but I can't take on anything more by myself. Wilder's exploding. I have time restrictions, and they need help," Dylan said.

"Yeah?" Greer asked, still not certain this wasn't some sort of big joke.

"Yeah. I like the product. I like the brother team. They're young, fresh, and focused. They need cash and they're overextended. They might have to pull the plug before they ever get truly started."

Okay. Dylan's explanation proved he did in fact know about BikeBro. The cogs in Greer's head finally fired-up and started turning. He wasn't quite ready to tell Dylan that he'd gotten an up-close look at the brothers' corporate office, shipping facility, and warehouse—all inside their tiny apartment. He wanted to know more of what Dylan had learned.

"How's their production?"

"They need guidance. An advisor and consultant. Help with all aspects of their business, but they're ripe, eager, and open to any help. They have big dreams. Tristan wants to buy the product and we can. It just all seems so personal… I don't know. I like these young men," Dylan said, thoughtfully.

Yeah, on a first impression level, Greer liked them too. "You know, there's no personal in business." Greer lifted his phone again, searching his schedule as Dylan chuckled.

"Except everything in life is personal."

"Well, I'm fascinated with the product and got a glimpse of their operation. They won't sustain much longer without some help—both financial and managerial. Where are you now?" Greer had managed to clear a couple of hours when he spontaneously came home to see for himself what kind of condition Dallas was in this morning, and whether he would show for his scheduled class. Seemed meeting Dylan now was as good a time as any.

"I'm actually standing on the front porch of your office. I like what you've done with the place." So those were real birds chirping in the background and not some piped in nature background noise.

"I'm about ten minutes away. Stay there. I've got a few ideas." Greer tossed the phone in the passenger side seat and worked the clutch, reversing out into the street.

"Will do." Dylan disconnected the call.

Greer fully understood his choice to break some of his firm rules. When dealing with business, he generally liked to stay in his lane. His firm invested in environmentally friendly for-profit businesses. He believed philanthropy was the only hope to make the world a better place.

But his true interest in BikeBro couldn't be called anything more than personal. Dallas had left his mark on Greer last night. He represented something deeper than obsession for Greer and had more meaning.

Greer took the curve out of his neighborhood, intrigued as hell at the prospect that had fallen into his lap.

CHAPTER 11

Greer tucked a pillow between him and the headboard of his bed, resting back with the laptop on his thighs. A Texas-size thunderstorm wreaked havoc outside, the wind whipping, tree branches scraping wildly against the side of his house. The forecasted cold front fought for weather dominance over the unseasonably warm temperatures. The storm was anticipated for the last several hours. He liked the cozy feel of being forced home under the bed covers with the low volume of the television keeping him company, and a nice bottle of white wine by his bedside.

He was surprised to learn network television was still a thing. He let it play in the background as he worked on the new BikeBro deal. He and Dylan had jotted down a shortlist of potential investors, understanding this was to be done outside of Greer's normal book of business. In a *what the hell* moment, they'd spent the afternoon together, creating a proposal for BikeBro and made preliminary calls to their potential investors, ticking off their list one by one. Together, they'd had the magic touch—everyone wanted in.

Greer had his analyst complete a quick needs-based assessment using Dylan's handwritten notes from his meeting with the brothers. The report proved stunningly favorable in moving forward, helping everything fall into place a little faster than normal. BikeBro had some product issues and their bookkeeping was a mess, but overall, they didn't require the resources Greer had suspected from the three minutes he'd been inside their apartment.

A ding from Greer's cell phone caught his attention. He looked down to see Skye's name in the notification bar. He picked up the phone, swiped a finger over the lock screen and read her text.

"Why do you want his number, Greer?"

Greer's thumbs flew over the small keyboard of his phone. *"I want to check on him. He was pretty messed up last night."* It seemed reasonable and truthful enough. He pushed send, dropping the phone back on the mattress. He hadn't completed two additional sentences in the rough-draft contract when the phone vibrated again.

Of course, he picked it up. *"I should ask permission before I give out his number."*

Greer's head started shaking *no* at the terrible idea. He couldn't make his fingers move fast enough in order to keep her from texting Dallas right then. *"You know I'm safe. I'm not going to bother him. I just want to check on him. Ducky seemed worried."*

He gave himself a mental high five for throwing Ducky into the mix.

The three typing dots kept Greer glued to the small screen

until no words ever came. Minutes passed with nothing more before he dropped the cell back on his bed. Greer refocused on the agreement. He read the same sentence three times, trying to make himself concentrate on anything other than Skye's pending text message.

Reasonably, he understood even if he didn't get the digits, he had his way into Dallas's life by way of the investment opportunity. He'd already decided to keep an eye on the entire project himself—at a distance, of course. Those three brothers had no clue how a business truly operated.

Skye didn't have to give him Dallas's number. He could get the phone number by himself.

Greer clicked the Wilder search engine icon and quickly typed BikeBro into the search bar. He expected to find a website link. Instead, he found a list of videos. Dylan had told him the company used YouTube as a marketing source, but he hadn't given it another thought. What an error that had been.

Drawn to the shirtless cover image of Dallas bent over his bike, his face showing the strain of the exercise, Greer clicked on their channel. Dallas dominated more than half of the video listings. He looked over the sizable subscriber count and average views of each video before clicking on the first one. Their branding seemed spot on. BikeBro was clearly the most prominent part of the video.

When Dallas started speaking, Greer lost the battle with his will. His gaze fixated only on Dallas. For someone who had managed his obsessive tendencies for most of his life, it was insane how badly he wanted him. The utterly handsome man, with the deep rich voice, caused Greer's dick to stiffen, pressing uncomfortably against the underside of his laptop.

At the sound of the text notification, Greer absently reached for the phone, barely able to take his eyes off the screen to see Skye's message contained ten numbers. If they weren't Dallas's digits, he would know soon enough. He started to type a message, but his gaze riveted back to his laptop's screen. Everything about Dallas just did it for him. He was hot as hell, no question, but also a good instructional trainer.

He watched Dallas for several seconds until the need to talk to him overpowered everything else. Greer paused the video and sent a text to the number. It took an insane amount of time for him to form a single introductory sentence.

"I'm checking on you." Greer pushed send, and started the video again, watching several more minutes as Dallas spoke to the class attendees. He seemed to have an infinite amount of energy. His voice barely seemed labored as he rode. In length and in intervals, Dallas explained the benefits of using BikeBro for a workout. It was damned impressive.

Greer's phone dinged, the vibration rattling in his hands. He casually lifted the device as if every one of his thoughts, all day long, hadn't been centered on this exact moment. The return message was simple and to the point. He suspected the trainer was very much the same way. *"I think you have the wrong number."*

It wasn't the message he hoped for. That would have been: *"Hi Greer, come fuck me, then do it again, then let me do you. I've been waiting for you."* But at least it was a start.

Greer typed quickly in response. *"If this is Dallas Reigns, then yes, it's the correct number. I'm Greer Lockhart. We met last night."* He pushed send, keeping the phone in front of him, staring down at the screen. His heart did a weird tripping thing as he waited. Greer again homed in on the desperate feeling that seemed to run rampant when he let his mind wander about Dallas.

Maybe as much as a minute passed before the reply came. *"Right. I should have gotten your number and messaged sooner. It's been a day. Thanks for making sure I got home last night. It wasn't the best idea to get so drunk. I understand you're responsible for the endless drinks. Not really thanking you for those."*

Greer read the message twice, pleased that Dallas's good

personality held. He was charming even in text message form. He started to type his own witty reply when another message came through.

"I'm afraid I gave you the wrong impression last night."

The furrow popped between his brows as he forced himself to forgo any other comment other than clarifying Dallas's last text. *"What impression is that?"*

Less than thirty seconds later, Greer's suspicions were confirmed. *"I'm straight. I appreciate the attention, but I'm one hundred percent straight."*

Hmmm. Maybe Dallas remembered more than Greer had hoped. More likely, Ducky had told him what he'd walked out on last night. Damn.

Then the devil's advocate that always lived inside Greer's busy brain reminded him how much Dallas's words landed in the deny-too-much category. His panic settled; he was back in the game. A smile touched Greer's lips as he typed. *"I believe you have the wrong impression of this message. I was just checking on you. You have to be hurting today."*

This time several minutes passed with no response. So many minutes, that he started to lay the phone down, strategizing his next move when the ding had him jerking the phone back up. *"The day started off rocky, but I'm good. Thank you, again. My little brother said you got me inside. I vow to never put another living soul in that position again."*

The genuineness of Dallas's words seemed to mess with Greer's game. Greer could see the true gentleman in Dallas through the text messages. Skye's descriptions of the trainer resonated. He sensed Dallas's truth and honesty. Greer typed slowly, trying to keep it light while wanting Dallas to know his own reality. *"It wasn't a problem. I enjoyed myself last night, more than I have in a very long time."*

A tinge of disappointment forced Greer to put the phone down. What had he expected? For Dallas to want to continue what they'd started last night? Not necessarily, but maybe something in him had hoped it would be that easy.

Then again maybe he didn't want easy. The chase was the best part, whether in business or pleasure. Most of the time, the end never met the expectation he'd built in his head anyway.

A resigned sigh slipped free.

Greer looked around the meticulously designed bedroom as if seeing it for the first time. The minimalist look didn't require a large amount of detail. Greer had never felt lonely before. He could say he even craved the selfishness of being alone, only doing what he wanted to do. So, what was he feeling right now?

He didn't know or couldn't put it into words.

When no other text came, Greer let it go for the night. He re-started the video he'd been watching, looking down the list of comments. There was quite a bit of interaction from the viewers. Dallas had a lot of female interest.

He mentally relived the full body, head-to-toe dancing he and Dallas had engaged in last night then the erotic feel of Dallas's fingers tracing the length of his lower lip. Man, that had been a sexy move. Greer's cock thickened again, turning into a hard, pulsing need, just like last night. He stared at Dallas's exercising form. He'd already jacked himself today, thinking about Dallas, but no more. He was saving this need for when Dallas finally gave in. He hoped it didn't take too long.

CHAPTER 12

"Is Mrs. Haven in?" Dallas asked quietly into the phone the next morning while peeking down the hallway leading into the living room of his apartment. Ducky had his back to him, headphones covering his ears with the muted sounds of hard-core metal bleeding through. At least one monitor looked to be in play over an epic battle of *League of Legends*. The apartment was almost silent except for the music slipping from Ducky's headphones and the furious pecking on the mechanical keyboard. He seriously had no idea when his brother ever slept.

"May I tell her who's calling?"

"Dallas Reigns. We used to work together at Florence Hill." He silently shut the door to his bedroom and went to the far side of the room. He didn't want Ducky to hear this conversation, even accidently. Ducky and Donny were still coasting on their high after meeting with Dylan. Their business had had too few milestones to let his newfound melancholy seep over into their good mood. Once these plans firmed—if they firmed—he'd let his brothers know he'd found another income source to hire more trainers. He'd rationalize this as his backup plan, nothing more, nothing less.

"Hi, yes, I remember you. Hang tight, Dallas. Let me see if she's in." He wasn't certain if going back to teaching full time was even an option. Maybe he could pick up some long-term substitute teaching gigs. Then he could actually pay next month's rent on time.

Dallas unknotted the damp towel around his waist and tossed it over the seat of his bike, going for his closet. He had his underwear on and one foot inside the hole of his athletic shorts when Mrs. Haven answered.

"Dallas, is that really you?" Mrs. Haven asked, sounding genuinely excited to hear from him. She'd always been just like that, truly interested in him and his life. Her greeting felt like a warm hug, even over the phone.

"Yes, ma'am. How are you?" he asked, pulling up his shorts and grabbing a T-shirt.

"I'm fine." Her bubbly warmth eased his anxiety like a healing balm. A real smile spread across his face. She had been his third-grade teacher, and how he'd met her son, Bennett. They'd been fast friends since then. Grand Prairie ISD had been his first and only choice of school systems to teach in when he'd graduated from college. All because of Mrs. Haven. She felt like home to him. "Did you hear Bennett's having his second child?"

"No. I didn't know he had his first child. When did that happen?" he asked, grabbing a pair of socks and his tennis shoes.

"Carver's almost two and has Jon Haven wrapped around his little finger. Dallas, I have a meeting in ten minutes. Tell me why you're calling or let me call you back when I'm done."

"I'm calling because I'm mulling over coming back to

teaching. I know it's the wrong time of year, but maybe a long-term sub position, if anything's available. I figured you would know best," he said, dropping down on the edge of his mattress, placing his shoes at his feet.

"Let me see what we have, and I'll get back to you. You know I never wanted you to leave in the first place," she reminded him, like she always did when they spoke.

"I know, but a personal trainer makes so much more money," he replied, like he always did. It just wasn't enough to sustain their lives and the new business.

"You know, Jon's retiring soon. I believe he has a couple of coaching positions open. Are you interested?" He could almost hear the wheels turning in her head.

"Sure, I'd be interested." Athletics had always been his interest. He anchored his phone on his shoulder as he put on each sock. "I'm not trained in any particular sport, but I can condition the heck out of those kids."

"All right, let me see what I can find. And, Dallas, did you know the Boys & Girls Club is having their dinner fundraiser in two weeks? They're looking for donations and Grand Prairie has a table. I can get you a seat. You know those ladies love you there. They pay a pretty penny when you're auctioned off."

Oh. Yeah. Right. How had he ever let himself forget?

This was where Mrs. Haven shined the brightest. She could get a person to do things they wouldn't normally do, all in the name of helping the community. The one time he'd been talked into a date-for-the-night auction, he had in fact raised the most money of any single person there—almost eighty dollars.

Maybe it was a good idea to sign up. He'd get a free meal, and some free advertising for BikeBro. And he was smarter this time. He wouldn't go in blindly. Skye could tag along and buy his time like other couples did.

"You have time to think about it. Is your email the same?" she asked.

"Yes, ma'am, and I'll do the auction again. It's for a good cause," he said, shoving his feet inside his shoes.

"Great! I'll send you the details and reserve your seat. It's so great to hear from you. I'll email you this afternoon." There was a small knock on his bedroom door. He looked over to see Skye peeking her head inside with her eyes screwed tightly closed.

"Are you in here?" Skye asked.

"I'll look forward to it. Reserve me two seats. I'll make Skye tag along. Thank you," Dallas said, his focus still on Skye who kept her eyes closed but looked confused by his response.

"Bye, Dallas." Mrs. Haven ended the call.

Dallas tossed his phone on the bed then reached for a T-shirt, tugging it over his head and down his chest. "You keep opening my door like that and you're gonna eventually see more than you bargained for."

"My eyes were closed." The door pushed open, and she came fully inside, looking around his room as if she'd never seen it before. "I thought you had a class this morning."

"I finished. I was going out to find some food. Wanna come?" he asked, tying his laces.

"We're thinking the same thing," she teased, coming to sit beside him on the bed. Her hands were tucked between her thighs as she crossed one leg over the other to get comfortable. Which was the exact opposite of his intent for them to leave and go find food. "I've been worried about you. You're off. More than just the hangover."

How could he tell her what was going on with him? He couldn't. Ducky had been walking around on eggshells, trying to keep out of his way. He didn't like himself this way either.

The past was in the past. The misery of learning unconditional love was a hoax, that his parents' love did have conditions, was all supposed to be buried away long ago. He and his family were all in a really great place now.

Except they would not hesitate to cut him loose without a backward glance if they ever found out about last night. There was no way Donny would be able to stomach working with Dallas either. BikeBro would be ruined.

Dallas would never turn his back on his family. But he knew they would turn on him in a second.

Skye elbowed him in the ribs. She changed her tone, probably because he hadn't answered. "It's chilly outside. You're gonna need more than shorts and a T-shirt."

"How cold is it?" Right. Life was happening around him. He had forgotten a cold front had blown through last night. He'd forgotten. Dallas let go of a deep breath and turned to look at Skye. Whatever she saw had her wrapping an arm around him, leaning her head on his forearm.

"It's gonna be all right. BikeBro's going to work, I know it is. And if that's not what's bothering you, then that'll work out too. You're a force of good in this world. You'll figure out what's right for you."

He suspected she spoke about Greer, and she had the same magic healing balm about her as Mrs. Haven. He lifted a hand, playfully patting her on the face with his palm in the same manner as she patted his thigh, annoying her as she swatted his hand away. "Were you the one who gave him my number?"

The guilty verdict came by way of those big brown eyes lifting to his as she sucked a lip between her teeth. They stared at one another for a few long seconds. "I didn't know if I should or not. Greer's a real good guy once you get past his self-image of being a baller, player. He's not really either of those things. Not really. He could be a good mouthpiece for the company. Did I do the wrong thing?"

"I don't know. Is he gay?" he asked, wanting her to say no, but hoping she'd say yes. His head was fucked up.

"He's incredibly open and proud about not allowing labels. He's super successful at whatever he does. I told him you're straight. You are straight, right?" Her direct stare held no animosity or judgment, and Dallas nodded with resounding yes. "If you're not, it's okay…"

"No, I'm straight."

She nodded, maybe not with complete certainty, but they both seemed willing enough to let it go. "Did he hit on you, because I seriously believe he's harmless. But he runs in some big circles. You should see his car. Maybe he might know someone to help fund BikeBro."

Dallas untangled her hold and rose to his feet, looking for his jacket. Everything Skye said was spot-on great, he just didn't want to be the one to deal with Greer. "I can't wait to give out your number without asking." He smirked her way.

"You better not give my number out. I'm a chick. You're a bulky, giant man." She waved her hand at him as if to point out the obvious.

Dallas just cocked his head in such a way to say, *we'll see*. Her face morphed into concern as she bounded off the bed, coming toward him in fight mode. With a move he'd done many times over the years, Dallas put his fingers to her lips, squeezing them shut.

"Of course, I'm not giving out your number. Go warm up the car."

Her eyes narrowed as she stared at him for several long seconds, probably trying to judge his sincerity.

"Heavy coat or jacket?" He let go of her lips, laughing at her irritation.

"Probably heavy. It's almost fifty degrees, but sunny." She left him there as if everything had been settled between them. She'd helped, and he had to get over himself. Nothing had changed. He grabbed his jacket and started through the apartment.

"Dallas, Dylan just asked if we could meet in the morning. He gave us an address other than the Secret office. He wants us there at eight. Do I accept?" Ducky asked.

"Whatever time is fine. Text Donny." He didn't stop his forward momentum of heading out of the house. He was starving. He hadn't had much to eat since his big night out. Absently, he looked back over his shoulder as he reached for the doorknob. "I'll bring you back something to eat."

Ducky had that same look of concern Dallas had seen for the last couple of days now. "Dylan wouldn't want to meet with us if he hadn't found some backing, right?"

"Either way, Dylan's helped us out a lot. Thanks to you." Dallas turned away, tired of the worry on his little brother's face. "I scheduled a re-run for the one o'clock class. I'll make it up tomorrow on my day off from the gym."

"Dallas…" Ducky started.

"Let it go. I have." Dallas let the door slam shut behind him, resolved to pull his shit back together.

CHAPTER 13

"I can't be any clearer. You're one hundred percent wrong," Greer announced, stopping the crazy man's prattle on the other end of the phone. He came to an abrupt halt in the middle of his office, dropping his head between his shoulders, staring up at the light gray ceiling, asking for patience from above. "We're not doing it. Big tech is entirely divorced from reality. They're overvalued and have damaged the broader economy. You know how I feel. I'd rather you turn to cryptocurrency than move toward big tech."

Kailey opened his office door, sticking her head inside. She gave Greer a momentary reprieve from listening to one of his biggest investors—a guy who'd had very little when he first came to Greer five years ago. He looked over his shoulder. The frustration of such a jackass phone call so early in the morning had him pinning her with his gaze, willing her to stay quiet.

Luckily, she did. Well, as much as Kailey ever could. At least she whispered. "Dylan's here. The brothers are pulling in. Should I put them in the conference room?"

He'd tried to split his attention between the call and his sister. It didn't go well. "Dammit, Richard, stop flooding me with a bunch of unfounded bullshit philosophies that aren't going to change my mind, and hold the fuck on." Greer stalked toward his desk, punched the button to mute the call and ripped the earpiece from his ear. "Have Dylan get them started in the conference room. The presentation is set. Show him how to work the remote for the slideshow, or hell, have him just explain the terms to them. They'd be fools not to accept. I'll be in as soon as I can. I put the contracts in a folder on the credenza."

She nodded and closed the door tightly behind her. Greer took a deep breath, centering himself, and forced his blood pressure down as he refocused on the matter at hand.

Remember, you hold the cards. The contract is ironclad.

Yeah, Richard Tenney could suck it. Asswipe.

Tenney's board was pleased with Greer's leadership and direction. Whatever was up the man's ass... Who the fuck cared?

The self-lecture helped. Greer rolled his shoulders, releasing the tension that had formed there. He pushed the earbud back in his ear and unmuted the call. He didn't immediately speak. Instead, he took two steps to the window overlooking the driveway. He released a deep heavy breath.

This wasn't as much fun as it used to be. Somewhere along the way he'd lost the momentum. Greer sensed the change inside. Not with his activism, which would take the biggest hit, but with the rat race of chasing after the capital. He felt like a traitor for even thinking such a thing. He tucked his chin to his chest at the realization of how badly he could hurt so many organizations who counted on him to survive.

"I can hear you fucking breathing, Lockhart."

Greer lifted his head to see the Reigns brothers leaving their older model sedan. They were all eerily similar yet completely different. Ducky and, he guessed, Donny were inches shorter than Dallas, but still tall men. They all wore dark suits and had the same look with that chestnut hair. Ducky's curly out of control locks seemed to have been tamed, or at least an attempt was made. Donny had a military-style buzz cut. Dallas had the flip over that was so popular today.

Dallas. The temptation hadn't diminished as he stared down at the handsome man. Maybe the most gorgeous man he'd ever seen, at least to Greer's heart.

Greer's gaze riveted to Dallas as he took in his long, confident strides up the front porch steps. Dallas called to him in just the same way as he had at the club. Greer's mouth actually watered as if Dallas were a delicious morsel made just for him. His stomach twisted as he followed Dallas all the way to the front door. With Dallas's hand on the doorknob, Greer started to turn away, but Dallas stopped before opening the door. Dallas ducked his head and let go of the knob. Donny seemed oblivious to whatever was going on with his brother, pushing past Dallas to step inside. Ducky made it up the steps and stopped beside Dallas, looking inside the office, but not moving forward.

The front door closed, leaving Dallas and Ducky on the porch. Ducky nodded. Dallas extended his fist, giving Ducky a quick knuckle bump. Greer had no idea what had been exchanged between them, but something about the moment had his heart connecting.

The slow seeping warmth returned, enticing Greer back into the world where only moments ago he'd disconnected. What an odd thing.

He remembered those first few years of starting his own business. Hell, he went back even farther. He remembered being a young teenage boy, making his first online market account, pretending to be his father. Greer had been overjoyed to make his first few thousand dollars in the stock exchange. The excitement had amped up several degrees when he'd given his treasure away to help save the seals.

Greer lifted a hand to his heart. The steady thumping produced contentment. He liked Dallas being inside his building.

Tenney whistled, one of those between the finger, ear-splitting sounds. Instant pain exploded in his ear. Greer winced, knocking the earbud from his ear. Anger had him reaching for the bud, ready to slam the guy. By the time he had pushed the earpiece back in his ear, the line had gone dead.

Fuck Tenney.

His phone rang. Tenney's name and number echoed through his earpiece. Greer let the call go to voicemail.

He sucked down a couple of aspirins then went for his private bathroom, forgetting all about the asshole on the phone. He found he wanted to look his best before seeing Dallas again.

Dallas. The constant chatter running through his head muted. It wasn't a bad thing.

He quickly brushed his teeth. Unfortunately, not because he planned to kiss anyone. He ran a brush through his hair then checked his face and nose for anything that shouldn't be there. He quickly adjusted his clothing, straightening his already plumping cock inside his tight-fitting underwear. Lastly, he added a touch of cologne.

Greer gave a side grin as he stared down at his shaky hands, quickly fisting them to control the tremor. He was nervous and excited. His anticipation was getting the best of him.

He went back into his office, grabbed his suit coat then decided against wearing it and started out his office door. He infused confidence in his long stride. The flutter of his busy staff downstairs carried to him as he crossed the landing, his entire focus centered on the closed conference room door. Did Dallas have any idea of Greer's involvement in this project? That moment of surprise would be a thing to remember.

With a push of the hand to the door, Greer strode into the conference room. Kailey turned his way with a big toothy grin forming. His brow furrowed, questioning why she was even in the room. Then he scanned the participants. Dylan sat at the head of the table, Donny to his right, Ducky and Dallas were to Dylan's left. All with their backs to the door.

Ducky was the first of the brothers to look up and turn his way. He gave a surprised gasp then nudged Dallas who was bent forward, studying the contract while speaking to Dylan. "This seems generous…"

With another knock of his elbow, Ducky stopped Dallas from saying more. Dallas jerked his head toward Ducky then followed the finger pointing behind them. From his angle, Dallas had to awkwardly glance over his shoulder to see Greer as he shut the door behind him. Greer had to work to school his facial features as their gazes met, then held. The shock of the moment had Dallas's mouth dropping open and a tinge of pink flushed his cheeks. No words followed.

The blush warmed Greer's heart. The connection he experienced was all still there, drawing him with wanton interest toward Dallas. Of course, Greer's cock stirred under the force of those penetrating, perhaps even accusing, green eyes. He couldn't help but grin at the look on Dallas's face. Out of nothing more than self-preservation, Greer decided to tackle the other side of the room before shaking Dallas's hand. Even though it cost him dearly, he turned away from Dallas and extended a hand toward Dylan as he circled the table.

"I'm sorry, I'm late."

"Not a problem. We're moving through the contract with great speed. You've done good work here, Lockhart. Guys, this is Greer Lockhart, the mastermind behind this proposal. Greer meet Donny." Dylan indicated to the only brother Greer hadn't met.

As he stepped closer to Donny, he stood, clasping Greer's outstretched hand. Dylan placed a finger on the table in front of Dallas. "This is Dallas and Duncan Reigns. They own BikeBro."

"He knows me as Ducky," Ducky added as Greer continued

around that side of the table. He worked to hide his smile and nodded.

"You know, him?" Donny asked Ducky.

"Yeah. He and Skye brought Dallas home the other night."

Dylan's gaze instantly shifted, first to Dallas, then to Greer where he leaned his ass against the credenza rather than taking his seat.

"But I don't think we knew he was a part of this. Right, Dallas?" Ducky looked to Dallas for confirmation, a small furrow marring his brow.

Dallas seemed to have gone mute and developed a *deer in the headlights* look. He shook his head. An uncomfortable silence descended over the entire group.

Greer crossed his arms over his chest and nodded. "Please continue."

Dylan gave him a *what the fuck* stare. Greer casually lifted a shoulder in a shrug.

They had in fact made fast time as Dylan lifted the second to the last page of the contract. "Dallas, did you have a question before we continue?"

Dallas tried to speak and had to clear his throat before he could continue. This might be the best moment of Greer's life. The good-guy Dallas Reigns was rattled by his presence. Straight, yeah right.

"So, you'll do all this for only fifteen percent of the company?" The deep tenor did all sorts of things to Greer's insides. He watched as Dallas flipped through the pages of the contract they had previously gone over.

"We'll also have a share of the profits as outlined," Dylan added with a nod.

"Guys, this is doable. We need help with manufacturing and handling the business. I say we take this offer, right now," Donny said eagerly, throwing his hands in the air, indicating this was a clear no-brainer. There wasn't a negotiating bone in Donny's body.

"Of course, I feel that way," Dylan said, agreeing with Donny. "But you all should look out for yourselves first. Take this contract to your attorney…"

Donny shook his head, disagreeing with Dylan, and caused Greer to grin as he jumped in, speaking before Donny could say anything more.

"I'll provide independent legal counsel if you don't have an attorney. We want you to be comfortable with the offer. Please take some time, nothing changes on our end."

"Is there something hidden in here that you haven't said?" Ducky asked. Greer appreciated the question.

"No, not at all," Dylan answered. "I read line by line with you, explaining our requirements. You hold the rights to your company, but we need to get the company out of your apartment and start building the company properly. We believe this will make you more successful." Dylan placed both hands on the contract. "It'll be a lot of work for you guys with quite a bit of change hitting you all at once. It's not a decision to make lightly."

"So, you're investing in our company. You'll continue building the Secret app. We'll have a new office and warehouse. Better, cheaper vendors for the hardware, and we'll have a shipping department. You're providing us with a business consultant to help with all this paperwork we're not doing. We'll have a bookkeeper, and more trainers, with a professional studio attached to the office for the workout sessions," Dallas said, summarizing the high points.

"Yes, and while that's happening, we'll begin a marketing and branding campaign to go nationwide," Dylan explained.

Ducky's eyes bugged out of his head. His delight was clear in the expression. "And if we fail, we owe you nothing in return?"

"Correct. But you won't fail," Greer answered for Dylan, adding his two cents while drawing Dallas's gaze back to him.

The endearing blush was still there. "I own this company. You're local to me. Dylan's asked me to keep an eye on you guys. This is what I do for a living. We won't fail."

"How did you become involved?" Dallas asked, skeptically. From the rustle under the table, and the wince on Dallas's face, Greer could only assume Donny had kicked his brother.

"Dallas, he just said this is what he does for a living," Donny explained for Greer as if his brother was the dumbest person alive.

"It's a valid question. Dallas,"—Greer let Dallas's name roll off his tongue like it deserved to be there—"Dylan reached out to me the day after you and I met. Now that we'll all be partners, I have a question for you guys." He waited until he had three sets of eager eyes focused on him. "Who the hell is Biker101? I don't like to lose, and he kicked my ass."

Kailey laughed, reminding him she was even in the room. "He's the worst loser you'll ever meet. That's why you need to take this deal. He refuses to lose."

"Ignore her. She's my sister. Her glowing praise is biased." Greer gave her the shut your mouth glare. "Now who's Biker101? My ego needs you to tell me he's either Lance Armstrong or Tom Brady."

Ducky laughed along with Kailey, sitting back comfortably in his seat, looking between his brothers. "If he's gonna own part of us, he should know."

"I already know the answer," Dylan teased, reclining back in his seat, looking proud that he had the upper hand.

"You knew and didn't tell me?" Greer's brow cocked in surprise. *Fucker.*

"I'm just learning you're Wild_Rider. I didn't know you had that performance inside you." Dylan chuckled when Greer lifted his middle finger in reply to that comment. It seemed the best response to give his almost partner.

"Dallas is Biker101," Donny stated proudly, drawing every eye to him. "And you just about kicked his ass."

Out of all the answers he could have been given, this one stole his voice. Greer's nemesis was his infatuation. The air in the room shifted as did every gaze. Dylan chuckled again, apparently very in tune to Greer's visceral reaction to the news.

"So, it's you," Kailey said happily before Greer had a chance to speak. "I knew there was something about you. When you threw the race, Greer was so upset. My husband and I were on Zoom with him before the contest started. I'm not sure I've ever seen Greer work so hard." Like normal, Kailey's cheeky attitude had even the stone-faced Dallas grinning.

"I think you're right. We need to take this contract and talk," Dallas said, reaching for his file folder. "Maybe we could take you up on the attorney offer."

"Hold up." Greer lifted a hand, near not ready to let the Biker101 subject go. "I want a rematch."

"Lockhart, I've been taking his advanced classes…" Dylan started as if he were the measure to beat. He wasn't. Greer wanted to beat Dallas or die trying.

"I've taken his class too. He's a good trainer, but I want another crack at him." Greer pointed at Dallas. "Just you and me. I've really developed a strong need to beat you. You can't throw it this time."

Donny's excitement was only surpassed by Ducky's. "Would we do it as a site-wide deal?"

"I don't care. I just want the match between him and me."

"I don't think it's a good idea." Dallas's attitude changed. He lost the hesitant edge. So, Dallas was competitive. Greer could see the wheels turning in his head even as he resisted the challenge. This look was filled with promises of honesty and integrity even while Dallas planned to kick Greer's ass.

His cock thickened, and he didn't try to hide his attraction from any of them, especially not Dallas. If Dallas lived his truth, well then Greer did too.

"I think we could make it into a donation drive. I see gamers do it all the time. We can make it a private event. To watch the match, there has to be a donation of something," Ducky suggested. "Maybe to a food bank. If people don't have cash, they can donate food with a picture on social media." Ducky lifted a hand for a high-five, clearly liking his own idea.

Dallas nodded, automatically slapping his brother's outstretched hand while adding, "I'd like the donation to go to either a local food bank or the Boys & Girls Club, if that's all right. We'll make it a private event with a passcode to enter. You can do that, right?"

Ducky nodded.

"Then set the rematch. I can do it this evening if there's enough time to make it happen," Greer suggested.

"I work in the evenings." Dallas turned away. He never looked up from gathering the papers in front of him, placing them inside the file folder.

"How about Saturday morning?" Donny asked. "Gives us two days to plan a strategy and spread the word."

"Perfect." Greer wasn't giving Dallas a chance to decline. He turned to Kailey. "See if anyone in Bill Hainer's office has time to see them this morning. Send the contracts over to him now. Ask for a rush." Greer pushed off the credenza and went around the table the way he'd come in. He stuck his hand out again to Donny. "I look forward to working with you. We'll make a lot of money together."

Donny beamed at the idea. When Greer passed by Dylan, he said, "Do you need a ride to the airport?"

"I could use one."

Greer nodded and kept going. He bypassed Dallas to stick out his hand to Ducky. He was really growing to love that guy. Greer couldn't help his good-natured grin at Ducky's sincere attempt to dress up for their meeting. But the disheveled hipster inside wouldn't be contained, no matter how crisply pressed his suit and tie were.

"Dylan's told me you're the glue to this operation, and we all wouldn't be here without you."

Ducky beamed as he got to his feet, eagerly shaking Greer's hand. "We're all equal partners. I just do my part."

Good answer. Greer patted Ducky on the arm. "At some point, I need to know how you came about your nickname." Finally, he turned to Dallas. Dallas stood, and Greer offered his hand. The shake was firm and solid. He shouldn't be considering how the weight of Dallas's hand felt good and right in his. Dallas's stare held Greer captive. Time slowed, his surroundings faded, his heartbeat the only thing he heard.

He wanted Dallas in every possible way. The gauntlet had been officially thrown. Greer would win their race and steal Dallas away in the process.

"He's always been able to read people like that." Kailey's whiney voice had him cutting his gaze her way, but he tightened his grip when Dallas tried to pull his hand away. Greer held on for only a second or two longer, letting Dallas know his intentions.

Greer let go of the breath holding him in place, and stepped back, speaking to the group. "You need to be sure you all want to work together like this. I've had my sister here since the beginning of EnviroCapital. It may have been the worst decision of my life." Greer grinned his most charming smile, all for Dallas's benefit, and pivoted around, heading for the conference room door.

Dylan laughed out loud. "On that note, take me to my plane."

"Thank you, Mr. Reeves," Ducky said as Dylan rose. They all expressed their thanks as his sister took over the final moments of the meeting.

"Gentlemen, take a seat. We have coffee and danishes. Let me see when Mr. Hainer has time for you. Give me just a minute."

Greer left them there, making his way to his office for his cell phone and keys. It was ridiculous how happy he was, and how he had loved every single moment of their meeting.

"I like the way Greer's clothes fit him," Ducky said from the back seat of Donny's compact car. Dallas, who sat in the front seat, let the words bounce around his head. He cast a questioning glance at Donny who already gave him a what-the-hell-was-Ducky-talking-about side-eye. "If my clothes fit me like that, I'd wear those kinds of clothes too."

"You're a dipshit," Donny muttered, switching lanes, following the directions from the GPS.

"I bet he makes bank." This time, Dallas turned as far as the seat belt would allow, looking back at Ducky whose thumbs worked furiously over his phone screen.

"Of course, he brings in a haul," Donny said. "His clothes look like that because they're made to look like that, which is something I'm gonna have when we start making some real money."

"He's a venture capitalist," Ducky added, turning the phone screen toward Dallas to show a professional shot of Greer looking stylish yet sophisticated. He had the same sparkle in his eyes he always did. A humor of sorts. A teasing of how life was nothing more than a game to him.

Dallas quickly scanned the caption underneath the photo. Of course, Greer was a venture capitalist. It all made total sense. Well, everything except why someone like Greer had lowered themselves to the level of Club Indigo then into being the DD who'd gotten him home safely.

He pushed back in his seat and dropped his elbow on the window's edge, placing his head in his hand. He'd been fighting all these feelings for a sexy hot, game playing venture capitalist. Greer didn't like labels. What a laughable thought. Someone like Greer could afford not to label himself.

"His company works with private environmental projects," Ducky explained, making Dallas's derogatory thoughts seem condescending and petty. "I guess that's why his offices had the solar panels. Greer bought that property and remodeled it into a living building. What's that mean?"

"I'm not sure. I think it has to do with all those plants. But that BMW's an expensive hybrid sports car," Donny added, exiting the highway.

"He's the real deal. He can help us. Dallas, you gotta let him win," Ducky said, shifting forward in his seat to stick his head through the center opening to look at Dallas.

"He'll know and won't like it," Dallas muttered. He trained guys like Greer all the time. Their drive to win had an innate understanding of what it took to fight the battle. "He'll know if I go light."

"Dallas's right," Donny said, taking the turn the GPS instructed. "It's better to be honest. And remember, lots of those guys are so in debt they aren't really worth what they say."

"If you think so…" Ducky said with doubt lacing each word as he dropped back in his seat.

"You're being quiet." Donny knocked Dallas in the belly with the back of his hand. He then executed a sweet maneuver, swinging them into the parking lot of Hainer and Associates before he missed the turn.

"Things are about to change." Something deep inside Dallas knew the changes weren't going to be what they had expected. Maybe not even what they wanted.

"Yeah, you think?" Donny mocked and pushed open his car door. "It's what we wanted. We did it." Donny got out of the car then happily ducked his head back inside the opening before Dallas or Ducky could make it out. "Look, Lockhart's helping with an independent review of the contract. That has to mean he's on the up and up." Donny stood, taking several steps backward. His arms spread in a king-of-the-world motion as he excitedly yelled, "We did it. Fuckin' A, we did."

"We did," Ducky beamed, pushing open his back door, but

stopping short of leaving the backseat. He stuck his head around Dallas's seat. His smile showed him to be as happy as Donny. "Mom's gonna be proud of us."

The tension coiling in Dallas's heart didn't unwind but thinking of his mother's joy helped. He suspected she'd want to reward them with a good home-cooked meal of fried chicken and real mashed potatoes. Dallas finally pushed open the door and forced himself to chill. They were a signature away from their dreams coming true. It had to count for something.

CHAPTER 14

Greer trotted up the center stairs of his office, feeling lighter than he had in years. Even Kailey's high heel shoes clicking on the steps behind him didn't bother him. "Greer, slow down and stop avoiding me."

He winked at one of his team members who particularly enjoyed his and his sister's never-give relationship and picked up his steps as he made his way to the office. The good mood handed to him this morning on a silver platter had lasted for several hours now. He needed to find a way to keep this new attitude. His annoying, needy dick sure seemed to home in on its true desire by way of an extraordinary man, who wore a suit like he wore his athletic wear: perfectly.

If he could somehow work Dallas with grace and precision, then maybe those perfect lips would eventually be wrapped around the solid erection in his slacks. Inside his home, in his bed, with Dallas's clothes hanging in his closet.

Yeah, that was rushing things, but it didn't freak him out at all.

Several steps ahead of his sister, Greer felt reasonably sure the door wouldn't hit her when he sent it flying shut. Greer clapped his hands, rubbing them together, eager to finish his day. He stood in the middle of his office, watching the monitors mounted on the wall, catching up with the highs and lows of the stock market so far today.

"I don't know why I put up with you," she said, busting through his office door.

"Me neither," he answered, reaching for the remote control on his desk. He turned the volume up a couple of notches, never looking at his sister. "What do you want?"

"Skye told me, and I'm not supposed to say anything." Kailey's cryptic statement gained his full attention. She had her arms crossed smugly over her chest as if she held all the secrets in the world. Greer narrowed his eyes at her, taking in her whole look. She tapped her foot against the floor impatiently drawing his eyes down to her ridiculously high, high-heeled shoes. No wonder she struggled to catch up with him today.

She could be lying, pretending to know more than she did just to get whatever information she thought Greer should share with her.

"What're you talking about?" he asked a second or two later, trying for indifference, but certain his keen sister had caught his pause. Greer turned back to the monitors, pretending to ignore her altogether.

"I suspected it was the tall one. Then I knew for certain the minute you walked in."

His steely eyed gaze snapped to his sister. She threatened to ruin the only good mood he'd had in months, maybe longer. "You need to stay out of it."

"Greer, tell me." Kailey stomped her foot, turning whiney, giving up her coy game. "I want to know. If you don't tell me now, I'll just bother you all day and night until you do."

"Why night?" he asked, confused in the way she posed her threat.

"We have the Groundwork Dallas Gala tonight. You're a speaker. Remember?"

"No, I'm not," he said, racking his brain. The mental schedule in his head had no recollection of the event tonight, but Kailey was never wrong about these things. Greer tossed the remote on his desk and reached for his office chair. He had his keyboard in front of him before his ass hit the seat. "Do I have a prepared speech?"

"I want to know about this guy. I think it's more serious than you're saying. You never forget these events," Kailey said, her voice softer as she came to the front of his desk.

"Kailey, there's nothing to know. He thinks he's straight," Greer said distractedly as his calendar filled the screen.

"But you don't think so," she surmised correctly. He saw the dinner listed in his day's activities. Damn, the good vibe holding him together took a slight hit. "Neither do I." His jaw tightened and he swallowed hard.

In a rare moment of honesty between the two, Greer lifted his gaze to his sister. "You caught that?"

"Of course, I did, and he didn't want to look at you either," she stated proudly.

He agreed those were all signs in his favor, but he had to stop Kailey from going into matchmaker mode. She'd make the whole deal a disaster.

"Regardless, Dallas thinks he's straight, and we'll be working with him, so I have to tread lightly and take *no* as an answer. You know that's hard for me." Greer checked his interoffice communication chain to find the link for a prepared speech from his public relations department. His whole day took a hard nosedive. He'd planned to make up these last few lost work hours this evening. "Keep your ears open for me. Don't let the brothers get frustrated without me knowing."

"I'm not sure you've answered one question I asked." The buzzer from his landline interrupted him from having to say anything more. The call came from Kailey's desk, but she stood in front of him. He pushed to accept the call.

"Greer, the Reigns brothers are back with the signed contract. Do you need to see them, or can I take the contract?" Evan, his senior analyst, asked. Good, things were sliding into place nicely if they had already met Evan, their designated senior account analyst.

"I'll send Kailey down to make copies. Make sure they know you're heading up their transition team and schedule time for the initial onsite review as soon as possible, this afternoon if you're all available. Also, have Ducky email me with the details of Saturday's rematch." Greer threw the reminder of the competition in to give Dallas something to stew over. He needed every advantage he could get. Playing a mental game was the only gain he had to beat a super athlete like Dallas.

"Will do." The call ended. Kailey had already vacated his office, leaving his door open this time.

Want, desire, or hell, just needing a final look at the sexy, all dressed up trainer got the best of Greer. He abandoned his document search and went to the railing of the catwalk, overlooking the foyer. The three brothers stood in front of Kailey's desk and garnered all Greer's attention.

Although he couldn't hear a word said, by their actions, he could see Kailey being her normal charming self. She touched Dallas's arm and laughed at something he said. Someplace deep inside Greer, a foreign place he hadn't known was there before meeting Dallas, had him wishing he had been the one to coax the smile from the man. He'd place money on the trainer being spectacular company if he wasn't bowed up so tight.

Greer tucked his hands in his pockets, enjoying the simple pleasure of watching. Dallas's kindness radiated with every tilt and nod of his head. What a gentleman. As if drawn by his presence, Dallas tilted his head toward Greer. Their gazes connected and held until all three men and his sister turned his way.

Greer didn't do any of the flirty, suggestive things he'd normally do to a prospective sexual interest. He let the stare be enough.

The air around him crackled. The room quieted until the noise faded. His bond with Dallas grew stronger with each second that passed. He couldn't deny he felt something deeply for this man. His palms grew sweaty, his heartbeat thumped through his veins, and his breath hitched, making it hard to breathe.

Sanity had Greer nodding an acknowledgement in their direction, then breaking the connection as he turned away from the power of that stare. He could obsess—on people, on projects…on life. He knew that about himself and took steps to rein it in, but this was different. Dallas presented a conundrum: something he wanted badly but was equally afraid to explore too deeply.

He went back to his office, casting a look over his shoulder before he was completely out of view. Dallas still stared after him. Good, at least he felt it too.

Saturday Morning, Two Days Later

"Just do your best, Dallas. Concentrate. This is nothing for you," Ducky said, coming to stand in the middle of his doorway, his hands tucked in his back jeans pockets.

"Way to wound the ego," Greer's grinning face said from the newly installed BikeBro mirror at his home. Donny stood a few feet behind Greer, a wrench in hand.

Yesterday afternoon, after another lengthy text message

exchange between Dallas and Greer, Greer had insisted he needed his own mirror to be on equal footing with Dallas for their big competition. Donny had taken one from his house and gone over to Greer's this morning to do the install personally.

Of course, it made no sense, but since Dallas hadn't gone more than eight hours without hearing something from Greer, Dallas decided nothing about Greer seemed sensible. So, he went with it because what else did you do with a crazy new investment partner?

Especially the one who had gotten solidly inside Dallas's head, fucking with him in a massive way. Dallas was utterly exhausted and in way over his head.

"I don't want you to hold back, Reigns." Greer stood close to the mirror with athletic gear on, his hands on his hips, looking pretty perfect and pleased with himself.

Dallas rolled his eyes at the happy look from a guy who could have had a lucrative career as an international male model or the center attraction for any Nike advertising campaign. Every part of Greer was muscular and defined, and like everything he wore, the gear fit like a glove. Greer pointed at the screen, keeping Dallas's attention.

"I'm serious. Give it your all."

Ducky came fully inside the room, arms crossed over his chest, his grin spreading as he looked at Greer. "You're good at trash-talking without ever raising your voice."

"I knew I liked you," Greer said with a wink, chuckling at Ducky's comment. Except it wasn't funny at all. Dallas's life had become a hellish nightmare since meeting this man who was actively making all their dreams come true. "How are the donations going?"

"Before I came in here, we were at two thousand dollars pledged to Grand Prairie Boys & Girls Club and two hundred donations to assorted food banks. Four hundred people have logged on. I was impressed," Ducky explained.

"Me too. We've only been promoting for forty-eight hours," Donny called out from where he was now bent over Greer's bike, screwing something in place.

"And it's Saturday mid-morning. That's usually our slowest time," Ducky added. Dallas watched his introverted younger brother speak openly with Greer.

As they shot the shit, Dallas clicked his shoes into the pedals, trying and failing to get into the proper mental zone. Like it had a million times already this morning, his gaze absently landed on Greer who seemed to always be looking his way. Greer's grin grew. The guy did that a lot, appearing pleased when he caught Dallas glancing his way. The whole deal was jarring to Dallas's psyche and made him unsteady. Thank God, no one else seemed to notice.

Luckily, Skye's image divided the screen with Greer's, making the unwanted focus of his attention a little bit smaller on the screen. She looked tired, as if she were barely awake, and wobbled a bit when she pedaled. She gathered her long hair, tying it in a tight messy knot at the back of her head. She'd agreed to be their trainer and officiator this morning.

"You got Greer's mirror working. That's exciting."

"Donny's got this down. He doesn't play around." Greer stepped back, letting Skye see the bike. This time Dallas got a better look at Greer's room. The floor to ceiling windows lining the back wall looked out over a swimming pool and perfectly landscaped lawn. The room itself was devoid of anything other than a few pieces of expensive exercise equipment.

"We've got four minutes before we begin. Are you ready, Donny?" Ducky asked.

"Yeah, Greer's on now and everything looks good." Donny looked directly into the screen at Ducky. "I've also got him wired directly to the monitor, so if something isn't right, we won't lose him."

Ducky gave a thumbs up and started out of the room. "I'll be at my desk, monitoring everything."

"I'll stick around here to troubleshoot any issues from this end," Donny said.

"Now remember, Dallas, you don't have to do your best…" Greer said, grinning as he started spinning his wheels. Skye burst out with a laugh and so did Donny. Dallas might not have been able to help his grin either, especially with as many times as Greer had told him to give it his all.

"You're right," Dallas said, the only piece of shit talking he'd allowed himself to do. "I only have to beat you."

The pushback met its mark. They all gave a burst of laughter.

"I'm calling a tie a win in my favor," Greer said.

"We'll give you that," Donny added.

The time ticker on the mirror started the thirty second countdown while Dallas, riding as Biker101, increased his speed. He'd already settled into position, grabbing the handlebars. He closed his eyes, praying for that mysterious place he only reached through exercise. If he could get there, nothing else mattered.

When the screen went live, the spectators' small profile pictures began filling the side of the mirror. Skye started the countdown. "Ten, nine, eight, seven, six…"

"For anyone listening. I'll double all donations posted by the end of the class," Greer said.

"Three, two…" Skye continued.

Fuck. Why was Greer such a good guy?

"Let's begin," Skye said.

Lost in thought, Dallas started a second or two late, and totally off his mark.

Fuck. Greer had done that on purpose. Helping other people was such a turn on to Dallas.

Dammit, concentrate.

Fuck.

Thirty minutes later, Dallas's chest heaved as he pedaled his heart out. The zing and whiz of metal meeting metal, spinning his wheel faster than anything he'd ever managed before didn't help Dallas feel secure in his place. He paid little attention to anything other than pushing himself, yet somehow, he instinctively knew this wasn't going to be enough.

Dallas was past being physically and mentally exhausted, and Greer was a force of nature. A mammoth distraction sent to destroy everything Dallas had worked hard to achieve over the entirety of his life.

"Time! Let's slow this thing down, you two maniacs," Skye called out, drowning all his thoughts and refocusing him in the moment. Dallas couldn't let it go, though. His feet pumped out the last inkling of his energy. "Look at these warriors still at battle. Slow it down, guys. Ducky, announce our winner."

There was hesitation in Ducky's words, a wonderment in his quietly muttered results. "Wild_Rider edged out Biker101 for the win…by less than a millimeter if that's even possible. I'm shocked."

"Check the numbers again," Skye said in an excited rush.

"No!" Greer croaked.

Dallas's lungs heaved, barely drawing in enough breath. He couldn't manage to push himself up. Instead, he tilted his head, looking into the mirror, sweat blurring his vision.

"It's…called," Greer panted.

The always put-together Greer, looked runover, much like Dallas felt. Greer tumbled off the bike, one cycling shoe still clipped to the pedal. His leg twisted as he hit the floor, sprawling out on the hardwood, dragging air into his lungs. Donny went racing toward Greer to keep the bike upright and off their main investor.

With a dramatic flair that was all Greer, he flung an arm over his eyes. His chest rose and fell rapidly with every breath. Dallas kept pedaling, barely, and dropped his head over the handlebars, letting the bike hold him in place.

The laptop sitting on the floor underneath the mirror showed him what the viewers were witnessing. A zillion heart shaped emojis splattered over the screen. The end total was seven hundred spectators signed on, watching him and Greer battle it out. The chat's rolling feed raced up the right side of the screen, showing the excitement of the community. Too bad he couldn't see what they were saying.

Conflicting emotions had Dallas closing his eyes, ducking his head between his arms. He had lost, but his company was having a great moment. And he'd raised money and food for charity.

"You okay?" he heard Donny ask.

They must have ended his and Greer's live feed. From the living room, he heard Skye and Ducky keep steady conversation going, engaging with the members. Good for them. As Biker101, his profile was still darkened. He should probably say something, but decided he'd make a statement later. He needed rest before he could form coherent thought. The sleep that kept evading him for the last week, looked a whole lot more achievable in that moment.

Dallas forced himself up. He grabbed his towel and water bottle, squirting a long stream directly into his mouth before tackling the dismount. Thankfully, his legs held him upright. He had one goal in mind: his bed. He took off his sweat-soaked shirt, tossed it toward his laundry basket, and opted to keep his shorts on, only because the mirror was still connected. He ran the towel over his head then down the length of his face and chest before he dove for his small mattress.

"We should say something on 101's account," Dallas said to Donny as his eyes drifted closed. "And ask Skye to take my class this afternoon."

"You were badass. If you threw it, you can't tell," Ducky said. Based on the position of the voice, he guessed from just inside his bedroom doorway. Dallas refused to look up to know for sure.

"He better not have thrown the fucking race," Greer called.

"When I'm dry, toss a blanket over me." Dallas was asleep seconds later.

CHAPTER 15

The step count from the back of the living room to the front door was exactly forty-seven steps. Greer paced the length of his living room, certain he'd already reached his daily step goal. He'd blazed a trail back and forth through the room while occasionally adding a lap around the deck of his swimming pool. He repeated the steps, over and over again. He was dressed for the night, choosing style over comfort. It didn't matter that it was only four o'clock in the afternoon. His obsessive-compulsive side had full control right now, and he was primed to begin his date-night with Dallas.

A date that Dallas either didn't know about or was purposefully dissing him on. Either way, Greer's frustration level had reached eight out of ten and was getting the best of him.

He and Dallas only had a few days' worth of text history, but in every exchange before this one, he could at least see that Dallas had read his messages. That was until the text messages Greer had sent as soon as he'd gotten the feeling back into his body after their match this morning.

Those texts were marked delivered, but not read. What did *delivered* even mean?

With a swipe of the thumb, Greer scrolled to the beginning, rereading every message sent.

"*Good rematch. I want my prize to be dinner with you tonight.*" Delivered.

"*I didn't take you for a sore loser. That's usually my job in any position I find myself in second place. Dinner tonight at M Street Grill say around six. My treat even though I won.*" Delivered.

"*Dallas, it's just dinner. I enjoyed your company. We're business partners. Have dinner with me.*" Delivered.

"*I don't know if you know this about me, but I don't like to be ignored. It's only fair to collect a prize. I'm harmless. Dinner tonight.*" Delivered. He had snickered at that one. Dallas should be the last person on the planet to consider Greer harmless.

"*Dallas.*" Delivered.

No matter how Greer had been acting since that first night at the club, and regardless of his recent revelation of his newfound boredom with his life, there was one thing staying consistent day in and out: Greer wanted Dallas. That had been abundantly, if not redundantly, made crystal clear to him.

Greer thought about the guy way too often and flat out needed to get to know Dallas better. For the most part, it really had nothing to do with sex, but if he could somehow swing Dallas into the sexual side of things, he wouldn't necessarily walk away. All right, he couldn't even pretend that lie was the truth with all the steps he'd taken. He wanted to fuck Dallas's brains out.

Greer had tackled his infatuation with a next-level determination. He'd been crushing on Dallas like a schoolboy. He wasn't certain he'd ever crossed those lines, even while in school. He was powerless to stop his thumbs from typing on the small keyboard, writing another text message.

"Look, I enjoyed your company. Maybe I crossed a line, and if so, I'm sorry. I believe we could be friends, even if it's nothing more than friendly work colleagues. A dinner at a nearby grill shouldn't be out of the question." Delivered.

Flashes of Dallas's discomfort at their meeting the other morning ran through his rampant thoughts. He'd relished those shy, hesitant glances without any consideration for Dallas's feelings. Greer started pacing again. From the very first exchange, all those days ago, Dallas had told Greer numerous times that he was straight. Dallas obviously wanted to be into women exclusively.

Greer could easily conjure the feel of Dallas's ass pressing against his rigid cock as they danced, and the way Dallas's fingertips caressed across Greer's lower lip. He could visualize the instant flush around Dallas's collar when Greer had walked into the conference room. Those things told a different story.

Hell, Dylan had even noticed Dallas's response to Greer. For the entire length of the forty-minute ride to the airport, Dylan had lectured the hell out of him about keeping the relationship professional.

The intentional pivot Greer executed sent him to his fully loaded bar for a shot of anything to help digest all this defeat. He poured a good, hearty portion of tequila, tossed it back, and absorbed the burn, before looking down at his phone again.

This time, magically, the text messages were all marked read and the three little dots at the bottom of the screen were drumming their notice of Dallas's pending message. Greer's heart leapt— not past the sting of the alcohol, but still landed close to his throat. He was back in the game.

As quickly as he could, Greer tried for funny and typed, *"I'm straight."*

Seconds later, the exact message came through to him from

Dallas. He laughed out loud, instantly relieving the tension and negativity that had consumed this afternoon. He hoped Dallas laughed too.

"M Street Bar and Grill at 6:00. I understand you're familiar with the place. It's two miles from the gym. When I was on the hunt for Biker101, Marisol said the owner of BikeBro had been in for dinner. I know a secret menu that'll appease any diet restrictions. Maybe Uber over, I want a celebratory drink for kicking your ass today. :) My driver can get you home whenever you're ready to leave. Hands to myself." Greer pushed send, ignoring the small little lies he'd texted. He read the words over again. Only one lie. He didn't have a driver. He'd be the DD again tonight and take Dallas home himself.

Stop right there.

Don't type another word.

He'd set the plan in motion and would not put another disparaging thought out into the world. Greer put his cell phone down, ignoring any other replies as he went for his office. He'd be at the grill on time. Until then, surely, he had enough unfinished business to keep him occupied for the next hour and a half.

The back door of the vehicle was barely shut before Dallas heard the wheels crackling over the gravel in the parking lot. He should have told the driver to hang on until he made up his mind. Now, he stood a few feet from the entrance, staring up at the M Street Bar and Grill neon sign, wondering why in the hell he had come. He shouldn't have.

Greer planned to fund and organize the complete rebirth of his company. How could he not show? But his always grounded and reasonable side mocked him for even allowing himself to take things this far. This was all very personal for Dallas, making Greer more a frustration than anything else. But he also had to find a way to work with the force of nature sitting on the other side of this restaurant's doors. They were partners after all.

Yeah right. He should go. Business hours were from nine to five, Monday through Friday. Not one in the morning text messages to see if Dallas was sleeping or another text message suggesting a virtual lunch date to talk production. Greer had Dallas hook, line, and sinker, messing with his head.

Dallas pulled his cell phone free of the logoed company joggers he'd chosen to wear tonight to help represent and drive home the point of this being a work meeting. The front door pushed open. Greer's blond head stuck through the opening. The guy had a way of keeping his head bent as his eyes lifted that made his piercing gaze reach inside Dallas's chest and give his heart a much-needed embrace. After Greer looked him up and down, he pushed the door wide open and held it with one hand as he stepped fully outside.

"You're late. I'd decided you weren't coming."

"It's six-o-five," Dallas said. At least that had been the time when he'd exited the vehicle.

"If I'm not five minutes early, I'm late." Greer's crooked grin tugged at the corners of his lips, amused by his little joke. "What's going on there?" Greer nodded to the cell phone in his hands.

"I don't know…" Dallas started to say, only to get a disbelieving cock of a brow and tilt of the head from Greer. "Maybe I should go."

"Why?" There had to be four feet of space separating them. Greer stepped forward, the door slamming shut behind him. Neither moved another step, but their magnetism, that physical phenomenon always pulling Dallas to Greer, was drawn taut. Held together so powerfully, it felt binding. Dallas just didn't understand the reason for their chemistry.

Dallas gave a nervous chuckle. Of course, Greer had to know why he should leave. There were a million reasons this was a terrible idea. Instead of voicing any of them, Dallas stuck with the most basic difference between them, and the one that mattered the least. "I'm in joggers. You're in slacks."

Greer looked down at his clothes then over at Dallas's, giving him a slow toe to head, full body inspection. Confusion contorted Greer's face, his expressive eyes turning perplexed. "You look great. Those are a great cut for your muscular thighs. I like the fitted look. No socks. Bold." Greer waggled his brows as he reached back for the door, tugging it open and extending a hand in a sweeping motion. "I hope you don't mind, but I've boasted my win to everyone within hearing distance. I haven't told anyone you're Biker101, but they believe you're here to celebrate my big win."

When Dallas didn't readily step forward, Greer took a single step toward him and extended a hand to his elbow in a slow, deliberate motion. "If you're a meat eater, Mac makes a burger for me that's out of this world. He combines several kinds of ground meats, but the bastard won't tell me the proprietary blend. You'd think twelve years of friendship and sharing a dorm room during our freshman year of college would count for something."

If Dallas crossed the threshold of this restaurant, his life would fundamentally change forever. He had no doubts about that. Cautious by nature, he'd never been one to reach out and touch the flame. Fear of the unknown was almost too much to bear. Yet, he still stepped forward with Greer's amber gaze holding his. What he saw in that gaze asked for his trust.

Time slowed. The subtle breeze cooled his heated face. A single bird chirped a sweet tune. Muted sounds of conversation flowed from those walking down the sidewalk behind him. Dallas was hyperaware of everything. Especially the man who held him loosely but refused to let him go.

Oh hell. When the time came for Dallas to regret this decision, he had to remember, he had no one else to blame but himself. With a deep, calming breath, he took the next step willingly.

CHAPTER 16

After three hours of dining, conversation, and game-playing, where Greer had systematically lost every round, proving today's cycling win had been a fluke, he could easily say that Dallas Reigns was a gentleman through and through. There was no surprise when Dallas reached past Greer's head, pushing open the front door before Greer could walk through. What he liked most about the move was that Dallas was close enough for Greer to breathe in the citrusy scent of his cologne.

Luckily, the unusually warm weather had held through their dinner. In the ever-changing plan dictated by each swing of Dallas's mood, Greer was thankful nothing inhibited their short walk to his house.

"You sure know how to throw a dart," Greer said over his shoulder.

"It was something my father taught us from the time we had the control to throw things. Some kids were taught baseball. We were taught darts and how to play pool. All three of us are fairly good. During the holidays, we've had some big competitions. There's been a time or two they ended in a brawl. Donny's got great aim; he can send a billiard ball flying right off the side of your head." Dallas chuckled at some memory that didn't seem all that fun, before he continued, "You know, real functional family stuff."

Greer had started walking through the parking lot toward the intersection. He slowed when he noticed Dallas's voice grew softer, pivoting a half turn to see him still close to the front entrance, tucking his hands inside the pockets of his joggers.

As Greer had thought many times over the last three hours, Dallas was seriously mesmerizing. Greer's heart did a little dip, trying to leap forward to stay connected with Dallas's, where it wanted to be. He had thoroughly enjoyed himself this evening but quickly discovered he had to hold Dallas's gaze while keeping his stare fixed on his face. Otherwise, Greer was too easily drawn to the tight material stretching over the nice-sized package in Dallas's fitted joggers.

"I Ubered here like you suggested," Dallas explained, rooted in his spot. His captivating grin broke across his extraordinary face. Those amused eyes sparkled with some untold mirth. Oh hell, Greer was quickly losing himself to the trainer. "You said something about a driver giving me a ride home."

Greer had to play the words over in his head and look away from Dallas to allow functioning thought back inside his crowded brain. Ride home. Right.

"The car's this way." Greer hooked a thumb in the direction of his house across the street.

He'd already learned to give Dallas space. If it were Dallas's idea, he seemed a lot easier to deal with in the end.

"I fibbed a bit. I'm my own driver. That's why I only had a

beer tonight and ate almost all my burger." This time, he didn't stop his forward movement when he cast a glance over his shoulder, turning enough for Dallas to see him pat his belly. "If I keep eating like that, I'm gonna have to take an extra class or two."

"Where's your car? I should probably go home, I need to be up early," Dallas said, but he did continue to follow Greer, who slowed as he got to the streetlight, not rushing to make it across before the light changed. He pushed the walk button and turned toward Dallas as he drew closer, now only a few steps separating them.

"Yeah, yeah. It's only a little past nine o'clock," Greer teased, tucking his hands in his slacks pockets, encasing his fists. It turned out to be the best option for as badly as his hands ached to touch this man.

"I know, but I've accepted a weeklong substitute position. I haven't been to bed before midnight in years. I should hit the sack early to get ready…" The streetlight changed. The walk signal turned green. Greer stepped off the curb only to come to an abrupt halt. He threw an arm out to keep Dallas from moving forward.

"What?" Greer asked, trying to make sense of those words.

Dallas looked around at the traffic-filled street with pedestrians jogging to make it across the crosswalk before the light turned red again. "Are we crossing the street?"

"Yeah, but explain that first," Greer said, making no move to cross. "I thought you worked at Elite Gym in the evenings with the rest of your time spent on BikeBro."

"That's right, but last week I called a friend at the school district I used to work for and asked for some part-time work. She found me some. A fifth-grade English class. It's a weeklong assignment," Dallas said as if his explanation made any sense at all.

"What about your training classes?" The ricochet of confusing thoughts running through Greer's head made it hard to know exactly which priority was the most important. They'd signed a large financial contract mere days ago. Dallas was the backbone of his business. He kept all facets running smoothly and had made a commitment to be available when needed. The next few weeks were crucial to the relaunch of the company.

"What I'll make next week will pay a month's salary for two new instructors to take on three new classes each day," Dallas explained as he reached around Greer to push the walk button again after the light had changed. "We'll give our members more classes with different trainers which has been our number one complaint. I'll go from school to the gym then come home and do some late-night classes and record for YouTube."

"Cash is coming your way, Dallas. If things aren't happening fast enough for you, you only had to tell me," Greer said with an edge of seriousness while keeping his all-business stare on Dallas. He couldn't have been more against any idea that took Dallas's focus off BikeBro at this stage.

"Everything's happening fast enough now. It just didn't before. I'm way overextended," Dallas said. Greer assumed Dallas's finances were dire since this was the second time Dallas had referenced them. The first time had been while they sat on the bench at the nightclub. He understood the stress of meager cash flow.

Greer had to dig his fingernails into his palms to keep from reaching out, wanting to give comfort to a man who sure didn't appear to want any. "We'll absorb all of the business's debt. I saw nothing that seemed unreasonable. You'll be taken care of. This will never work if we let the owner go belly up."

"Are we walking across the street?" Dallas asked, pointing to the new green walk arrow. Greer had to follow the line of Dallas's arm. His one-track mind had blipped momentarily, forgetting they were standing on a busy street corner having a very personal conversation.

Greer shook his head to dislodge his single-minded focus. He stepped off the curb again and started across the street. "We're not done sorting this out. I live about two blocks away."

"You really live around here?" Dallas asked, taking long strides beside him.

"Yeah, I've always liked this area. When I graduated from college, I decided to stay," Greer said, jogging the last few feet as the traffic light shifted from green to yellow.

"You live *here*?" This time Dallas's question stopped him in his tracks. The odd expression on his face had Greer looking around his neighborhood, trying to understand what Dallas found confusing.

"Yeah, why?" he asked. "It's a nice neighborhood. Quiet-ish. Friendly neighbors."

"You own an investment company. Google says you're a venture capitalist. People trust you to invest large sums of their money. You dress like a million bucks. I saw that car you were driving." Dallas threw his hands out toward the neighborhood before them. "This is nice but a normal nice. I expected you to live in a penthouse or some equivalent place that wealthy people congregate."

Greer added *charming* to the long list of Dallas's attributes. Hell, even if the temperatures dipped, he wouldn't have needed a jacket with Dallas's words warming him from the inside out. Greer ducked his head to keep his giant grin hidden and slowly walked toward his home. Dallas fell in line, easily catching up.

"I don't know whether to dash your image of me or not." Silence held between them. Greer cocked his head in Dallas's direction. That expectant stare had him answering. "Everything in my life's environmentally friendly and sustainable. My clothes are generally handmade and locally sourced. I guess that's also true about most of my material items. My home uses solar power combined with a hybrid energy system for minimal carbon emissions. My car's a hybrid. Travel's always difficult in today's world. I fly coach and I walk when I can."

So much for the suave and debonair persona he'd hoped might lure Dallas in. He wasn't sure reduced carbon emissions screamed bringing sexy back.

"And your investment company. How did that happen?"

The undeniable chemistry building between them just added another layer to the depth of his attraction. It pleased him more than he might admit that Dallas hadn't scoffed at him or laughed at his environmentally conscious ways. So many people did.

"My company's a personal motivation and a means to an end," Greer explained, knowing he came off vague. Dallas nodded, looking down at his feet as they walked. His date didn't verbally push Greer to say more, but Dallas's silence might as well have been a spoken directive to keep Greer talking. "You're ruthless with that quiet thing you do. It drives me crazy. Do you want the whole story or a condensed version?"

"Which is better?" Dallas's side grin set his heart in a pitter-patter. The playful emerald side-eye that followed had Greer vowing to always do exactly what Dallas wanted him to do from this moment forward.

"The complete version includes me stealing my father's identity at the age of twelve?" Greer said by way of a question.

Dallas laughed. "That one." His genuine grin was instant and alluring. The trainer's whole attention focused on Greer, encouraging him to continue.

"This story stays between us," Greer said, taking the right turn down his street.

Dallas nodded his oath, glancing around the neighborhood. Something about walking this well-worn path with Dallas by his side had Greer recognizing the romance of their stroll. The houses were smaller and close together, but the tree-lined street had a cozy, inviting feel with porches and streetlights creating the perfect cast of dim-lit shadows to guide their way. With spring right around the corner, soon he and his neighbors would go all out decorating their front yards with bright, fragrant blooms as the grass turned green and the trees began to bud. He really did love living here, and he appreciated seeing it from Dallas's fresh perspective.

"Well, I was twelve years old when my family went on vacation to Hawaii, and I found Kamilo Point. Have you been there?" he asked, turning on the walkway leading to his front porch. Dallas shook his head, following along beside him. "There were so many indicators that I didn't quite fit well with my family, but that vacation sealed my fate with them. Much to their consternation, I spent my entire vacation cleaning Kalimo's disgusting beaches. By the end of our stay, I had organized the locals and other vacationers. Together, we gathered what had to be tons and tons of garbage. It was a whole thing, and my parents thought I'd lost my mind," he explained, unlocking the front door as he spoke.

Greer pushed open the door, stepping in ahead of Dallas to flip on the row of light switches against the entry wall. The house instantly illuminated, lighting the entryway, adjoining living room and kitchen, all the way through to the backyard and swimming pool lights.

"It's beautiful," Dallas said, stopping Greer from saying more.

Greer went through his normal routine, tossing the keys and his cell phone on the center granite island separating the kitchen from the living room. Dallas went in the direction of the glass walls running the length of the back of the house.

"Thank you. Smaller is easier to sustain and feels homey to me. Plus, I grew up in one of those big sprawling homes. I found it's easy to lose the love when you don't have to deal with one another." Greer rounded the island, going for the refrigerator. "Do you want a drink? I have just about everything."

He had enjoyed his time with Dallas. He was comfortable and easy to be around. They'd shared an enchanting evening together and he wasn't near ready to let Dallas go.

Dallas shook his head, causing Greer to quickly add, "It's okay. I'll get you home. You had Dallas Blonde at the grill. It's Mac's personal favorite, so I keep them stocked." The open layout of his home made it easy to talk from just about anywhere in the main part of the house and be heard. "Besides, I'm not finished with my story. I told you it was long."

"Yeah, I want to hear about that stolen identity." Dallas strolled back into his living room, right where Greer wanted him.

He grabbed the can of beer and a can of water, shutting the refrigerator door with his elbow. "I came home from my vacation with a firm understanding that global warming was wholly a man-made problem. I understood that simple changes could reverse the damage we'd done to our planet. But I also understood the need for money to motivate people to make those changes. My twelve-year-old eyes were opened to a world that needed active conservation, and I saw big business as the earth's best bet for survival."

Dallas nodded until he gave a perplexing shake of the head. "Wait, what?"

"I know. What I saw so naively at twelve years old has taken me almost twenty years to even make a dent in. I still believe big business is the only way to save the world. They hold the excess capital needed to complete the thousands of projects currently working around the world to save our planet. When big business implements true change, they'll hold their partners accountable to the standards they create. If *they* require change, it'll trickle all the way down to the bottom. Every vendor, employee, and customer will eventually follow their lead. I've watched it happen."

Dallas took the beer as Greer motioned them to his sofa.

"I see the look of disbelief on your face. I get we point a lot of blaming fingers everywhere, but for me, all I see is what created the problem needs to fix the problem. Have a seat."

"You aren't drinking?" Dallas asked, his forefinger hesitating on the can's pull-tab.

"No, I've got precious cargo to get home," he said and popped his top.

"Keep going, then," Dallas encouraged. "I haven't heard environmental cleanup explained quite like this before."

Greer kept his distance, letting Dallas round the coffee table one way while he went the other. He counted it as a win when Dallas took the seat at the far end of the sofa instead of choosing the side chair. Greer sat in the middle of the couch, turning at a better angle to see Dallas.

"Here's where things get a little dicey for me. I found my father's credit card on his desk, and that started everything. I've always had a knack for understanding the stock market. I love numbers and negotiations. At twelve years old, I used his credit card to set up my first market account and began trading under his name. Things were different back then—it was almost twenty years ago. It couldn't happen that way today, but back then, I made ten thousand dollars in my first few months."

"Ten thousand dollars at twelve years old?" Dallas asked, stopping in midmotion of raising his drink. That astonishment had Greer chuckling. He sat back, completely relaxed with the secrets he'd shared.

"Yeah, I had quite a thing going until my father had some tax trouble. Even then, it wasn't horrible. I'd given all the money I earned to non-profits in his name." Greer chuckled again, then took a long drink of the cold water. His parents had been livid, and rightfully so, but not for the reason most people might think. His father had made his living in oil while Greer had donated thousands and thousands of dollars in his name to Greenpeace International. With such conflicting views, of course, he and his father were never going to see eye to eye.

"Is that a true story?" Dallas asked skeptically before taking a sip.

"Absolutely." Greer nodded solemnly, lifting three fingers in a scout's pledge. "My sister, Kailey—you met her at my office."

Dallas nodded and tilted the beer back, taking a longer drink. "She's taken a liking to you." Dallas's face turned quizzical as he swallowed. "Do you know her from the gym? She and Skye have gotten close over the last year or so."

"I've seen her once or twice. She has that same way about her as Skye. They draw people to them," Dallas said, relaxing back into the cushions.

Greer rolled his eyes, thinking about all the weirdos Kailey had attracted over the years with her kind nature. "Right? I've had to play big brother more than once. Let's talk about this substitute teaching position. What kind of salary do you need to have your main focus on BikeBro?"

Dallas's expressive face morphed again. He'd accidentally put Dallas on the defensive. He could tell immediately. Dallas had barely had two full beers at dinner, but he tilted the can back, drinking a couple of long gulps. Money must really be a serious issue. Greer didn't push for an answer, not yet, but he rose, going for another can of beer.

"Most people don't believe it, but Ducky does most of the work. Donny's our technical guy, but it's really Ducky who keeps everything going," Dallas said over his shoulder.

"But you're the face of the company, and Ducky seems better in a supportive role. His eyes always go to you for confirmation in everything he says," Greer said, grabbing the beer.

"He's young and needs to build confidence. He and I have always been close."

"How did Ducky get his name?" Greer asked, handing the beer to Dallas from where he'd twisted to look over the back of the couch. Dallas's over-the-shoulder gorgeous grin gave Greer all the feels.

"When he was little, he had a thing for Ernie on Sesame Street. He couldn't sleep without the Rubber Duckie song playing at night.

Greer took his seat, resting an arm on the back of the sofa as

Dallas slowly opened up, speaking intimately about his personal life. They stayed there, in just that way, each letting out small bits and pieces about their lives.

Surprisingly, Dallas showed a genuine interest in learning how Greer's home functioned. They toured the entire property, allowing Greer to talk in detail about all the small changes he'd made to make his home environmentally friendly.

His trainer was a sharp, articulate guy, and always leaned toward kindness. The way Dallas spoke, from the stories he told, he tried to see the best in people. Only as their night wore on did Dallas's hints of his anxiety begin to leak through. Greer interpreted those insecurities to mean Dallas wanted to be everything he could to those who held meaning to him.

Greer sat with one leg drawn up and his arm on the back of the sofa. He rested his head in his hand, openly staring as Dallas became animated while talking about his family. They were his foundation. He loved and respected all of them.

The undeniable draw between him and Dallas, the mounting attraction binding him to this beautiful man, had only grown stronger as the night wore on. The deepening connection said a lot, because Greer had obsessed over Dallas and Biker101 since before they'd ever formally met. Dallas checked off all the important boxes of Greer's ideal dream man. He honestly hadn't known these qualities truly existed in a person.

A faint needling of understanding made Greer somehow know this wasn't a coincidence. Fate played a part. Dallas belonged right here with him, and Greer had to find some way to make the trainer stick around in his life until they could sort it all out, make sense of their destiny.

"I can't remember, have you told me what kind of salary you need to make BikeBro your first priority?"

"No, and I'm not doing a pity party thing with you. Let me go to the bathroom, then I gotta be going," Dallas said, pushing to his feet.

Greer followed him up from the couch and watched Dallas walk away, eyes glued to the swing of Dallas's hips. That natural, sexy as hell swagger in his strut almost pulled a groan from him. Greer glanced down at his watch. It was already close to one in the morning.

On instinct more than any well thought out plan, he started for the bathroom, forcing himself to stop in the middle of his living room to wait. He prayed his shaky, uncertain insides weren't showing. He'd move forward with the truth, something this integrity filled man brought out in Greer.

Dallas rounded the corner, stopping short a few feet away from Greer. Something dark and uncertain crossed Dallas's features before his eyes narrowed and started to lower. Electricity charged between them, holding Dallas there with him. Everything Greer had ever wanted in a man stood right before him, even if he was uncertain and perhaps a bit afraid.

"Don't turn away." Greer took a step forward, wishing Dallas would too. When had the stakes so completely changed? Greer's hammering heart aligned with his mindful determination, something he wasn't sure had ever happened before. He let out a steadying breath, absorbing a natural, internal balance for the first time in his life.

Dallas's haunted gaze traveled hungrily up the length of Greer's body until it settled on his lips. The green alluring depths reflected immense desire, along with shame and resignation.

"You're gay," Greer said, barely above a whisper.

Dallas wasn't a liar, no matter the dozen *I'm straight* messages he'd received. Did he choose to be one in that moment? Greer waited for his response.

"I've tried not to be." The defeat of his confession had the handsome cyclist's shoulders sagging in despair.

An overpowering need to comfort Dallas had Greer moving forward, closing the distance between them. Greer didn't pause or close his eyes as he lifted slightly on his toes and chastely pressed his lips against Dallas's soft, warm mouth.

"You're safe here. I promise." Those words caused Dallas's big body to shudder and a small moan-filled puff of breath escaped his full lips. Greer felt Dallas's dick thicken. How in the fuck had Dallas held such tight control over the natural instincts of his body?

A whisper-soft caress coasted over Greer's mouth and skin, sending vibrating tingles racing along his body. "Kiss me."

Those long, soul-destroying eyelashes swept closed, and Dallas gripped Greer's hips with strong hands. His hold was so tight that Greer felt the fierceness of Dallas's internal battle.

Dallas tugged him flush against his body. Greer's heart slammed against his rib cage. He splayed his palms over Dallas's expansive chest, caressing a heated trail over each of those hard pecs, moving up until he could slip his hands around Dallas's neck. The entire move was designed to keep Dallas engaged and close as he gave his trainer time to reconcile his thoughts.

Greer tangled his fingers in the short silky strands of Dallas's hair, holding him in place as he lifted again. He traced his tongue across the seam of those perfectly proportioned lips. Their first genuine kiss. The imprint of this memory would last forever.

Determined to do it right, even if it killed him, Greer licked and nipped at the full lips, tasting and teasing with promises of all the sinful secrets to come. Now…if Dallas would only open his mouth.

The earth shifted under Greer's feet when those plump lips finally parted, granting him what he'd craved since he laid eyes on this man the very first time.

CHAPTER 17

Dallas hadn't intended to kiss Greer. He certainly hadn't meant to pull Greer against his body or feel his same overwhelming need reflected back at him. Yet, from the second Greer's haunting lips touched his, every bit of desire that had beat at him all evening—hell, that had tortured him since the minute he'd met this man—had Dallas opening under Greer's tender persuasion.

With no hesitation, Greer swept his tongue forward, taking ownership of Dallas's very soul. His heart melted despite all the reasons this was a bad idea.

Only one thing mattered, Greer's tongue moving over his, delving deep inside his mouth, chasing away all the self-condemnation. Dallas was helpless to fight against the longing. Something primal and carnal created a balance inside him, all from Greer's irresistible kiss.

All Dallas knew was he wanted Greer more than he'd ever wanted anything in his life. Greer's strong arms slid around Dallas's waist, holding him tightly, taking all the control. Their dance of tongue and teeth turned frenzied. He savored the domination, the force of Greer's determination eagerly guiding him through their shared moment.

The uneasy desperation of hiding from his true self slipped away, leaving his nerve endings igniting and sweeping desire skidding across each fiber of who he was as a man. Fireworks exploded behind his closed eyes.

Greer held too much power over him. More power than even the weight of all the discipline and lectured teachings, warning him against this improper behavior. None of that mattered one iota. For some reason, it helped justify the decision to have a one-night hookup. Tonight, Greer was in control, tomorrow Dallas knew the regret would come, and he'd deal with it then.

Dallas wrapped himself around Greer, bending into the man, taking everything offered while he nudged Greer backward toward the oversized sofa. His body's need guiding his every action.

There was a familiarity between them. They kissed like they'd been doing it for years. Greer countered every touch Dallas made with one of his own. The back of Greer's knees hit the sofa, and Dallas cradled Greer as he lowered them down, already addicted to the sweet kisses that were better than anything in his wet dreams.

Dallas crawled down on top of Greer, straddling his firm thighs, only breaking from the kiss to suck gulps of air into his oxygen-deprived lungs. Greer's jewel-toned gaze searched his face while his fingers threaded through Dallas's hair, drawing him forward again. He kept Dallas positioned just so, to better reach his neck.

His eyes closed as wet kisses and sinfully sexy swipes of the tongue traveled along his neck, up his jaw, until Greer's tongue traced the shell of his ear with expert skill, sending chills skating down his spine. Fuck, he liked that move. His hard cock leaked, no doubt leaving a wet spot in his briefs. He tucked his hips, driving into Greer's equally rigid arousal.

In a twist Dallas hadn't been expecting, Greer flipped them until Dallas's ass landed on the sofa. The guy pounced on him, pushing Dallas to his back. Greer panted. His red, kiss-swollen lips moved into a seductive smile as he followed Dallas, straddling his thighs to hover over him, making Dallas squirm under the intensity of his stare.

"From the first moment I saw you, I've only wanted you." Greer's words rumbled from his chest.

"You don't have to—" Dallas managed, but the fluttering of his heart cut off the rest of his words as it opened, giving itself freely to Greer and those sweet mutterings.

Greer pushed warm hands underneath the hem of Dallas's knit shirt. His palms blazed a tantalizing trail over each of Dallas's defined stomach muscles, up over his rib cage to lightly skim across each pec. Greer teased Dallas's sensitive nipples, rolling each bud between his fingers. Pleasure flared through his body, his nipples drawing up tightly. Greer pushed the material over his head. Dallas rose, lifting his arms to better help Greer pull the binding material off his body. Then tossed the garment carelessly aside.

"It's true." Greer's appreciative gaze scanned Dallas's face. "I feel something in this, something I need. It's hard to control myself with you, and I always control myself." Greer's plump lower lip tucked between his teeth as his hands traveled the length of Dallas's arms, touching every dip and curve as he went. Greer openly admired the view of his body. "I saw the chest hair on YouTube. I hoped it was as thick as it looked, and I'm not disappointed."

Greer sank on top of Dallas. His delicious weight pushed Dallas down again as Greer's mouth claimed his. That insistent tongue plunged forward through the seam of his lips. Greer's sweet taste may have touched Dallas's very soul. As the heat between them intensified, Dallas wrapped his arms around Greer, drawing him tightly into an embrace.

The seductive grind of Greer's slacks-covered arousal sliding against Dallas's equally hard cock had him moaning into the incendiary kiss. One second, he was melting into a kiss, and the next, Greer's palms pressed against Dallas's chest, pushing himself up, breaking Dallas's tight hold.

No, Dallas didn't want it to end. He could kiss this man forever, and that was what he'd planned to do as he reached for Greer, trying to pull him back into his embrace. Greer evaded his hold, his chest heaving as a knee pushed between Dallas's parted thighs. He tried to work the buttons of his shirt free. One leg on the sofa and the other dangling off the side.

Greer hastily moved his fingers from the shirt and fumbled with his own belt buckle. He still made record time, releasing the belt, unclasping the button of his slacks, and ripping his dress shirt free of the waistband. Dallas's dick jerked at the peek of one hard, dusky nipple, and he immediately wanted to run his tongue across the hard bud.

Ten seconds felt more like ten minutes as the sultry peep show continued. Greer was intoxicating, and Dallas was already drunk on him. He rolled his hips, driving his aching cock against Greer. Frustration was evident in the quick rise and fall of Greer's chest as he struggled with releasing the small buttons at his wrists. Greer's gaze lifted, locking on to Dallas. "I need to feel skin against skin."

Dallas sat up just enough to reach behind Greer, wrenching the tight-fitting partially unbuttoned dress shirt over the man's head. The brute force of the action sent the remaining buttons flying in Dallas's uncaring haste.

"Sorry." The word held no apology.

"I'm not." Greer chuckled as they tangled their hands at

Greer's waistband, trying to free his cock. Dallas's life hinged on the visual of what was hiding inside those slacks. Greer brought his palms to Dallas's chin, tilting his face up and into Greer's line of sight. "Look at me, Dallas. Those green eyes stay right here. I swear they'll be my undoing."

Fuck, Greer had him leaking with just his words. Dallas rose to meet Greer's descending lips halfway.

The power shifted. Dallas couldn't deny taking over as he devoured Greer's slightly parted lips. He was powerless to stop their frenzied momentum carrying them away. The kiss burned deep in his soul as Greer ate at his mouth like a starved man, neither seemed ready for it to end. Greer's fingertips slid inside the waistband of his joggers.

The first touch of Greer's calloused palm molding around the length of his shaft took him straight to the edge. He pushed up into the heat of the other man's hand.

The most perfect moment of his life was almost more than Dallas could bear. Nothing had ever felt as right to him as the feeling he got when he was with Greer. His hips surged up as he struggled to slow the kiss. He seared this moment into his forever memory. He'd had no idea how badly he'd needed to be free… to be himself.

Greer rose a few inches above his face, his lids half-closed, his full lips as pink as the flush on his face. He was as affected as Dallas. "Is this your first time with a man?"

He'd never done anything like this. Butterflies fluttered restlessly in his stomach, a mix of anxiety and excitement. Dallas's world had started spinning the moment he'd laid eyes on this man. Greer made him feel sexy and desired. These feelings were all so new and exciting.

And what Dallas had waiting for him was months of regret for what he was about to do.

So, he'd better make it good, because it couldn't happen again.

Instinct had him boldly pushing his hand between their bodies, gripping Greer's thick, long cock through the thin material of his slacks. He added just enough pressure to make Greer's amber eyes flash with desire. "Does it matter?"

Greer drove his hips into Dallas's palm, where he cupped and massaged the hard, unyielding length. The involuntary roll Greer wrung from his hips took him by surprise as Greer gave a hiss. Greer's forehead hit Dallas's shoulder, wet kisses trailing over his sensitive skin. Greer's heavy breath panted. "I haven't rubbed one off in a while…D…" The words trailed off as Dallas added pressure and rubbed his palm over the rigid shaft beneath the soft material.

Greer's pants needed to go.

Dallas worked the zipper, shoving his hand inside Greer's slacks and underwear. The heated air surrounding them shifted and Greer hurriedly lifted from his position.

"Do we stop?" Greer asked in a harsh whisper.

He reached for Dallas's wrist, his tight grip stopping him mid stroke and pulling his hand free. Dallas stared down the length of their bodies, his lungs heaving as he watched the exquisite man who'd easily broken down all of his lifelong defenses. At least for tonight, no more emotional protections were needed. Dallas was one hundred percent Greer's for the taking.

"I can stop if we do it right now. We can give you time," Greer murmured with sincerity in his eyes. So sensible and caring, and absolutely the last thing Dallas wanted.

Unable to say the words, Dallas answered by way of latching his lips around the dark brown disc of Greer's nipple. The exact one that had taunted him earlier. He circled and licked the tight bud, delighted when Greer's breath froze in his lungs at the touch of his tongue.

"God damn." Prickly little bumps rose over Greer's chest, racing to cover his arms. Then Greer lost all restraint, becoming a man possessed as he pushed at Dallas's joggers. Air hit Dallas's pulsing cock. It was too much. He cupped his palm around the back of Greer's neck, holding him in place as he sucked hard at the tight nipple.

This very moment was the rightest of Dallas's life. He never wanted it to end. But if something didn't change, he'd come before they ever truly got started.

He tightened his grip, both around Greer's neck and with the fingers that dug into Greer's thigh. He fought a losing battle against his control.

Greer pushed against Dallas's shoulders, urging him down. "Keep your hands on me, babe. Let me do this for us."

Dallas had never felt so physically attracted to anyone in his life. He took in the sight before him. His eyes swept over the blond hair, the firm expanse of Greer's muscular chest, then lowered to the most perfect cock he'd ever seen. Thick, blushing from the blood filling the deep blue veins spanning its length.

Greer flicked his tongue across Dallas's nipple. As his hand encased Dallas's cock, he reached the other low, skillfully kneading his sac. Desire raced along Dallas's spine, pushing his orgasm into his balls with demanding force. Dallas arched back, his head falling against the sofa as Greer worked him.

"Yeah, move your hand on me." Dallas panted, holding on as tightly as he could while drawing Greer flush against his chest. He thrust his hips up, pushing back and forth, fucking himself with Greer's fist. He was so close.

"Let me, handsome. I wanna be the one to make you feel good," Greer breathed against his lips. "Or we can slow…"

No. Dallas wasn't interested in slow. He nuzzled Greer's neck, mouthing and sucking the soft salty skin. He breathed in deep, taking in the delicious scent of the other man. It had been far too long since he'd known another's caring touch. Since his cock had felt anything more than his own fist. He relished each pull and squeeze of Greer's skilled hands.

Dallas growled in frustration at Greer's ability to duck out of his hold. Greer pulled away, a sexy grin splitting those well-kissed lips. Greer pulled a packet of lube from his pocket, coating his palm before grabbing his own cut cock with his hand.

The urgent frenzy settled within Dallas. This was happening. His gaze locked on Greer, committing every moment to memory. Dallas relaxed back against the sofa to watch Greer prime himself. The sight was better than any porn he'd ever seen. Dallas slid his palms over Greer's hips, pushing at the waistband of his slightly lowered slacks before slipping them down his perfect ass. He gripped each of Greer's ass cheeks, digging into the firm flesh. There was nothing soft about this man, toned from top to bottom. And he wanted to explore every inch.

Greer surprised him when he grabbed both their cocks in one fist and began to stroke them together. Perfection.

Dallas greedily watched it all. Greer's hot cock pressed against his. He jerked his hips back and forth in the rhythm Greer created. God, it felt so good.

"It's gonna be fast," he confessed. The heated pleasure swirling in his balls had them pulling up tighter and tighter against his body.

"Me too," Greer said, adding pressure as he fist-fucked them into oblivion.

The intimacy did all sorts of things to Dallas. He could have sworn his heart strings knotted with Greer's, binding them together whether Greer wanted it or not. Dallas grabbed Greer by the forearms, guiding his movements as Dallas continued to buck his hips.

Nothing had ever been this right before.

"Come with me, Dallas," Greer breathed, brushing Dallas's lips with his.

Dallas drove his tongue deep inside Greer's mouth, the need to devour this stunning man overwhelmed him. The spine-tingling feeling of Greer's cock moving against his was more than he could process. Dallas lost the battle, pumping his hips faster, screwing his eyes shut as he rode the pleasure until he lost control. His release tucked his hips, his body shuddered with gratification as warm come splattered his stomach and chest, coating them both.

"Fuck, Dallas…yes."

Dallas barely managed to crack his eyelids open enough to see Greer toss his head back. His hard, muscular chest arched as his own orgasm mixed with Dallas's to paint his chest. Greer was glorious to watch as the cords in his shoulders and neck flexed tight and tense.

Dallas closed his eyes, thankful he hadn't missed experiencing Greer in the throes of his orgasm. He could die a happy man right there on the sofa. Dallas released a long, slow exhale that honestly might have been the first real one of his life.

A sensual smile ghosted Dallas's lips while he coasted on the sated high of liberation. The fascinatingly crafty Greer had managed to get it all tonight: Dallas's mind, body, and soul.

Greer was a special man.

"We made a mess. Don't move," Greer said huskily as he leaned forward to place a simple kiss on the juncture between his neck and shoulder. The light touch caused shivers to race across his sensitive body. "Stay here."

Since those were exactly his plans, Dallas considered Greer's request to be more proof that they were truly in sync.

CHAPTER 18

Greer reached for the hand towels in the guest bathroom as an overwhelmingly strong voice inside his head made its greatest desires known. He didn't want Dallas to leave.

The realization made it more than clear that Greer needed Dallas to stay in this house, sleep in his bed, and wake in the morning by his side. This was more than wanting inside Dallas's hot ass, or Dallas in his. He envisioned a leisurely breakfast together with linked arms, sipping mimosas while feeding each other fresh strawberries. The romance of such a fairy tale had Greer's grin brightening as he swiped a towel up across his belly.

The possessiveness Greer had been battling for a while now had heightened to next level crazy. He craved ownership of Dallas in the form of matching rings and till death do us part commitments. How absurd. He'd only known his trainer for a couple of weeks. Even for Greer, that was moving way too fast, but rational thought didn't seem to matter.

He wadded the towel, placing it aside, and reached for another. Greer turned on the hot water faucet as he looked himself over in the mirror. His disheveled appearance, with his slacks barely hanging on his hips and his normally orderly hair standing on end, didn't bother him in the least. Dallas had caused this messy appearance.

A happier, sated broader grin spread across his face. This newfound inner contentment had been created by the level of commitment he was ready to give. To his surprise, the idea of a relationship hadn't freaked him out in the least. Based on his long, slow kisses and tight, powerful holds, Dallas had connected in the same way. Greer had never had a sexual partner respond to him in the way Dallas had.

He felt ten feet tall at the gift he'd been given.

The silly grin wouldn't leave Greer's face. He ran the towel under warm water before cleaning his chest and limp cock. He let the water run as he toed off his dress shoes, kicking them aside, and pushed his slacks and underwear down his legs. Those were tossed carelessly on the side of the sink.

Greer wet and wrung out a third towel before heading back to Dallas. Only a few feet from the bathroom, he heard loud snores. He remembered those from the car ride home from the club. They didn't bother him. On the contrary, they were part of Dallas and made his heart smile.

As he came into the living room, Greer drew up short, looking around the open space. It seemed Dallas had not only imprinted himself on Greer, but also his belongings. The room felt different, warm and homey.

Greer went to the side of the sofa and again lost himself in Dallas's good looks. A desire to protect this sleeping man bloomed within him. He wanted Dallas safe and happy for the rest of his life because he deserved nothing less. Just as Greer was relishing the tender moment, another open-mouthed, god-awful snore pierced the peaceful silence of the room loud enough to startle Dallas awake.

"Don't move," Greer said, dropping to a knee. He swiped the towel across Dallas's chest then back the other way.

"Shit, that's cold." Dallas jerked. The lingering effects of sleep were instantly erased as he lifted his head to stare down at the splattering on his chest. Greer chuckled, and folded the towel to swipe another way.

"It was warm before I came out here." They were silent, but not uncomfortably so. He felt Dallas's concentration centered on him as he lifted then cleaned Dallas's flaccid cock. "Pretty amazing to watch the control you had over this guy. I've been battling my hard-on since we met at Club Indigo. There's no controlling my rogue dick."

Dallas tucked one of his thick arms under his head and continued to quietly stare at Greer. His green gaze worked its magic and kept the chaos out of Greer's head. Dallas held him transfixed. He carefully folded the washcloth and placed it on the edge of the coffee table.

"You okay?" Greer asked as he pushed a stray lock of hair off Dallas's forehead. The slightest of grins tugged at the corners of Dallas's full lips as he cast a glance toward the dirty towel. "Ducky told me you were a clean freak. Want me to move it?"

"I don't want anyone else to find it," Dallas murmured. Greer settled back on both heels, pleased Dallas didn't try to cover himself from his greedy view. Greer lifted a hand to Dallas's oblique muscles, letting his fingers skim the length of the defined muscle. The comfort held between them.

"I live alone," he said, wondering why Dallas thought differently.

"Don't guys like you have housekeepers and yard people every day? Maybe a pool boy or two?" Dallas asked.

Greer burst out a laugh as he scrambled to his feet. He took

Dallas's hand, urging him up too. As Dallas stood, Greer reached for the washcloth and started for the laundry room, right off the kitchen. "Let me set the record straight about me. I have a housekeeper who comes in once a week, and that's only because I'm too busy to do a hard clean myself. My lawn guy is also my pool guy. He's here twice a week on Monday and Thursday because I need help maintaining all the landscape and greenery. For the most part, I don't like people in my—" Greer came back into the living room, seeing Dallas adjust himself back into his joggers. "What're you doing?"

"I'm getting dressed," Dallas said absently, looking down at his pants. "I can Uber home."

"No." Greer cut Dallas off with more force than he'd intended, stopping Dallas in midmotion of reaching for his pullover. Greer grabbed it, taking the shirt and tossing it back on the sofa. He sidled up to Dallas, pushing his hands inside the waistband of Dallas's pants. He shoved them down again. "Stay. We've only had a precursor to the real thing. I can take you home in the morning."

Dallas's heavy cock popped free, jutting straight at him, clearly liking his idea. "In the morning?"

Greer nodded, stepping into Dallas. He skimmed his hands over Dallas's ass, gripping each fleshy globe. "Take your shoes off. I'll take you home after breakfast. I make a mean omelet."

"Greer…" Dallas hedged, skepticism wrinkling his brow. But he didn't lift his joggers back in place or move away from Greer's suggestive hold.

"I've heard that tone of yours more times than I can count." Greer winked playfully and shifted his stance so his own hard cock lay next to Dallas's, between their bodies. Then he started the awkward steps toward his bedroom. "Take off your clothes and decide whether you see yourself as a top or bottom. I'll go either way." Greer pushed the joggers lower.

Dallas raised a single brow but seemed to appreciate Greer's attempts at coercion. He finally relented, stopping their backward motion when he toed at one shoe.

"I have to text Ducky. Make up some excuse," Dallas said, sounding resigned as one tennis shoe slipped off and one strong arm hooked around Greer's waist. The possessive command in the tight hold held all the promises of the great time they were about to have, amping up his desires by several notches.

Greer only left the hold to scoop up Dallas's shoe.

"Text him later," Greer suggested as he reached for the other shoe as Dallas toed it off.

"You always get what you want?" Dallas's question sounded more like a tease, not an accusation, so Greer gave a cocky little reply in return.

"We'll see." Dallas's pants pooled at his feet. Fuck, Greer had to ignore the hard cock jutting out at him to bend down for Dallas's pants. "Your body's incredible."

"So's yours."

Greer turned away. The plans forming inside his head might be the only thing that could have torn him away from Dallas's delicious body. He scooped up the pullover and started for the laundry room.

"What're you doing?" Dallas asked, slowly trailing behind him. Greer barely had the washing machine lid closed and the power button pushed when Dallas came into the doorway of the laundry room. "Did you put my shoes in the washer?"

"Can they be washed?" Greer asked, momentarily pausing.

"Yeah. Why're you washing my clothes? They were clean when I put them on." Dallas's perplexed stare barely edged out the nude body before him. That stare moved past Greer to his cell phone and wallet lying on the top of the dryer.

"You're stuck here now." Greer moved into the direct line of Dallas's gaze, giving a long, slow approving perusal of Dallas's gorgeous naked body. He was a sight to behold.

The trainer was solid and well-defined from head to toe. Every muscle sculpted by dedicated hard work. Greer's hard cock kicked up another notch. The sight had him leaking pre-come. He grabbed his dick, giving a slow tug from base to tip.

"I'm not near done with you, and I'm trying hard not to bend you over the kitchen counter and take you right there."

=♥=

Dallas couldn't take his eyes off the crazy, charming man. He moved back, letting Greer by. The guy had no shame. Greer slowly stroked his own cock as his eyes stayed glued to Dallas, even though he had to walk backward to keep his gaze where he wanted it. Greer's lack of inhibitions astounded him. He obviously had no reservations with being nude, on full display, inside his house.

This whole questionable night should have spiked Dallas's anxiety through the roof, yet, it didn't, and he didn't know why except to say Greer was so damn comfortable to be around. Intoxicating, compelling and addicting like a drug. Dallas's heart twisted and connected while loosening some of the tightness of his hard arousal.

Dallas's heart had no place in this arrangement. This was one night. When he woke from this dream and pulled himself back into his true reality, he was certain to pay the mental price for what he allowed to happen.

No one could ever know. No one would know. Just Dallas and his conscience.

"Beer or wine?" Greer asked, opening the refrigerator. When Greer glanced over his shoulder, whatever he saw in Dallas's expression caused his brow to wrinkle. "What's wrong?"

"Nothing at all." Dallas spoke the complete truth. His genuine grin spread as relief surged at the reprieve of fear for the repercussions of his actions. "I'm naked. Standing in the house of a man who's pumping cash into my company, guiding us on how to run a business, and who beat me in a cycling competition this morning. One I should have won, hands down. It's not my usual Saturday."

"Beating my nemesis might've been the second best part of my day," Greer quipped, pulling out a chilled wine bottle. He reached for two wine glasses in a cupboard.

"Ah, okay." The strong need to explore all the sexual deeds Greer kept teasing him with finally took a backseat. Dallas went to the edge of the island, maybe hiding a bit of his nudity, and anchored a hip there. "My second best part of the day was the cheeseburger at Mac's."

"Right?" Greer asked seriously as he poured. He picked up both glasses and came around the edge of the island, handing Dallas the fuller glass. "This is a wine Mac made. He's magic in the kitchen." Greer took a good hearty gulp, nodding at Dallas to take a sip. "A man that looks like you should never consider covering his body for any reason."

"You have a long list of good come-ons." Dallas chuckled, taking a drink. He quirked a brow. All the sweet-talking seemed unnecessary since Dallas was a sure bet.

"I'm speaking the truth." Greer playfully waggled his brows before he took another drink, urging Dallas again to take another. "You know, it took me a good thirty minutes to crawl to my bathroom after we finished this morning. You kicked my ass."

Dallas laughed and nodded. The battle had been epically intense. "I slept six hours afterward. I was exhausted."

"I know. Those six hours killed me, waiting for you to respond to my texts. We could swim if you want. I have a heated pool."

Talking to Greer was like playing volleyball. He had to be on his toes to keep up. Dallas lifted his glass again to hide his confusion. Minutes ago, Greer had been guiding him into the bedroom, asking his position preferences. Now, they were standing naked, feet apart, chatting in the kitchen.

Swimming? Really?

"Is that what you want to do?" Dallas finally asked, hoping Greer's answer mirrored his feelings. He wasn't about to let his nerves get the best of him now.

Greer shook his head, slowly. The wicked gleam in his eye had Dallas's heart doing a sudden flip-flop in his chest. "No, not at all. I wanna fuck you."

Greer's words slammed into him. His ass clenched at the thought. To have Greer be his first made him almost giddy with excitement, but he was apprehensive too. He'd only explored himself with his fingers. As badly as he wanted Greer to fuck him, he also wanted to fuck Greer. "Are you versatile?"

"Oh yeah." Greer drained the glass of wine, discarding it on the countertop. Judging by the grin on Greer's face and the twinkle in his eyes, he liked the idea.

"Condoms?" Dallas asked, proud that the neurons connected enough to say the word aloud.

"Of course." Greer walked his fingers on the granite countertop toward Dallas. He turned up his glass, wishing for more of the potent liquid courage as Greer's fingers trailed up and down his forearm.

"That's stronger than regular wine," Dallas said, placing his glass next to Greer's as the man took his hand, linking their fingers together.

"Yup, much stronger. Come with me." Greer pulled Dallas along behind him.

CHAPTER 19

Dallas would never be able to look at Greer's ass without remembering the hypnotic bounce of each fleshy cheek as he led the way to his bedroom. They slowed on the approach to the guest bedroom.

"Stay here. This room isn't for you." Greer let go of his hand, leaving Dallas standing in the hallway, right outside the door as Greer went for the nightstand. Greer returned with a twinkle in his eye as he gave him a wink. Condoms and a bottle of lube in one hand, Greer again took his hand, threading their fingers together, resuming the lead down the hall to his bedroom.

"Should I ask why those were in there?"

"No," Greer said playfully, explaining nothing more. When they toured the house, Dallas had been inside Greer's bedroom. They entered the darkened master suite, making their way to the large king-sized bed. Greer tossed the condoms and lube on the bedspread then reached for the lamp, turning it on.

That mesmerizing gaze landed on Dallas, the enchanting smile spreading. Greer gripped Dallas's cock, giving it a tug. "I can't wait to make you come again."

Dallas said nothing, words frozen in his throat at the contact. He stepped into Greer, his cock instantly growing harder from the touch. He hooked an arm around Greer's waist, unsure of what Greer wanted to do. All Dallas knew was he wanted to give Greer a blow job, an act he'd fantasized over forever. Greer's grip on his cock grew tighter with a more purposeful stroke. He started to lower to his knees. Dallas stopped him.

"But I wanna taste you so badly, D." Those words, as tempting as they were, didn't alter his plans.

"Me first," Dallas mumbled. With his arm locked around Greer's waist, he guided Greer to the bed. "Sit."

"Fuck, you're a wicked man. Full of surprises," Greer said. His fantasies sure were. Dallas's heart hammered against his ribs as Greer took a seat on the edge of the mattress, spreading his thighs, leaving himself open to whatever Dallas had in mind.

"Is this how you want me?"

Fuck yes, that was exactly how he wanted him.

Dallas had to roll his shoulders and grip the base of his leaking cock to keep from coming right then and there. The intensity of his arousal spiked to almost uncontrollable levels. The crazier part was that he wasn't stuck in his own head, berating himself over what he was about to do. Dallas was so in. So far in that he couldn't restrain his need, driving his aching cock into his fist as he bent to take a knee.

"My God, you're beautiful," he whispered as he drank in the sight of Greer's body. He was lost to see anything more than the thick, perfectly cut cock in Greer's fist, jutting up toward him and his for the taking. Happiness bloomed in his chest. Why did he feel like he'd found the pot of gold at the end of the rainbow?

"You don't have to, Dallas." Greer's fingers slid through his hair in a comforting caress that he nestled against.

"No, I want to. I'm just trying to memorize everything about you," he whispered. Greer's caressing palm came to his cheek, the pad of his thumb lovingly stroked across his sprinkling of a beard.

Greer's amber eyes held his. "Whatever you're thinking this is between us, you need to know, I'm all in. Memorize what you must, but I'm not going to be done with you tonight, not by a long shot."

The sweet declaration wrapped around his heart like a warm embrace, giving him the courage to wrap his fingers around the base of Greer's cock, bringing the tip to his mouth. The thump of Dallas's heart drowned out all other sound as he slid the broad head over his mouth, before drawing back and licking his lips.

Oh fuck yeah. A small burst of tangy pre-come hit his tongue. His eyes rolled back into his head as Greer's essence coated his tongue. He trailed the fingers of his free hand against the soft skin of Greer's thigh then moved to his sac, fondling their weight in his hand. He'd never explored another man before. Tonight would be filled with many firsts. Dallas rolled Greer's balls in his palm. The moan from the other man made him smile. He could do this all night. He tentatively licked across the thick head before taking Greer deep into his mouth.

"Damn, that feels good," Greer groaned, his fingertips scraped across Dallas's scalp. Dallas pulled off, letting the slick velvety steel slide from his mouth.

"Tell me if there's something you like. I haven't done this before." Dallas slid Greer's cock back into his mouth and down his throat, willing himself to go as deep as he could. He pumped his fist over the firm shaft, giving a good slow tug upward as he again backed off Greer's dick, stopping long enough to dip his greedy tongue inside the weeping tip, lapping at the salty beads collecting there. His reward was the deep sensual moan from above.

Pride bloomed in Dallas's chest. He lifted his gaze to meet that intense stare before sliding Greer inside his mouth again. More than anything, he wanted Greer to know exactly how badly he wanted him. This whole damn thing just turned him on too much. Dallas bobbed his head then backed off, using his hand to work Greer's length. He slid his nose along Greer's cock, inhaling the intoxicating scent of arousal, while kissing and licking the soft salty skin. He buried his nose in Greer's groin and inhaled deeply. God, he could get high on this man's scent. He continued to lick a wet trail along Greer's dick, kissing the tip reverently before mouthing the mushroomed head. Dallas glanced up for approval. The look in Greer's eyes was all he needed to see to keep going.

Dallas slid his hand low, gripping his own hard dick, giving a satisfying tug as he lowered his mouth back to Greer's cock again. He bobbed his head up and down, finding his rhythm, taking Greer deeper inside his mouth each time. The fleshy weight against his tongue and Greer's appreciative moans made his insides tighten and his own need ready to erupt.

"Damn, you don't have a fucking gag reflex. Loosen your jaw, babe. You can take more of me," Greer prompted, his fingers tenderly caressing his jaw and down his neck. The desperation in Greer's voice let him know he was doing everything right. Dallas closed his eyes, kissed the wet tip of Greer's broad head again, then relaxed his mouth. He swallowed Greer to the root, the tip of his nose mingling in Greer's soft thatch of hair.

What a fucking rush. Dallas's throat tightened around Greer's cock as Greer gave a slight roll of his hips. Dallas's eyes watered as Greer slipped farther inside. "My fucking God."

Oh yeah, his hand at his cock gripped tighter, moving faster. Never had he imagined it could feel this amazing.

Greer released the hold on his hair, and Dallas slid his lips up and down the smooth steel length in his hand. His own hand was wrapped around his cock, pumping. The wet slurping sounds were even a turn on. He rolled his hips, driving into his fist as Greer fucked his mouth. He chased the pleasure with every thrust of his hips and bob of his head. Greer's unintelligible words encouraged him from above. Fuck, he'd never imagined anything this sexy.

Dallas flattened his tongue against Greer's cock before curling around the tip and sucking Greer back inside his mouth. He took all of him again. Greer's pre-come coated the back of his throat and tongue. His senses were dominated by Greer's essence. God, he loved this. Dallas sucked and worked his tongue in tempo along Greer's length as he rode the sensation of the orgasm building in his balls. He was so into sucking Greer's dick that he was going to come from the sheer pleasure of it.

"Damn, that's so fucking good, Dallas. You've got to slow down, babe. I'm almost there." The haze of sucking Greer's cock had him trying to sort the words in his head. The grip on his hair tightened to a painful degree. Greer pulled him off and scooted back on the mattress, moving out from underneath his mouth. "I love that you're so fucking turned on by sucking my dick. My God, that was amazing. You're amazing, Dallas."

"What?" Dallas asked breathy. He was almost there. Greer was too. "Come in my mouth."

"Holy hell," Greer scurried to the center of the bed, grabbing the condoms and lube. "Here. Come here." Greer patted the mattress, his chest heaving, his gaze intense and that enticing smile spreading across his face. "Let me take care of you."

"Please, Greer, let me finish you," Dallas pleaded, his cock still in his hand. What was Greer doing to him?

"Not this time. I've got plans for you." Greer's voice was husky and deep as he pushed back on his heels. His dick jutted out in front of him, still glistening from Dallas's spit. Dallas licked his lips. He'd enjoyed every sound and shudder he'd drawn from Greer. He didn't want to stop. Never in his wildest imagination would he have ever thought he would crave something so much after just one taste. Even though he wanted to swallow Greer's orgasm and savor every drop, his curiosity as to what Greer had in store for him overrode everything else.

=♥=

"I want to do this right, even if it kills me," Dallas murmured.

Fuck. *fuck*. Why was that the only word Greer could think of? His dick throbbed as he watched Dallas climb onto the mattress, moving much slower because he hadn't let go of his engorged cock. Every muscle flexed in that hard body as he shifted into place. He never remembered being with anyone who was so ready to come just by sucking his dick.

What a fucking turn-on.

What an extraordinary find of a man. Caring, sweet, eager to please, and beautiful to boot.

Greer stared at the man of his dreams, taking in every slow stroke of Dallas's hand over that thick erection, and the moment ran rampant over his heart. He gave into his desire and leaned forward to kiss the wet tip of Dallas's leaking cock before swirling his tongue around the blushing head and sampling the moisture there. The little gasp of approval Dallas gave only made him crave more. Addicting was the word that flooded his mind.

Greer wanted to show this man how good they could be together. Luckily, he had the element of surprise on his side and enough episodes of WWE under his belt to take advantage of the situation. He knocked Dallas over to his back and never missed a beat, pouncing when he fell over.

"My turn. You come when I say you come," he teased. Challenge lit Dallas's intense gaze as Greer scooted between Dallas's parted thighs.

Greer's cock ached for the hard body splayed out before him. He was so owned by Dallas. His gaze stayed fixed on Dallas as he gripped the base of Dallas's dick. Wasting no time, he dipped his head, taking the arousal straight into his mouth. Dallas wasn't the only one who could go deep. Greer moaned his pleasure when Dallas's dick twitched in his palm. So damn sweet.

Greer gripped Dallas's cock in his fist, tightening his hold. He stared down the length of Dallas's big body. "Remember, D, we come together."

He could have sworn those green eyes flashed then Dallas's legs widened in invitation. "Do I turn over?"

His dick jerked at the curiosity and trust staring back at him. "No. Not this time." Greer reached for the bottle of lube, pouring a generous amount in his palm and on Dallas's cock. He wrapped his fingers around the shaft and stroked as he ran his other hand down Dallas's perineum until his slick fingers encountered the tight ring. He massaged around the rim.

"Ah. Feels good." Dallas said, his big eyes on Greer.

"You haven't felt anything yet." He pushed a finger inside that tight hole and slowly moved it in and out of his lover. Dallas's body arched, and a throaty moan escaped as Greer found the spot and curled his finger, working Dallas from the inside out.

"Fuck, Greer." He tightened his hand on Dallas's dick. Dallas's hips thrust up. The man was so responsive and eager for completion.

"I want your first time to be good." Greer grinned, adding more lubricant to his fingers, and inserting a second finger, scissoring them in Dallas's tight channel.

Greer resumed the slow stroking of Dallas's cock. Dallas's eyelids slid closed, his hips rolling in time with Greer's hand as he pushed in a third finger. His lover's body tensed as he lifted a leg, giving Greer a better angle. He lost himself in the ripples and flexes of Dallas's hard body.

"Greer," Dallas moaned and pulled back his other leg. Those big hands gripped the backs of his thighs. Dallas's pink pucker relaxed under Greer's gentle persuasion. Greer was so fucking drawn to Dallas his own cock begged for what Dallas offered. "Now."

"Just a bit more. I want it to be good for you. I want you crazy for this," Greer whispered on a rasp as he watched his fingers slipping inside of Dallas's tight hole. So beautiful.

"I just need you inside me. I want to feel you," Dallas whimpered, raising his body, dislodging Greer's fingers. Dallas reached for Greer, his strong hand cupping his neck, drawing him forward. Dallas pushed his tongue inside Greer's mouth. He shuddered at the urgency in the kiss. Dallas fucked Greer's mouth with his tongue, like Greer wanted to fuck Dallas's ass. As fast as he'd swooped in, he released him and dropped back down on the mattress. Dallas's gaze stayed transfixed on him as he gripped the back of his thighs, pulling his legs toward his chest again. "Now, Greer."

How could he resist such a demand? Greer reached for the condom, making quick work of tearing open the packet, sliding the latex down his length. He reached for the lube, coating his cock then dripping several drops directly on Dallas's hole, getting a hiss in return. He was focused on getting inside his lover that Greer couldn't even muster a teasing chuckle as he aligned himself with Dallas's rim.

His initial push met with resistance. He was so damn tight. Greer's body burned from the inside out, desperation caused a layer of sweat to form across his brow. An overwhelming need to claim Dallas had Greer pushing forward to end the agony. The battle between his head and heart waged—his heart slowing him down, reminding to do this right, give Dallas the best he could. At this point, his lover might just do him in.

Greer held back on his need to drive his hips forward, his gaze colliding with Dallas's. "I don't wanna hurt you."

The need reflected at Greer stole his breath like the man had stolen his heart. The meaning behind what they were doing swirled between them. This fine, gorgeous guy chose Greer to be his first. His chest swelled as he found his resolve. He wanted Dallas to want him. His brow wrinkled and his heart hammered. This meant so much to him.

"I'm going to take my time with you."

Dallas released his legs then wrapped those long limbs around Greer's waist, forcing him down on Dallas's chest. Dallas's strong arms encased him as his powerful heels drove into his ass. He reared back as far as Dallas would allow, tossing his head back as his cock sank deep inside the tight hot channel of Dallas's ass.

"Motherfucker," Dallas hissed. His whole body tensed, both his arms and legs locked around Greer, holding him in place. Dallas's snug heat gripped Greer like a vice. Nothing had ever felt this good in his entire life. Greer's jaw clenched as he took in Dallas's flushed neck and face. His lover's eyes were screwed closed as he adjusted to Greer's invasion.

"Babe, let me go," he whispered, pressing his lips to Dallas's chest, feeling the thumping of his heartbeat. Their intimacy had Greer relaxing into the hold. He rubbed his nose in the hair on Dallas's chest. "It'll ease if you let me move."

Dallas exhaled before drawing a slow deep breath into his lungs as his arms loosened their hold by the smallest of measures. An enchanting smile ghosted over Dallas's face before his eyelids split open, those green eyes finding his. "Move."

Oh yeah. Greer pulled his hips back only to have Dallas's strong legs help drive him balls deep back inside.

"Fuck. You feel so damn good." he panted, absorbing his visceral reaction. His feelings were all over the fucking place. How was this already the best experience of his life?

Dallas surprised him, taking charge of the moment. He canted his hips, forcing Greer to participate.

Greer wasn't about to stop. He didn't have the will to say no. So, he followed his trainer's lead, rolling his hips into Dallas's tight body. Dallas moaned as they moved together. A delicious carnal combination of give and take. The rhythm perfect. He was already too close. Greer fought his most primal urge to pound into all that tight heat. Show Dallas exactly who he belonged to. He steeled his spine and thrust with purpose.

"This feels so right," Dallas groaned, lifting his hips, urging him on. Greer changed positions, bracing both hands on Dallas's impressive chest. Dallas's long fingers dug into the mattress, fisting the material, writhing beneath him as he moved in and out of his lover's body.

"So fucking right." Greer concentrated on keeping his release at bay as Dallas's body enveloped his, holding them together. He made love to Dallas. This was the best sex of his life. Happily in over his head, he relished every thrust.

"Oh, God. Right there, right there. Please..." Dallas panted. The need in that husky voice would haunt Greer's wet dreams for the rest of eternity. "I'm ready for more. I need more..."

How could just the sound of the trainer's voice drive him to desperately want things he'd never wanted before? Greer bucked his hips, pistoning in and out of Dallas's delicious body.

"Me too," Greer managed between a clenched jaw.

With little control, Dallas pulled Greer down against his heated chest. Those strong arms wound around him, pulling him closer. Greer slid his hands under Dallas's back and locked his arms around Dallas's shoulders, holding them together as he plundered Dallas's tight ass. This moment with this man was the best moment of his life.

"Kiss me," Greer begged as he tilted his head and closed his eyes, losing himself in every twitch and shiver of his lover's body, never wanting this to end. Dallas brought their lips together and thrust his tongue forward, wild and owning, demanding entrance. He opened his mouth to suck on that glorious tongue as he rode his ass. That kiss vanquished all his resolve. Greer somehow increased his pace by finding the perfect rhythm. He pushed in, over and over. The seductive cant of his hips allowed Greer to go deep with every thrust. Fuck, Dallas's hot channel threatened to milk his release from his body if he didn't slow them down.

"So good!" Greer pulled from the kiss with a gasp. Fighting for a semblance of control, he grasped at Dallas's hard muscles to keep himself grounded. They moved together in perfect rhythm, their bodies moving as one. The erotic bliss never stopped, and the pleasure built into a heated frenzy.

Greer reared back, breaking their embrace. The way Dallas clung to him seemed as if he never wanted to let go. The knowledge had him pushing a hand between their sweat-slicked bodies. Greer wrapped his fingers around Dallas's pulsing cock and stroked him with a vengeance, determined to make his trainer come so hard he'd never forget the moment.

"Come for me, baby." Greer gritted through his teeth, thrusting deeply and deliberately into Dallas's body. It took all his willpower to control his hips as the wonder of Dallas swirled over his body, through his head, and emphasized the claim he held for this man deep inside his heart.

Dallas threw his head backward against the pillow, his back bowing off the mattress. His ass clamped down on Greer as he came with a silent roar. His muscles quivered with each thrust, and Greer was helpless in his pursuit, maddeningly driving himself harder into Dallas as he chased his own release.

His balls churned. His vision blurred as his heart thundered inside his rib cage. Dallas was everything right in this world. He'd waited so long for the validation. The spiraling heat rushing through him caused his hips to falter, and he eagerly tumbled over the edge.

Greer's eyes slammed shut as his orgasm exploded from him with a force that held him hostage with a desperate need to mark his territory. So right. Too right. He'd been given a gift and the bliss overwhelmed him.

Greer fell. Dallas's body easily softening the blow. Those strong, protecting arms circled Greer, keeping him as safe as he wanted to keep Dallas. His prince had arrived, and as wild as it seemed, Greer had fallen completely head over heels in love.

Lifting his hand, Greer reached to turn the bathroom lights

off, stopping mid motion, enraptured by the sight of Dallas lying in his bed. The moment marked a first for Greer. The scene was surreal as he etched the sight of Dallas wrapped in his duvet into the furthest reaches of his mind. He never wanted to forget the image of Dallas sharing space inside his personal domain.

The chill in the air sent a biting shiver prickling over his skin, making him move his feet a little faster. As he went for the bed, he caught a glimpse of the curtains billowing under the breeze. The retractable walls were wide open at his trainer's request. Much like Dallas sleeping in his bed, having the doors open while he slept was another first for Greer.

The best idea of his life.

Three o'clock in the morning.

What a life changing night they'd shared.

Greer lifted the edge of the duvet and scooted underneath. Dallas woke instantly. His shy, tentative, straight guy had lost his inhibitions. Dallas leaned to his side, lifting enough to invite Greer underneath his warm body. Without any hesitation, Greer slid into the warm place while Dallas grabbed the duvet, sending it flying. Dallas plastered himself over Greer's body, encasing him as the billow of the cover settled on top of them. They shared a pillow, and Dallas's fingers tangled in Greer's hair. Greer adjusted himself until he was comfortable, not wanting one single inch of his trainer's hard body to move off him. Apparently, he was a cuddler. Who knew?

"If I snore, turn me on my stomach." Dallas's sweetly whispered breath tickled Greer's ear.

"You stay just like this, and we'll be good. You good?" Greer asked. He ran his palms the length of Dallas's back, down to the curve of his ass, massaging and caressing as he went. His sated dick showed another side to this situation. Greer just wanted to be inside this man's arms for nothing more than the comfort Dallas brought.

"I'm not sore." Dallas's sweet lips pressed against Greer's

jaw.

"Good. I don't want you to be," Greer whispered, sweeping his palm back up Dallas's muscular back, breathing in the scent of his citrusy shampoo in Dallas's hair. He had loved sharing a shower with Dallas. "Tomorrow, I want you to fuck me. Promise me." Greer's answer came by way of those full lips kissing his ear.

Seconds later, Dallas lifted that handsome head, eyeing Greer closely, gauging the answer for himself before he ever asked. "Are you comfortable?"

"Never more. Are you?" Greer asked.

"Yeah," Dallas answered. Greer wished for a glimmer of light to better see the green in those eyes now staring down at him. "I haven't slept with anyone before. Am I doing it wrong?"

"I don't know. I haven't either. I think we're doing it right. It feels right." Greer tilted his chin up, puckering. Dallas obliged, sweetly kissing him with a soft, lingering press of the lips.

"You don't have anyone special in your life, right?" Dallas asked. He could see Dallas's insecurity in the tilt of his head and the firm set of his jaw. He stared directly at Greer, not hiding from the answer.

Straight away Greer started shaking his head. Another sincere truth tumbled from his lips. Dallas was magic in the way he ushered Greer's hidden truths out. "No, I never have."

"I don't have anyone special either…if you wanted to know." Appeased, Dallas lowered his head back to the pillow, so close he nuzzled his nose against Greer's hair, breathing deeply.

Well hell, his heart loved that move.

"I already knew you didn't. You wouldn't be here with me if you did. You're not that kind of man. I like you here, Dallas."

Dallas's scent, the reverence of his sweeping touch, his calmness, told Greer by every breath he took that he wanted to be right there with him. Yeah, this was right, and Greer closed his eyes, sleep starting to seep in around the edges.

"No matter what happens from here, this was right for me." Dallas's husky, tired voice whispered the sweetest of words he'd ever heard. All those foreign binding feelings wanted Greer to admit how badly he'd already fallen, but he held off. They had tomorrow and the many more tomorrows to come. He didn't have to rush them.

"Me too. I think you're my missing piece," Greer whispered. His roaming hand lowered to Dallas's lower back, the other hooking around Dallas's knee, keeping him right there. "Go to sleep." Greer took a deep breath and welcomed sleep with Dallas's lips pressed against his hair.

CHAPTER 20

With a tight grip on the doorknob, and as quietly as he'd ever moved in his life, Greer shut the bedroom door slowly behind him, letting the latch click in place. He listened with his ear stuck to the door for several long seconds, hearing nothing more than the heavy even breaths of Dallas's deep sleeping. Last night, or early this morning, when Greer had talked fast and furious, saying anything to get Dallas to stay the night, he had promised his trainer a home-cooked breakfast. He intended to keep his promise.

Greer padded through the house, the sunny day bleeding through every open window, warming his path, drawing his eye outside. The day held promise, making everything a little more dazzling than normal. Full of vivid hope, fine-tuning all his senses.

If he had time, Greer would plant himself on the back porch among the early seasonal blooms and fresh, spring breeze and meditate. It seemed the perfect day for deep reflection to help push away the bedlam that had become his life and allow all these sexy-trainer good-vibes to help heal his battered soul. But that would have to come in time. Right now, his priorities required clothes. He hadn't grabbed any to wear before he'd left the bedroom.

The residual warmth of Dallas's big body staying glued to his throughout the night had proved to be a bit of a brain buster. How he still felt Dallas's smooth skin touching his was a testament to the last hour as he'd lain there, memorizing the way his nerve-endings ignited with every brush of Dallas's sleeping body against his.

He hadn't shared just a bed with Dallas, but also a pillow. What a fascinating mind-fuck that had been. Just the thought of Dallas's sweet breath, puffing across his face made the tingles ignite all over again. Yeah, Greer had it bad for Dallas. And by bad, he meant, head over heels with the idea of getting to know every facet of that engaging man still sleeping a few feet away.

Greer went for the laundry room, found a used pair of jeans and a slightly wrinkled white T-shirt, and put them on.

First came coffee. He pushed the coffee maker's power button and flipped the top to see the machine was ready loaded to brew with fresh coffee grounds. He may have only slept a couple of hours last night, but the rest of the time, he had lain there happily awake, holding Dallas as he resisted the urges of his hard-on. He'd promised Dallas the next turn, and he intended to keep his word, no matter how badly he wanted back inside that addicting ass. But what he wanted more than anything was for Dallas's brute strength to own him, to fuck the shit out of him, to make sure Greer knew who the boss was between them.

Greer's ever-present smile took on a sinister edge. Being pinned underneath that man would come in time. Greer pretended to look at his non-existent watch. He'd give Dallas three hours before they were back in the bedroom, beginning the next round of their all-afternoon sexual quest.

As he drummed his fingers on the counter, Greer closed his eyes, thinking about the tentative give and take they had shared last night. When Dallas finally let go, he truly gave. Their kisses were mind blowing, and their sex was liberating. Greer wanted more of Dallas's honest touches. For those big eyes to look up at him with such wonderment as Greer pushed in and out of Dallas's perfect body. Fuck, he loved that move. He wanted those thick thighs wrapped snugly around his hips, guiding his moves. Dallas was exactly the embodiment of his Biker101.

The sudden shortness of breath and the steady increase in the beat of his heart had him wanting to name all this deluge of emotion. Greer had led a self-centered life. He never considered another living soul above himself. Yet suddenly, he wasn't seeing himself in a singular fashion. He no longer mattered.

When exactly had that happened?

Last night.

If he were being honest, his entire focus had been split between the enticing Dallas Reigns and the competitive Biker101 for a while now. Both attracted him in a basic, fundamental way. When the two men came together, Greer hadn't stood a chance. Nothing was going to stop him from developing a life-long connection with the beauty sleeping a few feet away. Either a long-lasting friendship or if he could convince Dallas to return his love…

Was it love? His heart sure felt it was. Logic argued it wasn't.

Greer had a long history of being impulsive. He was usually knee-deep before he realized what he had done. Whatever happened between them needed to develop naturally. This was far too important. Dallas's life would be upturned if he barged into his world. He had to prove his reliability, that he was worthy of that man's devotion.

He reached for his filled cup and turned, leaning his ass against the edge of the counter as he lifted the mug to his lips. As he blew against the hot coffee, he stared outside, thinking about how they'd slept with the patio door ajar last night. He'd never done anything like it before. A move designed to please Dallas who claimed to like the sound of the swimming pool's waterfall trickling right outside the door. The cool air kept them huddled together, searching out the other's warmth. Maybe having the door open wasn't the safest of options, but Dallas seemed to like it, so he'd work on the security measures to help keep it open for as long as the weather held.

Selflessness. It was damned perplexing. Dallas had not only touched Greer's heart, but opened a different, unknown side of him. Something rare and honest. A place Greer liked.

Since he didn't want Dallas to leave, that meant breakfast and a lot of influencing on Greer's part. He took a sip of his steaming coffee, then reached for the television remote control on the center island. With a click to a button, the wall-mounted television across the living room powered on. He rapidly pressed the volume button to lower the sound then searched out the Bloomberg channel.

Now for breakfast. He went to the refrigerator, finding the shelves more bare than he remembered. He didn't even have an egg, let alone enough to make his supposedly famous made-from-scratch omelet. He would have had to search Google for the recipe anyway.

Obviously, he needed groceries. He'd take care of that at some point today. Like everything else that had to do with Dallas, the plan changed by the moment. He went for his cell phone, abandoned on the coffee table last night, and called Ellen's Kitchen to deliver. Greer took a seat on his sofa, drinking his cup of coffee as he ordered most of the breakfast menu unsure what Dallas liked. His heart was overjoyed with the idea of how he'd learn all Dallas's preferences over time.

The incessant rattle and corresponding hum of his cell phone pulled Dallas from the best sleep of his life. He didn't have to wake or open his eyes to know where he'd spent the night. The perfect amount of firm versus softness of the mattress that fit both the length and mass of his body spoke of money. When he thought of such an indulgence, Greer Lockhart came instantly to mind.

Dallas opened his eyes and noticed the rumpled covers and the empty spot beside him. He propped himself up on an elbow, scanning the entire room. No sign of Greer. The digital Echo on the nightstand showed nine thirty in the morning. It had been years since he'd slept that late. He dropped his head back down on the pillow and stared up at the ceiling, thinking over everything he'd done last night. His cheeks warmed, remembering how much he'd loved every single minute of his and Greer's time together.

The very few times he'd let himself visualize sex with a man, he had always pictured himself being a top. The wanton ways he'd begged for Greer to never stop moving inside him sure proved what his fantasy had missed.

How did he feel now? The question was hard to answer. From the safety of this bed, surrounded by Greer's pretty things, he had no shame, which was weird. But he was certain the inner condemnation would eventually return. Dallas pushed those thoughts aside. He'd deal with them later. No one in his family needed to know what he'd done last night, and right now, he felt alive.

Don't overthink it.

Dallas flipped the duvet off and rolled to the side of the bed. The tender ache in his ass reminded him of the beauty of their sex. The most amazing night of his entire life. He could get lost in those amber eyes gazing down at him as if he were the only man in Greer's world. If only that were true. He sighed at the thought, searching the room for his freshly washed clothes. He spotted them neatly folded on a side chair next to a small table.

Greer had called the design of his entire home minimalist. Every item in the house had a purpose. Nothing frivolous just to fill space. Dallas thought it described Greer to a tee. What Greer had was incredibly nice and probably expensive, but no excess of anything. Dallas liked that about Greer. He liked a lot about the stunning man.

Dallas found his cell phone lay on top of his clothes just as it started to vibrate again. Greer had taken care with his things, a sweet and caring gesture. That pushy, arrogant man had been such a gentleman last night.

Stop the romantic thoughts.

Remember: One-night stand.

Instant sorrow and a deep feeling of loss followed that thought.

You're such a dumbass.

Dallas dropped his head between his shoulder blades and resisted the urge to scold and degrade himself for getting so attached so quickly.

Maybe Greer wasn't even in the house. His imagination ran rampant in a matter of seconds. Perhaps Greer had left because Dallas had stayed too long. Oh hell. He reached for his phone as the doorbell rang, stealing his frantic gaze from the small screen to the bedroom door. Something made him move faster now, forgoing the phone to quickly dress. Dallas made a mad dash to the bathroom, glad to see the hairbrush and toothbrush he'd used last night after their shared shower were still out. Not much would help keep this longer on top hairstyle back in place, but he gave his teeth a fast scrub.

His best course of action should be to walk through the house to the front door. If he saw Greer, he'd tell him he'd had a good time. If he didn't see Greer, it was probably designed that way for a reason, and he'd keep going. Dallas opened his Uber app as he left the bedroom. The smell of maple and bacon had his stomach growling as he rounded the corner, heading for the front door. The huge television was on, and several to-go containers took up most of the space on the kitchen island. Greer turned from the cupboards with plates and silverware in his hands as Dallas made his way toward the front entry.

"You're up. Good Morning." Fuck, the guy was so damned pretty with his bright smile and bedhead.

"Did I sleep too long?" Dallas asked. Greer left the plates and silverware on the counter, his brow furrowing as he started for Dallas who kept walking toward the front door. "The bed's comfortable. It's been a long few days. I guess I needed the sleep."

"What?" Greer asked in confusion, meeting him in the junction connecting the foyer, living room, and kitchen. He didn't slow or pause as he came flush against Dallas, placing a strong hand on his arm, balancing as he lifted for a kiss.

Dallas was confused at what was happening here and didn't immediately kiss Greer. They stared at one another until the awkwardness kicked his manners into gear, and he hesitantly bent for the chaste kiss.

"I'm glad you're finally up. I didn't want to wake you." Greer's gaze lifted to Dallas's with confusion knitting his brow. "What're you doing?"

"I scheduled an Uber," he said, waving his cell phone at Greer who hadn't stepped away. "I thought I'd wait outside until they arrived."

Greer reached up, moving the long pieces of Dallas's hair off his forehead, and smiled as the strands fell back in his face. "I'm taking you home. That was our deal. Cancel the ride. I got us breakfast." Greer did that thing he always did. He took charge in a subtle, persuasive, complete way. He clasped Dallas's elbow and started them toward the kitchen.

"You don't have to—" he started, but Greer cut him off.

"We talked about breakfast last night. I may have had bigger plans than the current inventory in my refrigerator allowed. I called Ellen's and had them make a little bit of everything for us. I wasn't sure what you liked." Greer only let go when they were in the kitchen. There were seven brimming to-go tins.

"This is for us?" Dallas asked, looking over each selection.

"Yeah."

"No one else?" There was an awful lot of food for two people.

Greer laughed and ran a hand through this hair. "Well, I wasn't sure what you liked, but I'll learn soon enough. I hope you're hungry."

Dallas's inner teenage boy sang a joyous tune at such a smorgasbord filling every spot on the large kitchen island.

"Grab a plate. Did you really schedule a ride?"

"Yeah, I should cancel if you're sure." Dallas's phone was plucked from his hand. Greer scooted around the granite island to the other side, reaching for his wallet, leaving his cell there.

"No, I will. I'm not risking you sneaking out the front door with the deer in the headlights look again. I'll go tell them. You fix your plate. They delivered coffee and cream. It's behind you." Greer took off toward the front door. "Don't disappear on me," he warned.

Dallas didn't have to be told twice when it came to food. He started pulling off the lids to find scrambled eggs, bacon, ham, pancakes, potatoes, two omelets, fresh fruits, sliced cheese and meats, biscuits and bread. Everything a person needed for a great breakfast. Dallas reached for a bottle of orange juice and pulled out one of the barstools as his phone began to vibrate again. In an instant, the reason for the alarm finally dawned on him. Damn. He had a class in fifteen minutes. How had that not occurred to him before now?

Dallas lifted from the bottom rung of the stool and extended an arm as far as he could for his phone. Barely back in his seat, Dallas quickly pulled up Ducky's number.

"Hello?" Ducky wasn't awake, but at least he answered. The front door slammed shut as Greer came back into the kitchen. His gaze was glued on Dallas.

"Hey, I'm not gonna make it home in time for a class. Can

you schedule one for me?" he asked.

"Yeah. You're out already this morning?" Instant relief flooded him. Ducky hadn't known he didn't make it home last night. An excuse fell into his lap without him really having to lie. A smile slid across his lips as his gaze connected with Greer's.

"Yeah, I had a thing to do this morning."

Greer nodded and reached for a plate, handing it over.

"But I'll be home for the noon class. Derek's taking the afternoon."

"Okay. Bye." Ducky sounded exhausted as he ended the call.

"That's not enough time," Greer immediately said, pausing with his plate in hand. "We made plans. Those plans require you to be here."

"What plans?" He furrowed his brow as he thought back over their conversations.

Greer gave him a cute pout, looking at him as if he were a forgetful child. "The plans of you in my ass this afternoon. I want that big guy making sure I remember where I belong."

Dallas's cheeks flushed with heat and his smile brightened. "I don't know. I have to get ready for work tomorrow," Dallas said, liking Greer's idea more than he should.

"Look, I'll drive you home, drop you off, then go to the grocery store," Greer said, following along behind him as he filled his plate. "You grab your clothes and come back here. We can have an early dinner. You need to punish me for being a bad boy, maybe twice." Greer's brows waggled with the idea. "I'll set the alarm and you can leave from here in the morning to go to work."

"You're insane. I have a million things to do for our company to get ready to be gone all week," Dallas said as he started filling his plate.

"Then put me to work. I can be an instructor or fill in however you need," Greer said. He placed his plate next to Dallas's and reached for the silverware and napkins. "I can feel you looking at me like I lost my mind. It's not a crazy idea. I have the equipment here."

"You're a busy man," Dallas said, trying hard to go with the idea without laughing straight in Greer's face.

"I am, but I work out every day. Remember, I beat your butt. I'm kind of a star on BikeBro right now."

He rolled his eyes and plucked the fork out of Greer's hand. Dallas didn't think Greer would ever tire of claiming his win. He scooped up a healthy portion of the eggs and took his first bite. The spicy flavor exploded in his mouth.

"You won because you got in my head. It's not a fair win. We should go again." Dallas liked that idea a lot, nodding his approval. Greer no longer held that control over his thoughts. He'd kick his ass this time.

"No way, I'm not that dumb," Greer said, taking a bite of the bacon, turning on the stool to face Dallas. "I can't believe I beat you to begin with. Tell Ducky I volunteered to run a class. That's the excuse why you come over here this afternoon. Seems reasonable." He lifted his shoulder in a shrug as if that resolved everything.

Dallas gave him the side-eye, considering the bad idea that might have potential to be a spectacular evening. They could use more classes. Greer could be a special trainer, leading the class as a prize for winning.

"Okay. Let me talk to Ducky and Donny."

Greer's brows dropped in a mock glare. "You caved too quickly. Should I trust it?"

"Not caved necessarily. Our members will like you teaching a class. The women especially."

Greer barked out a laugh, knocking him in the arm with his elbow. He acted like he didn't know that he was always the best-looking man in any room.

"That was a good one. Eat. We'll work it out." Greer turned away, concentrating on his plate of food.

Surreal might be the only way to describe Dallas's life in that moment. He didn't dwell on that, though. Instead, he twisted the top off the bottle of orange juice and grinned. They did have an ease between them that he genuinely liked.

CHAPTER 21

With a shift of the gears, Greer slowed his sports car as they reached the back gate to Dallas's apartment complex. In a day of firsts, Greer held Dallas's hand for the entire length of the ride. The weight and fit of Dallas's palm resting with his, those long fingers fitting with his perfectly, seemed proof of their fate. They fit together very well. Something so simple as holding his hand shouldn't have validated a long-term commitment, but for Greer, it did. He never wanted to let go.

On the flip side, from the second they'd left the solitude and security of his home, Dallas's body had become tense. With each passing mile, his body grew more taut, those expressive eyes now serious and weary as reservations clearly crept in. The easy smile that transformed Dallas's handsome face into a thing of pure beauty, a look Greer seemed ripe and ready to write long meaningful sonnets about, the joyfulness he had worked painstakingly hard to coerce from Dallas, was nowhere to be found. The chatty, friendly guy had withdrawn, only answering questions with one- or two-word responses.

Greer didn't know how to relieve Dallas's burdens. They surely felt like insurmountable boulders on his trainer's shoulders. So, Greer filled in the conversational gaps with nothing but mindless chatter. He talked endlessly about nothing, wanting to offer comfort over something he didn't understand at all.

"Confirming the plan. I'm going to Central Market. You're going in for your class and a shower. I'll be back here in an hour and a half to pick you up." Greer pulled his car into a parking space in the very back parking lot. He shifted into neutral and pressed on the brake, lifting the steering wheel. His body angled toward Dallas who stared straight ahead out the front windshield at the trees lining the fencing.

"I can drive to your place." Dallas gave Greer's hand a gentle squeeze. Those green orbs stayed focused straight ahead. Dallas's jaw firming in front of Greer's eyes.

"But will you, is the better question? Your anxiety's rolling off you like a steam engine puffing up a hill."

Dallas gave him an anxiety-filled side-eye but otherwise made no effort to relax. "No one can know what I've done. My family won't accept this."

Greer assumed it was something along those lines, but it made no sense with the glorious praise Dallas used in describing the members of his family. "The way you've spoken of them, what I've seen of your brothers, I can't imagine—"

"You don't know." Dallas shook his head and turned fully to Greer. The unrest lacing each of his three words spoke to the honest worry Dallas had and to the ache in the small piece of Greer's heart still left in his chest. The only thing he could do was try and reassure Dallas and put himself in the closet with his trainer—a place he'd never been before.

"Then we'll keep it a secret. I got it. But remember, straight guys hang out together all the time. Just because we're together doesn't mean we're fucking each other."

Dallas stared at him a moment before speaking. "I guess you're right." Those words didn't come out convincing nor did the slight nod Dallas gave as he reached for the door handle. Greer's hand tightened around Dallas's, keeping him from leaving the protection of the small sanctuary they shared. He didn't want to let Dallas go, not like this. The sweet man would beat himself up too badly for succumbing to his own needs.

"The windows are darkened. We're away from prying eyes. Kiss me."

Dallas turned back and started to shake his head no. There was so much turmoil reflected at him. Greer melted under its weight and wanted nothing more than to ease this man's burden. He just wasn't sure how. He reached for Dallas, his free hand cupping the side of his neck, his thumb caressing across that strong set jaw. All the want and desire that had brought and held them together charged the air, the currents zapping any restraint Greer clung to.

Dallas surprised him by meeting Greer halfway, his mouth opening without prompting. Dallas smiled seconds before he made contact. His guy needed Greer like Greer needed him. They would overcome their obstacles. Greer would commit himself to making sure they did.

He slid his tongue forward as their mouths meshed. Dallas's lips were soft and pliant, and he tasted of everything Greer needed. He'd willingly do anything to make sure this man stayed in his life. The kiss heated to combustible in seconds flat, tethering him and Dallas together. It conveyed all the hope and meaning of the new beginnings for something long-lasting; something he never realized he wanted. Dating, marriage, children, and growing old together—those moments played like snapshots through Greer's mind. He wanted it all with Dallas and would eagerly shoulder this man's burdens until the end of time.

The anticipation of making his dreams come true had Greer deepening the kiss, drawing him closer, but Dallas put a hand on his chest, pushing backward, breaking free. Dallas took deep ragged breaths. Greer refused to let him get too far away, clamping his hand on Dallas's strong bicep to keep him close. Every time they came together, the desperate emotions ran rampant. It was all too much. Dallas relented, resting his forehead against Greer's lips. The hand at his chest fisted tightly into his T-shirt. It helped to know Dallas felt the power between them and wanted to be as close as Greer.

"This was supposed to be a one-time thing," Dallas whispered, the puff of his breath warming his chest.

"Yeah right. Who told you that?" Greer grinned, pressing his lips against Dallas's forehead. He aimed for levity, determined to lighten the mood in the car. "How's your ass? I want you to think about me when you're on the bike."

Dallas looked up, staying close. His smile was instant. Humor finally erased that solemn expression. "Don't say it."

"But I did kick your ass a couple of different ways yesterday." That made Dallas bark out a laugh. Greer finally let go of his hand and leaned in again to press a chaste kiss against Dallas's lips. "Don't overthink this. Go do your class then come over. I can see where it's better for you to drive yourself, even though I really want to be the one driving you back and forth."

Dallas started to pull away. "I'll be there in a couple of hours."

"I'll stretch myself," Greer added for a naughty effect, hoping the mental visual ensured Dallas's hurried return.

His guy chuckled and reached for the door handle but stopped short of leaving the car. His serious side commanded this time as he glanced over his shoulder. "Don't. I want to." Dallas's simple words had effectively turned the tables on Greer, making his toes curl. His dick thickened, pushing against his zipper.

"You and I could have something, Dallas. Same page." Greer truly believed his words. Dallas leaned toward Greer who bent for another sweetly given kiss.

"Same page, then. I'm glad you were my first. I really enjoyed our time together."

"Me too. Now, go before I bend over and take care of that." They both looked down to see Dallas's cock at half mast, tenting his joggers.

Dallas quickly adjusted himself and chuckled. "Since I let him go, I'm not sure I'll ever get the control back." He squared his shoulders, pushing open the door. When his guy looked at Greer, the masks were all back in place. Passive, as if Dallas didn't have a care in the world.

The kind, gentle man had captured Greer's heart so completely, when Dallas stepped out of the car, his heart went too.

"I'll see you in two hours," Dallas said, looking back in through the open door.

"Yeah," Greer replied before Dallas nodded and shut the door. Greer watched him through the rearview mirror. A small part of him wished Dallas had looked back at him, but he didn't. He jogged toward his building, disappearing inside his apartment. That was okay. They were making headway.

Was it really a lie when he told Ducky he planned to spend the afternoon working with Greer on how best to lead a class? Maybe not, but when he added Greer wasn't a natural leader, that was probably where his lie solidified.

It was him. Dallas sucked at lying and used too many words while most likely tipping his little brother off to the truth. But luckily, Ducky didn't voice any of the confusion so clearly visible on his face. He only nodded and asked Dallas to bring food on his way home.

Dallas pulled his older model Camry along the curb in front of Greer's house, and like magic, all the worry and concern of his entire life faded—just like it had the previous night. Greer was right. They were safe behind the walls of his home and his heart's most secret desire waited for him on the other side.

He twisted the key, killing the engine as memories assailed him again. He couldn't go a minute without remembering something about last night. He grinned, thinking about when he'd taken the seat of his bike that morning. The tender ache did in fact pulse, reminding him of the best sexual experience of his life with every turn of the pedal. He'd loved it so much and never wanted it to end.

How could something so fulfilling be so wrong? While there with Greer, Dallas's life-long problem with anxiety had completely faded. His worry was non-existent. His body hummed, remembering the relief of his burdens. Maybe Greer's constant finger play on his abs had something to do with the smile building in his haggard soul.

When the bubble of this weekend burst, when Greer went on with his life and Dallas went on with his, he'd have to learn how to balance his true self against the biases of those who were important to him. He promised himself he'd figure it out. He could no longer let family ties dictate who he wanted to be as a man. None of that seemed important anymore.

Greer Lockhart. Dallas closed his eyes, thinking of the wonderment of the man. Everything about Greer attracted him. The stunning man's caring soul, the tenderness he showed last night while gently making love to Dallas, was forever locked away in his memory. He had concerns that he might not ever truly get over Greer, but no matter what, he'd always appreciate how that man had pushed him to be his authentic self.

Dallas wished for the life his parents had always wanted for him, except he wanted Greer as his partner. Marriage, children, growing old, grandbabies. How wrong he'd been to never fully visualize such things. A knock on the passenger side window startled the shit out of him. Dallas jerked his gaze toward the window, seeing Greer's wide grin and handsome face staring at him.

Greer opened the door, sticking his head inside. "Are you nervous? Do I need to talk you inside?"

Dallas chuckled and pulled the keys out before reaching for his door handle. From the minute he was first introduced to Greer, that man had talked Dallas all the way into his bed. Greer didn't need to this afternoon, though. Dallas willingly opened his door and stepped out, clicking the key fob to lock the doors—you know, because someone in these expensive homes might want to steal his fifteen-year-old car.

"Your car's super clean," Greer said, over the top of the car. "I doubted the truth of your clean-freak status based on the condition of your room."

"Har, har. Now you have jokes," Dallas said, rounding the trunk. "I like order, but BikeBro might be beating that out of me."

"Will it help to move the offices outside of the apartment?" Greer asked, meeting Dallas on the sidewalk, neither touching the other.

"Ducky's already said he doesn't want to move his office, and if we make him, he plans on living at the office. Per him, it just makes it easier," Dallas said. The news made Greer trip as he started up the walkway. He looked uncertain, opening his mouth then closing it when no words came, Dallas chuckled. "Don't worry, he'll do whatever needs to be done."

"Did you tell him I wanted to lead a class?" Greer asked, seemingly accepting his answer, falling in step beside him.

"I did. That's why I'm here. Remember? It's concerning to let you take over, you're going to need a lot of help before you go live. You know, because you're not a natural born leader." Dallas winked, opening the front door, pushing it wide, letting Greer walk through first.

Barely inside the door, Greer reached for Dallas's T-shirt, tugging him through the doorway. "I'll show you a natural born leader." Greer shut the door with a push of his foot. He was barefooted, how had Dallas missed that before, and why did it seem so sexy?

Dallas bit his lip as Greer's grip tightened, fisting his T-shirt. The light breeze coasting over his already heating skin drew Dallas's gaze toward the opened retractable walls along the back of the living room. A feature of the home that had fascinated Dallas last night. He barely got to see the cool view, though, because Greer's face was in his. That was a much better view in his opinion anyway. Greer wrapped his strong arms around Dallas's waist, lifting his smiling lips for a kiss.

"I've been bad and started without you. Come join." Greer's naughty grin and teasing words did all sorts of things to him. He was definitely putty when Greer's mouth captured his lips in a smoldering, addictive kiss. Dallas heard more than saw Greer's jeans drop to his feet. Foreplay was a thing of the past. Dallas was so right there with him. Why waste a second of the time they had together?

Dallas gathered Greer in a gentle, but strong embrace, drawing Greer's hot body flush against his chest. One of his hands lowered to grip Greer's naked ass. He squeezed the firm globe, letting his fingers sink into the perfect flesh. The other hand lifted to cradle Greer's head, angling him just so to deepen the soul-destroying kiss.

Greer's hips tucked into his. A moan eased past his lips as their cock's were forced together. They were pressed tight from knees to chest. Maybe Dallas had played a large part in driving Greer's groin against his own. Fuck, Greer was a hot guy. Dallas's tongue pushed forward, and Greer's fingers tangled in his hair. The battle for dominance drove the kiss from sultry to incendiary.

Bedroom. They needed the bedroom.

As if Greer read his mind, his handsome guy wrenched from the kiss and whispered in his ear, "Bedroom. Now."

Those fleshy, demanding lips came for him again and he surrendered. He deepened the kiss, giving as good as he got. It took about ten seconds for his haze-filled brain to finally connect the dots, then Dallas started to blindly lead them to the bedroom, because he would *never* willingly break from a kiss like this.

CHAPTER 22

From the first moment Dallas opened for his kiss, Greer was lost to his man. The feel of his trainer's strong arms wrapping securely around his body, the scent of citrusy spice cologne and male arousal swirling around his senses intoxicated him. The taste of this special man tantalized and enticed him.

All kinds of carnal visions exploded in Greer's head as he and Dallas shuffled across the tile floor toward the bedroom. The slow-moving pace was awkward, neither wanted to let the other go. Then Dallas's big arms locked around Greer's waist before he bent at the knee and hoisted him off his feet, holding him about a foot off the ground. His gasp interrupted the kiss. He was suspended inches above Dallas's handsome face.

Oh, fuck yeah. He wanted to be owned and manhandled. A dream fully materialized by his strong trainer. Greer smiled his sultry grin, lifting the corners of his mouth as Dallas's chin tilted up and his mouth opened. It was all the instruction he needed to resume the scorching kiss. Desire welled, heating Greer's body.

Greer wrapped his arms around Dallas's thick shoulders, then ran his hands up the back of his neck to thread his fingers through those silky strands. He tilted his lover's head for a better angle. Thank God he'd taken the time to stretch himself. Less time he'd have to wait to have that big, thick cock moving inside him.

He wrapped his legs around Dallas's slim hips, locking his ankles together. Dallas had such a strong body. He rolled his hips into Greer, seeking more contact. Desperate and impatient Greer grasped the fabric of Dallas's pullover, dragging the material up until his hands could reach the warmth of Dallas's bare skin hidden underneath.

It wasn't enough. Greer tore from the kiss, dragging Dallas's shirt up over his head. Greer's heavy, needy pants puffed across Dallas's kiss-swollen wet lips. He hadn't thought the move through. If he removed the shirt, Dallas would have to let go of him. He didn't want that. Instead, he moved Dallas's head out of the hole, left the arms inside the sleeves and plunged his tongue hungrily into Dallas's open mouth. How they had gone from laughing outside to dry humping each other in less than two minutes spoke to the overwhelming attraction they both seemed to share.

"You're so fucking hard," Greer hissed, breaking from the kiss to haul his own shirt over his head. His back hit something hard, most likely the hall wall, and he grinned as his shirt came over his head and off his arms.

"Sorry. Misjudged," Dallas muttered, latching on to his neck, mouthing a wet trail up to Greer's ear. The Kellus Hardin original piece of art, rocked on its mount beside them. Greer glanced that way, thankful it stayed on the wall.

"Being carried is turning me the fuck on."

"You aren't light," Dallas whispered, tracing the shell of

his ear with his tongue. Dammit, Dallas made it hard to keep perspective.

"Then get us to the bed," Greer hissed, sliding his hand between their bodies, driving into the waistband of Dallas's jeans, seeking that hard cock.

Dallas thrust against the pressure of Greer's hand molding around Dallas's weeping cock. His mister was so responsive, rutting shamelessly as he tried to move them into the bedroom. Dallas jerked away from his ear, his face in Greer's direct line of vision. "That feels good."

"Yeah?" Greer asked, moving his hand lower, making the jeans taut around Dallas's waist as he cupped his balls. "I think you're happy to see me."

"You're still in your clothes."

"I wasn't, but I was afraid you weren't coming in, so I threw my clothes on to come retrieve you." Greer waggled his brows. "I think I'll always have to chase after you."

"I was coming in, just thinking about you and got a little lost." Dallas's breathless words drove his desire higher.

"Really good fucking answer, Mr. Reigns." Greer dropped his legs, and Dallas let him go. His trainer pulled the shirt off his arms while kicking his shoes off. He made record time pushing his jeans down his legs.

All that bare muscular flesh had Greer grazing his palms appreciatively over Dallas's sculpted stomach, around his rib cage. Dallas's hips pushed forward, drawing them together until they were nestled tightly against the other.

"I also have lots of good ideas. Like you using that pouty mouth on me." The tone of Dallas's voice was full of raw hope. Damn, he wanted his mouth on him too. Greer brushed his lips over Dallas's throat, placing a kiss on the juncture between his neck and shoulder before trailing wet, open-mouth nips and kisses down his chest. Greer took tender care with each taut nipple, licking and sucking while his guy moaned his approval. Dallas's responsive body rippled and flexed as he went.

Greer smiled at the standard Hanes tighty-whities Dallas wore. His mister was a briefs guy, but they didn't fit him or his personality…at all. Greer would purchase something a little sexier for him next week. He cast a playful glance up the length of Dallas's expansive chest. He ran his fingers along the elastic waistband and slowly lowered Dallas's tented briefs. Greer dropped to his knees as he worked Dallas's briefs down his legs. That gorgeous cock sprang free, and he couldn't help but steal a taste.

Oh hell. The slow, torturous pursual he planned was forgotten as he fixated on one target and reached for that perfect jutting length.

"Fuck, Dallas. I'm so into you. Like set ablaze, scorching, five-alarm into you." Greer gave a long, slow tug on the cock in his hand, running his fist tightly from tip to base. Dallas's dick showed appreciation at those words with the bead of pre-come that gathered at the tip. Greer dipped his thumbnail into the slit. His mister hissed out a breath, and his large hand cupped the side of Greer's cheek.

"Taste it." Dallas drew in a shuddering breath. "Do I taste as good as you?"

Fuck.

Fuck. How did Dallas keep stealing the upper hand? Greer licked his lips and brushed them across the tip before curling his tongue over the wet head. He swirled his tongue around the tip before he opened his mouth and slid Dallas all the way in. Greer was determined to give his guy everything Dallas had given him last night.

Dallas's grip on his jaw tightened, the hand in his hair tugged, guiding Greer back and forth. The panting from above urged Greer on. Greer cupped and caressed Dallas's sac, fondling the balls in his palm. He flattened his tongue, gliding Dallas in and out of his mouth. This time, he loosened his jaw and opened his throat. The moan he earned made him smile around his trainer's length. Dallas liked that move. Pre-come coated his tongue, Dallas's unique taste dominated his senses, making him crazy for more.

"Shit," Dallas grumbled, forcing Greer forward. Dallas's hips snapped, his cock taking a deep dive down Greer's throat. Oh fuck, this was hot. Greer's eyes watered as he forced himself to calm.

He grabbed Dallas by the ass, digging his fingers into the fleshy globes and swallowed more of his big guy. Dallas's hips rolled then seconds later relaxed, but Greer kept his face pressed tightly to Dallas's groin.

"How do you do that?" Dallas asked in awe. Greer released him, taking deep pulls of breath through his nose as he sucked and worked his tongue in tandem with Dallas's canting hips. His fist went to his own dick. He couldn't ignore the need any longer. He stroked himself as he bobbed his head, devouring his lover's cock. His release built at warp speed. Dallas's moans spurred him on. He was on a collision course with his orgasm if he didn't slow his eager ass down.

Greer was certain he had about a million orgasms ready to go at this man's hand, but he loved the anticipation, and he wanted Dallas to experience the build-up too. He squeezed his cock, denying himself the release that threatened his plans, and ran his tongue along his trainer's shaft, pulling him from his mouth. He raised his gaze, happy he'd stopped just in time. Dallas's cock wept in front of him, calling him forward again, threatening his willpower.

"You're truly beautiful, Dallas," Greer murmured, slowly kissing up his lover's body. "I was transfixed at the club. I couldn't look away. I haven't been able to look away since."

"Your mouth's amazing," Dallas said, ignoring his compliment, but Greer hadn't missed the blush crawling up his cheeks. His guy didn't have an arrogant bone in his body. A flash lit Dallas's green eyes, and a sly smile bloomed on his face. His chest rose and fell as if he were calming his nerves. Then he bent, kissing Greer sweetly on the lips.

"You feel good against me." Greer rutted shamelessly against Dallas, wrapping him in his arms, taking Dallas's mouth in a toe-curling kiss. Dallas kissed him harder, delving deeper, reflecting all the sexual crazed need racing through them. Dallas thoroughly and completely explored his mouth, pushing Greer toward the mattress. His knees went weak as he was consumed from the inside out.

Greer wrapped his arm around Dallas's neck, fusing their mouths together, deepening the kiss. Nothing could compare to the way Dallas made him feel. He licked at that skillful tongue invading his mouth, seeking more as Dallas pushed him down on the mattress. The arm around his back urged Greer to the center of the bed.

"I like it rough." Greer let his desires be known.

Dallas forced him down, covering him with his heavy body, crudely taking his mouth in a demanding kiss. Greer screwed his eyes closed at the feel of Dallas's answer to his request. Dallas sank his teeth into Greer's bottom lip, then ground against him in the most delicious way. Greer cared for little else than to keep Dallas's mouth on his. He craved Dallas's heated touch, the searing need ravishing him with every brush of his tongue.

"Let's see if we can give you what you want," Dallas rasped against his ear. A naughty grin tugged at the corners of his mouth. Anticipation raced across every nerve ending in Greer's body. It didn't matter what happened from this point forward because Dallas owned him, body and soul.

The hints of vulnerability this man evoked caused wanton need to rush down Greer's spine and land heavily in his balls. He lifted his palms to Dallas's cheeks, drawing him down. Love more than need had Greer capturing Dallas's mouth fast and rough. Dallas's big body pinned him in place. Yeah, they were back in business. Greer's hands were all over him, stroking and teasing, encouraging Dallas to take his fill of Greer's needy body.

Damn, his man knew how to kiss.

Dallas's pulse thumped wildly. He could kiss Greer forever. His damn cock though had other plans. After a life of denial and restriction, Dallas needed to experience it all. He wrenched from the kiss and pushed himself to be bold, to give what Greer so clearly wanted: anything Dallas desired. He nibbled and bit at the soft skin on Greer's long neck. "Turn around. I wanna taste."

Greer used those damn palms to bring his face in his line of vision. "You sure?"

"More than sure. I'm pretty sure it's something I'll be doing quite a bit of. I've always wanted to." As much as he'd fantasized about the tight confines of fucking a guy's ass, it couldn't compare to how many ways he'd thought about eating ass. God knew he'd sneaked around to watch it a time or two and come so hard he'd been embarrassed to come out of his room for fear Ducky had overheard. It seemed the ultimate carnal indulgence, a decadent treat. Something he could lose himself in. Give his partner pleasure before plundering hard and deep. Fuck, the thought made his mouth water as much as his damned dick leaked with anticipation.

Dallas lifted, pushing back to his heels. He panted, salivating at the body sprawled out for his view. Greer was the most beautiful man he'd ever seen. That sight only got better without his clothes, which said a lot because Greer dressed to impress in a big way.

"Get on your knees, ass up for me. I want to play with you."

Greer gave a wicked wink and a sinister smile as he seductively turned, ass in the air, both knees firmly on the mattress. He wiggled his ass in challenge. Dallas reached out as hyperawareness flowed through him, determined to remember everything he'd seen on the porn site.

Dallas spread his ass cheeks. Time slowed as he stared at the tempting pucker waiting for him. How did Greer keep turning more and more enticing by the second? With the heel of his hand, he instinctively pushed against his own erection, trying to ease the ache. His body vibrated with excitement at the thought of tasting Greer. He gripped himself and slid his length along Greer's crevice. Dallas sucked in a breath at the warm and tempting instant pleasure blowing his mind.

"Feels good. Finger me," Greer encouraged as he turned his head over his shoulder, watching him. "You want it, don't you?"

"Yeah. But first I'm gonna eat your ass, and you're gonna like it. Hands on the mattress. Don't touch yourself. That's my job."

"Oh, hell yeah." Greer's genuine enthusiasm fueled Dallas. Greer moaned huskily and lowered his head, angling his ass into a better position. Dallas slid his hands over each globe of that firm ass, his fingernails scratching the soft skin as he spread Greer open. He lowered his face to the tempting sight, ghosting his lips over the sensitive flesh. A groan vibrated from his chest as he sent a puff of breath over Greer's sensitive skin.

Fuck, Greer was so damn responsive. Dallas's confidence soared as he pressed his lips against the top of Greer's crack and kissed and nipped a trail toward the center, kneading the ass cheeks with his palms and thumbs as he drew nearer to his destination.

"Come on, D. Do it," Greer hissed, his body quivering with anticipation.

"I'm not rushing through this. I've been waiting my whole damned life to do this. And don't touch yourself." Dallas didn't waste another second. He licked across Greer's hole. Holding himself back from burying his tongue in his lover's body.

"Holy fucking hell." Greer pushed his arms out on the mattress, fisting his hands into the blanket underneath him.

The tremble in Greer's body urged Dallas to do it again.

He licked the edges of Greer's crease and bit at the soft skin surrounding his pucker. Greer turned pliant underneath his tongue, gasping and encouraging.

Dallas wanted to drag this out, give Greer everything he'd given him, but it was so damn good. He buried his face in Greer's ass and thrust his tongue forward, fucking him. He nipped, sucked, and molded the tender opening, lost in the intoxicating intimacy of the act. He loved the taste of Greer, the feeling of power he wielded and the desperate gasp of breath every time he forced his tongue through the tight quivering flesh.

He ran his hands up and down Greer's thighs, over his ass, hips, and down the long spine of Greer's back. Dreams hadn't done any of this justice, not even close. When he looked at all that gorgeous flesh flexing at his fingertips… Knowing this man wanted his touch sent a rush through him that would have dropped him to his knees if he weren't already there. He used the pad of his thumb to circle the relaxing muscle. He licked and massaged Greer gently open. Dallas lifted, pushing back on his heels, watching his digit slide inside Greer's perfect ass. Warm tightness immediately gripped him.

"Yes, baby. Yes." Greer praised. Hips rolling with his face buried in the mattress was a fucking sight to behold. Dallas easily found the same bundle of nerves that had made his toes curl the night before and grinned when Greer pushed back against him, lifting his head to look over his shoulders, his hand reaching to his cock. "Fuck yeah, D."

"Don't… Not yet, Greer. Together. We're coming together." He withdrew his digit, spreading Greer as he buried his face in Greer's ass again. He was a man possessed. He fucked Greer with his tongue, grabbing Greer's hips to keep his lover right there against him. Unintelligible whimpering fueled every swipe of his tongue.

When his own cock began to beg, Dallas finally let go, pushing back, reaching for the bottle of lube. Greer crumpled to his thighs. The blissed-out moan and quick rise and fall of Greer's chest as he sucked in deep breaths was all the confirmation Dallas needed that he'd done this right. He hurriedly slicked his fingers, laying the bottle close. Dallas dragged his tongue across Greer's back as his now-slippery finger found his lover's relaxed hole and glided easily inside.

Greer stretched his back and neck, elongating his torso, before arching his back and lifting that ass. All combined with the most delicious moan Dallas had ever encountered, as Greer said, "What're you doing to me?"

"Hopefully everything." Dallas chuckled, moving his fingers, adding drops of lube. Each slick thrust caused a visible shiver to race over his lover's body. Such a fucking turn-on to watch Greer writhe under his simple touch.

"Fuck me, Dallas."

Dallas forced two fingers into Greer, curling them over his gland and earning a strangled moan.

He scissored his fingers, stretching and working Greer open in fast, quick strokes, doing everything Greer had done to him the previous night. He wanted there to be no pain, just all pleasure. Greer's desires became a chant as he fucked himself on Dallas's hand when he added a third finger. "Fuck me, Dallas."

Dallas kept moving his fingers as he reached for the condom. He looked down at his heavy cock, come leaking from the tip. He was almost afraid if he touched it, he might explode. He wanted this so bad. Dallas gripped the packet, ripping the top away with his teeth. "Fuck, Greer, you're so fucking hot. Your greedy ass grips my fingers…"

Greer pushed back on Dallas's hand, rolling his hips as he lifted. Greer sat with his back to Dallas's chest, pumping his hips into Dallas's fingers. Greer's head dropped against Dallas's shoulder, his arms lifting, hand threading in his hair. Greer was the sexiest guy on this planet. He tilted Dallas's head, capturing his mouth. He thrust his tongue forward into the awkward kiss, caught completely off guard when Greer's hand reached between their bodies, grabbing Dallas's engorged cock.

Greer tore from the kiss, his eyes narrowing, his face twisting into something stern and commanding. "Condom. Now."

To drive Dallas's unspoken retort home, he curled his fingers directly into the orgasm-inducing bundle of nerves as a reminder of exactly who was in charge.

Greer sucked in a breath, that tight ass clenching around his fingers. Greer panted as he scrambled off Dallas, dropping down on all fours. "Own me. Now!"

Dallas chuckled, rolling the condom down his cock. "I'm pretty sure that's what I've been doing."

Greer's grin lit up his face as he looked over his shoulder to give him a seductive wink. "You sure are confident for your first time."

Electricity, chemistry, and just plain desire crackled through the air. He could feel it sliding across his skin. Dallas swatted his lover's ass. The anticipation practically sizzled between them as he took hold of his hard cock and positioned himself at Greer's entrance. The moment was here. His heart slowed to a steady thump. Dallas grabbed the lube, quickly giving himself a good coating. What he'd always wanted. All his focus centered at the tip of his cock, circling Greer's hole.

The overwhelming intensity held him in place as Greer eased back. The tight ring of muscle gave the slightest hint of resistance.

"Oh God…" Dallas hissed. Swamped with so many feelings, his hands shook as he guided himself in. "Oh yeah…" Dallas's eyes rolled back in his head. He sucked in a breath and held it as Greer's tight, warm channel surrounded the head as he slowly pushed forward. Greer's body tensed, his hands fisting the material on the mattress again as he moaned his name repeatedly.

Then his guy did something Dallas had never thought possible, he visibly relaxed and pushed back, fully seating Dallas. Tight heat encased him, gripping him like a vise. It was fucking heaven and hell. Torturous, maddening, and oh so sweet.

His body trembled, his brow furrowing as the power of that sensation had darkness edging his consciousness. He had to breathe. He was going to pass out if he didn't draw in air. Being balls deep in Greer had him on overload. The pleasure took all his senses.

Move. He couldn't. Every muscle in his body quivered and tensed simultaneously, leaving him helpless. *Move.*

Greer took over, pulling off Dallas's dick and sinking back down in the most lust-filled moment of Dallas's life. Greer's movements were deliberate and depraved. The thought brought a smile to his lips.

"Come on, babe." Greer's eyes were laden with lust. His lips parted slightly before curling into a sexy sneer. "Fuck me, D."

Sex. Greer. Hard and fast. Right. His brain finally caught up after glitching out.

"You feel too good." Dallas's voice sounded raspy and raw even to himself. He ran his palms up Greer's hips, caressing the smooth, soft skin, before digging his fingertips into the hard muscles.

Greer squirmed, circling his hips, meeting him move for move, urging Dallas into action. Dallas thrust deep, hips snapping back and forth, in and out, in a maddening motion into Greer's pliant body. His hands moved of their own accord, sliding over any skin he could find. The steady rhythm built as he canted his hips. Crazy heat began to boil at the base of his spine, spilling into his balls.

This was too much, so good. He wouldn't last. His orgasm was building too fast to control.

The muscles in Greer's sides moved under his fingers as he held on to Greer's waist for leverage before sliding his arm across Greer's chest and locking his lover in place. In his wildest imagination, he hadn't even come close to envisioning the feeling of his body pushing deep into Greer's. He held Greer against him, skin on skin, so much friction and heat. In his dreams, he'd topped, but never like this. Greer felt insanely good.

How could he ever go back to pretending to be the person his father demanded he be? He couldn't live the lie any longer. This was right, so fucking right.

Fuck, being with Greer…was everything.

Greer worked his hips, keeping the tempo, building the sensations with him. His thighs burned from exertion, but he had no intention of slowing. The air thickened around them as he continued to bury himself in Greer's perfect heat.

Grunts and pants filled the air. "Fuck, Dallas. God. Damn."

"I know," he managed to grunt out, screwing his eyes closed, never wanting this to end. Greer squirmed on him, lifting, and seating himself on Dallas, his movement forcing Dallas's dick balls deep. Dallas's ass rested on his heels as he rode the pleasure, struggling to fight back the orgasm racing like liquid fire down his spine. "Fuckin', hell. Greer."

Greer arched as Dallas clutched his waist, drawing him even tighter against his body. He couldn't get enough. Every part of him needed every part of Greer. Dallas thrust deeper, changing his pace. Insistent and demanding. He drove himself into Greer hard and fast, guiding Greer up and down on his cock.

Sweat-soaked hair fell across his forehead as he worked his body into Greer. The sound of heavy breathing and flesh meeting flesh filled the room.

"Let me touch myself," Greer pleaded. His bouncing cock slapped rhythmically with every thrust of his hips. His breaths were as uneven and just as ragged as Dallas's.

Dallas loosened his hold around Greer's chest to reach down and stroke the cock of his dreams. He tightened his fist, wanting to coerce Greer's orgasm from him. The weight and feel of Greer's thick cock sliding against his palm felt almost too good, too right. Smooth steel covered in silky velvet, much like Greer himself. Greer's hand came down on his, helping Dallas keep the rhythm of his hips. The move was intimate, proving they were truly in this together.

"Gonna…come." Greer gasped, rocking his hips, driving hard onto Dallas, meeting him thrust for thrust. His arm reached back and circled around Dallas's neck, locking there to hold him as he continued to ride over the edge.

"I can't sto—" Dallas pressed his fingers into the soft skin of Greer's hips, holding his lover in place while he drove his dick deep inside Greer's tight channel. His body set ablaze, every nerve ending firing as his release churned hotly in his balls. There was no stopping the orgasm that hit him like a bolt of lightning. His body shook and shattered with every pulse of his own cock, exploding into a million pieces as he emptied his load into the condom in Greer's perfect ass. His muscles seized and his toes curled from the force of the orgasm that punched through his body. Spots danced behind his eyes as he rode out the intensity.

"Yessss!" Greer hissed as his dick jerked wildly in Dallas's grip. His ass clenched tightly, milking the last remnants of Dallas's climax from him. Dallas panted, working to draw oxygen into his burning lungs, heaving in and out as the edge of oblivion crept around his consciousness.

"I knew it was going to be good, but fuck," Greer managed. How he could form a sentence was beyond Dallas. He couldn't even catch a decent breath.

Dallas nodded his approval. It was all he could do to hold Greer close while his heart threatened to pound out of his chest. Dallas kissed the back of Greer's neck. He never wanted to let him go. He teetered on the edge of bliss and unconsciousness as his eyes closed.

CHAPTER 23

The day couldn't have been any more special. Dallas floated naked in Greer's heated swimming pool, lost to the relaxation of the gentle lapping water. The cool breeze tickled its way across his exposed skin in the most decadent of ways. He barely lifted his arm, dragging it under the water to help keep him drifting along the surface. Skinny dipping, such a normal part of life, yet another first he'd experienced at Greer's prompting.

Dallas treasured all the lack of rules in Greer's reality. His guy liked to be nude and wanted Dallas nude along with him. Greer had no inhibitions about anything.

The warm water stirred, drawing his attention to Greer's similar swimming approach. Greer seemed a master at swimming idly with purpose. His determined hand reached out to Dallas's, threading their fingers together, messing with Dallas's suspended balance. It was too hard to deny Greer anything, especially when he turned, getting to his feet. The fingers of his free hand traced the ridges and valleys of Dallas's tight stomach muscles. His dick stirred, plumping, but not really becoming a real hard-on with the sharp chill in the air stunting its growth. Well, that was until Greer added his tongue and mouth, following the path of his fingers. His cock liked that move a lot.

"Another margarita?" Greer murmured, his enchanting gaze scanning Dallas's face.

Greer's seductive efforts at romance made the last twenty-four hours a thing of fairy tales. He'd never been so looked after or cared for in his life. He didn't want it to end, but real life beckoned. "I've got to go soon. I should have already left," he said, making no move to actually leave.

Greer dribbled warm water over Dallas's exposed skin. He hovered close, holding Dallas, keeping them together in one spot. "Stay the night with me. We can set the alarm and get you up by five. You said you slept better in my bed."

Dallas watched Greer rise above him. "I'm already shirking my responsibilities." He'd only briefly told Greer of the interrogation Skye had pummeled him with this afternoon when he'd texted her, asking her to take his class for the evening. "This weekend's been like a mini vacation. I have a world waiting on me to reengage."

Greer mashed his lips together. The piercing stare and furrowing brow showed his disapproval of Dallas's response, but there was something more to the annoyance. "Next weekend, I have a political dinner in Houston and a beach cleanup on Sunday in Guatemala. Come with me? We'll leave Saturday morning and be home Sunday night."

The well of laughter manifested into Dallas reacting as if Greer had lost his mind. "I can't go out with you in public like that. I thought of this as a one-night stand. Besides, I have too much to do—"

Greer reared back, rising out of the water, fully coming to his feet. His face contorted in a range of emotion until it settled on anger, and he let go of Dallas completely, leaving him to flounder in the water. "This is *not* a one and done situation. Don't you dare trivialize us like that."

"Us?" He'd barely gotten his feet underneath him when Greer's frustration turned to full-blown outrage. Dallas hadn't meant any offense and certainly not in the way Greer had apparently taken it. Greer shoved back. His harsh glare came with no words, and the guy always had a ready arsenal of persuasions to spew. Then he abruptly turned and waded toward the steps. "Greer, come back."

Greer ignored him, taking the steps up, water cascading a trail down his nude body. He didn't look back. Dallas watched Greer's purposeful stride. The heat of his body mixed with the cool night's air, causing steam to rise off Greer in waves. The sweet, gentle man he'd spent the last twenty-four hours with had turned into a sleek, predatory animal in complete control of his surroundings. He was impressive as hell, much like he'd been their first meeting in Greer's office.

"Do you want me to go?" Dallas asked, standing in the shallow end of the swimming pool. The suggestion felt like a battering ram to Dallas's heart. Just mere seconds ago, Dallas had started this argument by saying he couldn't stay. Now, it was all he wanted to do.

Greer whipped out a terry cloth beach towel from a stack on a towel warmer and rubbed it over his face. "Of course, I don't want you to leave. How is that not crystal clear?"

The relief was staggering. Dallas released a breath he hadn't known he held. He kept his gaze glued to the hard body at the edge of the other side of the pool. Greer ignored Dallas as he made his way to the pool's steps. Neither spoke as Greer dried off. He was such a handsome man; he stole Dallas's breath like he stole his reason.

They stood about three feet apart, Greer kept his back to Dallas but reached for a second towel and handed it over. Dallas took it, bringing it to his chest, but his entire focus remained on the man now running the towel over his damp hair. "Then tell me what you think this is?" Dallas whispered.

Greer had no hesitation. Not a moment of pause or consideration. "I believe I've found a man I want to spend a significant amount of time with." He finally turned, wrapping the towel around his waist, scooting past Dallas without touching him. "I see a future with you."

On every level, Dallas loved every single one of those words. Greer spoke directly to his aching, fragile heart, that had just begun to heal all those battered rough edges. The barrier Dallas had constructed between himself and his sexuality all those years ago was crumbling under the wrecking ball known as Greer Lockhart. Dallas had never expected Greer to see the same value in him as he saw in Greer. He had honestly believed their ending came tonight.

Yes, the demons of Dallas's world lurked around the edges, waiting to steal all this happiness. Of course, whatever they were doing couldn't continue, but it did ease some of his burden of being defective. Never truly being good enough for the people around him.

"Nothing's changed for me." Greer turned at about three-quarters of the way to his bedroom. The towel in Dallas's hand hung limp at his side.

He stood there, dripping wet, goose bumps springing up on his damp flesh from the cool air, but otherwise, he felt none of it. All the anxiety of his entire life ran anew through him. "I'm definitely not out. And I'm not sure I'm gay as much as I'm really into you." Even as he said the words, they tasted bitter on his tongue. He denied what he knew deep down was the truth. He'd tried to convince himself so many times he wasn't gay. He'd felt the guilt every single time he had those runaway thoughts. God, he hated being this fucked up.

Greer's face softened; his chest fell on a slowly released exhale. He reached a hand up, pushing at his perfectly in place hair as if it didn't naturally fall there. "If that's so, then why're you turning this into a one-time forbidden tryst?"

"I can't ever be seen with you. My family would never forgive me."

Greer's blond brows crinkled. He took a couple of powerful, determined strides toward Dallas. The predator was back in his gait. Greer's lips pressed together, showing he didn't understand. How could he? Those were secrets Dallas had never shared with anyone.

If his own blood didn't want him, how could he expect anyone else to?

"I'm not sure I believe they would. You're all very close." Greer challenged the façade he held in place.

"No." Dallas shook his head and lifted the towel. The lifelong shame that had taken a brief hiatus came rushing back, somehow stronger. The incrimination staggered him under the heavy, emotional weight.

"Tell me, Dallas." Greer's voice changed to a soft encouragement as he came within a foot of Dallas. The tone promised everything would work out as it should.

Dallas didn't want to say. Greer had it all. He didn't get hung up on things like family opinion. He started around Greer, heading toward the bedroom. He needed to dress and go home. Greer's arm shot out, blocking his retreat.

"Tell me what I'm competing with."

The weight of the world sat heavily on Dallas's shoulder, kicking its dangling feet in a renewed exuberance. Turmoil had him looking over at Greer. He was everything Dallas had ever wanted in life. Desire, commitment, and friendship stood within his grasp.

Dallas had to force his gaze away for fear of getting lost in Greer's amber depths. His heart drummed in his chest as he scanned the dazzling surroundings that represented Greer's unparalleled success. Things like this stunning backyard and magnificent home all happened when a person lived by their convictions, not their doubts.

He shook his head before his thoughts sucked him under. Whatever Greer declared he wanted would come to an end. Greer wasn't the kind of man to hide from anything.

Greer watched Dallas then slowly schooled his expression. A trick Dallas had used himself. "You're eventually going to have to tell me, Dallas. Until then, I'm sorry I lost my cool."

The strong-arm holding Dallas in place, curved and wrapped around his waist. Greer didn't pull him forward or come closer. It was a tentative hold. Something new for Greer. The past week leading up to right now had been hard, perhaps on both of them. He'd never considered Greer's feelings, only his own.

Damn, he didn't want to hurt Greer. Dallas's chin hit his chest. His truth tumbled from his lips. "It's easier for me to take this day by day without looking forward. I'll always have to be careful being seen with you. It seems an awful lot to ask from someone who bends life to fit his will."

Greer stepped into Dallas, crowding him, helping to bring some much-needed positive relief. "I don't always get what I want. I compromise more than you know. I want you, Dallas. I'll play by your rules… I'll try. I have a full steam ahead approach to life, so you'll have to remind me when you become uncomfortable. We can see where this is headed while locked behind these walls. When we're out in the world, we're friends." Greer waited for Dallas to look at him. Dallas agreed, finally giving a nod.

"I'm sorry," Dallas whispered.

"No, I'm sorry. You might not believe this, but I've tried not to push you. Then you were great company and easy to be around and so fucking sexy," Greer said, staying inches from Dallas.

"That's what I think about you." Dallas angled his head, scanning Greer's face as he spoke the words. "You're charming and hard to stay away from."

"Then I believe you owe me a blow job and a promise to sleep here tonight." It took a second for Dallas to roll his eyes and wrap an arm around Greer's shoulders, pulling him close.

"I like being honest with you," Dallas murmured. Greer adjusted his position, staying in the circle of Dallas's arm while starting them toward the bedroom.

"Good. Just continue to be."

Dallas hoped it was that easy.

The vibration underneath Greer's pillow had his tired, gritty eyes opening wide. The Dallas-infused insomnia of the last few days was catching up with him. Forty-eight hours ago, Greer had engaged in the biggest athletic competition of his life. The adrenaline high of his great win and the resulting prize of gaining his heart's desire had taken their toll. The stiff, aching muscles had finally set in. Did rigor mortis only happen after death? His brain was a funky place.

The room was dark. Way too early for any living human being to be awake. He lay on his side with the warmth of Dallas's broad chest and strong arms wrapped securely around his body. The whole disastrous situation of waking at such an ungodly hour was made instantly better with Dallas by his side. Greer's own arms were tangled with Dallas's, as were his legs. No surprise there. Apparently even in the depths of deep sleep, Greer held on firmly for fear this extraordinary man might try to leave him... again.

All of Dallas's rejection might be showing in the cracks of Greer's carefully built confidence. He fully understood the hurt of being rejected by those who were supposed to love him. Greer had made a dauntless effort at protecting his heart for most of his life.

Yeah, until his gaze had landed on a tipsy hot trainer at a local dance club.

It was laughable at how freely, if not carelessly, he'd given his heart away. What if Dallas's fears couldn't be overcome? Dread gripped Greer, solidly waking him.

No more negativity. Insecurity was Dallas's deal, not Greer's.

Greer did what he did best, forced those thoughts aside, never to be considered again. He'd already decided he'd be or do whatever Dallas needed. His mister was scared, and he had to tread carefully to relieve Dallas's burdens.

That simple.

The obvious truths began to splinter his plan. Not once in Greer's life had he ever been enough to make someone love him. Now that the stakes were higher than ever, Greer's arms instinctually tightened as worry swirled his belly.

"What?" Dallas mumbled against his hair. "Is it time to get up?"

Greer cleared his head and neutralized his tone. Dallas was a perceptive man. He'd sense Greer's worry, most likely interpret them as a disconnect and cause Greer to spill his truth before he was ready.

"No, we have fifteen minutes." Greer smiled as Dallas burrowed against him, content to sleep.

Greer had other ideas. There was a reason he'd set his alarm fifteen minutes early in the first place. He shifted until he was chest to chest with Dallas. He pressed his lips to Dallas's bare shoulder then mouthed his way up Dallas's neck, leaving a trail of tender kisses as he went. His nose skimmed the short, silky dark hair surrounding the shell of Dallas's ear.

"I wanted to give you something to remember me by today. Let me kiss you."

"My breath," Dallas muttered, keeping his head buried in the pillow. The slow even breaths showed Dallas wasn't getting

Greer's intentions at all.

"You're ruining the romance," he teased quietly and took Dallas's jaw, positioning him so he was at a better angle. "You brushed your teeth before bed and that wasn't all that long ago. Kiss me, D. Show me how much this matters."

Dallas's eyes slowly opened, a sleepy, honest gaze met Greer's and his whole world stopped. Greer reared back several inches, staring at this kind, generous man. He wanted to be the only man Dallas ever kissed again. Dallas was his and he was Dallas's.

An irrational, desperate cave-man edge made Greer want to claim Dallas right this minute. Demand that Dallas feel the same way about him. Fuck day by day, he wanted decade by decade. Greer's move-mountains approach to life dictated forty-eight hours was long enough to declare his love. Why wait any longer? He had to stop all this treading-lightly and stalling to give Dallas time.

Seconds before the words tumbled from Greer's lips, he glossed them over, easing the intensity. "I want you to be mine."

Dallas's face softened as Greer encouraged him to his back and sank down on top of him. Dallas wrapped himself around Greer. He brushed his mouth across Dallas's lips. Dallas opened, and Greer plunged his tongue forward, gently but thoroughly making love to Dallas with his lips, tongue, and teeth.

Time stood still as Greer lost all sense of reason. He absorbed the understanding that every part of him wanted every part of Dallas…till death do they part. Greer kissed Dallas like his very life depended on their intimacy. He gathered Dallas in his arms, working his way between his parted thighs. His cock was like a steel rod between their bodies. The kiss deepened, turning frenzied in seconds flat.

Greer had to wrench himself from Dallas's tight hold, trailing licks and nips down his trainer's neck before his guy seemed to understand his intention. After swirling his tongue around

Dallas's pebbled nipple, he sank his teeth into the sensitive skin above Dallas's rib cage then lifted his head and enclosed his hand around Dallas's stiff cock.

"We don't have much time. Let me do this." Greer pushed back on his knees, spreading Dallas's thighs as the bedcovers slid down his body. He pumped the thick length in his fist, enjoying the feel of Dallas's desire sliding through his hand, cherishing the profound knowledge that he could make Dallas want him this much.

Greer's gaze slid down his lovely trainer's alluring body to the drop of pre-come glistening on his lover's broad tip. Drawn there, Greer willed himself to memorize the sweet feel of Dallas's cock entering his mouth. *So beautiful.* His lips touched the warm fleshy tip, kissing Dallas there before opening his mouth. Slowly, but thoroughly he took Dallas to the back of his throat on the very first swallow.

"How do you always do that…" Dallas hissed.

The awe in Dallas's tone made him chuckle. Then he almost moaned as his mister's taste assaulted his senses. He could consume this man all morning if they had time, but sadly they didn't. He trailed one hand up the side of Dallas's thigh, reaching for his sac. He toyed with the soft skin before rolling his lover's balls in his palm. With his other hand, he fisted Dallas's shaft, using his hand to stroke as he used his mouth and tongue to pleasure his lover.

Hell, he was lost to Dallas.

The body under him tensed, Dallas's feet and hands clutching at the mattress as he fought the bucking of his hips. Greer licked a trail up Dallas's engorged cock, teasing the squirming man beneath him. He swirled his tongue around the swollen tip before dipping inside the slit, coaxing more of his lover's essence from that powerful body. Greer lifted his gaze to Dallas.

The desire darkening Dallas's riveting gaze was all it took for him to want to devour his trainer. He deep-throated Dallas, swallowing around the length in his throat.

"I love your mouth," Dallas moaned, scraping his blunt fingernails against Greer's scalp as he fisted his hands in Greer's hair. Dallas's hips rolled, finding a cadence Greer eagerly followed, bobbing his head with the rhythm Dallas set.

Using his left hand, he massaged and cradled his lover's balls in his palm while gently squeezing Dallas's shaft with his other. His fist slid suggestively over the wet trail his tongue left behind as he moved on and off his lover's aroused cock. Dallas's hands grew more insistent, forcing Greer's head lower. The decadent feel of Dallas's broad tip shoving down his throat left Greer fighting for breath in short gasping intervals. His guy seemed to like it naughty every single time they came together, which was exactly the way Greer wanted it.

Dallas's moans came by way of an indecipherable chant, made louder with every thrust of his hips. Oh, how he wished to spend the day together in this bed.

His lover plunged forward one last time. The pulsating cock lodged enticingly in his throat until Dallas tried to pull away. Greer wasn't having any of that. He gripped Dallas's hip and took him to the root, burying his nose in the soft hairs at Dallas's groin before pulling back to sample his prize. Dallas's salty release filled his mouth and throat. What a fucking turn-on.

Dallas's hips locked in place, the hand in his hair holding Greer there. He couldn't breathe and that was fine by him. If he died right there, at least he'd go a happy man. Before he could make good on that offer, Dallas released him. Greer rose, swallowing and gasping for breath at the same time. Dallas's hand came to his cock, the other tossed over his eyes as his chest heaved. His long hard body tensed, the muscles rippled and tight.

Oh fuck, he was in so much trouble. Greer wiped at the side of his mouth, crawling up his lover's body. Soon Dallas would leave him. His hands pushed under Dallas's body, reaching for his shoulders. Greer held on tight as he cushioned himself head to toe on that big body.

Dallas held him, turning to the side, cradling Greer with his arms and his legs. He loved that move. Then Dallas amped it up a notch by burying his face in the crook of Greer's neck.

"How do you do that?" Dallas whispered.

"You turn me on." Greer kissed his shoulder, pleased he was able to satisfy his guy. "Today, when you're gone. You remember I'm right here waiting for you."

There was a quiet pause, something Greer wasn't sure he liked. When Dallas finally opened his mouth to speak, his cell phone's alarm cut him off. The loud chirp ruined the moment. Dallas turned, having to completely release Greer to reach his phone on the nightstand. He put it down and turned back to Greer who smiled and lifted his arm. "Snooze with me for just a little longer."

The phone started ringing. Dallas reached back, looked at the screen, and answered on the second ring. He laid back on the mattress, his hand covering his eyes. The invisible wall between them dropped into place at record speed, keeping Greer where he lay, utterly silent.

"I'm awake," Dallas said, most likely to Ducky. They had agreed last night that Ducky would call Dallas at five thirty this morning. He'd claimed to be at another friend's house, with one too many beers under his belt. Luckily, Ducky seemed oblivious to the truth. "Thanks."

Dallas dropped the phone and lay there a few seconds before he rolled to sit on the edge of the bed farthest from Greer. "I'm exhausted."

Tentatively, Greer reached out, trailing his palm down Dallas's broad back. A doubt Greer couldn't quite voice kept him quiet. Dallas finally tilted his chin over his shoulder, looking down at Greer. The gaze did look more tired than turmoiled.

Dallas laid a heavy palm against Greer's cheek, then trailed the outer edge of his face. "Thank you for all this."

Greer left the words he wanted to say unspoken and decided on a small smile instead as Dallas stood. His nude body on full display. A delightful distracting treat for Greer.

"Do you mind if I get some coffee?"

"I'll make it for you," Greer offered. This man brought out his nurturing side of wanting to do for another.

Dallas gave him a smile and started for the bathroom. Any insecurity faded as he watched that ass until it disappeared through his bathroom door.

CHAPTER 24

Exhaustion coupled with a classroom full of ornery fifth graders couldn't remove the constant smile from Dallas's face. He'd had the patience of Job all day. Maybe being the best substitute teacher of anyone, anywhere. He happily watched the last of the students leave the classroom for lunch before he pivoted around and headed straight for the teacher's office chair. He tugged his cell phone free from his back pocket before his ass hit the rolling seat. His thumbs flew over the small screen until he reached the text messages icon.

Twelve new messages. Four from Greer.

His grin widened as if Greer stood right in front of him. Man, the guy was a trip. A fall Dallas willingly took. He chose to open Greer's message first before either Ducky's or Donny's. What did that say about Dallas's business-mindedness? He didn't care in the least.

Greer's message began with, "*I feel like I know you can't open messages while working.*"

The second followed about thirty minutes later. "*I hope this isn't bothering you. I'm in my office, thinking about you. I feel like I should tell you how much I miss you.*"

The third came about forty-five minutes after that. "*As a possible boyfriend, I'm finding I'm a needy guy. What are you doing right now? I'm working but still awfully distracted. Bright green eyes keep robbing me of my thoughts. Did I tell you I miss you?*"

The fourth and final message read, "*I was thinking dinner at your place tonight. I could bring pizza or something, enough for us all. I'll keep my hands to myself. Ducky can think we're working on my class leadership etiquette. Thoughts?*"

Another message from Greer came as Dallas stared at the screen, rereading the words as if Greer's deep, masculine voice spoke every word directly to him. "*I know you're at the gym until almost nine, but I spoke with Ducky today. I told him I'd like a run through of everything before I take my first class. Maybe I should have waited to hear from you. I'm not good at waiting.*"

Dallas barked out a laugh. Seconds later, another of Greer's texts came through. "*If I've crossed a line, I'm sorry. It's like I'm jonesing for my next hit and you're my crack.*"

The message in progress bubbles flashed at the bottom of the screen, and Dallas grinned happily as he waited for the next message. "*I've never really done drugs. I'm guessing what that might feel like. Don't worry.*"

He laughed a hearty chuckle this time, picturing Greer walking and typing, explaining everything to a quiet office like he had this weekend when he spoke in detail about his home. Dallas let his thumbs fly, answering all the text messages in one of his own. "*I don't think it's a good idea for you to come to my place tonight. Maybe I can stop by after I finish my shift at the gym, but*

I can't stay long. I have a class at 10 tonight."

Dallas pushed send and switched the screen to Ducky's messages, who had a very distinct style of texting of his own. He wrote a single sentence in each message. Dallas had learned to read them all together to understand whatever his youngest brother wanted to say.

"Hey, everything's running smooth here today."

"The new trainer had his first class."

"The numbers were good."

"Not as good as you, but good."

"Greer Lockhart wants to come over tonight to see how we do things and prep for his class."

"I don't know if it's a good idea or not, but you can't hardly tell him no."

"Should I message Donny to come over?"

The good vibes spread. Dallas sat back in the seat and chuckled at Ducky's accurate observation of Greer. The only thing he might change was to say that Greer was impossible to say no to. Dallas started to reply then decided to check Donny's message first. Greer had already dinged him back. Dallas ignored it just to prove he could after spending the last six hours with Greer bouncing around the forefront of his mind.

Dallas stared down at Donny's paragraph, appreciating his single message. *"They found a warehouse and office space. 4,000 square feet off i-20. The lease is one year. I'm going to authorize. You should be here right now. You went missing this weekend and now this? What's right, bro? You need to get over yourself and put our company first. You know you're a nutcase and this is no time for your fucking head games. They're why I stalled before getting involved to begin with. I'm sick and fucking tired of carrying the load. You don't want to do your share, then fine. I'm cutting you out. Decision made."*

An unexpected sucker punch wouldn't have sent his good

morning reeling any faster. Of course, Donny was the buzzkill of the day. The sudden spark of intense guilt had his brows pulling together. His smile melted into a frown. The weight of the world rested like a boulder on his shoulders.

At the time, taking this substitute position had been the right decision to make. Hell, it was still the right decision. He needed cash. He'd been covering his and Ducky expenses for too long now, but Donny hadn't been wrong about the headcase he'd become, or about the distance he'd placed between taking care of his responsibility and figuring out all this obsession he had for Greer.

Dallas had acted like he didn't have a care in the world. And ultimately, exploring the forbidden side of his sexuality was always going to cause a divide in his life. Greer could never be an established, accepted part of his world like Cari or Skye or any female for that matter. When Dallas left to spend time with Greer, his responsibilities would always be left suffering and undone.

His heart sank back into the familiar hollowness he'd experience pre-Greer. A place it seemed destined to reside. He tossed the phone on the desk and scrubbed a hand down his face, trying hard to erase the haunting pain of his thoughts. He'd been truly content and happy this weekend. Maybe the happiest he'd ever been before.

Dallas reached for his lunch sack. In his haste to get out of the house, he'd managed to grab a protein bar and a coconut water before he left. He lived off those two things. Yet today, both were unappetizing and ultimately left untouched. He dropped his head in his hands and let his eyelids close. What did he hope to accomplish by continuing to see Greer? They could never be out or long term. The bold Greer wasn't the kind of guy to stay hidden or wait in the wings for anything. Dallas was so naïve. The culmination of him and Greer came to a spectacular thirty-six hours, nothing more.

That realization caused a sharp slice of pain to lay his heart open. Hell, his back hit the seat cushion. He couldn't catch his breath under such anguish.

Why had he ever gone with Greer in the first place? In Greer's house, the moment he'd turned the corner from the hall to the living room to see Greer standing there asking him if he was gay, when honesty of his secrets had dropped from his mouth, that was when he should have started for the front door and never looked back.

What did he expect? For Greer to fall as hard and fast for him as he'd fallen for Greer?

Oh fuck, he was going to cry. He had let himself believe in fairy tales. A gorgeous prince charming come to swoop him from the drudgery of his life.

One hundred percent, Greer would tire of Dallas.

"Reigns, you need anything from the lounge?"

Panic had his gaze colliding with Mrs. Tobler, another teacher. Her smiling face leaned around the door to his classroom. He'd known her for years. All the chaos must not have been reflected on his face, because she didn't look freaked out or concerned. Dallas scrubbed his hands over his face, rubbing at his tired eyes, hiding to steel his spine.

"Nah, I'm good. It was a long weekend," he said, dropping his hands and pushing to his feet.

She laughed a throaty, commiserating chuckle. "I think it's going to be a much longer week for you. I watched the big competition. That was something else. Very motivating."

A jaw-cracking yawn he hadn't known was there ripped free, making them both laugh. "I'll go with you. I could probably use some coffee."

"The coffee isn't great." She stepped away from the doorway as he walked through. "But they have energy drinks."

"You're on." The blessed numbness of his life, the one he'd spent much of his teenage years cultivating, settled over him like a cold, unfeeling blanket. He prayed it stayed in place. It was the only way to get through the loss of someone like Greer Lockhart.

The timed-out darkened screen of Greer's open laptop sat untouched in front of a barstool on his kitchen island. The device should be holding every bit of Greer's focus. To say he was behind in his work was a substantial understatement. Greer's constant internal self-discipline lecture had him committing to following the same work schedule and load as Dallas. No more days spent wasted, daydreaming over his exquisite trainer.

Greer's inner being mocked his new plan. His obsessive side knew Dallas's place in both his head and his heart took center stage of his life, hopefully for the rest of his life, but he had to try and salvage his sanity. Surely, with enough mental effort and time under their belts, Greer could find a reasonable work balance. Maybe.

For fear he might be missing something important, Greer had done something he'd never done before. He'd farmed out most of his personal client base to the senior analysts in his firm. What a hard pill for him to swallow. Greer liked to be involved in everything, but no matter how hard he tried, he couldn't get his head in the game. With his eyes opened or closed, vivid images of Dallas were all he could see.

As he scanned each of his memories, he realized there were things he missed. Like the fine lines around Dallas's smiling lips or the tilt of his head as he ducked away seconds before he laughed. Winning the trainer over then keeping Dallas by his side seemed to be all he wanted to do with his life.

Hence the many candles burning around the living room. The expensive sparkling wine chilling in the ice bucket. The lube and condoms lying within reach of both the sofa where he'd envisioned Dallas bending over and the lounger close to the swimming pool, a place Dallas naturally gravitated to.

With a snap of his fingers, Greer remembered the back retractable doors. He went there, pushing each large pane open, allowing the fresh air to filter through the living room. The twinkle of the quiet night sky added another romantic element to the ambience he tried to create.

Greer looked around the room, satisfied. Pepperoni pizza was the most prominent aroma, stronger than the fragrant candles. That couldn't be helped. He'd grabbed something fast just in case Dallas hadn't eaten, but he hadn't wanted to waste the little time they had eating a full meal before Dallas would have to leave to make his scheduled class on time.

He went to the champagne bucket, pouring himself a single glass. He took a hearty gulp, trying to muster his work motivation. The chrome laptop was the only eyesore in the room. He drained the glass in one big swallow and manned up, taking the stool.

He abandoned the crystal flute on the granite counter before logging into EnviroCapital's proprietary server. If nothing more, he needed to add an additional note to the preliminary changes he wanted to implement with BikeBro. He planned to allocate additional funds for a team of instructors to help Dallas's workload balance. Based on the research data gathering now, Dallas needed to remain the face of the company—because, boy, what a face— but Dallas's time restrictions made fast growth difficult. And with a quick tilt of the head, he admitted he wanted to help free Dallas's time for everything Greer had planned for them to do. He wanted dates, traveling, and pockets of strategic alone time.

Greer's cell phone lay on the island next to his laptop, drawing his gaze there. He looked at the screen and had to remind himself, like he had several times today, that Dallas was a busy man. Texting Greer wasn't yet a priority. He hadn't heard from Dallas since noon. He'd have to ask Dallas to respond a little more frequently. His needy side, the one Dallas brought out in him, craved more communication.

Greer's eyes shifted to the corner of his computer screen to check the time. Eight twenty-three. The gym was a three-minute drive from his house. Four, if he caught a light. Dallas would be there soon. Greer forced himself to focus on the laptop.

An hour and fifteen minutes later—he knew the time with all certainty because he'd watched every minute pass in painful misery—Greer closed the lid to his computer and swiveled around on his barstool to face the living room. Half the candles had burned out. The others still flickering began to mock him as he finally let the realization of Dallas standing him up settle into his realm of thinking.

He tucked his hands between his thighs and let the heavy weight of disappointment slump his shoulders. With the constant highs and lows of the last few weeks, his heart was becoming the most annoying organ in his body. This time hurting like it had never hurt before.

"What happened to spook him?" Greer tucked his lips between his teeth, worrying them as he tossed around different scenarios in his head.

Maybe he had come on too strong. That made him bark out a humorless laugh that somehow made his heart hurt worse. Of course, he had added too much pressure to Dallas. That was his standard MO, but his swirling gut told him that wasn't the problem.

When Dallas hadn't texted Greer back, that should have been the bright neon arrow pointing to something being amiss. He should have forced their conversation. Of course, he should have.

More on instinct than any real plan, Greer reached for his cell phone, snapping a photo of his living room. He scooted off the stool and first went to the oven. The overbaked pizza smell had him turning off the warmer. He reached for an oven mitt and single-handedly pulled the large, blackened pizza stone out, and dropped the burned pizza in the trash. He carelessly tossed the mitt and the stone toward the stove as he went for the back doors, shutting them tight. Greer blew out each of the candles. It seemed overly dramatic to toss those in the garbage too, so he'd wait until morning.

His kind, considerate, giving trainer hadn't called. Dallas had willingly left him waiting alone. Greer's first time being stood-up, and it fucking sucked.

His heart required—no, demanded—he go and drive the route from the gym to Dallas's apartment to ensure Dallas hadn't been stranded or hurt somehow. His sweet, assertive gentleman didn't have it in him to leave Greer waiting without a single word.

His head knew better and won this round.

Greer went to the workout room, turned on his BikeBro, and signed in. On some sort of morbid kick, he activated the mirror. Standing fully dressed in the casual wear he'd painstakingly chosen tonight, Greer split the screen, knowing Dallas could see him if he was there. If Ducky, Skye, and Donny were on, they'd see him too.

No one else but Dallas mattered. Greer tried to mask his feelings, hide the emotion from his face when Dallas's image filled the other half of the mirror. He watched the slightest turn of Dallas's mesmerizing eyes as they met his gaze. Their usual warmth gave the most subtle shift, turning icy cold and resolved. Dallas's jaw firmed, his brow furrowed, and his trainer looked away, concentrating on the class.

Greer glanced over at the list of cyclists signed on. Dallas had a large following. How did he attract so many riders at ten o'clock at night? From a business perspective, Dallas should be teaching in a group setting during prime-time hours.

He forced himself to turn the BikeBro off, because seriously, how pathetic was it that he stood there staring. The screen darkened and he still stayed planted in his spot.

What happened next?

After a long, slow exhale, he closed his eyes, absorbing the shocking hurt. In his heart, he knew that he and Dallas were more than a one and done. They just were. They connected and fit together like pieces of a complex puzzle. He had to do something, so he lifted the cell phone still in his hand and tried to form the right words to dial them back in time to this morning.

"Babe, what happened?" Greer typed then immediately deleted those words.

Dallas had felt their solid connection. Greer knew he had. Images of them barely staying above water while swimming together because neither wanted to let the other go… Dallas curling around Greer, sleeping right on top of him with his hand stroking his hair and Dallas's sweet breath dancing over his face… Dallas sitting on the sofa, free of his burdens, laughing at whatever story Greer told… They were in sync and meant to be.

"We can figure this out," he tried again then abruptly deleted those words too. They weren't right either. Greer couldn't solve what he didn't understand. Dallas didn't need more guilt or shame in his life. He also didn't want to fall into any category that involved those two emotions. He absolutely refused to be another burden to Dallas. But he had to say something. Communication was his life, and this desperation racing through him sought an outlet.

Leave him alone.

Let him be.

They could talk tomorrow.

Decision made. Greer left the room with long, purposeful strides. He made it as far as the entry to the living room before he stopped again. Dallas needed to know how badly Greer wanted him, and that they would, in fact, figure this out. He typed another message after twisting the lock to his front door.

"I miss you." Greer attached the picture he'd taken of his living room. The loneliness radiating from the photo said everything Greer wanted to say. He hit send and went for the garage door, heading for his sports car. He tossed the phone in the backseat and shut the door tight.

Knowing him, if he didn't keep the phone away, he would certainly break and send a zillion pathetic messages, begging

Dallas to stay in his life. Next, Greer went for his key fob. He clicked the car's locking system button and listened for the faint honk, guaranteeing it had locked. He never broke stride as he went to the backyard and tossed the key fob into the flowerbed. He wouldn't be able to easily find it under the darkness of night.

The hysteria overriding every other emotion set his clamped jaw ticing. He must find a way to win Dallas over. And he would. His heart would allow nothing less.

CHAPTER 25

Apparently, Dallas had started his own form of pacing to keep from crawling out of his skin. He had purposely ignored the text from Greer last night, but it was gnawing at him again. He wasn't ready to deal with any kind of fallout. He went from one side of the classroom to the other, making a square, easily getting his ten thousand steps for the day. Dallas listened as the students read aloud.

Even he rolled his eyes at that lie. He wasn't listening, not to one single word. His entire focus remained fixed on trying to stay awake from a night of fitful sleep and this irritability that had settled on him since yesterday afternoon. Both were contenders for the first-place prize of darkening his already sour mood.

Regardless of the reason, Dallas had refused to take any shit off anyone since he'd made the decision to end things with Greer.

When Greer's image appeared in his BikeBro mirror last night, the hurt he saw reflected in Greer's eyes sent Dallas's wretched mood into a hard nosedive.

It seemed the always combative Donny took the brunt of his anger. Unfortunately, his antagonistic brother relished an argument. From the second Dallas ended his session last night, Donny had started in on him for being MIA yesterday. His older brother was the kind of guy who picked at an open wound. Dallas was nothing more than a fresh, bleeding gash, needing a little bit of time and care to heal.

Who was he trying to kid? He'd never recover from losing Greer Lockhart.

Desperate and jittery. The fear became real. He might seriously crawl out of his skin.

What the fuck?

All the reasons he couldn't see Greer didn't amount to jack compared to how badly he wanted to be with that man.

Dallas's eyes shifted to a student making fart noises. He'd give it to this class, they had master level success at giving the substitute teacher hell. Dallas had turned those tables on the little instigators today, being relentless in his discipline.

"Fourth one down on the second row, this is your third warning. Gather your things, put them on my desk, and go to the principal's office. Explain to her why you continue to disrupt this class. I want a note from her office before you can retrieve your belongings."

The scolding shouldn't come as a surprise. He'd been doing about the same thing for most of the day, but the air in the room shifted as all the students' heads swung Dallas's way, giving him a wide-eyed astonished stare.

This particular kid gave all the grunts and groans as he stomped to Dallas's desk then out of the room. Dallas allowed the weight of the repercussions for disruption to settle in, then said, "Does anyone else have anything to say?" A few shook their heads. Others did their best to avoid eye contact. "Continue reading."

The monotone rhythm started again.

Dallas started pacing again. He had to regain his inner balance.

How he wished he'd never met Greer or known his sweet, caring nature. Greer's kind coercion led to Dallas abandoning his long-standing boundaries, giving him the best two days of his life.

He'd found utter contentment and happiness… Greer's soul-destroying kisses and gentle warmth. The way Greer made him feel wanted and cherished. Greer actually saw him.

This rock and a hard place Dallas lived within was closing in on him. His values had shifted. He had to get out of his isolated life. If not with Greer, then another man.

His heart truly hoped it would be Greer, but that was up to Greer.

This decision would tear his family apart. Maybe better now than before they got too far involved with expanding BikeBro. He had to talk to Greer.

Dallas had spent more than half his life keeping secrets. When Greer started talking about a relationship, he should've laid it all out, warned Greer before too many dollars were spent on BikeBro. There was no scenario where Donny could handle Dallas's truth. That thought sent anxiety racing through his veins. He would lose Donny, his father, and his mother. His choices would implode their family, but Greer would be there to help him navigate the fallout. At least Greer had painted that picture for him.

Dallas had to talk to Greer, face to face. Those sad eyes staring at him last night were his complete and total undoing. He could love Greer. Hell, he already did.

=♥=

If his life didn't suck so badly, he'd probably congratulate himself for staying off his cell phone last night and through this morning. Greer now better understood the constant control required of a recovering addict. His respect grew leaps and bounds. Sixteen plus hours into his self-imposed exile and he desperately needed to talk to Dallas.

Although tossing the key fob last night had cost him a few minutes this morning when he had to search the flower bed before work. Now, in the midday hours, Greer gave himself props for hiding the key fob. By about three o'clock in the morning, without doubt, he would have given in and driven to Dallas's, ruining everything by exposing their relationship to Ducky.

Greer's edginess and quick temper couldn't be contained. He stood in the center of his office, his arms crossed tightly over his chest with his leg bouncing, watching the television monitors. The normal rhythmic vibe of competing business channels, relaying the day's stock market reports, didn't draw him in like normal. But he kept staring, shifting his gaze between the screens. He'd get himself back, learn to balance. He always did.

"Greer, Mr. Tenney's trying to reach you. He's been calling your cell phone all morning. Do I tell him you're here?" Kailey asked through the speaker phone on his desk.

"No. Send him to Evan."

"Okay?" She sounded confused. He didn't care.

Tenney hadn't liked the idea of Greer giving his account up to a "lesser" analyst—Tenney's words not Greer's. He'd almost given in and taken the account back. But at four o'clock this morning, with no more than a few restless hours of sleep, he decided all his efforts needed to be laser-focused on winning Dallas back.

His best plan of attack was through BikeBro. By six o'clock this morning, he'd been fully briefed on the Reigns brothers' day to day operation and the changes his investment firm intended to make to get the company off the ground.

Obsessive, compulsive, dominating, neurotic—any of those words could describe the craziness of his scheme. BikeBro didn't begin to fill the hours of Greer's day hence him standing idly in the middle of his office right now. The Reigns brothers ran a haphazard operation.

If Greer dug in, committed the time, he'd certainly have the company operating in its true growth potential. All he had to do was wait to hear back from Ducky after the email he'd sent in the wee hours of the morning.

He looked down at his wristwatch. Eleven forty-five. When did Ducky start his day? Kailey interrupted his thoughts when she beeped in again. "Ducky's on line two, asking specifically for you. Do you want me to reroute him, too?" Greer flipped around, taking two long strides to his desk. He reached for the handset with his forefinger on the line button when Kailey said, "If you're still in there, I've got a doctor's appointment this afternoon. I'll be out for a couple of hours."

Greer took note of her tone. Her quiet cadence drew his concern. He ratcheted back his hard-edged tone, aiming for gentle and kind. "Is everything okay?"

"I don't know. Beau's making me go. I've been having headaches. He thinks it's allergies, but you know how he is," Kailey said. Greer's brows came together. Thoughts of Dallas took second place behind Kailey's possible health complications. What was Beau thinking?

Don't borrow problems.

"Call me when you're done. Don't forget. I'll be waiting to hear from you." Greer had to remind himself Beau wouldn't let anything happen to his sister. He was crazy about Kailey and had been since the moment he first laid eyes on her. It had taken Kailey longer to settle into the idea of a them than it had Beau. Greer smiled at the chase Kailey had given his best friend.

"Do you have your cell phone on you? I haven't heard the annoying ring this morning." She had a point. The whole office had to appreciate the silence from his ear-splitting ringtone. Greer had left his cell phone in the car, knowing he was barely keeping it together. In a moment of sheer weakness, he wouldn't hesitate to break down and beg Dallas to give him another chance.

Greer let go of a heavy resigned sigh as his day just grew more complicated. "No, but I will. Call me when you're finished with your appointment."

He didn't dwell, pushing the line button to take Ducky's call. The BikeBro's oversized file folder splayed its contents across his desk. They'd already done so much work in preparing for a national launch. His team impressed him on a regular basis. "Greer Lockhart."

"Hey, Greer, it's Ducky." Ducky's voice was husky and low. He clearly hadn't been awake too long.

Greer reached absently backward for his office chair, needing to take a seat before his legs gave out and toppled him to the ground. Ducky's voice gave him an odd sense of calm and comfort. The squeezing pressure around his heart eased. All the questions he really wanted to ask zinged and zipped through his overcrowded head.

How's your brother?

What happened to cause him to pull away?

Why is he so afraid to be himself?

Does everyone he dates fall so quickly for him?

Maybe there was a club Greer could join, one filled with broken hearts trailing after Dallas's affection. At least then he wouldn't feel so alone.

Of course, Greer couldn't ask any of that. Instead, he cleared his throat and stuck to his hastily created plan. "Good morning. Thanks for giving me a call. I wanted to let you know I'm taking over your project personally. Evan's had...something come up." The lie rolled convincingly off Greer's deceitful lips.

"Yeah. I read that in your email. I forwarded it to Donny and

Dallas. I don't know if they've had time to see it yet," Ducky said.

Greer swallowed the craven lump forming in his throat. "That's fine. I saw the corporate name change."

"Yeah, StreamTrainer felt right. Everything's moving fast. Secret's badass. I'm waiting for Dallas to sign off, but I think he will. They've got the new logo mockup and a new website ready to launch. I'm stalling for Dallas. I want him to see it all. I think he's going through something right now…" Ducky abruptly stopped speaking, causing Greer to look at the landline phone display to see if they were still connected. "Wait. No, I didn't mean it like that. Dallas is the one that has a good feel for our members—"

"No, it's fine. I understand," Greer said, cutting Ducky off from making any further excuses. He wanted Ducky comfortable with him, especially since he just proved to have loose lips. "There's a lot coming at you guys all at once."

Greer gave a dramatic roll of his eyes. The Reigns brothers had no way to know how completely their lives were about to change.

Something as basic as a branding redesign left undecided for several days while every part of the business's operational relaunch sat waiting would have been a hard-disciplinary line for him. Enough to question whether he should be involved in this project in the first place. He'd never give a passive '*oh well*' to that kind of delay. "I'm calling about the class we talked about. I want to get it scheduled."

"Yeah, Dallas said he'd gotten you ready, but never committed to a time. If it goes well, Donny said he'd like to make it a regular class even if it's once a week. Can you do it this evening? Or even tomorrow? Tomorrow's probably better to give me more time to spread the word."

"Tomorrow's fine," he said, without looking at his schedule. He had canceled everything for the week. "What's the best time?"

"We have the most participants logged on right after work.

That's six o'clock our time. Is that good for you?"

"Sounds great. Set me up." Greer jotted the note on the legal pad in front of him since he didn't have his cell phone handy. "I also have some free time early this afternoon. I wanted to tour the new facility. Get my bearings. Are you and your brother available to meet me around one o'clock? I know Dallas's unavailable so that's not a problem."

"Yeah. Okay." Ducky's voice grew softer, clearly uncomfortable with this turn. "I'll call Donny."

Greer didn't give Ducky a break. He was back, happily pushing past people's boundaries, getting what he wanted. And what he wanted the most was to get these brothers in front of him so maybe they'd spill some beans on Dallas's past.

"Good. You two can get me caught up."

"Okay." He grinned at Ducky's use of the single word.

"Perfect. I'll see you two then." Greer disconnected the call. He wished he could be a fly on the wall when Dallas found out about these plans. A small smile formed at the stalkerish lines that he might be crossing.

In the quiet morning hours, when his desperation peaked, Greer had promised himself one week. If he couldn't make it work, or convince Dallas to give them another chance, he'd leave the man alone.

Maybe.

Doubtful, but the only way he could justify such an intrusion was with a time limitation. He'd have to reassess later.

How three brothers could be so different was beyond Greer. Donny blatantly had zero patience for his younger brother, who didn't seem to care for Donny's opinion in the least.

Greer had spent two hours with the brothers, going over every detail of the changes being made to StreamTrainer. Ducky seemed to be doing his best attempt at stealth mode. With his cell phone always in his hand, he would trail behind or step completely away while constantly working his thumbs over the small screen. Then he'd come back to the conversation, with specific questions, and more fully engaged again. Ducky was master-level good at being sneaky. It took Greer a while to understand Ducky was most likely texting with Dallas, keeping him updated on everything they discussed.

After two hours, Greer had come away with the understanding that each brother had a job to do, and they didn't tread on the other's toes. Group decisions fell to Dallas as the deciding vote. Greer was certain Dallas sided with Ducky in every situation, giving the two of them the majority. Donny didn't care for that one bit. His hot temper generally came with a bite even as he tried to be professional in this meeting.

While taking the tour, Greer had only been able to glean small bits of information about the Reigns family structure. He'd learned Donny had enlisted in the United States Army the day he'd turned eighteen years old. Dallas on the other hand had graduated from high school with enough college hours to begin classes just shy of being a junior. Ducky hadn't chosen either of those paths. He'd worked odd jobs, mainly in different commercial kitchens, as he taught himself computer coding. A field his father had little regard for and apparently made those feelings abundantly clear.

Whatever Greer had hoped to accomplish today had fallen short. The oppressive melancholy hanging over his head had only grown more encompassing while being in the company of the people Dallas loved.

His gloomy outlook had him calling it a day early, heading home with a bottle of sleep-aide in the passenger seat. His self-absorbed shitty attitude had no place around people, especially those who worked for him.

To Greer's surprise, Beau's sports car was parked at the curb in front of his house. He hadn't seen his best friend, face to face, in a good long while. His and Beau's relationship had changed significantly when Beau married Kailey. The hospital and his wife kept the doctor far too busy.

Greer pulled his car into the driveway, watching Kailey step from the passenger side. Her doctor's appointment. Damn, he hadn't let himself near his cell phone all day. The thing had probably lost its charge by now.

What a selfish bitch he'd been. Greer watched her closely, trying to judge the look on his sister's face as he put the car in gear and killed the engine. Other than her eyes looking red-rimmed from crying, he couldn't read her expression.

As Greer slowly stepped from his vehicle, Beau came around the trunk of his car. His arm reaching then wrapping around Kailey, drawing her close to his side. Whatever was happening had to be fresh because Beau still wore his scrubs. Kailey though was in a pair of pressed blue jeans and a lightweight sweater, makeup free. His worry elevated. He had no idea she owned such simple clothing.

"What's going on?" Greer asked, walking toward them as they headed to his front porch.

"Do I have to have something going on to come see my brother?" she asked, her playful tone not quite hitting her usual teasing cadence.

"I believe so, yes." Greer stuck out a hand, shaking Beau's extended one. "And you, it's not even five o'clock, and you're not at the hospital." Greer pushed the house key inside the lock. They seemed to want inside his home before they broke whatever news. The way Greer's luck was going, this wasn't going to be good news.

"We tried to call you from the doctor's office. We went by your office, you weren't there, so we came here," Beau explained.

The three and a half minutes it had taken for him to pull into the driveway and walk the twenty or so steps to the front door were a true killer. "Like I said, what's going on?"

Kailey entered the house, turning off the security system,

then partially blocking the entryway. Greer stopped dead in his tracks as he somehow seemed to understand what was happening. He shifted his gaze between Kailey and her husband. His grin stretched his cheeks as he said, "You're pregnant."

His sister's wide-eyed stare burst open in a floodgate of tears. Buckets of them rolled down her cheeks, causing Greer's grin to falter. Perhaps he'd gotten it wrong. He cast a quick, wary glance over his shoulder to see Beau smile bigger than Greer had ever seen from him in his life.

Kailey brought both hands to her eyes, covering her face. "Ignore me. I keep doing this. I'm four months pregnant and had no idea."

Beau nodded, backing up Kailey's confession. Greer guessed that was all right by him. A sweet baby coming to their small inner circle. Tears formed in Greer's eyes too. Beau put a hand on Greer's shoulder, drawing him into a hug, one he readily took. What great news.

"She does keep crying. After everything was said and done, they called me to come get her. Worried she wasn't safe to drive herself."

"I tried to call you first," Kailey said through her tears. Not too forlorn to give an accusing poke to Greer's chest as he shuffled them all inside the house. "But you didn't answer your phone."

Kailey came into Greer's arms, hugging him tight. Beau shut the door behind them. "I told you when you married him, you needed to start calling him first. What am I going to do with you?"

More than anything, Greer wished he'd been able to be there for his sister today. Kailey held on to him tightly, and he gave as good as he got. They both seemed to have a desperate edge. Neither of them knew too much about nurturing and love. Greer closed his eyes, placing a kiss on the side of her hair.

"Congratulations. I'm really happy for you guys."

=❤=

The crazy way Dallas's heart hammered in his chest made him worry about a pending heart attack. What the hell was wrong with him? Fear made his anxiety crippling. Dallas made the turn onto Greer's street. He had exactly twelve minutes before his shift at the gym began. That left him about five solid minutes for him to beg Greer's forgiveness. If he couldn't get that, at least he'd be in Greer's presence. Dallas needed to be around Greer like he needed his next breath.

The unreasonable suffering of the last thirty-six hours required Dallas to put his bullshit aside and beg. For what, he didn't know. But Greer scheduling the BikeBro meeting without Dallas turned out to be his undoing. No doubt, he deserved to be discarded.

Maybe…hopefully, Dallas could apologize and promise to do whatever it took to show Greer he was worthy of that beautiful man's words of relationship and commitment. Everything else could fall however it landed.

As hard as Greer fought to bring them together, Greer deserved some sort of explanation as to why he had freaked out yesterday. Why Dallas treated everyone in his life with respect, except for the one man who had opened a side of him he'd been too afraid to explore.

What if it was too late? Greer may have reached his limit of rejection. Dallas could hardly let the thought form without an impending freak-out clawing at his gut.

At least he and Greer could move forward professionally.

Who the hell was he kidding?

The sport's car parked at the curb in front of Greer's house caught his attention first. Greer's expensive vehicle was parked in the driveway. Dallas tapped his foot on the brake, slowing down. It may have only taken a second in time to pass by Greer's house, but damn, that was the longest second of his life. His gaze landed on the two men standing on Greer's front porch. His heart sped up. He tightened his grip on the steering wheel. Who was that handsome guy with Greer?

His heart cracked as he memorized everything about the guy with his arm wrapped around Greer, pushing him inside the house. From this angle, he could see the two were well-suited for each other, a pretty couple. Greer embraced the guy, his hand, sliding suggestively down the other man's back before they both stepped inside the house.

Broken-hearted, Dallas's gaze slid back to the road in front of him. He needed to get away. How could he have ever thought Greer—

Dallas shook his head. Stupid, he'd been so stupid. The truth settled in around him. Only autopilot had him pressing on the brake at the end of the street, stopping at the stop sign. His hands dropped from the steering wheel, landing in defeat in his lap. The blow to both his head and his heart took a moment to absorb. Dallas gave a slow, shaky exhale. He had to calm down.

Of course, someone like Greer had an arsenal of men waiting in the wings.

They had never talked exclusivity.

Dammit. Dallas couldn't help the well of tears gathering in his eyes. What had he expected?

He had believed Greer when he spoke of wanting something long term.

Did Dallas really think someone of Greer's caliber was at home, pining away for him? That Dallas, the established nutcase, with all his hang-ups, could capture the heart of such a fine man? Greer had made him believe so.

"You ride a bike for a living with a mountain of debt stacking up daily. What did you expect?" Speaking the words aloud didn't help. His shoulders slumped under the weight of such a loss.

Maybe he'd been played in some rich guy's shag-the-straight-guy fantasy?

The honk from behind him had Dallas lifting his eyes to the rearview mirror. Power was knowledge. He steeled his spine. At least he knew the truth and had made the right decision to back away. Dallas flipped on his blinker.

Lessons learned. He took the turn without looking back.

CHAPTER 26

Two days later

Under the cover of early morning darkness, Greer did something he hadn't done in weeks. With more speed than necessary, he whipped his sports car into the parking lot of Elite Total Gym. It was five forty-five in the morning. A familiar figure caught his eye as his headlights illuminated the dark lot. Skye bounced through the parking lot with her ever-perky stride, her ponytail bobbing with each step. Her startled leap followed by a quick jog forward let him know he'd caught her off guard.

For a man who lived a solitary life, Greer hadn't liked being alone this week. He needed company. Someone to help make sense of everything that had gone so painfully wrong.

He barely had the driver's side door shut when she said from two parking spots away, "You're here. I didn't expect you. I haven't seen you in a long time."

"It hasn't been that long." Except it had.

Their normal routine of her calling him out and him countering with a flimsy excuse didn't roll as easily off the tongue as it used to. He supposed that had more to do with his mood than any lost chemistry between them. He slung the duffle bag over his shoulder and tried for casual.

"I almost didn't come today. I watched your class. You're a natural instructor. I didn't know you had it in you." Greer walked to her, standing about a foot away. She didn't try to move or urge them inside the building. She scrutinized him with her keen stare.

He'd seen this same concern and confusion from anyone who courageously tried to speak to him. Most of his colleagues kept a wide berth. He had no idea what they were seeing, but the gentle way they used when dealing with him implied it wasn't good.

"Hmm," he said, sweeping a hand toward the building and nodding that direction to encourage her inside the gym.

She didn't take the hint. "You look awful. What's wrong?"

He could only keep the *I'm fine* façade up for so long. He closed his tired eyes, and they wanted to stay shut. Except, he knew too well the crazy mental destruction lurking behind their closed depths. *Dallas.* Everything Dallas. The extraordinary man played the starring role of all his dreams. Skye stepped closer, her hand reaching for his arm to give a gentle comforting caress.

"You look exhausted. Are you sure you should be here?"

"Probably not." He forced the lids back open. Not able to muster a smile, even to ease Skye's worry.

"Does this have to do with Dallas?"

What a laughable question. Fuck yeah. And only had to do with Dallas.

Greer didn't want to lie, yet he couldn't tell the truth. Hiding was a bitch. He sealed his lips, not saying a single word. After a long, dramatic pregnant pause, he finally ducked his head, and started around her, heading toward the gym's front doors.

"You know, Dallas looks just like you. We're all worried about him," Skye said from behind him.

"Who's everyone?" Greer stopped short a few feet away, allowing himself this one inquiry. Maybe if Greer didn't look at Skye, didn't let her see how badly he wanted her to explain, then it wouldn't count as breaking his oath of keeping silent for Dallas.

"So, it is him. What happened?" Back to being her energetic self, she bounded forward, rounding on him, getting right into his personal space.

"Skye, I can't talk about it. I promised. Can we go work out?" He again tried to move around her toward the building, but she cut him off, stepping in front of him for a second time, blocking his getaway. One of her brows arched in challenge.

"Or we could go get a cup of coffee and talk. You look like you need a friend. He does too." Her kind smile and encouraging nod had Greer shaking his head absolutely not.

"I don't think that's a good idea."

As if he hadn't spoken, Skye started for his car. He watched her go. "Come on, Greer. You're not in any condition to workout. Your head's not right. You'll hurt yourself."

"But I'm paying you," he reminded, meaning he should be dictating what was best for them right now. If he did lunges for the next hour, that was fine by him.

She tossed her hand out carelessly, without looking back, leaving him gaping at her. At his passenger side door, she made a more dramatic hand gesture, waving him over. "Come on. This is getting ridiculous. Coffee. We're wasting talking time."

"He doesn't want anyone to know."

Skye nodded toward the other side of the vehicle while she put a single finger to her lips and said, "*Shh.*" The metaphorical lead rope that the women in his life guided him around with tightened, pulling him in her direction. His desperate edge had him latching on to the idea of Skye being a close personal friend to Dallas. Maybe she had some insight that might help point him in the right direction.

Going against everything he knew was right, Greer started for the car, giving himself an internal lecture to keep his mouth shut. If Skye spoke, he'd listen, but he didn't have to add to the narrative.

"I have an hour. Let's go by Starbucks," Skye said as she dropped down into the passenger seat before he ever opened his door.

Greer's control had clearly fled. He debated this decision all the way to Starbucks. Neither spoke of the elephant riding along with them until they had made it through the drive-thru line. He parked and cut the engine.

Skye turned to face him, coffee in hand. "I suspected he was with you this weekend. Marisol said y'all had dinner together Saturday night."

The gossip circle. Right. How had he not considered that? Marisol, Kailey, and Skye were so clever. Marisol's observant eye would absolutely have picked up the undivided attention Greer had placed on Dallas. Greer jerked his head in her direction, thankfully the coffee had a lid to keep it from ending up in his lap.

"You didn't tell her what you know, did you?"

Skye's musical laugh mocked him, and he wasn't sure why. "Tell her you're over yourself about Dallas? Those were Marisol's words, and she thinks Dallas is that way about you too. Apparently, there was lots of longing in y'all's stolen stares. Again, her words."

Damn. Maybe they couldn't pull off being buddies out together having a good time. Greer had really thought they'd been low-key and discreet. He should point out Marisol had been wrong about him and Dallas, but he couldn't find those words.

"He doesn't want anyone to know, Skye. And he's already

broken off all contact with me. I don't need anything else getting in my way."

"Dallas is a hardheaded one." She nodded as if commiserating and blew on the coffee before taking a small test sip. "So, what happened to make him bolt?"

"I don't know. You tell me. You've known him longer." He took a sip of the coffee. Tasteless and bland, much like everything he put to his mouth these days. He discarded it in the cup holder. He was wrecked on every level.

"He's always kept his cards close to his chest. Until right now, I would have thought nothing ever got to him," she explained, settling back in her seat.

"How is he?" Even through all this overload of confusion and pain, Greer didn't want Dallas hurting. His need to care for Dallas, to wipe away his sorrow, was almost Greer's undoing. He was ready to crawl out of his skin from wanting to beg Dallas to trust him enough to let him help.

"Just like you. He looks like hell, and he's more closed up than normal. Ducky's going crazy because Dallas doesn't seem to care about anything."

Greer paused, thinking over every one of her words. He cut a side-eye glance toward Skye, judging her sincerity. "He looks tired. I've been watching his class." This time, Greer directed a hard, no-nonsense stare her direction, wanting the truth. "You haven't been surprised about any of this. Why not?"

"Under *what's said in this car stays in this car*, right?" she asked, her demeanor becoming serious, a side he hadn't seen before, even during her personal training sessions.

The seconds ticked by; her questioning eyebrow raised. She wanted his oath before saying anything more. Greer gave a single confirming nod.

"In fifth or so grade, Dallas kissed one of our guy friends during a party. It turned out to be a whole thing. That then caused years of a whole thing."

"I thought I was his first kiss…" he said, voicing his first disappointing thought aloud.

Her singsong laugh returned. Skye reached a hand over to push at his shoulder. "Don't look so dejected. We played spin the bottle. Back then, Dallas was an extrovert and a daredevil. One of the guys—Jacob McLaney, a few years older than us—boldly stopped the bottle in the middle of the spin and pointed the tip toward Dallas. I think every girl in the circle was disappointed. Dallas always had that slightly distant thing. None of the girls could draw his attention. Dallas didn't back away from Jacob, though. Kissed him in front of the whole party. Not a closed-mouth deal. They used tongue."

What happened to get Dallas from kissing guys so young to hiding his true self so completely? Greer's stomach churned over the possibilities. Poor kid.

"So, what're we gonna do to make this right?" Skye asked, sweetly implying her willingness to help in the matter.

"I don't know. I send him a text message every morning and every night. I've sent a snap a couple of times when my antsy side gets the best of me, but he's not responding to any of it." He couldn't shake the desolation laced in every word he spoke. Greer stared down at his lap, watching his fingers fiddle with each other, revealing his anxiousness. His shoulders slumped. Everything made him edgy and unsure.

"Greer, that's seriously sweet."

Now he just wanted to cry. He gave a shuddered exhale, linking his fingers together to stop their worry. "I asked him to go with me this weekend. I need to cancel my trip. I'm in no condition to be around people."

The flutter of his heart had him giving another side-eye glance toward Skye as the possible pieces of Dallas's life fell together.

"What happened when he kissed the guy?"

Evidently, the memory didn't come easy for Skye. She took a second or two longer to form her answer. "It was all everyone talked about for days. Dallas was grounded for a long time. He changed. I know he got a hard time from some of the kids at school. Then he was taken out of school by his parents. I think they put him in some kind of church school for a year. He came back a different guy. He was more withdrawn and kept to himself. I don't remember him going to the parties or hanging out with us again."

"What're his parents like?" he asked.

"His dad's super strict, but all the other parents would say things like, *'he had three boys, of course he's got to have a firm hand.'* Dallas's mom is a housewife. She always fed us. My parents go to church with them. That's where I would see Dallas while he was going through his Christian school year." She nodded, staring off, seeing some unknown memory in her head. "I was the only one they let him hang out with during that time, and he never spoke about what he was going through. They thought I was a good Christian girl. Can you imagine?"

The bleak years Dallas experienced in his youth exposed a picture in Greer's head that he didn't want to see. What all had Dallas gone through? Did his parents put him through some form of pray-the-gay-away therapy? It explained so much. "I need to talk to him. What's he doing this weekend? Do you know?"

"I don't know. Ducky's asked me to train the new instructors. He's worried about Dallas. Other than that, Dallas is volunteering for an auction at the Boys & Girls Club Friday night. He's not in any condition to make small talk with anyone, so I agreed to buy him in BikeBro's name. We also plan to film for YouTube. We're running out of pre-recorded content—" Skye abruptly stopped speaking. Her serious face morphed into something excited. Her fingers landed on his arm in a slap. Her eyes grew wide as she spoke her thoughts aloud. "Greer! He's being auctioned off for a date."

She bounced in the seat at the implication. Greer nodded before understanding what she wanted him to do. Buy Dallas's time? Greer immediately shook his head no.

"No, Greer! Buy Dallas. That'll force him to have to talk to you, and it's so romantic." Her hands came together close to her heart and her head tilted. Her doe-eyed stare lost in the romance of her suggestion.

Outside of being something that might happen on the Hallmark Channel during the holidays, Greer did see the significant romance qualities of showing up unexpectedly and buying his man. "I don't know. He doesn't want anyone to know."

"He's doing it to build exposure for BikeBro. You're BikeBro too. And if we make a big donation and buy him, the company looks like it's supporting local charities. Greer! I think it's a great idea." She slapped him in the arm a bit harder this time in her unbridled excitement. "You have to do it."

If he purchased Dallas as a show of company support for the community, that BikeBro was the one making the purchase, maybe it might work. A relieving sense of hope filled his heart and drove him to say, "Would you take his classes this weekend?"

Skye's eyes grew wider. "You're going to surprise him with an overnight trip? Greer…"

If he took Dallas to Houston, they'd have distance and time to sort this out. Two things they both genuinely needed.

"I don't know." Greer tucked his lips between his teeth, gnawing against the tender flesh. He needed time to think but showing up unannounced to buy Dallas for a date seemed reasonable. His heart instantly connected, hanging on to the dreamy idea. "You can't tell him or anyone for that matter. And I'll need your help. I'll have to get him proper clothing to wear. I have meetings on Saturday. I could give him a spa day Saturday to relax and get him ready for the gala. You'll have to help me with sizes. I could have a bag packed…"

"I'm in, Greer." Skye gave her supporting allegiance and sat back in her seat, looking incredibly pleased with herself. "Dallas deserves happiness. You deserve happiness. What's our plan? I can sneak into his room and get clothing sizes today while he's teaching. That won't be any problem…"

Greer let Skye talk as he said a simple prayer to the universe. *Please don't let this blow up in my face.*

"What the fuck, Dallas?" Donny shouted, shoving open Dallas's closed bedroom door. His brother's ominous shadow darkened the doorway.

Dallas had barely signed out of the class he'd just finished. Sweat flew when he jerked his head in Donny's direction, caught off guard by his brother's outburst. His spine instantly steeled at the harsh, judgmental tone.

Why the fuck was Donny even in his house at ten forty-five at night?

Donny stalked toward Dallas, getting all in his personal space. Donny had always been a bully.

Now was not the time.

Anger easily licked along Dallas's spine, building into an instant defense against his brother's rage. Dallas refused to be backed into a corner ever again. He pushed past Donny, forcibly knocking his brother in the shoulder as he went. Donny's intimidation tactics no longer affected him.

Dallas's intentions had been to shower before bed to make the last morning of his sub assignment a little easier. But Donny bounded forward, blocking the entrance to the bathroom. His brother's chest swelled, declaring nothing was getting past him without a fight. Fine by him.

"It's close to eleven. Leave me the fuck alone. Go home," Dallas roared, bending to put his face within inches of his brother's, showing his own brand of intimidation.

"I'd love to be in my fucking bed, in my fucking house, but your lazy-ass is holding everything up. Why aren't you responding to any of the emails?" Donny shouted.

Fuck him. He didn't answer to his brother no matter what Donny thought. Dallas turned away, giving Donny his back as he started down the hall.

"Donny," Ducky hesitated, removing his headphones. They were absently placed on his desk as Ducky got to his feet. The faint sounds of music explained why Ducky hadn't known Donny was in the apartment, let alone about to bring all this down on Dallas.

"Shut up." Donny's aggressive tone and sharp point of the finger stopped Ducky from saying anything more. "Dallas's been an asshole all week after being an asshole for several weeks. He's gonna ruin every damn thing we've been working for." Donny waved his hands through the air in a show of theatrical frustration as Dallas cast a menacing stare back over his shoulder.

"Nothing's ruined," Ducky said calmly. "Greer says it's fine."

Ducky's reassuring gaze followed Dallas who at the mention of Greer's name suddenly felt like a caged tiger.

Dallas started for the kitchen then pivoted toward the center of the living room. The damn walls were closing in on him.

Dammit!

He lost the battle of restraint.

Dallas spoiled for a fight. He balled his fists at his sides. He rounded on Donny who stayed disarmingly close. Dallas had inches of height and brawn on his brother who wasn't the least bit daunted by the threat of Dallas bearing down on him. Donny came within half a foot of Dallas's chest. His brother's balled hands came to rest at his waist. Donny's chin tilted up. He wanted answers, and if they came by way of fists, that was clearly fine.

God, his family was so fucked up. Donny had taken a hard, determined turn into their father's aggressive footsteps.

How did they always end up right here?

As Dallas stared down at his brother, the faces of his father and brother began to mix in his head. The two men were so similar. His father had done this exact same move countless times throughout Dallas's life. Thrown either a mental or physical punch to get inside Dallas's head.

Fuck that. Dallas was done with this life.

He matched Donny's angry move with one of his own. He stepped into his brother, bumping his chest.

"Relax. Everybody, relax. We're good." Ducky wedged his body between him and Donny, pushing apart their bowed chests. Dallas kept his death stare on Donny's troubled eyes.

"Every fucking thing is waiting for your goddamn approval. We can't even begin the rebranding or the move into the new building or make changes to the fucking website, because you aren't doing what you're supposed to be *fucking doing*. Do you even know we've hired four new instructors?" Donny yelled, his hand coming over Ducky's shoulder, pointing in Dallas's face. "Skye's working with them to get them ready because you've gone MIA. What the fuck?"

The only thing that saved Donny's finger from breaking under Dallas's grip was Ducky moving Dallas backward. Of course, his asshole brother followed, not taking a clue to defuse matters.

There was no way anyone could understand the awakening happening within Dallas. The pain of living an unwanted life, of being miserable over something he couldn't change no matter how hard he had tried, of finding ever-lasting love in someone who wasn't meant to be his.

Dallas wanted out. Off this merry-go-round ride he'd been on for years. Every minute of every day for more years than he could count, Dallas had been going through the motions, hating himself for being so weak, and hating everything about his life.

Ducky, his kind, compassionate, misunderstood little brother, kept Dallas balanced. Ducky cared about Dallas as much as Dallas cared about his younger brother. Donny only ever looked out for himself in every damn situation.

"Nothing's waiting on me, asshole. You two agreed on

everything. It's the majority, like we agreed upon from day fucking one," Dallas countered. "Stop trying to jump my ass for no good reason."

"Not anymore." Donny threw his hands in the air as if Dallas were the dumbest shit on the planet. The shouting upped a level as he said, "We all have to sign off on everything." Donny's frustration shifted to Ducky who reared back against Dallas's chest. "You told me you were going to talk to him. I trusted you to take care of this."

"After tomorrow," Ducky said defensively. "I said I'd talk to him after tomorrow when he's done teaching."

Donny's angry gaze blazed a fiery trail back to Dallas's. "Why is your ass not right here when we need you the most? This was the worst possible time for you to go crazy nuts."

Dallas's anger exploded inside him.

They'd been over this a thousand times.

"Because I can't pay my fucking bills. We wouldn't have a place to live if I didn't do something. I need to be taking as many sub positions as they'll give me or we won't have a roof over our heads. Why can't you get that through your head?" The banging overhead began. Each drop of the broom on the ceiling above was like nails on a chalkboard to Dallas, grating on his last nerve. Dallas couldn't take anymore. He pushed past his brothers and grabbed his keys off the kitchen counter. He was out the door, jogging to his car.

He had no idea where he was going, but he couldn't stay there another second. He was crawling out of his skin.

Fuck his whole life.

CHAPTER 27

"You could at least smile and pretend to be happy you're here," Skye whispered in Dallas's ear.

He looked over at his date for the evening, Skye, who stared up at him with bright eyes and a giant grin. Skye looked pretty in her clingy dress. How long had it been since he'd seen her in anything other than athletic gear and an occasional pair of blue jeans?

What he appreciated most about Skye was her gallant attempt to compensate for his foul mood. She'd been charming and fun to be around all evening. She always had his back. Something that meant the world to him.

Dallas dropped his brow into a hard V to tease her playfulness. Unfazed, Skye used her fingers to lift the corners of his lips. He did smile which showed exactly how much of a healing balm she was to him.

"You look handsome. I'll be fighting off the ladies tonight."

"Don't let anyone outbid you," he whispered, like he'd done about twenty-five times already this evening.

"I have two hundred dollars. Make yourself look ugly so we don't go over our budget." She winked at him, giving a knowing look as if he had it in him to turn into a troll. He couldn't help the burst of laughter, disrupting the current speaker at the podium.

"I'm thinking it'll be twenty-five dollars, max," he whispered.

"We'll see." She cocked her head to his almost untouched plate of food in front of him. "Eat. It's a free meal."

After the week from hell and navigating the aftermath of a not-so-subtle heartbreak, he could say that some of the over-the-top emotional overload had begun to settle for him. Eating wasn't an option yet, though. He'd completely lost his appetite. He supposed he'd eat again before he starved to death. At least it made sense to him that his body's survival mode would eventually supersede his fucked-up hurting heart and head.

Dallas listened as Mrs. Haven was announced and took the stage. She ran the auction. His nerves promptly got the best of him as showtime neared.

Skye scooted from her seat, taking his attention with her. "I'm running to the bathroom."

"I'm the ninth one. Don't be gone long," he instructed, resisting the urge to clasp her wrist and keep her there with him.

"Two minutes."

His inner introvert didn't like Skye's timing one little bit. Dallas watched Skye go as Mrs. Haven's voice drew him back to her. Like always, she was her normal, funny self. He let go of a long, uneven exhale. How had he let himself get into this mess?

=♥=

"I placed his suit with your suit in the garment bag. The weekender has a change of clothes for both of you as well as the logoed beachwear for Sunday's cleanup. You leave early Sunday morning at six a.m., so don't dawdle. Cars are arranged to take you to the airport, then to the cleanup. You're scheduled to leave the cleanup at two after a group lunch with the NPR reporters. You should be home by about five. Your car should be waiting at the airport back here in Dallas. So follow the itinerary," Kailey said through Bluetooth.

Greer nodded, committing the plan to memory as he stared out the front windshield of his sports car. "Did you contact Ducky?"

"Yes. I kept it vague and told him you were taking Dallas on an unexpected photo op over the weekend. He sounded oddly relieved and said Dallas needed to get away. He'd been real stressed lately. Then he rambled about Dallas working too much, and that he'd finally figured it out. I didn't press him as to what he figured out."

Greer had no idea what Ducky meant. He'd been so solidly stuck in the idea that none of this was a good idea that he hadn't really considered much else. "How did he sound? Questioning or like he was buying it?"

"I don't know how he normally sounds, but he seemed fine," she explained. Kailey had been extraordinarily patient with Greer. He appreciated her effort, and nodded, staring at the darkened brick of the building. If something didn't happen soon, his internal freak-out might get the best of him.

Even expecting Skye's text message, the loud chirp of his phone, letting him know it was game time, startled the shit out of him. The bright light of the screen illuminated the inside of his vehicle.

"I gotta go in," he said in a rush. Greer's heart hammered as he reached to kill the engine. The give and take of the wisdom of whether he should move forward with this desperate hairbrained idea was getting the best of him.

"Good luck, brother. Let me know how it goes."

Fuck. He couldn't seem to make himself reach for the door handle. What the hell was going on with him? Greer's forehead hit the steering wheel and he closed his eyes, demanding he calm the fuck down.

"Did you leave me? It shows you're still connected," Kailey said.

"Thank you for all this. You really moved mountains."

"That's why you keep me around. I'm sending the itinerary to you. Stop worrying and go be you! Get your man, brother. Be charming. You've got this."

Nothing more than sheer tenacity had Greer forcing himself to leave the security of his vehicle. He walked the length of the Ruthe Jackson Center building. His stride was full of confidence even under all this worry and reservation. His life's happiness depended on his ability to win Dallas over. He had never been this unsteady before. Thankfully, Skye stood in the doorway with an instant grin when he opened the door.

"He doesn't expect a thing. Come this way." By the path she took, she had cased the joint beforehand. She snuck him past the ticket attendants, down another hall, then through a side entrance. The dimly lit oversized room was filled with guests, most sitting at the many large round tables. Servers worked discreetly to remove dinner plates as the auction took place on a small stage at the back of the room. Skye took him to the front of the room and whispered in his ear. "He's number nine. I think most of these are husband and wife pairs. Stay here until it's time. I've got to get back. He's nervous."

"Thank you for this." Greer reached for her arm, giving a gentle, appreciative squeeze. She had gone above and beyond to help get him ready for this weekend. He owed her everything and would most certainly make up this debt as soon as his heart settled down and he could think properly again. She gave a nod, looking genuinely pleased, and left him there.

Oh hell, Greer was nervous. He could feel the heat creeping up his neck. He had to find a way to calm down. Greer forced his cool, collected facade in place, pushing his hands inside his slacks pockets to keep from fidgeting.

The next fifteen minutes may have been the longest of his life.

Everything that was said after Mrs. Haven called Dallas's name was drowned out as he rose and took the dread-filled steps toward the stage. Humiliation roared like a freight train inside his head. Dallas's practiced smile and measured steps were all rehearsed. He wondered if the audience could see evidence of the heat rushing up his cheeks. He did *not* like these types of things at all. How he continually ended up right here, mocked all his efforts of always wanting to be a good guy. He had to learn how to say no.

Pockets of his scripted introduction pierced through the sounds of his thumping heart.

BikeBro.

Recent donation.

Local business.

Okay, he had this. Dallas took a steadying breath and climbed the final step to the stage. He wished he'd remembered this sacrifice last night when he and Donny had been warring. Being here tonight had to mean he wasn't the complete lump of nothing his brother claimed him to be.

Dallas headed to the rehearsed marker on the stage. The bright beaming spotlight focused on him as the lights in the audience were dimmed, casting the rest of the room in shadows. He waited while Mrs. Haven continued her witty monologue. She was exceptionally good at engaging the audience. She read his interests, kept it light, and added one of her own: long walks on the concrete beaches of Epic Water Park. Of course, she'd promote a local attraction.

An older female's bid of ten dollars came from the other side of the room where he'd been sitting even before Mrs. Haven set the opening bid. The bidder's eagerness caused a low-level chuckle to permeate the room. He couldn't see who made the offering, but Skye's voice rang out next, taking the bidding to twenty dollars. Someone in the middle of the room shouted thirty dollars.

Of course, he couldn't see any of the bidders, but he recognized the voice as the woman who'd bought him last time. Skye outbid her by going to forty dollars. The far side of the room again upped the bid, calling out fifty dollars. Skye raised her offer by another ten dollars.

The small increments were a good sign for his wallet. This whole thing should tie up soon, and maybe they wouldn't ask him back if he didn't hit the hundred-dollar mark.

"Five hundred dollars."

Dallas whipped his head in the direction of that all too familiar voice. A battering ram couldn't have bowled him over more than the force of Greer's alluring voice. How was he still on his feet? He couldn't see Greer, but his heart sure seemed to know the path. It lurched from his chest, doing a happy dance on its way across the large room. Seconds felt like days. What was Greer doing there?

"Now we're talking," Mrs. Haven exclaimed proudly. Dallas looked back at her. She had her hand covering her brow to shield her eyes from the lights as she tried to see who had made the astonishing offer. "Shoot, I wish the lights were on so I could see."

Dallas made a small motion with his hand in Skye's direction, willing her to up her offer even though Greer had eclipsed their agreed upon highest bid by more than double.

"Five hundred and one dollars," Skye said, and his head

rejoiced for the ten or so seconds before Greer spoke again.

"One thousand dollars," Greer said from much closer, to the happy gasps of the room.

Dallas's heart threatened to beat out of his chest at the thought of Greer being there, bidding on him. Married couples of the Grand Prairie elite didn't fetch that kind of payout. There was an immediate, hearty round of applause from the room.

"I'll double the offer if we end the bidding right now."

Mrs. Haven didn't give either Dallas or Skye a chance to respond.

"Sold!" She slammed a small gavel down on her podium to affirm her announcement. "Dallas, I think it's the best offer we're going to get. You're sold before the buyer has a chance to back out." She received a solid round of laughter at her excitement.

Rooted to the spot, his mind raced, his thoughts turning frantic. What was he supposed to do with this?

"Step off the stage, Dallas. You're done."

That stage—a place he hadn't wanted to be—now felt like his only safe place in the world. Mechanically, he forced his body to move as his head screamed *no*.

How had his life become so fucked up and out of control?

Dallas should have never hidden behind silence. Of course, Greer was too bold of a man, he'd want a face-to-face answer.

Dallas took the steps down, anxiously searching for some excuse to bolt.

Calm down.

Maybe Greer had heard about the fight between him and Donny last night. Over the last week, Greer had apparently become Donny's and Ducky's confidant on the road to best friends forever. Perhaps, Greer was here to make sure his investment stayed intact.

When Dallas rounded his table, Skye was no longer in her seat. The woman who sat next to her handed him a folded piece of paper. He slumped in his seat and opened the note.

Dallas,

Please don't be mad when you learn the part I played in all this.

I want you to have the time of your life this weekend, you deserve it. I've got you covered here. I'll handle what comes your way. I've planned to be available all weekend.

I love you so much. You're my dearest friend.

Skye

PS: Ducky unknowingly helped, but I don't think he has any idea what's going on.

Dallas read the note twice as some understanding replaced all the apprehension.

"That was so exciting. Is he your boyfriend?"

He lifted his eyes to the woman who'd handed him the note. The implication in Skye's words didn't freak him out like they should have, but maybe that was because all his panic had been used up. More so, all of him wished he could say yes. The fairy tale image of his life had Greer as his forever boyfriend. The knight who swept him off his feet and committed to a forever-life just with him. The sadness of reality had Dallas swallowing a lump in his throat, and he shook his head with regret.

"He's my new business partner. It's a company sponsorship."

"Oh, what company?" she asked.

Had Greer not said BikeBro's name while offering so much money?

The turbulent clash of his heart and his head grew more fierce. Dallas looked over his shoulder, searching for Greer. He found him at the payor's table, bent over, scribbling on something.

How did he always look so damn good?

Somehow Dallas instinctively understood that he stood at the crossroads.

He didn't have to go with Greer. That would be the safe decision. He'd traveled that path his whole life. He knew each step of that lonely, unfulfilling road. A route with no depths, just the gray of the world passing him by.

The other direction was filled with uncertainty. No clear path, but the allure of freedom spoke to him in whispered invitation. That way had a life splashed with bright, vivid color.

Greer wasn't meant to be his, but the draw of living a full life was too hard to resist. Greer was his guide, nothing more. He'd owe Greer for eternity for his gentle persuasion, leading Dallas to find his more authentic self.

The obstacles, his defiance, all the matters he'd debated all week finally came into a semblance of order. He could keep his values and chose a colored-filled life.

He could and he would.

He fisted the note in his hand, holding on to her words. At least he wouldn't lose everyone. Skye supported him, and Ducky was more intuitive than anyone gave him credit for. No one else though, and that was fine. He didn't need anyone else. He depended on himself.

A hand clamped down on his shoulder, giving a firm, gentle squeeze. All the tingles and currents of excitement associated with Greer's touch were there before the whispered breath at his ear sent a shiver sprinting down his spine.

"We need to be going."

Dallas glanced up to see every eye at his table on him. The possibility of a perceived judgment automatically cast doubt on his choice. He firmed his resolve and rose. Not anymore. He wouldn't let others' opinions darken his new life.

"Excuse me," he said to the table in general.

The overwhelming empowerment had him squaring his shoulders. His confidence built as he looked at his dream-making, stone-faced savior. Sadness, fatigue, and weariness lurked in the depths of Greer's jewel-toned eyes. The firm set of his mouth and jaw created a crinkle of small lines at the corners of his lips. Otherwise, there was no expression on Greer's striking face.

Greer didn't touch him again. He swiveled around and started for the exit.

It seemed Dallas was destined to always follow.

CHAPTER 28

As the miles passed in the rearview mirror, Greer sat behind the steering wheel, brooding. He refused to be the first to speak. He had upended his entire life to the culmination of swooping in and doing his best Prince Charming interpretation, yet his love hadn't fallen into his waiting arms. Oh no, not Dallas. He sat in the passenger seat with his face scrunched-up, staring out the side window with his bulging arms crossed tightly over his chest.

By God, Dallas would be the first to speak.

Hopefully.

Why wasn't Dallas fighting for them in the same manner as Greer? Did he truly not feel all this chemistry drawing them together? Greer's biggest fears played on a loop in his mind, in meticulous detail, mocking him as each mile passed. Perhaps the bitter truth was the one thing he had refused to consider—Dallas just wasn't that into him.

"Where are we?"

All right, at least Dallas had spoken. Greer tuned back into his drive, looking around for an interstate mile marker. Dallas's silence had lasted longer than he'd thought it would—at least thirty minutes from where they'd started—and they drove on a now-deserted highway, surrounded by complete darkness.

Even with all the trepidation about his stunt to get Dallas alone, his cock was a greedy bastard. The damn thing had turned hard and demanding the second he'd laid eyes on Dallas at the auction. The fucker even seemed to like Dallas's tone, even if it held none of its normal warmth. Desire had his cock twitching, pressing against his zipper, desperately seeking attention.

"I believe we're close to Ennis," Greer muttered, unsure.

"Ennis?" Dallas asked, livid.

Okay, well that broke the uninterested tone Dallas had used. Greer couldn't find the question in the single word Dallas asked, so he kept his lips clamped shut and continued to stare out the front windshield.

"Why aren't you answering me?" Dallas demanded.

"I did answer you." Greer gave himself points for keeping his eyes straight ahead.

"Why're you being like this?" Dallas asked.

"Like what, Dallas?" He felt the burn of Dallas's laser-eyed focus boring through him.

Greer spared a glance in Dallas's direction. Dallas's self-righteous indignation got the best of Greer. What the fuck did he have to be put out with? Greer forced himself to settle before those exact words tumbled from his lips. It wasn't easy.

"I'm sorry if something isn't to your liking. You've got me running a million different directions, trying to hold on to what I thought we shared. You're going to have to be more specif—"

Dallas gave a disgruntled humph and turned away, back to

staring out the side window, his arms crossing tighter this time.

"What's that mean?" Greer asked, confused. Dallas's silence turned deafening. Boy, the guy knew how to imply a million different things without saying a word. "I've spent the entire week doing everything I could to get your attention. You've gone practically MIA. The class participation is down—"

Dallas's hands shot out as if none of that mattered. "I'm tired of apologizing to everyone because I can't pay my damn bills. Where the fuck are we going, Greer?"

"Houston." The word was clipped and final.

"Houston? I can't go to Houston," Dallas bellowed.

"Sure, you can. You aren't doing anything else." Greer instantly regretted his words, wishing he could take them back. Dallas was a hard worker. Greer took a deep steadying breath and dropped the pretense between them. "I'm sorry. I didn't mean that. You've got me crazy. I don't know if this is a good idea or not. We're going to Houston for a fundraising political dinner tomorrow night then a beach cleanup by a company I'm working with in Guatemala."

"I can't go to Guatemala, and before you ask why, for all the reasons you just said," Dallas explained in whatever octave hit right below a yell.

"I've worked it out. You're covered back home. And you're supposed to think of all my effort as gallant."

The harrumph followed by the invisible wall of distance snapped back in place between them. Dallas turned away from Greer, again staring out the window.

What the hell was happening?

"You're going to have to share with me what I did wrong that caused you to dismiss me so carelessly."

"Me dismissing you?" The quick whip of Dallas's head jerking toward Greer had him fearing whiplash. "I hadn't left your house for thirty damn hours and you're huddled up with another guy?"

The accusation was impossible to understand. Greer had made himself sick with all the worry and pain of being rejected by his one. Another man? He wished he could think of another man. Every thought, every day was of Dallas. Only Dallas. "What're you talking about? I haven't been with anyone but you since the first night I saw you at the club."

"I saw you, Greer." Dallas's haughtiness laced every word. "I drove to your house before my shift because I couldn't stay away. I missed you. I believed your lies. When I pulled up, you were in the arms of another dude. I fucking saw you."

Of course, he hadn't been with anyone and surely hadn't had another man at his house. "What day was it?" Greer shot back, racking his brain for what Dallas could have possibly seen and misinterpreted.

"Because it happened more than once?" Dallas gave an exaggerated roll of the eyes and turned away. "I'm dealing with a lot right now. You really fucked with my head. It's not right. Why does everyone fuck with my head? I try to be a good guy. I don't play your games. Can you just take me home or drop me off in Corsicana? I can't do this with you. I'll get myself home."

"Dallas. I sat home alone every night waiting until your ten o'clock class began. I sat on my sofa and watched you teach your class then sent you a single text message. I only allowed myself to say good night, not the millions of words I wanted to use to beg you to pay attention to me. Outside of going to work, that was the entirety of my week. I'm honestly telling you the truth. I haven't been eating or sleeping. The only people who came to my house were my sister and her husband—my best friend, Beau. That was Tuesday afternoon. Kailey found out she's pregnant and they came to share their news. I swear those are the only people who have been at my house."

It took several long moments before Dallas finally turned, looking at him, blinking. The uncertainty staring at him had to

BREAKAWAY

mean Dallas wanted to believe Greer, but the guarded man was scared. Greer slowed the car until he was able to pull to the side of the road.

The relief was staggering to know Dallas had in fact come to Greer this week. Everything Greer had done to bring them together had been the right decision. All the crippling tension from such steep rejection began to ease. He let out a stabilizing breath, absorbing yet another twist in the path to their relationship.

Greer had pushed forward, remembering their extraordinary time together, trying to ignore the glaring fact that Dallas had walked away from him without a backward glance. Yet, he hadn't. Dallas had come to him.

All the restraint Greer had used to stay quiet, shattered like a break in the dam. His truth tumbled from his lips. "Tuesday afternoon, after I took over the management of your account, I met with your brothers. I did both of those to be closer to you. To show you we could work together while being on the downlow. When I got home, my sister was at my house. My family isn't close like yours. She's all I've got. Kailey had been to the doctor that afternoon. Beau's a physician who works a million hours. When I saw them, I thought the worst. It never occurred to me that they came to tell me good news. I was relieved and Beau probably hugged me, I usually don't instigate those things. I may have hugged him back. Kailey was there. She must have been the first through the door if you didn't see her. That's all that happened. It's all verifiable. I'm super aware of you. I can't believe you drove down my street and I didn't feel you there."

As Greer spoke, Dallas visibly eased. Yet, his words still held a hint of skepticism. "It makes sense that you don't believe in monogamy. Not that we're to that point…"

Greer reached inside his breast pocket for his cell phone. He quickly found a picture of Beau. "Is this him?"

Dallas took the phone, blinking and squinting as his eyes adjusted to the bright light illuminating his stunning face. Greer

285

gave a small smile. All between them was not lost. Dallas had come to him. Greer put the car in gear and started them back onto the highway. "Take a look through my phone. You'll see some pictures of you in there. Look at all my social media. I have Twitter, Facebook, Tinder, Scruff…" Greer chuckled at his little joke. "You pegged me. I've liked to slut around, but not since I've met you. Monogamy's an easy commitment to give to you. I feel like it's a given for anyone who enters into a relationship with you," Greer said, picking up speed, watching the road through his mirrors. "We've got a long way to go, and it's late. We'll talk it out when we get there."

Dallas handled the cell phone for several minutes, only flipping through the gallery, never looking at any of Greer's apps or messages. His trainer placed the phone into the dashboard caddy then adjusted in his seat and leaned his head back on the headrest. "If you need me to drive, let me know."

"Okay." A tentative truce. His heart's desire did in fact want him. Greer could drive all night and be content as long as Dallas sat in the seat next to him.

CHAPTER 29

The extravagant opulence of the hotel added another layer to the many facets of Greer Lockhart. The foyer was quiet, most likely due to the time being a little after one o'clock in the morning. Greer was met at the front doors with access codes and directions to their rooms—yes, he'd booked two rooms.

Greer chose to carry their bags even though no less than five attendants tried to take them as they walked from the car to the lobby's elevator bank. Greer lugged a solidly packed garment bag and a large leather duffle, both slung over one broad shoulder.

In those first few minutes, the grandeur of the hotel suited Greer very well with its monstrous radiant crystal chandeliers, gorgeous unique contemporary artwork, and highly polished floors. He looked at home, in charge, and confident.

Dallas worked not to fidget with his nervousness. He shrugged out of his suit jacket, careful to keep it from wrinkling. Once inside the elevator, his silk tie came off next, then he released the small button at the tight collar.

"Skye was my partner in crime." Greer's eyes twinkled as he met Dallas's gaze. "Tonight's a formal event and will be held downstairs. I have a tuxedo for you. Skye helped pillage through your closet for the correct sizes. I have a tailor coming later today to make whatever alterations you need."

Dallas raised his brows but otherwise stayed quiet while releasing the buttons at his wrists. A tailor. Huh.

"Kailey handled the rest. She sent you a change of clothing in here." Greer patted the duffle bag. "Our gear for the cleanup is still in my car."

The elevator doors dinged open. Greer swept an arm forward, encouraging Dallas out before him.

When Dallas stepped out into the same level of grandeur as the lobby downstairs, he had two choices—right or left—but no idea which way to go. Greer edged past him, keeping his hands to himself. That blond head nodded toward the right then Greer started that direction.

This wasn't like any hotel Dallas had ever stayed in before. The room doors were far apart, only three down the long hallway. At the second door, Greer stopped. He entered the code into his cell phone. A buzz released the lock's latch. Greer pushed open the door, holding it with his foot, and again motioned Dallas through first with the nod.

The overhead lights automatically lit as he walked into the exquisitely decorated space, the size of a small apartment. The drapes were open, showcasing the muted landscape of downtown Houston at night. The room was highly decorated in modern blacks, grays, and chrome. Splashes of vibrant color popped out from every direction. A full kitchen ran the length of one wall. The bedroom door was open. The lights were off, but he saw the edge of a mattress just beyond.

"I didn't think this through very well. Take the bag. It has everything you need that's not already provided by the hotel. I'm in the room next door." Greer stood in the entry doorway and again did the head thing, nodding to the right. "There's a virtual assistant. It's a hologram. She'll get you whatever you need. This is an Escape property. I believe Tristan Wilder's behind a lot of the technology. Who knows if I'm remembering that correctly or not." Greer shrugged a carefree shoulder. Even tired, he was by far the most handsome man Dallas had ever seen.

Greer grinned as Dallas took slow measured steps back toward him. He came to a stop about six feet away and tucked his hands in his slacks pockets. Greer put the leather bag on the floor between them. "We aren't sharing a room?"

"No. I want to do this right. There's no implied sex. I did worry you might bolt in the middle of the night, but apparently, I'll follow you wherever you go, so I'll find you." Greer's playful brow cocked in challenge. "That's a warning."

"Okay." Dallas smiled at Greer's tease. One thing about Greer, he always threw a curveball. Dallas had no idea what to think of this latest round of surprises. All he knew was that there was an invisible, impenetrable barrier keeping them apart. And this time it was all Greer's doing.

"Tomorrow's a workday for me. I'll be tied up for most of the morning into the afternoon. Kailey scheduled you a spa day in my absence. You can take it or not, but they're instructed to help get you ready for tomorrow night."

"Okay." Dallas nodded, deciding Greer was in fact serious about leaving the room.

"Okay." Greer parroted and smiled, nodded then shook his head and forced himself to step out into the hall. Dallas came forward, catching the door, waiting for the punchline. Greer stepped another foot away then another. "Text me when you wake."

"Greer?" Dallas asked, brow furrowed. Greer took determined

backward steps toward the last room on the hall.

"No, I'm doing this right. We moved too fast last time," Greer said, moving backward until he stopped in front of the furthest door. "Everything in the room is available to you. Use what you want. Call room service if you're hungry. It's a full menu."

Food held no interest. His straining cock was turning just as confused by Greer's retreat.

"Go inside and shut the door, babe. Remember, I'm trying to woo you with my gallantry. I want to keep you safe. Sexy men standing alone in the hall could attract all sorts of unsightly debauchery."

Dallas didn't do as instructed, too mesmerized by Greer's enchanting smile. Greer lifted a hand and disappeared behind the door.

He narrowed his eyes. Somehow, Dallas had wound up in an alternate universe. Minutes passed. When Greer didn't open the door, claiming a big prank, Dallas finally retreated to his room, grabbing the bag, letting the door shut in his wake.

He stared at the bolted door separating their rooms.

Greer didn't knock, laughing at his funny joke.

All right. Dallas guessed this was really happening.

He started for the bedroom while reaching inside his suit jacket for his cell phone. The automated lights illuminated his path as he went. The bedroom mimicked the coordinating decorative theme of the main room with color splashing out everywhere. Especially off the large, intricate print hanging above the bed. The hotel's art was strikingly impressive.

Dallas placed the bag and the suit coat on the mattress and took a seat next to it. He first texted Ducky, who weirdly hadn't messaged him all night. Ducky always kept Dallas up to date, to a fault. On a slow day, he sent fifty text messages, making sure Dallas knew everything happening.

He knew his little brother too well and got straight to the

point. *"I'm not angry. You can talk to me."*

The three dots flashed on the bottom of the screen until Ducky's reply came through. *"I keep saying the wrong things."* Another text followed immediately afterward. *"I support whatever makes you happy."*

Dallas smiled at the honest simplicity of Ducky's accepting soul.

"I'm sorry I've been awful. Check out this place I'm staying." Dallas went to the doorway and snapped a picture of the bedroom then turned, snapping one of the living room. He attached both to the message, sending them to Ducky. *"It's the nicest place I've ever been."*

"It's an Escape property, right?" Right. Ducky had been in on the setup. Any momentary reprieve from his anxiety vanished.

"I think I need to keep this quiet. Donny wouldn't understand."

"Fuck Donny." Ducky's rage-against-the-machine attitude came through loud and clear in that text message, instantly easing Dallas. Then in rapid-fire succession, six messages came through. His brother was quick draw with the texts.

"He was wrong last night."

"You don't have to sign off like he said."

"It's a majority and you and I are a majority."

"We already agreed to that."

"I just held off because I wanted you to see how great the new logo looks."

"You have a good eye for things like that. It was better to wait until your head was clear."

Dallas could hear Ducky's protective nature through the words on the screen.

He smiled as he responded. *"Let's talk tomorrow about it all. Catch me up on what I missed when you get up. I'll go through my email before then."*

Ducky sent a thumbs-up emoji and said nothing more.

The nightstand had a built-in cell phone docking station. The place was cool as shit. Dallas plugged in his phone and again sat on the edge of the bed, unzipping the bag. Whoever packed this case knew what they were doing. Every bit of the inside space had been optimized. They had two pairs of shoes, a pair of blue jeans, some joggers he supposed were his, a sweatshirt, and a rolled Henley. There were undershirts, underwear, socks, and toiletries—everything from Dallas's preferred hair products to the toothpaste brand he liked the best. Skye had been busy as well as sneaky.

Dallas did have people that loved him even when he didn't deserve them at all.

He kept digging through the duffle. No lube or condoms.

Greer told the truth about pushing their reset button.

Dallas grabbed the toothpaste and toothbrush and went to the bathroom that also had everything he needed there too. He quickly brushed his teeth then moved the pieces of his hair that had fallen onto his forehead. He pulled his shirt tails from his slacks then decided to remove both his shirt and undershirt.

On a plan only now solidifying, Dallas remembered how much Greer liked his bare chest. He knew very little about the art of seduction and could use all the distracting help he could get.

Dallas stared at his reflection in the mirror while building his nerve.

The anthem playing inside his head sang its chorus loudly. He could live a lonely life of fear and regret like he'd been doing, or he could be bold and take what was blatantly being offered. His heart was clear in its final decision.

Dallas had jumped to conclusions. Greer told him the truth about Beau. He'd seen Kailey and Beau's wedding photos in Greer's gallery… Greer looked dashing in his tuxedo as he stood by Beau's side as his best man.

He grinned as his chest puffed in the mirror, proud of his bold resolve and his building determination. Dallas kicked off his shoes, removing each sock by hand.

With this newfound confidence, Dallas headed straight for the door separating their rooms. He stopped inches away, letting out a slow steadying exhale and looked down the length of his body. He removed his belt, tossed it over a nearby chair and unfastened the button on his slacks. He reached inside to adjust his eager cock, highlighting his need through the tight material.

All the troubled anguish from his week of hell culminated in this solid black door keeping him from what he wanted most in the world. He unlocked the deadbolts and lifted a fist. It loosened on the descent with his palm resting on the cool wood.

Maybe his new courageous attitude would come in baby steps. His forehead rested beside his hand and he spoke to Greer. "Open the door."

Greer paced. His exhaustion levels were a solid nine out of ten.

The relief of learning Dallas had in fact come to him this week, of seeing that he and his love did have a chance at a future, had left Greer utterly relieved and thoroughly drained. He needed rest to regroup and start again tomorrow. More than that, Greer had to give Dallas space to become comfortable with the idea of a relationship with him.

The balance was tricky. Too much space and his trainer might bolt.

Fuck. What was he thinking, leaving Dallas alone like that?

Dumbass.

Dallas was the last person he should leave with time on his hands. How had he not considered the obvious problem between them when reserving two different rooms? When they were together, life couldn't be better. It was when Dallas left that things went to shit.

His steely gaze riveted to the door separating him from Dallas. Greer walked the length of the suite from the bedroom through the living room, calling himself every name in the damn book. He clearly recalled the confusion in Dallas's heart-stopping gaze when Greer left him standing in the doorway to his room. Greer gave a grunted groan when his memory plainly conjured the image of Dallas's flawlessly cut cock outlined so enticingly in his slacks.

His only consideration had been the sense of pride he had in knowing he was the reason for Dallas's obvious arousal. He'd wondered if Dallas even knew his suit slacks revealed so much.

Even now, Greer's lip tucked between his teeth as he stared at the black door separating their rooms. Fuck, it turned him on to see Dallas's desire for him.

And not the point.

His fucking thoughts were all over the damn place. He had to focus.

Greer had had Dallas in his grasp, and he'd fucking walked away.

He took brisk steps away from the door. Regardless of his stupidity, he had to stop bulldozing Dallas. Give the guy room to make his own decisions. He'd made the right choice to leave Dallas's room. Greer's gaze snapped back on the door.

The right choice for a fucking idiot.

Defeat was a suck-ass bitch.

Greer disrobed, letting most of his clothing fall to the floor. He should go rub one off then go to bed.

But his heart's desire was just on the other side. He was helpless to do anything more than move closer to the door.

The click of a lock drew every bit of his focus to the deadbolts. Time slowed. Had that been his imagination?

In no time flat, Greer's curiosity had him within inches of the door. The drumming of his heart pounded almost too loudly in his ears, and his excited breathing caused a rapid rise and fall of his chest. His eyes shifted back and forth as his mind raced with all kinds of hopeful scenarios. Had Dallas really unlocked his door? Was that an invitation?

Fuck yeah, it was. Greer extended a hand to the deadbolt and stopped just short of unlocking his side.

On second thought, he pulled his hand back. He refused to push Dallas, no matter how desperate and erratic his thoughts.

As quickly as that thought came, another pushed forward, playing out in vivid detail. The story of his and Dallas's lives created a slideshow, flipping through his mind.

Dallas by his side as his lover, his partner, and his best friend.

Domesticated bliss.

Marriage.

Children—probably several.

They would travel, build a loving home, and love one another for the rest of their lives.

He saw their destiny intertwined. Never breaking. For all eternity. Truly that was all he'd ever wanted. Pushing Dallas wasn't the answer. Dallas had to want those same things.

"Open the door."

Greer couldn't be certain if the words were a manifestation of his greatest desire or Dallas's actual voice instructing him to do exactly what he wanted to do.

His thundering heart sped up even more. He could accept the fact he was impatient and tended to want things that were completely out of his reach. In business, those qualities were always a plus. But, not so much in his personal relationships. He pushed, and pushed, and never stopped. A trait that annoyed everyone in his life. Yet, Dallas appeared to want him just the way he was.

With nerves vibrating with hopefulness, Greer flipped the deadbolt. The door popped open on its own. The final sign he needed. He hastily opened it the rest of the way. Dallas stood on the other side. And in that moment, his bare-chested trainer took his breath once again, just like he'd taken his heart.

Greer took a determined step toward Dallas, reaching for him, seeing everything he'd ever wanted from life and so much more reflected in those alluring eyes. His hands lifted of their own accord, cupping Dallas's whiskered cheeks between his palms. He drew Dallas forward. With no hesitation, Greer pressed his mouth against those supple lips, drawing Dallas into a blistering kiss.

He drew Dallas flush against his chest. The moment became so much sweeter when Dallas enclosed both his strong arms around Greer, cradling him tightly against his hard, enticing body.

With the last shred of his willpower, Greer tore from the kiss, drawing back a few inches away from Dallas's face. He searched for any kind of reservation. "I want you like this, but I also want you in my life every day. I can wait."

"I want that too," Dallas whispered, desperation lacing his tone. His mesmerizing gaze reflected something Greer had never seen before. Dallas's soul was laid bare for him, inviting Greer in.

Their panting puffs of breath met and mingled as Dallas's words settled in his heart. Greer had never heard better words spoken in his life. The fight to have this man was well worth the effort as Greer let his heart's deepest wishes tumble from his lips. His voice was soft, assured, and filled with devotion.

"I love you, Dallas. It's real for me. I know we belong together."

Dallas's eyes widened. Seconds felt like hours as Greer watched a range of emotion that he couldn't quite decipher play across Dallas's face. Dallas's heart pounded against Greer's chest, thumping frantically, each beat matching his own. Regret narrowed Dallas's brow before something like resolve settled in, smoothing his features. His probing green gaze pinned Greer.

"I love you too. You're the man of my dreams. Of course, I

love you, but it won't be easy for us."

Greer's heart burst wide open, rejoicing in such a sweetly muttered declaration. If there were any boundaries he'd managed to keep in place, they broke free, lassoing him to Dallas, binding them tighter together. Greer tilted his head, whispering as he leaned in for a kiss. "Easy's for wimps."

CHAPTER 30

Bed. They needed a bed right now.

Greer took small, measured steps backward while his hands shoved into the waistband of Dallas's slacks, pushing them down as he devoured his love's addictive mouth. How did every single one of their kisses get better and better?

He slid his tongue wantonly against Dallas's as he grabbed the fleshy globes of Dallas's perfect ass and walked him toward the bedroom. Dallas's hips rolled, grinding his rigid arousal against Greer. Fuck, he liked that suggestive move. And the bedroom was so damn far away.

Something stopped their motion. He opened his eyes, spotting the oversized leather sofa, and immediately adjusted his plan. They could take a minute there, a small break per se, before continuing the long trek across the suite.

Dallas's arms locked around Greer. His mouth tore from the kiss as his feet came out from underneath him. Greer barely had time to grip the back of the sofa and anchor a strong arm around Dallas's back, holding most of his body weight as he settled Dallas onto the sofa with a small bounce. Dallas's surprised gaze flew around the room, getting his bearings as to what had just happened as Greer wasted no time at tugging Dallas's slacks off each leg. The pants went one direction while the tighty-whities went another.

"I didn't see that coming," Dallas whispered huskily as his cock sprang free, thick and hard as stone.

Greer tucked his lip between his teeth. His mouth watered as his single-minded focus set in. He hastily worked his belt and zipper free. "Scoot up and grip yourself for me."

They were so damn in sync. Dallas's eyes twinkled, and he smirked, making his gorgeous features even sexier, while he edged up the soft leather. His shameless, personal porn star did exactly as he asked. Dallas's fist gave a slow steady tug on that beautiful cock and his other hand reached for his balls. "Like this?"

"Yeah, just like that." Greer's slacks hit the floor, and his knee hit the armrest. He climbed his ass over the edge, refusing to take the time to walk around to the front of the sofa. Dallas's parted thighs invited Greer in. He nestled there, taking over the stroking of Dallas's cock. He began to climb up Dallas's expansive chest. Dallas lifted, meeting Greer halfway, with his mouth open and his hands locking around Greer's neck, drawing him into a soul-destroying kiss.

He gripped both their cocks together and rutted against Dallas as he devoured his man, driving his tongue deep. He made love to Dallas with his mouth and his hand. Dallas's hips rolled. His love was so damn strong.

Dallas angled Greer's head, returning his own mind-blowing sensual strokes of the tongue. God, he'd missed this man. He craved Dallas's delicious taste and fucking loved the way Dallas countered every one of Greer's moves with one of his own. His perfect lover.

He hadn't lost him.

Now, he just had to keep him.

Dallas wrenched from the kiss, the hand at Greer's back wiggled its way around to his front, pushing between their hips until it closed around Greer's stroking fist. "Feels good."

The strong palm at Greer's neck moved him as if he were a rag doll. Dallas's hot lips sealed and mouthed against the tender flesh of his neck and jaw. Dallas's hand easily engulfed Greer's, circling around both their cocks. They worked together, giving the other pleasure. That sinful tongue traced the shell of Greer's ear before plunging inside. Greer gave a full body shudder, lost in ecstasy as Dallas chuckled knowingly against his wet skin.

"Fuck me, D," he said.

"I'm tryin'," Dallas drawled, whispering breathily before he turned Greer, capturing his mouth again. Greer opened as Dallas's tongue met his. Slow and deep, teasing him with every swipe.

Dallas circled Greer's tip with a thumb. He lost sight of the kiss as he hissed and thrust his hips against Dallas's in the rhythm his lover created.

The strokes were bold, firm, and fast, and it all became too much. Dallas was the seducer, not Greer… "It feels too good. I denied myself this week. Probably not the best idea," Greer hissed against Dallas's mouth.

"Let go. Come for me. We have all night," Dallas whispered. How Dallas managed the twist of the wrist with their bodies melded together, he would never know, but fucking hell, his breathing became erratic and he started to pant. "I changed my mind. I want to taste you."

Before the words registered in Greer's foggy brain, Dallas twisted, and Greer was dislodged. His ass hit the cold leather, sending a shiver over his heated skin as Dallas dropped to his knees. Their gazes locked and time slowed. Greer couldn't help but reach out. His palms encased this striking man's cheeks, the pad of his thumb gliding across Dallas's kiss swollen lips.

"I love you," Greer murmured and would have taken a kiss right then, but Dallas smirked and slid his palms along Greer's thighs, blazing a heated trail to his sac and cock. Dallas took him in hand, gripping him roughly as he toyed with his balls, rolling them in his palm.

All his defenses faded as he watched Dallas lick his lips. His warm mouth opened. That sinful tongue swiped across the tip, sending a hiss through Greer's clenched teeth before Dallas took him deep inside his mouth, swallowing him until Greer's tip hit the back of Dallas's throat.

Greer slid his fingers into Dallas's hair, tangling with the longer strands as his gaze riveted to the mouth rising and falling on his cock. Holy fucking hell. Dallas's mouth was amazing. His lover gave to him so unselfishly. His orgasm took a backseat as he basked in the gentle lovemaking Dallas gave with his mouth. He wanted this to go on forever. Of course, being with Dallas had been the most intimate experience of his life, but what they were doing now was everything he'd ever wanted from life. They were making love. Truly loving the other enough to put the other's climax before their own.

What a heady fucking thought. Under hooded eyes, Greer watched Dallas slide a little farther down his cock on each swallow. That had been something that excited Dallas before. Dallas was such a fucking natural at sucking dick. Greer tightened the hold he had on Dallas's hair and lifted his hips.

"You got it. Relax your jaw."

As reverently as he could, he skimmed his fingers along Dallas's jaw, wanting him to have what he tried so hard to give.

"Loosen."

Reality slammed back into Greer as Dallas swallowed him to the root. His balls retracted, and his hips rammed forward while his hand fisted in Dallas's hair, locking him in place. Steely green eyes lifted to Greer's, and he released Dallas, letting him bob on his cock.

Dallas sat back on his heels, his concentration split between Greer's leaking cock and taking in gulps of air. Dallas's skilled tongue curled around the tip of his cock and the sight and feel made Greer weak.

"Fuck. That's hot," Greer growled, drawing Dallas up by the arms. "My man."

He sealed their love with a blistering kiss, loving the taste of himself on Dallas's tongue. Dallas melted against him, deepening the kiss. Greer wrapped Dallas in his arms. There wasn't a chance in hell he'd be able to live without this man in his life.

As if Dallas read his thoughts, he tore away from Greer, his searching eyes scanning Greer's face. "I need commitment and monogamy. I wanna love and be loved. I want all those things with you."

Greer's heart ached at the lack of pretense and game playing in the softly spoken declaration. It was just the way he wanted it too. "I'm never letting you go. I'll fight to keep us together."

Before they left this suite, Greer would fuck Dallas on every surface, but right now, he wanted them in the bedroom, on the bed with Dallas underneath him. Greer pushed to his feet, drawing Dallas up with him. His resolve took a hit as Dallas rose, kissing a trail over his groin, stomach, chest, neck, and lips. He loved that his guy was taller than him. Greer stepped away, moving out of Dallas's hold and started for the bedroom.

"Come on, big guy," Greer rasped.

"Is something wrong?"

"No, it's too right. We're moving to the bed." It still took a second. Greer didn't blame Dallas for his confusion.

If he hadn't lost his head, he'd be coming inside that hot mouth right about now, but not this time. He heard Dallas's bare feet padding on the tile floor behind him.

Greer went for the nightstand, grabbing the condoms and lube from the drawer. He might not have planned to stay in this room, but clearly, he'd hoped for the inevitable and arranged accordingly. Greer moved the duffle, whipped the bedspread off the bed and tossed the condoms and lube on the mattress. He gave a devilish smile and sat on the edge of the bed, scooting back as he patted the mattress beside him.

"Right now, this is where I want you."

No more words were spoken. Dallas came toward him. With one knee on the mattress, he reached for Greer. Tongue, teeth, and lips met, and instantly ignited the heat again.

Greer wrestled Dallas onto his back, climbing over his body before he wrenched free, moving quickly to reverse his position before Dallas got other ideas. He got on all fours, situating Dallas's head between his knees. Greer gripped his own cock, rubbing the leaking tip over Dallas's full lips. "Open for me."

Oh, his mister did in fact open. Dallas was mastery level good at a fucking blow job. With a blistering touch, Dallas skimmed a heated trail to Greer's balls as he took him deep into his mouth. Shit. Greer's hips slid forward, his vision began to blur and his toes curled as his cock slipped deeper into Dallas's throat.

He gripped Dallas's cock, leaned down, and nestled his face in the soft hair at Dallas's groin while he stroked the thick length in his fist as he tried not to focus on the way Dallas so easily swallowed him whole.

Dallas planted his feet on the mattress, knees bent. Warm fingers lightly tickled the back of Greer's thighs before Dallas gave him a playful little slap on the ass. He arched his back, angling himself just enough to watch his cock disappear in Dallas's talented mouth. Greer rolled his hips, fucking into Dallas's welcoming wet warmth. Dallas took him all, sucking him with every thrust of the hips.

The way his orgasm was building, he didn't have long. Greer slowly ran his tongue up the length of his lover's cock before he took Dallas into his mouth. He slid his hand around Dallas's legs to grip his muscular ass cheek.

He did his best to match Dallas's naughty mind-blowing suction, move for move, as his fingers searched out Dallas's tight pucker. He panted and moaned, his heart drumming at the wicked way Dallas used his mouth, throat, and tongue to coerce Greer's release. God, he would never tire of having Dallas's mouth on his cock.

Greer made himself focus. His sure fingertips slipped inside Dallas's hole, relaxing him open as he slid his mouth up and down Dallas's hard as steel cock. Dallas's salty essence burst across his tongue, letting Greer know he was doing everything right. His palm molded around his love's retracting balls, fighting his own need as he listened to Dallas moan, urging him on.

His cock popped free of Dallas's mouth. Seconds later, warm fingers gripped his ass and spread him open. Dallas's hot breath puffed against his most intimate spot, making his head spin.

"You're perfect, Greer."

Greer's eyes slid to the back of his head as Dallas's tongue lapped across his hole. What the fuck. Oh man, he loved to be rimmed. Dallas's fingertips worked in tandem with his tongue, the sensation so intense Greer swore he was going to come on the spot. It felt so damn good. Dallas added another finger, and Greer groaned from the intensity.

Electricity sparked at the base of his spine and flowed over him, making his body tingle in the most delightful way. He would definitely come if they continued down this path. Dallas kept working him, not letting up on the oral assault. Greer's knees shook, he was so fucking close.

Greer forced himself to move and fisted his swollen cock, hoping to slow his impending orgasm. He reached for the lube and condoms. "I can never get the upper hand with you."

"Hey, I like licking your ass. Come back here."

Greer dared a glance at Dallas who looked genuinely

disappointed.

He liked Dallas's idea too, but he had something else in mind.

"I need to be balls deep in you, babe. Grab your legs." Greer positioned himself between Dallas's parted thighs, rolling the condom down his leaking cock before hastily flipping open the top of the lube. He poured a generous amount on his cock then directly to Dallas's hole. He worked a finger into Dallas, pumping in and out. After a few seconds, he added a second digit. "You're making me so goddamn hard. I don't think I can be tender with you.

"Then don't. I want to feel you. Just fuck me, Greer."

They were speaking the same language. Greer tucked his lip between his teeth and positioned his cockhead against all that heat before he pushed past the tight ring of muscle. His eyes never left Dallas's as they slowly became one.

Dallas let go of a long, loud moan and gripped the back of his thighs a little tighter. The burn of Greer stretching him sent tremors of desire rocketing through him with each deliberate inch Greer pushed into him. His eyes rolled into the back of his head, the tendons in his neck and shoulders tightened, and he released his legs, wrapping them around Greer's ass, helping to push Greer deeper inside his body.

Greer dropped forward, his lips searching Dallas's as his hips sank deeper, locking him inside. This was perfect. They fit together so well. Dallas relaxed. His eyes opened to amber orbs staring intensely at him. He couldn't help but get lost inside their depths as Greer's body filled his.

"I love you, Dallas." Greer panted and started to move his hips in small, measured thrusts. His fingers caressed Dallas as his hips rolled in the rhythm Greer created. His man anchored his knees on the mattress and took complete control.

Greer's palms moved steadily over each of Dallas's pecs. Insistent fingertips toyed with his nipples, sending shock waves reverberating all throughout his body. His lover's exploration continued down his stomach muscles, reverently loving him until Greer finally reached lower to grip his aching cock.

The pressure of Greer's tight grip was almost too much as Dallas's fingertips dug into the bedding. His ass clenched around Greer, pulling a moan from his lover as Greer drove in and out of his ass. Dallas couldn't stop his body from moving, matching Greer, taking what it wanted.

"You're so tight." Greer buried himself in Dallas with strong, deep, soul-searing thrusts. Heat built at the base of his spine and engulfed his body in warmth. This moment was so tender, so right. He never wanted it to end. "I love you."

Dallas reached for Greer, drawing him down, pressing his mouth against Greer's full lips as his ass clamped snugly around his love. Greer shoved his tongue forward, brushing and tangling with Dallas's, fucking his mouth like he fucked his ass.

Pleasure built with every snap of Greer's hips. They rocked together as one, their bodies perfectly in sync as Greer increased the tempo of his hips. He tore from the kiss, his forehead falling to Dallas's chest. Dallas wrapped Greer in his arms. The frenzied pace was laced with all the love and commitment they shared.

Greer pushed an arm under Dallas's back, gripping his shoulder, holding him in place. Greer's hips began a wild piston that had Dallas's toes curling in ecstasy. He released Dallas's cock, sliding an arm under Dallas's knee, urging his leg back and to the side of his chest.

Greer reared back on his knees, changing their position, setting Dallas on fire with every move he made. Pleasure wrung a moan from his throat as Greer thrust harder, hitting Dallas's prostate, making stars sprinkle his vision.

"Touch yourself, babe."

It was all too much. If Dallas did, he'd lose it right then. "I won't last."

"Then tell me you love me," Greer demanded. His warm palm wrapped around Dallas's cock. The friction of Greer's fist was all it took.

"Love… *you*," he panted, barely getting the words out before his back arched off the mattress. The orgasm swamped him. Ribbons of hot come splattered over his stomach and chest. Dallas lost his mind. His body shook with bliss as Greer rutted into him.

"I love you, too." Greer collapsed, dropping to his chest, his wild hips still bucking. Dallas soared as liquid heat filled the condom in his ass.

This was the best moment of his life. He did love Greer.

Dallas encased Greer in his arms, never wanting to let him go. Everything with Greer was always so damned perfect and right.

Dallas's breathing slowed, and he could feel Greer's racing heart pounding against his chest as their bodies settled onto the soft mattress. Neither one spoke as they lay there in elation. He could stay like that forever.

Moments later, darkness sucked him under.

"D, are you asleep?"

Dallas had no idea how much time had passed or how long they had lain there together. His tight hold kept Greer against him. He was so out of his element and didn't care in the least. Greer pushed off him. Not far, just enough to dispose of the condom and swipe a warm wipe across Dallas's chest. This hotel was amazing.

Greer reached for the bedspread, sending it floating over them as he settled back over Dallas. "I'm a needy bastard. Sleep for a bit, then I need you in my ass. I like you there."

Minutes passed in comfortable silence with Dallas riding the sated high before he whispered huskily, "Thank you for coming for me tonight."

Full lips pressed against Dallas's shoulder as Greer tucked

himself into the crook of Dallas's neck. "Thank you for loving me."

CHAPTER 31

After being pampered and spoiled all morning, Dallas was in an exceptionally good mood. He now understood why people were always going on about needing spa days. The massage had chased the tension from his muscles and made him feel like a million bucks.

"I've never had clothes fit so well," Dallas said, looking at himself in the floor length mirror inside the small walk-in closet.

The subtle shifts in Greer's expressions were becoming more familiar. The way his alluring face peered over his shoulder into the mirror, the slight tapering of his eyes as he scanned the length of Dallas's body made Dallas forget all about his tight-fitting tuxedo.

Since Dallas had unleashed his love, let the damn emotion run rampant, it seemed all he could manage was to keep his obsessive devotion from constantly tumbling from his lips. The exotic spicy scent of Greer's cologne didn't help him keep perspective.

"What just happened?" Their stares met in the mirror. Greer's held a decidedly scrutinizing glint. "The blush on your cheeks. What's that mean?"

Dallas had to tear his gaze away and step aside. Remarkably, Greer let him go. The steps only took Dallas as far as the bedroom, where the tangle of the sheets on the slightly crooked mattress spoke to the aftermath of Greer's focused attention this afternoon. Dallas had had more sex in the last eighteen hours than he'd had the previous three years, with five of those hours spent in a full-service spa.

Greer was a lustful man and brought that same side out in Dallas. Especially with as fine as Greer looked in his bespoke tuxedo. Dallas couldn't help the peek he gave, looking over his shoulder at Greer. "We're already late."

The fidgeting was hard to control. He looked for something to do with his hands. He spotted his wallet and cell phone, relieved with the small distraction. He went to the dresser and tucked those items inside his jacket's breast pockets.

Greer followed behind Dallas, tracking his same path. "We can stay in. I'd rather stay in." His all too skilled hands moved with purpose, circling Dallas's waist. "You're a handsome guy. I love the auburn lowlights they added, and the scruff is sexy as hell. I won't forget how the whiskers felt against my thighs as you sucked my balls. We need a repeat."

The description might as well have been Greer's hands fisting Dallas's dick. Any restraint he had scattered. His cock grew ramrod stiff in two seconds flat.

"Greer, I can't walk in like this." Dallas didn't have to look down to know how his tight-fitting slacks outlined his overzealous cock.

Luckily, Greer chuckled and gave him room. He stayed a shadow's length away. "That's where you're wrong. I want everyone to know I'm the reason." Greer pointed to Dallas's junk with a smirking grin on his face. "Stop looking so putout and use your magic power to shrink it down."

That might be the single best way to describe his over-the-top attraction to Greer. Half his life ago, he'd learned to control what aroused him—at least the physical evidence. Greer's charms seemed enough incentive to never hide another hard-on again.

"This silence thing needs to stop. You're incredibly hard to read." The firm set of Greer's lips had Dallas taking a giant step away. Sex brought words out of Dallas's mouth that he never intended to say. Greer's expression meant that he knew exactly how to make Dallas talk.

"We need to go so we can be back here a little sooner," Dallas said reasonably. It worked. Greer turned away, looking about the room until he found his wallet.

"All right, you have a good point. The deal about this evening… It's a work event. I'll be different tonight. This oversharing I seem to do with you is not really who I am with others. I equate tonight to a game of chess." Greer tucked his few items into his tuxedo jacket as he spoke. "If I walk away, just hang tight. I'll come back for you. It's rare for any of these attendees to feel comfortable talking business with their significant others around."

Dallas nodded, glad for the change in topic. He clasped the button of his jacket, stepping back in front of the mirror in hopes the panels hung low enough to cover his never-ending arousal.

"I'll seem cold and distant to you, at least that's the way Kailey describes it." Greer's pause had Dallas nodding his understanding again. "Let's play a game. We need to get to better know one another. Your favorite color, tastes, preferences to everything. When I see you start to get bored, I'll ask a question. You must respond. If you choose not to, I pick the punishment."

"Can I ask you a question?" Dallas asked, challenge showing in the cock of his brow.

"Absolutely."

311

As if the transformation to rigid professional happened in front of Dallas's eyes, Greer took a deep breath, squared his shoulders, and stood taller. His purposeful bearing carried him out of the bedroom in long, confident strides. He took on a secret agent vibe.

"Come on, babe," Greer called, standing with one hand tucked inside his slack's pocket, expressionless at the room's open front door. His cool, aloof stance was a thing of beauty. Greer should grace the cover of GQ with such a stunning pose. Instant trepidation made Dallas's heart beat a little faster.

"I think my game plan for tonight is to stay quiet." Dallas didn't break stride as he went through the open door.

"Not too quiet. Talk StreamTrainer freely."

Dallas nodded. The long, relaxing massage that had rubbed away much of the tension he'd carried in his shoulders for weeks lost its effectiveness as his muscles began to tighten again.

"What's your favorite color?" Greer asked out of the blue.

"Favorite color. I haven't thought about it. I guess blue. I search calming colors. I like my mood to stay even."

"Good choice. I don't have any blue in my house and now I see your point. I need blues," Greer said. The elevator doors opened. Dallas wanted to be a gentleman. It wasn't instinctual to walk ahead of anyone. Greer finally broke mold and laughed at their stalemate. His arm extended, preventing the elevator doors from sliding closed again. "In the vein of learning about one another, I like to get your doors. Not everyone's, but yours. So, please, go first."

The request came with a wink. Of course, he gave in and walked through.

"What's your favorite color?" Dallas asked.

"It used to be hues of red until I met this emerald-eyed man. Now I'm solidly a green guy." Greer waggled his brows, entering the box. "Pretty good answer, right?"

Dallas's grin split his face at how proud Greer seemed with his response.

"It's weird to be in such a private space and not be all over you." Greer stood on the opposite side of the elevator with his hands in his pockets. "You're gorgeous." Greer's approving gaze slid down his body then lifted to meet his. "I like the joggers and knit shirts a lot, but this… Damn, I'm a lucky guy."

"Greer, stop."

Of course, Greer did the opposite. He stepped toward Dallas, pulling his hands from his pockets. Dallas extended a hand, as if that would ever stop Greer, but luckily the doors opened. The gala had spilled over into the foyer. Elegantly dressed men and women were sprinkled across the room in small clusters.

Greer reached for his hand and whispered, "You're my boyfriend. We're committed. It'll be a surprise."

"Why's that?" he asked.

"I've never brought anyone other than Kailey," he whispered. These hints into Greer's life were like little bombs to his heart, obliterating the small amount of perspective he'd managed to keep.

"Fuck, Dallas," Greer hissed, looking back at him. "I like that blush."

Exactly two hours from crossing the threshold of the downstairs elevator bank, Greer was back, pushing the call button to take him and Dallas to their rooms. He stood silently, staring at the indicator lights, waiting for their lift car to arrive. Dallas's hand rested in his. Their fingers had been entwined for a majority of the last one hundred twenty minutes. The comfortable fit and weight never grew old. His hand craved the touch, seeking out Dallas anytime he strayed too far away.

All his well-placed forewarnings, putting Dallas on notice

about the whys and hows of how the evening would progress, were all for naught. Greer kept Dallas right there beside him for the entire length of the gala.

Usually, these political fundraisers were as effective at generating new investors as was the chatter on the greens of the golf course. Not tonight. Nothing measured to the irresistible man by his side or his profound sense of pride that such a fine man chose to spend any time with him at all.

As Dallas projected, he had remained quiet, barely speaking to anyone. When he did, Dallas solely spoke of StreamTrainer. He'd been a perfect spokesperson for the company, building enough excitement to create a low-level buzz all evening.

Greer had fielded questions about Dallas and saw all the weighted assessment from his peers. Interestingly, he never saw condemnation in those sly stares. Instead, Dallas was a draw for both men and women. Dallas had no idea of his value, seemingly unaware of any of the interest cast his way.

His leg bounced at the overlong wait.

Greer's somewhat aloof composure became harder to maintain when all he wanted to do was be alone with Dallas. It wasn't even sex that drove him this time. He wanted to finish their getting to know each other game, and he needed to understand better why Dallas's family was such a problem. He couldn't develop a strategic master plan to move past Dallas's biggest hang-up until he knew their true obstacles.

He looked at his watch. Ten o'clock. In a few short hours they would leave for their quick jaunt to Guatemala. That was how much time he had to gain all the confessions and explanations. He planned to ply Dallas with alcohol to loosen his lips. If he could manage it, he hoped for a bit of lovemaking on that fantastic balcony before they left in the early morning hours.

This elevator was taking too long.

Finally, two elevators beeped at once. Dallas took a small step forward, but Greer took a giant side-step backward, letting the others who gathered behind them on to the closest lift. He turned to race to the second car at the end of the elevator bank. He rapidly pressed the *close* button before Dallas ever stepped inside.

Greer released Dallas's hand for the first time in the last hour and watched the doors close while seeing another couple trying to make it to them before it was too late. He did have some guilt for not delaying the elevator, but new love and the desire to be alone with his man outweighed doing the right thing. He gave an apologetic wince and a shrug as the doors sealed closed.

His enticing Dallas took the ledge on one side while already reaching for the knot in his silk tie. "Are we done for the night?"

As much as Greer liked Dallas all dressed to impress, he also liked him warm and welcoming in his casual attire. Better if Dallas's big powerful body, with all its defined heavy muscle and tight cords—

Stop, Greer. Talk first. The honeymoon phase of their new love had to wait.

"Done downstairs? Yup."

Dallas released the small buttons at the top of his dress shirt then pulled the silk tie free of the collar. "I think you pretend to be tough, but you're really a kind guy." Dallas's steely gaze assessed him, but the knowing crooked grin spoke of sex appeal.

Oh hell. His own libido needed no help.

Greer shook his head, trying to clear his mind of the rogue thoughts. "You're not getting out of here without telling me what's going on with you. I'm not leaving until I know, because you'll bolt again otherwise." *Good.* Greer sounded firm and in control. They didn't automatically have to fall into bed anytime there was one nearby.

Dallas took a step toward Greer. A purposeful seduction-worthy step. Then another. "I've thought of a question of my own. When you swallow me, what do I taste like?"

Greer hissed, throwing a hand out to stop Dallas when he took the next step forward.

The shock of such a question coming from his reserved-to-a-fault mister added another layer to their relationship. Greer was in trouble with this one. His cock swelled rapidly, stiff as a board. His mouth watered, ready to confirm whether his memory was a correct representation.

He fisted his fingers into Dallas's dress shirt. Words failed him as he fought his most basic instincts. Luckily, the doors dinged open to their floor. He kept a hold of Dallas, pushing him out backward as he followed. Greer made it to the darkened entrance of the hallway leading to their rooms before Dallas's strong hands reached for his hips, stopping his forward movement. His mister's brawn owned Greer in that minute. He was wrenched against Dallas's solid chest, those large biceps locked around his waist.

"Thank you for coming after me. To lose you would've been the greatest loss of my life." The devotion-filled words were whispered against Greer's ear. His whole body turned into a tingling mass of nerves. Greer's forehead hit Dallas's shoulder as that sweetly given oath healed the fractures in his heart.

"I was afraid you didn't want me," Greer confessed, his eyes closed as Dallas tightened his hold. Possession seeped into every pore of Greer's body, showing him exactly where he belonged. Greer felt loved and protected in the embrace.

For the first time in his life, he understood the security of what a genuinely loving embrace meant for both his heart and soul.

"I'll want you until the day I die. Even longer if it's possible." Outside of the giant steel cock pressing into his, this moment wasn't about sex. They would end there. Greer was too sexually attracted to this man not to, but right now, they were about sealing their future together.

"Tell me what we're up against," Greer whispered. He pressed his lips to Dallas's jaw and reared back to look him in the eyes. Dallas's Adam's apple bobbed.

"I need a drink."

"Me fucking too."

Dallas's husky chuckle sent goose bumps springing across Greer's neck, chest, and arms. Dallas owned him. The elevator dinged behind him. Who knew if it was coming or going? Dallas released him, and they started for the room.

"Change," Greer said over his shoulder, trying to walk away.

Dallas wrapped an arm around Greer's stomach, drawing him backward. They were just shy of the hotel room's door as it swung shut behind them, closing them into the privacy of their room. Did they really need to talk? Dallas's mind was made up. He'd deal with his family when the time came.

"You're making it too hard, Dallas."

Dallas's chuckle reverberated throughout his chest. "You know how to make it soft again."

Greer's chin tilted over his shoulder. "I want you to talk first, then fuck me out on the balcony. I've been thinking about it all night. You can bend me over the oversized chair and fuck the shit out of me while promising you won't ever disappear again."

Dallas ground his hips into Greer's ass. One of those involuntarily, lust-induced gyrations. In contrast to his words, Greer turned in Dallas's arms, lifting on his tiptoes to seal the promise with a kiss. With no hesitation, Dallas opened, sweeping his tongue forward. He kissed Greer like they had been kissing just this way forever.

The latch on the door clicked, Dallas felt more than heard the door swing open then a startled gasp behind him.

"Excuse me." The unexpected voice didn't automatically make Dallas tear away from the kiss. Instead, he finished with a slow removal of his lips as his gaze fixed on Greer's. "I'm sorry to interrupt. I have the platter. I understood you wouldn't be in the room."

"Did you order food?" Dallas asked, inches from Greer's

face. He almost refused to let Greer go.

"I did. I haven't seen this side of you." Greer did let Dallas go, taking a small step backward as his brow arched with suspicion as he spoke. "Had I known you had that in you, I'd've planned differently." Greer's shoulders squared in resolve. "Go change. I'll take care of this."

Dallas relented, ducking his head and started away, looking back over his shoulder, hoping Greer would cave and follow. He didn't.

Dammit.

Greer unbuttoned his jacket, shrugging it off his shoulders as he murmured to the attendant, "I apologize, I didn't think we'd be back yet. Set us up, please. I'm going to change."

Even though all their belongings were together in Dallas's room, Greer went the other way. He wasn't accustomed to going against his urges. Leaving Dallas's seduction felt as wrong to him as anything he'd ever done. Greer rounded the corner to the bathroom, berating himself as he went.

What the fuck was he thinking? Well, he wasn't thinking. At least not with the right body part.

Fuck it. Greer started to go to Dallas. They could talk later, but his reflection in the mirror stopped him in his tracks, startled by what he saw. Everything else was forgotten.

He looked the same but somehow completely different. He took in the blond strands and the subtle flip of his styled hair. His perfectly shaped brows. His almond shaped eyes. His nose, slightly too wide for his narrow face, and his full lips. It was clearly him, but no longer belonging to him.

Everything felt different. He was a man in love. Greer truly loved Dallas. It showed in the gleam of his amber eyes, in the glow of his smooth skin and in the natural upturn in his lips. It was etched in his being.

He poked a finger through the knot of his black silk tie as the contentment of his commitment eased some of the urgency to have Dallas moving over him. He removed the tie, released the button at his neck, and placed the cuff links on the sink's counter.

"Are you coming into the living room? It's nice outside. I could move everything to the balcony," Dallas asked.

"Before I come out, are you dressed?"

"I am." Dallas's husky laugh told a different story.

Greer peeked around the corner to see if he was telling the truth. Dallas's wonderland of a chest was bare. His bottoms were the joggers he'd worn today. Greer noticed the condoms and the bottle of lube in his lover's fist, which of course, tightened the connection they shared. He grinned and decided to match his mister, quickly disrobing his dress shirt.

"Let's go, Romeo."

CHAPTER 32

The cool night breeze held none of the usual balmy warmth of Houston. The stars twinkled above as Dallas bent with his forearms resting on the railing and a half full cocktail glass in his hand. The ice clinked against the crystal as he took a hearty swallow, sucking down the smoothest whiskey he'd ever tasted. He'd had enough to drink this evening that the burn of the liquor was a distant memory.

He could get used to such a posh life. Downtown Houston was mesmerizing at night. The city lights hypnotized with their brilliant sparkle. Perhaps the whiskey helped build the allure. Greer's strong hand came to the base of his back, gliding a coercing path up his spine. His touch as comforting and warm as always. Tonight, he could add persistent to the long list of Greer's good qualities.

Greer stepped close, reaching for Dallas's hand. His hip rested against the railing and his head angled in such a way to better see Dallas's face.

"Stop avoiding and tell me," Greer whispered huskily.

"You have to have figured it out by now," Dallas said vaguely, refusing to let the worry of home destroy the ambience Greer had created.

The large balcony, twenty stories in the air was a cozy setting with a crackling faux fire pit and a soft, modern instrumental playing quietly in the background. Greer's additions, the delicious bite-size foods, the alcohol—enough for twenty men—and the plush pillows and coverings set the romance mood perfectly.

Greer lifted Dallas's palm to his lips, kissing him before stepping away.

With each passing minute in Greer's precious company, every fiber of Dallas's being had tied itself to Greer. His spirit tangled with Greer's spirit, hoping to never be parted. Greer had captivated his soul, and it refused to ever be untethered from him again.

What more needed to be known?

"Here," Greer murmured. He held a piece of bread slathered with something sweet and savory on top.

For the last hour or so, Greer had plied Dallas with alcohol and food. It had worked. Dallas was loose and relaxed with his belly full. He took the offering by leaning on one arm and opening his mouth. Greer's smile was enough to have him sucking the morsel into his mouth, bringing the tips of Greer's fingers inside with the bite.

"My guess is that your parents don't approve."

Dallas chewed and swallowed, taking Greer's hand in his, threading their fingers together. "That's an understatement."

"Skye told me a story about when you two were younger. It led me to believe there might have been some form of conversion therapy." Greer gave Dallas room. Not a lot, but he also didn't crowd him. Greer's concern was evident in his worried brow and serious stare.

"Not like the horror stories. I wasn't physically abused by the programs they put me in or taken off to work camps like so many I've heard about. That's where my mother drew the line, but it was still enough to..." Dallas stopped speaking and lifted the glass to his lips, remembering the months he'd spent inside the church, listening to the scriptures damn something he had zero control over. The bible verses they chose to focus on condemned him for his most basic desires. "The mental shit and the shame can be just as crippling."

His physical abuser hadn't come from outside the family but inside. His father never believed Dallas could get past his "defects." Anytime life got tough, Dallas was his father's punching bag. To this day, the smell of Miller Light had his back tensing, preparing for the blow and envisioning the humiliating trail of bruises he'd have for days to come. They represented the embarrassment Dallas posed to his family.

Even as Dallas had grown broader and stronger than his father, he hadn't stopped the physical abuse. He'd let it happen. How fucked up was that? He had so much regret.

"The worst part was my father. My mother was complicit. My father believed in the spare the rod scriptures. He felt like my 'defect' was his fault for being too lenient."

"Defect?" Greer asked.

"Yeah, it's what he called it. If I didn't get over it, I wouldn't have a home. I was taken from my bedroom and given the sofa to sleep on. To this day, if I sleep in their house, that's where I sleep. But if I didn't get a hold of my defect, they'd put me out." Dallas gave a dislodging shake of the head, hoping to dispel the memories. No good would come of rehashing his past. "It was half my life ago. I thought I'd gotten past it. Occasionally, I'll think some guy is attractive, but I ultimately decided I was asexual."

Greer's sad smile made Dallas give one of his own. "I'm sorry."

"I've had to come to terms with it all since I met you." Dallas lifted his glass, swallowing the rest of the watered-down whiskey. "I'm not normally this erratic."

"I suspected. I'm not close to my family. But my sexuality is the least of their problems with me." Greer stayed close, but turned, anchoring his ass against the railing. He crossed his arms over his chest. "So what're we going to do?"

Dallas eased away from the rail, staring Greer directly in the eyes. "I've been manic about it all week. Sometimes bold, sometimes cowering. When I thought you and I were done, I decided I still wanted to live my life in the best way for me. Then I began worrying about StreamTrainer. You've spent your time and money…"

Greer lifted a hand, stopping Dallas from saying anything more. "Your company's a concern, one I'll handle. You leave it to me. What would your brothers say about us?"

Dallas stared silently at Greer, assessing him. How could he reasonably drop this truth after all the time and money Greer had spent on their company?

"Let me guess to make it easier on you. Ducky's good. Donny's a younger version of your father." Greer had summed it up quickly and concisely.

Dallas nodded. "Donny thinks I'm a nutcase. He'll want out or for us to sell or he'll try to push me out. Probably want to push me out. He feels like you'll make us millions and millions of dollars."

Greer gave another small smile and pushed off the rail, nodding his confirmation. Most likely to the money comment. His love paced a circle around the furniture on the balcony.

"Here's my truth," Greer said, lifting his head to make sure Dallas was listening. "I want you with me. We need time together so you can see what I see…" Greer's feet clearly did his thinking for him. He never stopped marching. Even when Dallas interrupted him.

"We barely know one another. I cover my and Ducky's rent…"

Greer lifted a hand, stopping him from saying more. "Let me finish. For your company, we have one of two options. We can buy Donny out or we can push forward, go nationwide, and put some heat on the heels of your biggest competitors. At some point, we'll put enough pressure on them that they'll want to acquire StreamTrainer."

"Sell?" Dallas asked. Greer nodded. His shrewd calculating expression softened.

"For a substantial profit," Greer added. "Donny's not wrong about that."

"What if I wanted to keep the company? Could Ducky and I buy Donny out?" Dallas paused before deciding he might as well lay it all out. "Donny and I have already come to blows. I won't be able to hide this thing between us forever."

"All I care about is you being with me. We'll play it however you want. I'll adapt and we'll adapt. But ultimately, this investor team holds the cards on StreamTrainer. Donny causes a problem and he's out."

The pressure on Dallas's heart eased. The uncertain future of his dream company had added a heavy load to Dallas in an already dire situation. As long as Ducky was taken care of, nothing more really mattered.

Dallas went to Greer, needing a kiss and maybe one of Greer's expert healing touches. As he leaned in, Greer put a hand to his chest, stopping his descent. "Promise me, Dallas, whatever happens, we're together. We'll figure it out. No more cutting me out."

"You aren't the kind of guy to go on the downlow—" Dallas started, but Greer cut him off.

"You might've been right about that a month ago, but not now. I was a wreck last week. You've changed me. I honestly believe this is love between us. I can't imagine what else it would be. The pride I had with you by my side tonight…" Greer's fingers drifted over Dallas's chest as he stepped in, closer to him. "Dallas, I've lost my free will. I have no other choice but to protect you and us."

The sweet words were said with wonderment. Not an ounce of trepidation or fear.

"You have a choice," Dallas said, his insides growing warm with Greer's sweet tone. He had already made peace with removing Donny and his parents from his life, but he wasn't ready to step away from StreamTrainer or Ducky. Yet, nothing eclipsed his draw to Greer.

Dallas placed the now empty glass on the small table. Their future looked packed with pain, but he agreed. He had no other choice than to stick by Greer's side. "What did Skye say about us?"

"She's known about you and me since we danced together the night we met at the club."

"Really?" That surprised him, and he became instantly conflicted. The old fears and reactions came too easy.

"Whatever just happened, you have to ignore it. Skye loves you. So does Ducky. So do I. We'll work through the rest," Greer said, coming chest to chest with him. Greer picked up Dallas's arms and wrapped them around Greer's waist until he participated, the lighthearted action had him smiling.

"I'm not sure I'm worth the trouble."

"I'm positive you're worth any bit of trouble. And you've given me plenty." Greer's commiserating playful head nod caused Dallas to laugh.

"Kailey's your only real family?" Dallas asked.

"Pretty much. It's not ugly. We're all cordial when we see one another. It just is what it is."

"I have to get right with losing my family," Dallas said, tightening his hold.

Greer's palms moved to Dallas's chest. "I've always had chaos in my head. I stuttered as a child because I think so fast." Greer's fingertips tapped his temple. "You end the chaos. Everything slows to a manageable pace when you're around." Greer's lips pressed against his ear. "We have three hours before we leave." Now that tone was most definitely lust-infused, and Dallas perked up.

"I'm hard as stone. Your voice does it for me." The moment took on an urgency. Not of unbridled lust, but of something deeper and binding. Dallas had told his truth, Greer knew everything there was to know, and he still wanted Dallas around.

Any space he might have been able to keep between his heart and Greer's cinched closed. Dallas pushed at Greer's slacks. His willingness to be with Greer outside for anyone watching to see spoke of how much he trusted Greer's word. A feeling of liberation came over Dallas, solidifying his decision. It felt so damn good to be the man he always wanted to be.

"Your touch…" Greer started, releasing the hook and bar closure on his slacks, before lowering his zipper. Dallas's hands snaked down, dragging the underwear down Greer's thighs until they slid past Greer's legs on their own.

Greer's hands were all over him, claiming him with every touch. Greer undressed him, caressing as he went. In a bold move, Dallas took charge, shuffling Greer across the concrete balcony floor. Dallas's slacks dropped lower to match Greer's. His lover drew back and grabbed their cocks in his fist, squeezing them together. Fuck if that wasn't becoming his favorite move and the only reason Dallas allowed any space between them as he kicked away his joggers and cupped Greer's neck, bringing him in for a kiss.

They made it a few feet to the patio furniture. Dallas had planned on the outside sofa, but only got as far as the lounge chair when his lover's arms circled his neck, clinging to him for balance. He liked the move so much he used all his strength to guide Greer down right there on the lounger. He followed, their bodies fitting together perfectly on the oversized cushions.

Greer ravished Dallas's mouth as his blunt fingernails scorched a path down his back to grip his ass. Greer's hips drove forward, grinding against his ready cock.

Nothing in the world mattered as much as this man beneath him. Nothing. Greer had given him everything. He was being consumed.

He inched his hand lower, his fingertips skimming over each of Greer's stomach muscles until his fingers found what he searched for, and he gripped Greer's hard, swollen cock. Greer tore from the kiss with a hiss, and Dallas watched his lover's eyes close and his face etched in desire as Greer again thrust his hips forward, bucking into Dallas's fisted hand.

"Fuck, I can't get enough of you," Greer panted. "You're all I think about. Inside me, Dallas."

The sweet declaration had Dallas rising, pulling free of Greer's tight hold to reach for the lube and condoms he'd left on the small table nearby. He returned, this time more fully in control. He leaned down, gripping Greer's cock in his hand and hovered his lips close to Greer's. Greer lost no time in meeting Dallas's waiting lips. His tongue kept time with his hand, stroking to a frenzied pace. Greer's hot body quivered with need. Dallas loved being in control, guiding Greer to where he wanted him to be. He wrenched again from the kiss, Greer's mouth chasing his.

Dallas kept up the friction of his fist gliding over Greer's cock. "On all fours," he demanded.

"I changed my mind. I'm close. You can get me off."

Dallas slowed his strokes, his grin tugging at the corners of his mouth. "You know how this works. We come together."

The contradictory emotions crossed Greer's expressive face. Dallas could see the struggle. Greer's hand flew to his cock, encasing Dallas's hand there, working to keep the friction going. Dallas loved to see the disciplined Greer straining for control.

"Let me give you what you really want. Turn over."

A change overcame Greer. It was almost a tangible force. When he turned, the lounger proved the perfect angle for everything he had in mind. He took his time, admiring the sight in front of him. Greer's ass on display in the cool night air, his expressive face full of anticipation as he looked back over his shoulder.

"Fuck me, Dallas."

The need coursing through Dallas's body sent his racing heart into overdrive as he dropped to his knees and positioned himself behind Greer. He quickly tore open the packet and rolled the condom over his cock. He grabbed the lube, flicked the top open and squirted a generous portion on his fingers. He kept the bottle close, placing it on the metal table next to the lounger. Greer made an impatient hiss and wiggled his ass. That was his lover's subtle way of telling him to hurry it up. He laughed and swatted Greer's bare ass.

"Patience is a virtue."

"I'm not virtuous."

"We can discuss that later. Right now, I want you begging." Dallas placed one hand on Greer's back and brought the other to Greer's hole, circling the tight ring, teasing his man as he massaged Greer's muscular back. He slid his hand up and gripped Greer's shoulder as he breached the tight opening of his ass.

Dallas increased his pressure on Greer's shoulder, forcing his lover's chest to the cushion as he worked to open Greer. He curled his finger, easily finding the gland. Greer's body arched so beautifully as he pushed up on his arms, chasing the pleasure.

"Fuck. Dallas."

He chuckled and added a second finger, scissoring Greer open, aiming for the gland with every other stroke. Greer dug his fingers into the plush cushion, his body trembling as he reared back on his knees, fucking against Dallas's hand. The sight of his fingers disappearing into Greer's body mesmerized him, and he pushed at Greer's shoulders, urging his lover down again to get a better view of Greer's ass stretching around his digits.

Damn, he was so fucked over this guy. Greer's hips responded with every push of Dallas's fingers. Greer panted and ground his ass down, forcing Dallas's fingers deeper.

"Dallas, take me."

Dallas felt he had tortured them both enough. He removed his fingers to position his cock. Greer didn't give him a chance to ease inside his tight ass before he bore down on him, immersing Dallas's engorged cock in white-hot pressure. The delicious warmth squeezed him so good it forced a loud moan past his lips.

His thoughts seized as his body instinctively drove his hips forward. Greer's hot channel took all of him. Helpless to slow his hips, all he could do was give in to the urge to claim Greer, own him, as he plunged deeper into his lover's body. Greer belonged to him just as he belonged to Greer.

Goddamn, it was good. Dallas's eyes nearly rolled to the back of his head as he pulled Greer back against his chest. Greer hung on to the chair for balance. Dallas kept their bodies fused together as he sank into Greer over and over. He kept up the demanding thrusts, his thighs burning from the position. But he didn't care, his hips forcibly rolling into Greer.

The invasion was too good. He never wanted it to end. Heat swamped him. Sweat broke out across his body as he continued to drive his hips into Greer. This was so perfect.

Greer's body quivered against his as they rode the pleasure together.

"My perfect lover."

Dallas smiled at Greer's words and kissed the heated skin at the juncture of his neck and shoulder. "You ain't seen nothing yet."

Dallas dropped his fingers to Greer's hips and guided him

down as Dallas thrust up.

=♥=

Greer's eyes slowly slid closed as Dallas thrust into him, absorbing the visceral reaction of his body stretching to take all his man had to offer. His body heated and strained in the most decadent of ways. He was so fucking owned by Dallas.

Dallas's arm wrapped around Greer's waist. His other hand trailed a light caress to Greer's sac. He fucking squeezed, sending a shiver racing up Greer's spine. He curled his fingers into the cushion as pleasure shook his body. So consumed with the sensations, he had to consciously draw oxygen into his lungs.

"Move, baby." Dallas's voice was raw and needy, exactly what he wanted to hear. He lifted, Dallas's slick cock almost slipping from his channel until his man pushed upward, driving Greer against the back of the lounger. Oh, fucking hell that felt good. The burn of the mind-blowing stretching and filling gave him over-the-top pleasure.

"Fuck, do it again," he panted, hanging his head as his body lurched back down only to snap forward again, harder and faster this time. The grunts from behind caused his cock to leak. Greer reached down, clamping a fist around his cock, fighting the extraordinary orgasm building at lightning speed as he was bounced by powerful thrusts in a decadent pace Dallas created.

Grunts and frenzied pants drowned out the usual night sounds, adding to the heated excitement. Dallas's thick cock found his prostate with every punch of those amazing hips.

His ass burned. His lungs seized. His brain buzzed. "Fuck, Dallas. Fuck."

"Like?" Dallas drawled.

Being manhandled as if he weighed nothing? Hell yeah, he fucking liked. He never wanted this to end. He gripped the chair, his thighs straining as he worked to keep pace with Dallas. Greer canted his hips, matching Dallas move for move, losing himself in the feeling of his lover filling him so deeply.

He rolled his hips, forcing Dallas to thrust harder while he crashed back against Dallas's chest. He reached his hand wildly behind him, grasping at Dallas as if his lover could help anchor him. He managed to grip Dallas's head as that thick cock moved so enticingly inside him. With his fingers clinging tightly to Dallas's silky strands, he hung on for dear life.

Even if he wanted to, he wouldn't last much longer, not with the way Dallas hit his prostate with every push forward. He trusted Dallas to hold him up as he used a free hand to grip his cock, hoping he could hold out just a minute or two longer. It was too much and not enough at the same time, and it felt so fucking amazing.

"Fuck, you feel good. Stroke yourself," Dallas instructed. He didn't need to do more than release his fist. His orgasm rushed through his body at lightning speed, swamping him with pleasure as Dallas pushed into him. His fingernails scraped against Dallas's scalp as his hand fisted involuntarily when his mister reached forward, barely touching Greer's cock.

Dallas's hips faltered, his rhythm becoming erratic.

"I'm coming…" Greer panted breathlessly. He slammed his eyes shut, and his muscles locked in pleasure as his orgasm charged forward. Greer was so fucked in all the right ways. Dallas barely managed to keep them both upright as they came. His sated haze made him useless as he sagged back against his lover, lost in their perfection, and closed his eyes.

CHAPTER 33

Their early flight to Guatemala hadn't offered them much time to sleep, and before Dallas knew it, they were on the beach, taking part in the cleanup initiative.

Greer was a force of nature, and it fascinated Dallas to watch him live and work by his convictions. He set a high bar for himself and demanded the world around him do the same. And he clearly didn't need much sleep. Where Dallas was exhausted from a hard morning of manual labor—after a long night filled with…manual labor, so to speak—Greer thrived in the fast-paced work environment he created.

For such a polished man, Greer wasn't afraid to get his hands dirty. He worked as hard as anyone else on the beach cleanup crew. Moreover, he motivated the volunteers, wasting no time in rallying the troops. The global news media had been invited and gave Greer all their attention. Dallas got why. Greer was charming, photogenic, and well-spoken. He took the attention as giving him a forum to sing glowing praise about the company organizing the event, C.A.R.E.—Community. Action. Resources. Environment.—one of the first businesses Greer funded. Today marked four hundred million pounds of garbage collected from beaches worldwide.

Through action, Dallas saw what Greer tried to show the world. The smallest effort had significant effects on climate change.

Greer was such a mix of a man. He mingled comfortably with the world's wealthy and elite. He also worked side by side with the everyday man, creating the same personal connections between both groups. Greer hauled trash, worked the recycling equipment, and offered a strong-armed hand for all the heavy lifting.

The love blooming inside Dallas grew stronger by the second, nearly consuming and overwhelming him. Greer was such a good man. Not anything like the player Dallas had thought he was. He gave hope to many startup companies, much like his own, helping to make dreams come true.

They'd spent the day picking up trash on a beach, but Dallas had picked up so much more. He'd seen shining bold and bright the truth of the man he'd fallen for.

"What do you think?" Greer asked, dropping down in the airplane seat next to Dallas.

"There's been a lot. What specifically?"

Greer leaned into Dallas with a giant grin, puckering for a kiss. "The plane," Greer said, and kissed him again before settling back into his seat.

A guy named Ryan, who'd owned C.A.R.E., took the seat across from them.

The bits and pieces Dallas had overheard about the small, intimate private plane, hadn't made a lot of sense. He was new to the world of trying to save the planet.

"Ryan, have I introduced you to my boyfriend?" Greer asked as the plane accelerated down the runway.

Ryan chuckled, grinning at Dallas. "Several times."

"Just making sure," Greer teased, intertwining their fingers. "This plane has been a project a long time in the making. It uses synthetic fuel. Emitting zero carbon. It's a prototype. Not the inaugural flight. I missed that one, but still very new."

"I'm just catching a ride," Ryan explained, and as if on cue, the plane lifted into the air. "And to see this plane that's going to change the aviation industry."

Dallas had only flown twice in his life and nothing this small or intimate. There were eight seats—two groupings of four seats. There were two other passengers in the seats directly behind theirs.

With a squeeze of the hand, Greer drew Dallas's attention to him. "I have to take care of some business. Are you good here?"

"I am." He nodded. Hopefully, he could even get some shuteye.

"Ryan, have you met my boyfriend?" Greer said cheekily, unbuckling his seat belt. "He's had me on a run. As a therapist, you might counsel him on the importance of staying with me."

"That might be pushing my ability to influence," Ryan said, teasingly.

Greer gave a hearty laugh as he used the armrest to lean toward Dallas again, regaining all of his attention…again. "You sure you're good?"

"Stop. Do what you need to do." The gleam in Greer's eyes should have been the first clue something outrageous was coming.

"Mile high club?" Greer whispered, his brows waggling in excitement at the absurd idea.

"Of course, not," Dallas countered.

Greer stayed close but turned toward Ryan. "The blush gets me every time."

"Go," Dallas said, knocking his arm off the armrest.

"I'll take that as a maybe." Greer winked, a sensual grin slipping over his lips. He kissed Dallas before he flipped around to the seat behind them.

"He's a force," Ryan said quietly, his grin as big as Greer's.

"I have that playing in a loop inside my head." Dallas tapped his temple.

"I bet." Ryan gave a commiserating nod. "How did you two meet? He's investing in your company, right?" Ryan crossed one leg over the other. "Greer sent me one of your boxes. I haven't started yet but plan to."

"He did?" Dallas asked, surprised.

"Yeah, last week." Ryan smiled. Dallas's confusion must have shown on his face. "My guess is he's sent them to many, many people. He's great at creating a buzz. I was on the brink of bankruptcy when I met him. I wanted an environmental company that operated as a for-profit business. I was selling recycled necklaces. It started off great, but hard to expand. Greer found me and changed everything. He gave me cash, but also guidance. I was wise enough to follow his suggestions."

"I think we feel the same way," Dallas said about him and his brothers, omitting the horrible, last week from hell.

Ryan looked at him closely. Silence held for several long moments.

"So why did he ask me to fly home with you?" Ryan lowered his voice, looking Dallas directly in the eyes. "I can usually tell, but I'm not sure with you."

Ryan's gaze slid over Dallas's face until it dropped to his chest. He scanned Dallas's arms then his bare legs.

"What do you usually know?" he asked just as quietly, not sure why he didn't feel set up by Greer. He liked Ryan. They had worked together for most of the morning. Once you'd sweated together on a beach in South America, you had some new type of bond.

"Conversion therapy." Ryan's voice lowered to almost a whisper, barely able to be heard. Ryan leaned forward in his seat, his tone a little above a whisper. "I spent two summers in a conversion therapy camp when I was fifteen then again at sixteen. Once I got out of my father's hold, I spent years in counseling to overcome the shame. I attempted suicide twice before channeling my energy into education. I'm a clinical psychologist."

"How old are you?" Maybe Dallas had misread Ryan. He looked young and professional with no hints of the baggage something like that might cause.

"I'm thirty. I poured myself into my education and conservation work. I filled my voids with an insane workload."

Dallas nodded his understanding. Had he had access to money, he'd probably have gone on with his education. Instead, he had turned his energies into working out. He exercised an insane amount of time. He had suspected it was to keep his plate full. Too full to consider much else.

"I've had a small dose of..." Dallas lowered his voice to barely more than a whisper. "Conversion therapy through my father's physical abuse and a significant time spent in church. Enough that I've had a hard time learning who I really am. Being with Greer is very new for me. I came with lots of problems. He really had to push for this relationship."

Ryan's serious expression turned amused as he settled back in his seat. "I heard him tell someone that he bought you at an auction, so you were obligated to be here with him."

Dallas chuckled, nodding his agreement. "There's truth in his words."

Ryan kept his smile as he studied Dallas. "I won't pry. My door's always open to you. I counsel conversion therapy patients. From a healing from harm approach."

Dallas nodded, having no real idea what that meant.

"My only piece of advice to you is to give yourself a break.

What's been done to you will take time to overcome. You'll have lots of ups and downs. Stay patient with yourself. If you and Greer are in fact a couple, lean on him. He's flashy and showy, but underneath, there's no better man. He says he loves you."

"That's what he says," Dallas said, a small amount of anxiety wiggled around his heart. Could he truly get past himself to be enough to keep a man like Greer?

"I promise, living a truthful life will be a better life for you and Greer."

Dallas nodded again and took a deep breath. He prayed that was true. He appreciated Ryan's willingness to help, but avoidance seemed the best option to handle his life right now.

His goals were set. He'd given his commitment to Greer. He never wanted that to change.

The anxiety within him built. Avoidance. That dark side of his life would be handled when the time came.

Dallas turned his head, staring out the small window, watching the clouds fill the sky.

Greer sat on his bed, back against the headboard, legs underneath the blankets. The mounted television was on, the volume lowered to almost silent. They had agreed on some Netflix show, and the credits just began to roll. Dallas had lasted for about ten minutes before he fell sound asleep. His loud snores had made Greer chuckle. He then promptly coerced his love onto his stomach where Dallas had slowly gravitated to Greer's side, curled up there against him.

His laptop sat open on his thighs. Greer spent the last hour and a half adding notes and directions to several of his EnviroCapital accounts. The weekend had been such a success on so many different levels.

The alarm on his laptop dinged. A notification appeared on

the screen. Dallas's pre-designated time to go home. Not Greer's though. He looked down at the chestnut-colored head tucked in against his hip. Greer let his finger rifle through the thick strands. Dallas didn't move a muscle, so he whispered very low.

"Babe, the alarm went off."

Greer only got a grunt with Dallas shifting to turn on his side. His back angled against Greer's legs with a pillow tucking to his chest. The snores were a little louder this way.

Oh lord, Greer had it bad. Like so in over his head in love.

Greer reached to close the lid of the laptop and pulled a pillow from behind his back, pushing it between him and Dallas. As he stood, he got lost in the beauty in his bed. His heart filled with the romance of their great love. The overwhelming need to take care of Dallas had him pulling the blankets snugly around his guy. It was unreasonable how much he liked Dallas in his bed, in his room, in his house.

Laptop and cell phone in hand, he left the room, quietly closing the door behind him. One of his most favorite memories of the weekend, one that would stay with him for the rest of his life was Dallas's sleepy whisper confessing how Greer made his life full of color. He'd never heard love described quite that way. After reflection, he agreed Dallas was his life's color, vivid and vibrant.

Greer discarded the laptop and cell on the island and closed the retractable doors, wondering if Dallas would require them open during the heat of the summer. Maybe in those future summer months, they might spend that time in the Seattle area.

He'd secured the funding for the Washington State project this weekend. It was a huge accomplishment. Perhaps the biggest of his life. It proved his investors believed in him. He couldn't be happier.

He'd have to travel back and forth. Soon, he planned to show Dallas the architectural plans. He wanted someone to share the excitement with. He was so in love. Dallas had been remarkable by his side today. The children volunteering for the cleanup were drawn to him. Dallas had gravitated to them too. He guided them, taking a genuine interest in their part of the cleanup.

Dallas would be an excellent father. Little chestnut-haired children, both sons and daughters. A big family. Greer rolled his eyes at the beauty of the picture he painted inside his crazy head.

Tomorrow, life would return. Their future began. He concentrated on his cell phone and searched Ducky's number. In all their rushed planning last week, Kailey had said Dallas would be home tonight. Greer couldn't bring himself to wake Dallas to leave.

Greer pushed call and brought the phone to his ear. On the fourth ring, Ducky answered.

"Hey, Greer. What's up?"

He decided on the truth, at least with Ducky. "Dallas's sleeping. We had a long weekend. I would prefer not to wake him. I didn't want you to worry."

Straight forward, clear…vague. Why did he suddenly feel like he was telling Dallas's secrets?

"Cool. He signed off on everything on Saturday morning. The website's gone live and we're connected to Secret now. Sales have already doubled. Tell Dallas for me. We have to ship those out tomorrow."

"That's great news. I'll tell him in the morning. He should be home early," Greer said.

"Cool."

Greer smiled at the single word. His sign it was time to end the call. "Goodnight."

"Yup." The phone went dead. Greer lowered his, chuckling. What an interesting guy.

He heard footsteps on the floor behind him seconds before two strong arms wrapped around his waist.

"You're so free, walking around naked." Dallas's chest

pressed flush against his back as Greer slid a hand over Dallas's arm until their fingers linked together. "I like you in bed with me."

Dallas pressed his lips against Greer's shoulder, sending a full body shiver racing along his skin. "I wanted to call Ducky and let him know you'd be home in the morning. In our planning last week, we told him you'd be home tonight."

"Come to bed. You need to sleep," Dallas said against his ear, letting him go until they were holding hands, Dallas's naked body on display as he tugged Greer toward the bedroom. "You don't take care of yourself properly. Sleep's good."

Greer grinned, watching the bounce of Dallas's ass in his natural strut. God, his guy had swagger.

CHAPTER 34

"Where is he?" Kailey asked, swinging around on the barstool until she faced his front door. Greer looked over at the Echo to check the time. Almost seven thirty. The day hadn't been easy. Greer's carefully hidden anxiety had finally gotten the best of him.

He texted Dallas approximately an hour and a half ago, stating very clearly if Dallas didn't arrive back there in a timely manner, Greer would be forced to come to Grand Prairie and find him. He'd tried to say it in such a way that he came off as witty and fun. Who knew if he'd accomplished a playful tone? They had parted ways twelve hours ago. Anything could have changed in the interim.

"He'll be here," Greer said, trying to sound convincing as he flipped the steaks over on the pan and seasoned the other side.

"*Trust me.*" Those were Dallas's words in his last text exchange with Greer. He needed to believe in Dallas. Requiring an all-day Facetime session seemed stalkerish. He had wanted that though, even if he couldn't figure out how to sell the idea to Dallas.

"Beau's on his way," Kailey said. He looked up to see her cell phone in her hands, her body still angled toward the door. "He wants to meet Dallas too."

"You look ready to pounce, Kailey. He doesn't even know you're here. Don't face the door like that," Greer said, washing his hands then reaching for the full tray of food. With measured steps, hoping to tamp down his worry, Greer started toward the grill on the patio when his front door opened. He snapped his head that direction, air leaving his lungs in a whoosh of relief at the sight that met him.

Dallas's handsome face appeared through the crack of the door he opened. He looked around until his gaze landed on Kailey, where it froze.

"Is this note for me?" Dallas gave a sidestep all the way in, holding the note Greer had hastily written. The one telling Dallas to come inside and meet them on the patio.

Greer's shoulders relaxed now that Dallas had arrived. So much relief coursed through him that he pivoted around, heading toward his honey.

"I was afraid you'd knock instead of coming straight inside." That information had Dallas closing the door. Greer met his guy in the foyer. Only now would he let himself admit he strongly doubted Dallas would come back. With everything Dallas had to deal with, it felt like a monumental step in the right direction. Greer lifted to steal a quick kiss. "I'm glad I didn't have to come searching for you."

"The army you said you'd deploy to find me made me nervous." Dallas's lighthearted banter spoke volumes about his lover's head space. Dallas bent to kiss Greer, his smile beaming at him. Since his threat of a military manhunt had been so successful, he'd have to keep that tactic ready to use.

"How was your afternoon?" Greer asked. Dallas's hand rested on Greer's hip, keeping him close.

"Busy. We moved into the new offices and we didn't miss a scheduled class or a shipment out. We have twelve classes a day now. And Skye says thank you for her office."

"Did I give her an office?" Greer didn't remember that detail.

"No, it's a closet. She claimed it." Dallas nodded to the tray still in Greer's hand. "What's all that for?"

"Kailey and Beau are stopping by to meet you. I hope you don't mind. Kailey's a pain in the ass who doesn't understand how new love requires private time to adjust." Greer lifted again for a kiss, grinning broadly at his joke, but Kailey's annoying voice drew Dallas's attention toward her, which left Greer hanging.

"I'm right here, turd."

Greer had to angle his head toward his sister who had gotten to her feet, her shoes clicking on his polished floors as she approached. "And since I waited all weekend to hear from this guy." She pinched Greer in the ribs with her pointy fingernails, sending him into a spasm to get away while keeping the tray of food upright. Kailey took Greer's place in front of Dallas. "I had to come see you for myself."

Of course, Kailey didn't care about things like personal space. She wrapped her arms around Dallas, holding him tightly until he reached around her waist, returning her hug. His gaze collided with Greer's.

"You're so nice-looking, Dallas. I can see why my brother's crazy about you."

Oh Lord. He didn't want to give the wrong impression, so his eye roll stayed inside his head.

"Come on. You'll give him the big head," Greer said. Luckily, Kailey did let Dallas go, but she stayed in his face.

"Marisol thinks you hold power over my brother. You're going to have to teach me your skill."

Greer let the eye roll go this time and left them standing there, heading for the grill. Of course, she would embarrass him, but he also knew he would never be able to keep her away from Dallas. So, she needed to get it all out tonight. "Don't listen to her, Dallas. Pregnancy's affecting her brain."

"Hush, brother."

Greer cast a quick glance over his shoulder to see Kailey lifting a fallen piece of hair off Dallas's forehead. She lovingly moved it back in place, happy to be there with Dallas. His mister had an incredibly awkward *"help me"* or *"don't walk away"* expression. He was about to learn what it meant to have a sister in his life.

"Come on, you two. I've got baked potatoes, vegetables, and these steaks. Grab the bottle of wine when you come."

His gentleman extended an arm, urging Kailey to go first. Her response was to wrap her arm around Dallas's outstretched one, causing Greer to laugh out loud.

"She's hard to shake free."

Kailey gave a perfectly executed *tsk*, not daunted in the least. "I'm Skye's friend which makes Dallas my friend. He just doesn't know it yet."

"I won't let her inside the house next time," Greer called out, ducking out onto the patio.

"Don't worry, *Dallas*." Kailey said loud enough for Greer to hear. "I have all the keys. I can get in here at any time."

He couldn't find it anything other than comfortable around Kailey and Beau, and boy, had he tried. They were both very much like Greer—upper crust in both education and pedigree—

but they all did *normal* so damn well that, somehow, they made Dallas feel relaxed and as if he could relate.

Beau had arrived about twenty minutes after Dallas. He was Greer's equal in every way. Reasonably, Dallas understood there was no attraction between them. He got it. They were just so damn fluid together it was hard not to speculate about their past.

Greer, Beau, and Mac had all shared a small dorm room at SMU. They'd tailgated together, served as each other's best men—well, for Mac and Beau—and were everything Dallas had wished he'd had in a male best friend. Dallas was no longer jealous of their bond, just envious of the connection.

Kailey on the other hand had been glued to Dallas's side for the evening. As Beau instructed Greer on the proper way to clean a grill, something grill master Greer resented, Kailey had her eyes on Dallas. He felt them burning a hole through him.

"Why do you keep looking at me?" he teased, finally glancing over at her.

"Nothing really. Greer wouldn't tell me anything about you. I had no idea how far things had gotten between you two. Once I figured it out, Skye started spilling the tea. I'm glad my brother has such a good man. He deserves a genuine, gentle man."

Dallas lifted his drink and had to force himself not to react. Ryan's conversation yesterday on the plane had resonated within Dallas. He went home with fresh eyes this morning. Ducky was already at it, hard at work, expertly managing the move into their new offices. Dallas didn't waste a second before jumping in to help.

Their new team of staff members were efficient. Everything ran so damn smoothly. Skye hadn't held back either this weekend. She had trainers scheduled around the clock for the entire month. Their YouTube filming schedule was also set. Their new studio was big. Greer had allocated funds to set up for in-person classes, giving the home user a bigger sense of community for their workout.

"He's a force," Dallas said about Greer. "He can move mountains. I felt like baggage today. He's done so much for our company."

"You aren't baggage, at least per Skye." Kailey's singsong laugh had him smiling too. "She said you two made a pact when you were younger that if you weren't married by the age of thirty-five, you would marry each other."

He'd forgotten their childhood oath. Thirty-five had seemed so old. What a nice memory. "We did. In elementary school, I think. Greer told me you're pregnant."

Kailey's eyes sparkled as her hand went to her belly. "I am. I'm nervous. Greer and I didn't come from a loving home. We weren't raised with a lot of nurturing and attention. It's why I hang on to Greer so closely. He's the only real one of my family. He's the only one who's ever been willing to get out and work with his hands. My grandfather hit it big in the oil industry. Most of our family lives off him. Greer's an anomaly. How much he cares about the world is exactly how much our family doesn't care."

"That's hard to believe with the way I watched him work this weekend. He doesn't stop for anything," Dallas said, casting a glance at Greer still arguing with Beau.

"That's a huge understatement. Greer never stops. I'd guess he's made more money in his short life than my parents have their whole lives. But Greer gives all his money away. He feels like that's why he's been put on this planet. My parents don't respect him at all," she said, lowering her voice to an almost whisper.

"Gives away?" Dallas asked in the same hushed tone. "I thought his investment company funded for-profit environmental businesses."

Kailey nodded and leaned closer to Dallas to be better heard. "That's right, but he donates and funds many charities. He doesn't think of money like normal people. It's a game to him. He could charm the jewels off a person. He's like a modern-day Robin

Hood. He doesn't see it that way, but I do."

On a small scale, Dallas had witnessed and connected with Greer's generosity, how much Greer cared about people. He kept his gaze focused on Greer, watching him burst out in laughter at something Beau said. "He's mentioned to me about the discord with your parents."

Her chuckle said his words were an understatement. "Greer is the best man I know. My parents don't value goodness. My brother's never said it out loud, but I feel like they did a number on him. The way he's dated in the past. The way he fills his plate so full, so he doesn't have time to reflect. I'm not sure he believes he's worthy of love."

Dallas couldn't help his involuntary burst of laughter. Greer was everything good and right with the world. Everyone had to love that man like he did.

"No, listen," she said, her hand coming to his forearm. "I didn't know how to give or accept love. I heard you met Ryan yesterday. I've spent a lot of time and money with him to figure myself out. Once I got right, I turned my attention to Greer to figure him out. I decided Greer doesn't see himself as a valued, suitable partner for anyone. I came to that conclusion without Greer's help. He wouldn't participate. So, I could only guess." Her little shrug made Dallas smile again, thinking about what Kailey said.

It was hard to believe Greer might not see himself as worthy of love. But Dallas could probably say the same thing about himself. The tightness in his chest grew as he realized they might be more similar than different. What an incredible thought.

"How much older is Greer than you?"

"Four years. I'm the youngest. There's a brother between me and Greer. When I was in high school, I'd run away from home and go stay with Greer in his dorm room. My parents never even knew I was gone. I moved into Greer's apartment his sophomore year. Again, my parents didn't know I was gone. Greer's always been my one, but don't worry, I've decided I'll share him with you." Her elbow knocked him in the arm at her playful joke. "Has he told you about the Washington State project?"

"Bits and pieces," he murmured. Kailey held all his attention now. He appreciated these little insights into Greer's life.

"Get him to tell you about it. His face lights up the same way when he looks at you."

"Why do you look like that? What did you say?" Greer asked accusingly. Dallas hadn't even heard Greer's approach, let alone that he had rounded the table to Dallas's side. His mister's eyes narrowed teasingly toward Kailey as he extended a hand to Dallas's shoulder. Dallas did one better and lifted his face, puckering his lips for a kiss. The idea Greer didn't feel worthy of anything resonated with Dallas. He didn't like it at all.

"I told him I've never seen you this happy," she said cheerfully.

"Omigod, you're messing with my game." Greer's hand gave Dallas's shoulder in a gentle squeeze. "Don't listen to her. I'm irritable and hard to get along with. Guys like the chase—like you gave Beau."

Beau who had followed Greer over, nodded toward the front door. "It's true, we do. And it's almost eleven. I have to be at the hospital in six hours."

Kailey rose, grinning suggestively. "I think they need time alone anyway."

"Probably do," Beau agreed.

"Omifuckinggod," Greer said, "Shut your mouth."

Dallas tried to stand but had to dodge Greer's flying hands. Dallas had taken Kailey's words to heart. Greer worked so hard to make sure Dallas felt loved that Dallas needed to give that back. He wrapped an arm around Greer's waist, thrilling when there was no hesitation as he relaxed into the hold. From this day forward, Dallas promised to show Greer exactly how loved he was.

CHAPTER 35

Two Weeks Later

"What an incredible experience. We already look so much more professional," Dallas said to Ducky while climbing off the bike they'd set up in the center of the stage. The lights flipped on automatically and the cameraman, a friend of Ducky's for many years, nodded before exiting the studio without another word. Most of their new staff came from Ducky's world. None of their new employees ever wasted time standing around and chatting. They were introverts, doing their jobs and moving on.

"Sales are crazy. We had to hire temporary workers to fill shipments from the weekend. The current inventory won't hold us through next week." Ducky stood at the edge of the stage, a few feet from the door with his arms crossed over his chest.

They were alone in the studio, making Ducky more comfortable to speak freely. They'd had a scheduled leadership meeting this morning, but Dallas had to take a class for a trainer who'd run late.

"What's Donny have to say about that?"

"He's still not speaking to you? What a puss."

Somehow, even between Dallas's labored breaths, he still managed to laugh straight out at Ducky's disgust. He grabbed a towel, running it over his face. Because the air conditioner was set at a cool sixty degrees inside this room, his sweat was down by half.

"Don't knock it. It hasn't been a hardship." Dallas bumped Ducky on the elbow and motioned his head for them to leave the studio.

"He's in Maryland now. I wondered if he told you. He's touring the company Greer found for hardware production. I think it's a formality. We ordered five thousand boxes from them yesterday. Another ten thousand next quarter. Greer works in numbers that scare me a little bit."

Dallas smiled because he agreed. The order quantities seemed overly optimistic, but the cash from all those corresponding sales would truly change the course of their company.

"We agreed to have Skye add a morning class of personal training and a cardio class to the schedule six days a week. We tossed out the idea of adding them to YouTube too. What do you think?" They moved around a painter currently working on their new StreamTrainer logo being added to the hall wall.

"Who's doing the cardio classes?" Dallas asked.

"She will. She's hoping you'll pick up one or two a week. She's offered to cut back on her time at Elite gym and sent us a proposal for a salary increase. I think Greer's behind it, but he's letting you decide since she works under you." Ducky glanced his way, a brow arching, as Dallas thought about his answer. For him, that was a no-brainer. He wished they could afford for Skye to work full time.

"What about the technical staff? How many have you added?" he asked. Although business had begun to boom, his debt load hadn't decreased in the slightest. Cash was still a major obstacle.

"We have a customer service person who's going to sit out front as the receptionist and two guys I game with to help monitor the social site part time. Secret's also giving us one person on their end, but we have to pay their salary. I'm still working on monitoring it too, but now we'll be covered twenty-four seven. It's weird to have an exact schedule. It's gonna take me a minute to get used to it."

"I bet." What an understatement. Ducky hadn't lived by the time of day since they had started working together. "We have two people filming, right?"

"Yeah. We're gonna start doing the split screen thing, getting different angles rather than the single shot from a stationary camera. That'll add another cost." Ducky's arms were still tightly crossed over his chest as they walked. "One of the film guys is going to help me edit the videos for the website and YouTube. He's not charging extra for that. And he went to Full Sail so he knows what he's doing. It's funny that Greer has an office here. He's taken a big interest."

"Yeah," Dallas said as they rounded the corner into the area housing a cluster of individual offices. He started toward the one he shared with Ducky. About twelve days ago, Greer had started showing up at their corporate office regularly. He combed over the bookkeeping, watching every dime spent. He monitored their growth personally. Greer's approach to business seemed as if he moved chess pieces around on a board. His mister absolutely had the Midas touch.

In short order, Greer had maximized their growing bank accounts. He had also maneuvered Dallas out of his second job at Elite gym. Last night had been his last shift.

Donny had no idea what was going on except Greer had little

time for him. He'd voiced his frustration over Greer's apparent friendship with Ducky and for giving Dallas a salary large enough that he could quit his second job. Of course, Donny hadn't shared any of that with Dallas, only with Ducky. His older brother could hold a grudge almost as well as their father.

"I'm calling for a pizza party at my place tonight. Call Skye, have her meet us there," Greer said, coming through his and Ducky's office door. He looked dashing, and his enchanting smile always pulled one from Dallas.

"Why's that?" Ducky asked, simply turning Greer's direction, his arms still crossed over his chest. Dallas could hear the smile in Ducky's voice. Maybe more than anything else Greer had done, his friendship with Ducky was the most endearing to Dallas.

"You're looking at quite possibly the best salesman on the planet." Greer tooted his own horn while tossing a legal pad with handwritten notes titled *bill of sale* on to Dallas's desk.

Dallas scanned down the page until he reached the bottom where the total boxes sold were circled in black ink. "Sixteen hundred boxes. Are you serious?"

"And sixteen hundred monthly subscriptions. All to Belo. And that's not all." Greer flipped over the page showing another handwritten bill of sale. "Dylan's ordered seven hundred boxes, paying full price."

"He's paying full price?" Ducky asked, concerned. "Shouldn't we just give them to him?"

"Absolutely, not," Greer declared as if that were the craziest idea ever. "I had to pay. He has to pay." Greer delivered his theory with a wink directed at both of them.

Ducky must have agreed since he grinned. His fist came out to Dallas, and he obliged with a knuckle tap of his own.

"Did we think of corporate business like this?" Ducky asked.

"I'm not sure we did."

Greer sat on the edge of the desk between him and Ducky.

"It's the way to grow StreamTrainer in a big way. Here's what I've been thinking. Dallas needs to move into the position of a corporate salesman..."

What? Dallas couldn't have heard Greer correctly. He didn't know how to sell anything. With an immediate objection rising to his lips, Greer lifted a hand to cut him off.

"Hear me out. I'll open the door for you, get you the introductions, and train you on how to close the deal."

"Then why don't you just do it," Dallas countered. Greer's lips pressed together as if he were talking to a simpleton.

"Because I'm a busy man. I'm only here for now. You guys have given me a break from my reality, but I have my fair share of work being left undone." Greer left his perch on the desk, lifting the tablet to Ducky. "Can you call Donny and see when these two shipments can be delivered? Orders this size will be easier to ship directly from the distributor. Then call the contacts at the bottom of the pages. We need both companies invoiced as soon as possible. For both the boxes and the year's membership."

"This is great," Ducky said, his eyes growing wide. "No discounts and all the membership fees up front. This will end our cash problems."

Greer reached over to teasingly knock Dallas under the chin, urging him to close his gaping mouth.

"I thought it was great too. So, pizza, swimming, and margaritas at my place tonight. Invite Skye. We should offer her a full-time job to take over the training department. We have a lot to celebrate."

"I agree. That sounds great to me," Ducky said distractedly, taking the chair behind his desk. "People like Dallas. I can see he'd be a good salesman."

Greer clapped his hands, rubbing them together, clearly very proud of himself. Dallas's eyes narrowed.

Had he agreed to be a salesman?

He had no idea how to sell anything to anyone.

What had just happened?

Greer strode toward Dallas, his stride long and confident as he slid his sexiest grin in place. The sounds of "Ain't No Rest For The Wicked" began to play on the surround sound. His gorgeous honey sat at the center island, taking a long drink from his cocktail glass, eyeing Greer's progress.

He knew Dallas loved him, but damn, the man sure kept him on his toes. Every evening, when Dallas first arrived home, they played a game of cat and mouse. Dallas voiced his concern of wearing out his welcome by being there every night, and Greer worked to learn the art of romance. He wined and dined Dallas. Maybe Dallas didn't fully understand where he belonged, but Greer did.

Tonight, candles glowed and the living room furniture had been pushed out of the way. Greer had planned dancing for the evening. Of course, Skye and Ducky didn't come for dinner. Greer had introduced Skye to Evan five days ago. The two were currently on their fourth date, utterly taken with one another. Ducky had a League of Legends tournament he didn't want to miss.

"I knew they wouldn't come tonight." Greer stopped in front of Dallas, reaching for Dallas's half full glass of Grey Goose and brought it to his lips.

"You look handsome," Dallas murmured. Greer swallowed the hearty sip, stepping closer as he handed the glass back to Dallas. "Your clothes always fit you very well. I remember that from the first night we met." The smile on Dallas's face made his heart beat a little faster.

"That was the night I fell in love with you," Greer admitted. The night would be etched in his memory from now until eternity. Dallas offered him another drink without any prompting even as the slightest flush hit Dallas's cheeks. His Adam's apple gave a small bob. His mister liked his words; Dallas was so damn endearing. Greer took the glass and stepped between Dallas's parted thighs, caging the trainer in against the counter. He reached for the bottle of vodka and poured a good portion into the glass.

"Have nothing to say about that?"

"I love you too."

Greer laughed, putting the shared glass to Dallas's lips. "Not the night you fell for me too?"

Greer's phone went nuts, drawing their attention down to his slacks. He pulled the cell free. Generally, he tried to silence the thing before he began his few precious alone hours with Dallas. He muted his phone and absently tossed the phone on the counter beside the bottle.

"Social media."

"What social media do you have?" Dallas's strong arm came to Greer's waist, keeping him snugly there. "Are we friends or followers?"

"Twitter, Instagram, Tinder, Scruff. I thought we had this discussion," Greer said teasingly, trying for cheeky. Dallas completely missed his joke. His eyes narrowed until a quirk lifted one side of his pouty lips.

"That's right. I need to join Tinder." The words flipped Greer's smile into an automatic frown. How quickly and efficiently had his guy turned the tables on him?

"No, you don't. And I'll delete mine." The idea of Dallas signing on to Tinder and seeing what he might be missing had Greer giving the glass back to Dallas as he reached for his phone again. Working quickly, he deleted both apps with Dallas watching. "Now come dance with me so I can forget the mental image of your possible Tinder hookup."

Greer tucked his phone away as Dallas discarded the glass, giving a chuckle. He took Dallas's hands, drawing him to his feet and the few steps to the center of the living room. He came flush against Dallas's hard body and hardening cock, wrapping himself around his man.

"Tell me what you're thinking about this sales position idea. I've never sold anything in my life," Dallas said.

"You as the national sales advisor means we can travel together." Greer ignored the snappy tune playing overhead and pressed his cheek against Dallas's as he started to sway. "Don't worry. I watched you in Houston. You're a natural. You'll figure it out. I wasn't lying when I said national sales is where your true growth will come from. Corporate accounts are a no-brainer. They'll promote physical health with their staff at a very low cost to them."

Dallas drew back to look him in the eyes as if that idea had never occurred to him. "That's not a bad idea. We can have exclusive corporate competitions every quarter. Maybe an annual tournament with prizes. Would the companies donate prizes to give to the winners?"

"See? Perfect salesman," Greer's said, winking at Dallas. "You'll figure it all out."

"Why do I feel like there's more to this?" Those speculative green eyes narrowed, and Dallas resisted Greer's efforts to draw him closer again.

"You're a hard one to get things past, aren't you?" How could Greer explain all this change inside him when he didn't truly understand what was happening inside him in the first place?

Greer had to stop shirking his responsibilities. He started every morning at EnviroCapital. He worked closely with his analysts, requiring daily briefings on all their accounts, but he could tell his heart was no longer in it. By early afternoon, Greer gravitated to the StreamTrainer offices just to be around Dallas a few more hours during the day.

Greer was looking for a new life. Something different. EnviroCapital could handle itself with Evan as his managing partner. Greer loved his company, but the Washington State venture had broken ground. Outside of Dallas, that project held all of Greer's interest. With each dig of the shovel, he wanted to be there to watch personally.

"They broke ground on the Washington State project," he murmured.

Dallas's eyes lit up with excitement. Any attempt Greer had made to start their dance ended. He wasn't even frustrated when Dallas stepped completely out of his hold. "You've started?" he asked, enthusiastically.

"I have and it's exhilarating to me." Any excitement Greer had managed to tamp down exploded through him. He stepped back, scrubbing his palms down his face, his grin as wide as ever. "I have an excitement I haven't had about work in a long, long time. If my team can do this right, it could be a game changer."

"Show me the plans," Dallas encouraged.

"I'm supposed to be wooing you. Let me." Greer fisted his hands and started back for Dallas. *Perspective.* They had done nothing more than shovel some dirt around for a photo op today. They had time to go over all the plans. It didn't have to be now.

Dallas kept a distance, and it wasn't easy with the way Greer tried to pull him back into the hold. "Greer. Tell me what's on your mind before this goes too much further and we're in the bedroom."

"Are you complaining?" Greer asked, cocking a single brow.

"Not even a little bit." Dallas drew Greer flush against his chest. "You don't have to keep doing all this."

Greer's attention split between his honey's palms traveling a tantalizing trail down his back and his words causing a puff of breath to hit his heated skin.

"I choose you. Nothing will change that." Dallas reared his head back again, trying to look Greer in the eyes. "It's an oath easy to give. I feel like you should've been there for the groundbreaking, not here babysitting me. Go to Washington, focus on EnviroCapital. I'll be here, waiting for you."

"Do you promise you'll be here? In this house, away from all that chaos of your family," Greer asked, moving face to face with Dallas.

"If that's what you want." Dallas's voice was husky as he gave his promise. "Now, show me the plans. I'm interested."

"Wait." Greer placed both palms on Dallas's cheeks as he started to pull away. "Thank you for reading me so clearly." He angled Dallas's head for the sincerest kiss of his life.

CHAPTER 36

November, eight months later

With his arms crossed, Dallas leaned against the wall at the entrance of the studio, watching the inaugural cardio class with a room full of active participants. Skye led the class; a film crew followed her every move. She was such a natural in front of the camera. An incredible motivator and leader. Today, Skye had an extra bounce in her step. Probably due to the company vote last night making her a full-fledged partner of StreamTrainer. A place she'd deserved from the beginning.

The decision hadn't come without problems. Dallas and Ducky had strong-armed the vote, leaving Donny outraged at the idea of splitting the profits four ways.

Of course, the offer came with inherent risk. Their business was growing at an astronomical, almost inconceivable rate. Most days felt like a tightrope of balancing inventory, shipping, and monitoring the hundred thousand daily users. The only part of StreamTrainer that ran like a well-oiled machine were the classes. Those were always top tier, and Skye needed all the credit for those.

Dallas barely had an extra minute for a stationary bike these days, and those few times came during the long, lonely evenings when Greer was in Washington State. Greer spent three days a week there; he loved that project. Every so often, Dallas found the time to tag along, but the national sales position had become a small department of five salespeople and two assistants. They were growing faster than any of them thought possible.

"You should be giving up part of your shares to Skye," Donny hissed in his ear. "You're the one never around."

Dallas's shoulders tensed. He hoped Donny hadn't noticed. He ignored his brother and didn't budge a muscle to let him pass by. He and Donny had never truly gotten over their ugly fight after signing the investment contract all those months ago. Every time he looked at Donny, he saw judgment and aggression, remembering the fucked-up way Donny treated him while he was at the lowest point of his adult life. Dallas couldn't seem to let it go. He'd barely seen his parents since then either.

A war brewed underneath the surface between them. Dallas felt it in his bones. Until it came to a head, he wouldn't borrow problems.

Dallas never took his eyes off Skye as he spoke. "We sold twenty-three thousand boxes last month. I'm doing my share."

Donny gave a humorless laugh. "Yeah, with lots of help. Cari should've been a partner before Skye. She's family."

Dallas said nothing as the class came to an official end. He loved Cari. She was a sister to him, and she could at times calm Donny's rage. But she hadn't been much more than an occasional instructor in the early days. His brother had kept Cari at a distance on purpose. His growing arrogance demanded he be the bread-winning king of his castle.

"You're changing, brother. The clothes. The car. You're always gone. Ducky sees it too. This won't end well if you keep trying to live the high-life off the back of this company."

Dallas was certain his neck flushed under his indifferent pose. His jaw locked and ticced as he repeated Donny's usual slur. "Because I'm a headcase, right?"

"You always have been." Donny dropped his insult and turned away. Dallas listened to the measured step of his retreat. His brother had delivered the mean-spirited blow and didn't need to say another word. He was certain Donny had planned his attack, wanting to hurt Dallas after losing the vote against Skye.

Anger licked along his spine, begging him to confront Donny. Make the jerk eat those words by way of a fist to his hateful mouth.

The secret of juggling his life weighed heavy on his shoulders. Many days, most actually, Dallas kept his head down and lips sealed, doing what he should.

The pretense of his and Greer's relationship was almost non-existent. They kept it professional when Greer came to Dallas's office. Outside of that, they were a devoted couple. No matter how Greer tried, he couldn't keep his hands to himself, and Dallas didn't want him to. The life they shared was wonderful. They were so functional and loving.

Greer was his best friend. And he never wanted that to change.

"What'd you think?" Lost in thought, Dallas focused his attention on Skye, standing right in front of him with a beaming grin. "Don't let him get to you."

"I'm not. You don't either," he said, pushing off the wall.

"Not today, for sure." She squirted a long stream of water from her water bottle into her mouth. "The other studio's almost ready. Have you seen it?"

"It's been a few days," he said, nodding toward the new

filming studio, in the opposite direction of the way Donny had gone. "Show me?"

"Come on." The studios were side by side. They walked through the class participants while they gathered their belongings. He loved they were to the point of having full classes and smiled at many as they passed by.

The second studio was designed for professional filming—YouTube, the website, and commercials would be videoed there. It was smaller than the original studio, but sleek and brand new. Their logo lit the backdrop of the stage with professional lighting angled in all the right directions.

"I might have to come back and film classes," he said as he climbed the steps to the stage.

"You know you're the most requested instructor still to this day. I'd put you on the schedule anytime," she said, following him up.

All the happy feelings of success tingled along his skin. His pride in what they had accomplished swelled his chest. Less than two years ago, Dallas had absently brought the idea up to Ducky during a holiday dinner at his parents. Donny had inserted his contribution. A dream stated offhandedly, and here they were…

"We did it."

"You did it," she said, knocking him in the arm, heading toward the stationary bike.

"You too," he shot back, tucking his hands inside his slacks pockets. "You jumped in when we needed you the most. You made sure we had classes even when I couldn't pay you or handle the load myself."

"Best decision I've ever made." Her pretty, smiling face beamed up at him while she patted his belly. "Are you getting enough exercise? You seem to have a pretty cushy life." The laugh she gave caused him to laugh too.

Now that he was a man in love, in a life that he loved, he and Greer only worked out three days a week. What they did do very well was eat and drink together. Greer loved to share all sorts of new foods and wines with him. His body wasn't quite as hard as it used to be.

"All right, I'll take on a class or two when I'm in town. We finally seem to be leveling out in orders. At least until next month. I keep hearing about the January rush."

Skye stood with her feet apart, arms crossing over her chest, gaze calculating. "Do a YouTube class for me. It'll be a big deal that you're back. I heard we're having a twenty percent off sale for Black Friday weekend. Do a cameo that weekend too. It'll push those sales, I'm certain."

"You're like a dog with a bone," he teased, waving a hand in the air as if she were blowing smoke up his ass. "I think you give me too much credit."

"I don't think so," she said, trailing after him with a distinct whine in her voice. "Ducky and I miss you. I took a pizza over to his place a couple of nights ago. He actually ate with me. He keeps talking about wanting to wear his clothes like you and Greer do."

Greer had spent a significant amount of money on Dallas's clothing. His usual uniform of joggers had become slacks and a suit. Everything fit perfectly. Snug like a second skin. He'd seen Ducky give him the same eye he did Greer, scanning his clothes when he came in the room. He'd wondered what Ducky had thought.

"I have some news I haven't shared," she said.

"What's that?" he asked, watching her excitement grow.

"Evan and I are getting a dog." She looked so damn proud of herself.

Dallas kept his disparaging thoughts to himself as he remembered every dead plant she'd ever had. Plus, a goldfish or four that had to be flushed.

"A dog?"

"A little Boston. Someone Evan knows is selling them. He

should be old enough to move in when I move in with Evan." Now that was a long way of getting to the real point. Dallas's grin was immediate. He took her into his arms, giving her a big hug. One she gave back.

"Congratulations," he said against her hair then promptly dropped his arms, wanting her to step away. "You're sweaty. Girl sweat. Ew."

She didn't let him go. Her arms wrapped tighter around him. "You've made me very happy, Dallas. You didn't have to do what you did today. Thank you."

"A smart guy once told me, 'Go to your attorney. Run everything past him.'" After a second more, he made her loosen her hold to look her straight in the eyes. "There's risk involved, Skye. Evan will know someone independent to talk to."

"Are you sure you just don't want to give me a great big salary and call it done," she asked. After how excited she'd been when they offered her a partner position, he knew she didn't really want that.

"We're a family business. You're family. Stop trying to get out of it." He tucked her against his side, and she easily wrapped an arm around his waist. They walked side by side for several steps before she hip-bumped him. He looked down at her upturned face. She looked happy and content. All the things he'd ever wanted for her.

Stepping from his vehicle, Greer listened to the garage door churn closed as he stifled a yawn determined to happen. His normal parking spot had moved several inches to the left to make room for Dallas's new Tesla.

Every part of Greer's entire life had changed. Half the garage space, half the closet space, half the bathroom storage space. Dallas had made his house into a home. A loving, happy, sex-filled paradise.

Since boarding his flight this afternoon, Greer had thought of little more than his man and his bed. He hoped to talk Dallas into a quick nap before dinner. Then maybe they could get a fast bite to eat before a hearty round of fornication, and before a much longer overnight sleep.

The pace he'd been keeping was getting the best of him. He needed some downtime, a vacation. A trip somewhere relaxing. A beach with Dallas by his side wearing one of those tiny speedos.

His grin beamed as a fantasy played out in his head. A nude beach. All the sand and blue ocean and naked Dallas on display.

Greer reached for the doorknob, only then seeing the yellow sticky note stuck to the door. The simple words *"To the fridge"* scribbled in Dallas's efficient penmanship.

The fatigue seeped away. He cradled the note as if it were a love declaration. Dallas was so particularly good at those. After all this time, the romance between them had only grown. The excitement of knowing his love had prepared for his arrival home erased the concerns of his world.

He twisted the knob to open the door, feeling the love inside the home. Greer did as instructed. He went for the refrigerator to see his favorite IPA with another sticky note attached to a bottle opener that simply said, *"Exercise room."*

Greer took the beer, removed the cap, and took a long swallow. It hit the spot and he started down the hall to their workout room. The door was closed with two sticky notes stuck to the door. *"Shhh. Filming."* And *"Bedroom."* He removed both, stacking them on top of the others.

Carefully, Greer placed his ear to the door, hearing the rapid spin of the cycle's flywheel. Dallas's deep breathy tenor huffed out the workout. Greer smiled. His guy was out of breath. They both barely spent three hours a week working out and those hours were always together.

As much as he wanted to stick his head inside the room to get the visual of Dallas's hard body pumping out a workout, Greer again followed the directions to the bedroom where he found a folded pair of jeans and his beloved SMU sweatshirt on the bed. Socks and walking shoes on the floor. On top of the sweatshirt was another note. *"Dinner at Mac's. He's expecting us. The dresser."*

He turned to see a book there with a note that simply read, *"Page 241."*

Greer thumbed through the pages to see another sticky note. The word *I* was highlighted with a bright red arrow pointing to the letter. Dallas wrote *"Page 363"* beside the arrow. He turned there to see the word *"Missed"* with another red arrow pointing to that word with further directions scribbled on the note. *"Page 497."* He followed that instruction to see another sticky note with an arrow pointing to the word *"You."* Dallas's efficient script said, *"Welcome Home."*

All the effort made when a simple *Hello* would have sent Greer's toes curling. He removed those sticky notes to save in his secret place where he hid all Dallas's special notes.

He undressed as he went to the closet. He fished an old shoebox out of the farthest corner, surprised when he lifted the lid to see a box of Dude Sweet Chocolates sitting on top of his secret treasures. Dallas must have found his hiding place. There was another sticky note with Dallas's writing on top of the chocolates. *"Don't be mad. I wasn't snooping, I was stress cleaning. My special box is the Nike box in our office. <3"*

It wasn't hard to imagine Dallas embracing him, whispering those words in his ear. That was how his mister spoke of love. His whispered breath would send shock waves of shivers from his ear down his spine, tingling every nerve ending in his body. His life was complete. He found it hard to contain his joy. Greer took the chocolates out, he loved a sweet treat, but these were made better by knowing Dallas had gone out of his way to purchase them.

Greer stuck the notes together on top of each other inside the box then quickly dressed. In the bathroom, Dallas walked inside, and startled at the sight of him. "You're home. I didn't hear you come in."

He stood in front of the mirror, trying to push his thick blond hair back in place as he stared at Dallas in the mirror. "I wanted to bother you, but I got the *Shh*." His hair was forgotten as he turned away and met Dallas in the middle of the room. "Thank you for my notes and my chocolates and my cold beer."

"I promise I wasn't snooping. I clean and organize when I get antsy and that's hard here because everything is already so orderly." Dallas kissed him and pulled away, tugging his sweaty T-shirt over his head as if that drop of information wouldn't require explaining. "Give me ten minutes and I'll be ready."

Greer grabbed Dallas's wrist before he could get too far away and pulled Dallas back toward him. "What were you antsy about?"

"Nothing." Dallas shook his head then rolled his eyes. The look telling Greer more than the words that his mister was making fun of himself inside his own head. "I was here and alone and freaked out about the car payment."

Greer couldn't help the chuckle. Dallas was the thriftiest person he'd ever met. They had spent hours on a video call with Dallas fretting over the cost of the midrange Tesla.

Greer let go of Dallas's hand and swatted him on the butt. "Go dress."

"I should be paying more of my living expenses," Dallas started again for the zillionth time. His guy never gave on anything. He worried himself, and Greer, to death.

"Not having this conversation again. Go dress. I'm starving." Greer left Dallas alone in the bathroom and started toward his bed. A ten-minute catnap wasn't exactly what he wanted, but it would have to do.

CHAPTER 37

Two hours later, Mac's grill was hopping. As much as he missed his alone time with Greer, Dallas found himself relaxed and comfortable. The bar felt like home, and he couldn't find it in him to want to leave. Greer had moved them from their regular spot at the end of the bar out to one of the pub tables in the game room.

The plan had been to play a round of darts and listen to some classic tunes on Mac's new jukebox, but neither of them seemed too interested in starting a game. Instead, they stayed planted in their seats, listening to some old school songs they'd selected and made Marisol walk the length of the large room to continue waiting on them.

"Has he told you about the time he was robbed walking home?" Marisol asked, placing a new drink in front of Dallas.

"He what?" Dallas asked. His frantic gaze collided with Greer's irritated one as she put a clean napkin in front of him before placing his new glass there.

"My friends suck at having my back." Greer's frustration rang in his tone as he gave Marisol the stink-eye.

"So, it did happen?" Dallas encouraged.

Greer gave an exaggerated eye roll and slunk down in his seat as he lifted the glass to his lips. "We need to move. Another strong shove in favor of relocating to Seattle."

The only thing that could have redirected Dallas's thoughts from something as worrisome as being robbed was learning Greer had considered relocating. "Move? We haven't discussed moving to Seattle."

"It's a plan formulating right now, and I wasn't robbed necessarily…" Greer started, but Marisol cut him off with a sharp laugh, one Dallas had only heard once before. That one had been directed toward Greer too.

"Totally robbed," she confirmed with a single nod, driving her point home.

"Robbed," Mac agreed, sliding onto the empty stool between them.

"What happened was, I took the alley way home because it shaves about a block off the walk. It was my fault for being lazy. All they got was like twenty bucks," Greer explained, giving a shrug as if it were nothing and took another drink.

"Don't forget the right hook," Marisol added, holding the tray with their used glasses. She circled her eye for Dallas, indicating where Greer took the hit. "His eye was bruised for weeks."

"Greer…" Dallas started. They had walked to and from many of the restaurants on this street a hundred times now, because Greer insisted it was safe.

"Now, hang on, Dallas." Greer lifted a hand, stopping him from saying anything more. "During that same time, several people were mugged. Mac hired an undercover off-duty officer who's out there right now, I'm sure. So, it wasn't just me and the problem's solved. Marisol should have never brought it up," Greer said, swinging his head toward Marisol, giving her a punishing glare as Mac busted out with a hearty, loud laugh.

"He's telling the truth. We haven't had another problem," Marisol added, before turning away from the table. "Probably should've hired the officer before there was a problem, right, Mac?"

"Hey, now. Better to keep the focus on Greer," Mac said, losing the smile, drawing a laugh from anyone in hearing range. "How's that little baby girl doing?" Mac effectively and completely changed the subject.

Greer never missed a chance to brag on the newest member of the family, Olivia, Kailey's newborn baby girl. Greer pulled out his phone, quickly working the screen to bring up her latest picture. Kailey was sweet to include Dallas in the picture of the day. Every day, Kailey and Olivia dressed in matching outfits. He and Greer always got a slideshow of how cute the two looked together. Olivia was three months old and already a fashionista in training.

"Kailey feels like Olivia is a mini her, but I'm pretty sure I see a lot of me in that baby girl," Greer explained, handing his phone to Mac who started scrolling through his pictures.

"You think?" Mac asked, doubtingly.

Greer snapped the cell away as if Mac were too dumb to look any further at his pictures. "No one needs your negative energy." He lost himself again, staring down at Olivia then lifted his love-struck and slightly inebriated gaze to Dallas. "She looks like me, right?"

"Absolutely," Dallas nodded, hiding his smile by finishing his drink. Greer nodded his assertion and looked back down at the phone. Dallas started shaking his head *no* to Mac. Beau marked their baby. She was the spitting image of her father. "We should go. I have work tomorrow."

"Code for I'm about to get lucky," Greer said and lifted a hand across the table for a high five. Dallas left him hanging as he pushed off the chair.

"I'm glad you're home, Greer. Dallas always seems a little lost when you're out of town," Marisol said, coming back to the table. She took her job seriously, right there ready to take Dallas's empty glass.

"I like when we give Greer's secrets away better than mine," Dallas said to Greer's suddenly serious look. Greer didn't respond with one of his snarky comebacks. His expression turned thoughtful and focused. His gaze remained glued on Dallas as he pulled his wallet free.

"Lovesick," Mac added, chuckling, and knocking Dallas in his arm. "Did Dallas tell you he took that guy's money at darts last week? Had the whole place watching them play. He's a natural born hustler."

The serious look turned hard and had Greer's brows dropping into a hard V. Those amber eyes became laser beams as he said his teasing words. "You been playing fast and loose on me?"

"I won twenty bucks." Dallas nodded proudly and waggled his brow. "I decided I had a legit way to keep paying my car payment if things go south with StreamTrainer."

"Well then that changes everything. Daddy's got the big bucks." Greer reached across the bar, pushing Marisol her tip as he got to his feet.

"Y'all be safe getting home," Mac said, pushing off his barstool.

As Dallas started toward the front door, Greer's hand wrapped around his. They made it about three feet before Greer tightened his fingers around Dallas's, giving a firm squeeze. "Guy, huh?"

Dallas cast a quick glance in Greer's direction. Even then it took a second to decide if Greer was in fact jealous. Then a few more seconds to get past the absurdity of such a thought. Of course,

Greer wasn't jealous. What did he have to be envious over? That was Dallas's job in their relationship. "Straight, arrogant, asshole of a guy. Reminded me of Donny. I couldn't help myself."

Greer pushed open the door, urging Dallas out ahead of him. "I'm traveling too much if you're lonely and hustling other guys."

Dallas turned around, taking a couple of steps backward until he came to a stop in the middle of the parking lot. "Are you serious? I can't tell." What a laughable thought. Greer was messing with him. Dallas turned and started for the streetlight to cross. "Come on. The light's green."

He took off jogging and made it across the street before the streetlight changed to red. He looked over his shoulder. Greer wasn't there. He turned quickly the other direction, only to do a one-eighty to see Greer still on the other side of the street. Both Greer's hands raised in a what-the-hell gesture as they stared at one another.

"What's wrong?" Dallas called out.

"I don't know, Dallas." The tone and posture said that Greer did in fact know what had him upset and refused to budge a single inch.

What was happening?

Perhaps he was consumed with the green-eyed monster. Dallas was a beautiful man. Of course, other men would pay close attention to his guy.

Greer crossed his arms in frustration and pushed back on one foot, tapping the other. He stared at Dallas who glared right back at him. His brows dropped into a hard line as his annoyance at himself bloomed. Greer's fists went to his hips in frustration.

Dallas was soundly out of the closet now.

Ah, that was it.

He wasn't jealous but insecure and worried. He didn't like Dallas being lonely and out looking for something to fill his time. Greer should be there with him.

"Are you sure about us?" Greer called out.

"What?" Dallas asked in such a way that he might have really meant *that was the dumbest question a person could ask.* "Greer, I played darts with an asshole."

"Am I tying you down prematurely?" Asking the question out loud caused unbearable pain to slice across Greer's heart, causing him to lose his brazen attitude. Greer found it hard to breathe and lifted a hand to his heart, absently rubbing at the pain in his chest.

"Prematurely to what?" Dallas asked, either dodging the question, or he countered back with another really good point. Dallas wasn't heading in the same direction as Greer.

The light changed and Greer stepped off the curb at the same time Dallas did, coming for him. "I just played darts with a guy that kept taunting me because Marisol told him I could play."

"It's not that," Greer said, meeting Dallas at the halfway point and having the foresight to take this conversation to the other side of the street. He turned Dallas, taking his arm, and jogged through the three second beeping timer. "You haven't had time to find yourself. Should we give you more time?"

"Greer, it was darts," Dallas said, turning angry. He tore his arm from Greer's hold and stepped several feet away in the opposite direction of their home. "This is ridiculous."

"No, listen to me. We committed fast, maybe too fast." In a life dedicated to pleasing this one man, the weight of the implication of losing Dallas had Greer's shoulders slumping, and a heavy, pitiful sigh slipped free. He closed his eyes. The unbearable pain of his thoughts was too much to absorb.

"Are you saying it's too fast for you?" Dallas asked. His soft, hurt voice caused Greer to move past his own bullshit. Dallas was hurting and confused. His expressive face showed he had no idea what was happening. Greer took a deep cleansing inhale, letting the exhale release all the sudden bout of negativity and doubt, sobering him right up.

"Of course not. I'd marry you today if you'd let me. This is new for me too. I just don't want you to resent me later because you felt I pushed you too fast." The three feet separating them was the most Greer ever allowed between them. What was he doing? He started for Dallas, reaching out to take his hands in his. "I trust you. I don't know what just happened…"

"Greer, stop," Dallas said, twisting his hands until he entwined their fingers. "There's no one else I want. I would marry you today too—"

"Then marry me." The cool November breeze and the sound of traffic zipping past just feet away faded as he stared at the love of his life. His world revolved around this man. Dallas gave Greer the strength of peace and the drive of personal purpose. The disruption of chaos that had always run rampant through his head had settled into a distant memory. He never wanted to live a single day without Dallas in his life.

"Greer." Dallas lifted Greer's knuckles to his lips and pressed a kiss there. "The guy reminded me of Donny. You never get jealous over any…"

"Dallas." The calm Greer had grown to thrive within stared him straight in the eyes. His company's current growth and the projects he personally developed were benefiting wildly from the way Dallas had centered Greer. Dallas could have no real understanding of what he made possible in Greer's life. "I say this with all certainty. I'm ready to start our future. I'm so crazy in love with you. Marry me."

He sensed a distancing happening, not physical but emotional. Dallas stepped into him and clutched his hands tighter. Silly words slipped from Dallas's full lips. "Greer, you're such a good guy. We haven't even known each other a year."

Greer took better control of their moment. He was serious. This had been their course from the very beginning. "We're close to a year and we've been together every day for months and months. In gay years that's like fifty years. Marry me."

Confusion clouded Dallas's face. Greer had to remind himself that uncertainty didn't mean refusal. Greer stepped into Dallas, crowding him with determination. "I want to spend my life with you. I want what we have to last every day for the rest of our lives."

Dallas released his hands, lifting a loving palm to Greer's cheeks. The pad of his thumb left a sizzling trail over Greer's lower lip. "We're already doing that."

His sweet guy was giving Greer an out—one he didn't want at all. "I want you to be legally obligated to be there with me. I know you'll take your vow seriously. I will too. I love you. Say yes."

Dallas's green gaze turned from perplexed to tender. His pouty lips relaxed into a smile. All his love's telltale signs of giving in. "You know I'll follow wherever you lead. I guess that means down the aisle."

"I love you." Greer captured Dallas's mouth with his. Dallas opened for him, and Greer didn't hesitate, his tongue searching Dallas's, sealing their fate. The kiss was meant to be light, but Dallas wrapped a hand around Greer's bicep, drawing him snugly against his body. The other arm anchored around his waist, exactly where Greer wanted to be.

A long loud, honk from a passing vehicle had Greer tearing from the sweet kiss. A guy hung from the window as he yelled, "Get a room!"

Greer turned his heated gaze to the car. "He just said *yes!*" he yelled as if the occupants of the speeding car could hear him.

Dallas's hand came to Greer's jaw, turning him back. "Let's go home. Then ask me again there so we don't have to have our special place be out here on the street."

"I can do that." Greer slid under Dallas's arm, letting his warmth guide him all the way home.

CHAPTER 38

Warm lips pressed against Dallas's temple, drawing him from a deep, sound sleep. He always slept better when Greer was home. Maybe because Greer had a gentle touch when turning Dallas to his belly when he got too loud. He smiled and started to roll to his stomach only to find he was already there. He opened his eyes to see Greer sitting on the edge of the bed.

"Time to wake up, handsome."

Dallas closed his lids and rolled to his back, throwing his arm over his eyes. Why were the overhead lights on?

"The god-awful sounds that come from you…"

A giant jaw cracking yawn made it hard to say, "Ha. I'm awake. What time is it?"

"Seven fifteen."

Dallas's eyes popped open, and he turned his head to see the sun peeking from underneath the curtains. Greer's long-sleeve knit-covered arm came around Dallas's waist and he gave a hip bump to scoot Dallas's further over.

Greer's natural state of gorgeousness was set off by the casual look that didn't really feel relaxed. The amber knit pullover matched the color of his eyes. His hair had the perfect swoosh and his arm dangled with the leather strap bracelets Dallas had purchased for him on one of their overnight trips to a beach cleanup. As pretty as his guy was, they were at the beginning of a workweek. Greer's work uniform was always a tailored suit and silk tie.

"Why're you dressed that way?"

"I've taken some liberties," Greer started, waggling his brows. His mister overstepping himself happened so regularly that Dallas was completely desensitized to the probable invasion to his life and nodded for Greer to continue. "I sent an email to your assistant to reschedule your day. I got us in for a marriage license." Greer tilted his head, looking proud of himself. "Not to brag, but I pulled strings. We can marry today if you want. Lucky you."

Greer's sexy smirk and waggling brow drew a smile from Dallas. Excitement vibrated through him and his heart started a steady thump. "I am lucky. Are you serious?"

He gave Dallas that look that told him he wasn't kidding. "I have the rings. Did you already find them?"

"You have wedding rings?" Dallas asked. Any lingering sleep faded. He sat up, pushing back against the headboard and rubbing his eyes. His fuzzy brain grappled with all these love-infused bombs Greer tossed around.

He'd meant every word when he'd said he wanted to spend the rest of his life with Greer. Clearly, Greer wanted that too.

"Yeah. I'm weird, I know. I bought the set in May because I wanted them on hand when the time came. You know I always knew you were the one," Greer explained as if it was the most normal thing in the world. "They're serviceable plain bands to get the job done. You can take your time to pick something else out that better suits you."

"You're always thoughtful." Dallas gave Greer's thigh a gentle squeeze.

He hoped he hid the surprise at how quickly Greer had put his plans into action. They'd only talked about getting married last night with no mention of today being their wedding day. He should have known once Greer got something in his head there would be no holding back.

"Should we invite our families?"

Maybe for the first time ever, Greer didn't have a ready response. His honey blinked at him for several long seconds. He opened his mouth, closed it again and blinked. A mischievous twinkle hit Greer's gaze as he grinned. "Do we really like anyone well enough to want them there?"

Greer had a point, but obligation and responsibility always needled at Dallas's reasoning. "I think I should tell my family. Marriage is a big deal. We shouldn't start our lives together with lies and secrets."

"Babe, you're being a downer. You feeling okay?" Greer brought his hand to Dallas's forehead, testing to see if he might have a fever. "If you've changed your mind..."

"No, I haven't." Dallas laughed, moving out from under Greer's teasing touch. He rolled out of bed from the other side. "I thought about this a lot last night. I should at least tell my family, even invite them. I was wondering about having a small ceremony here. Invite our families. If they don't come, then that's on them."

"Okay. So, something small here this weekend then?" Greer asked, not really requiring an answer. He was in thought mode. As Dallas started toward the bathroom, Greer followed without giving any of his normal morning gropes or pats. He must really be caught up in thought. "I'll agree to the day change if I don't have to invite my family. Just Kailey because no one wants my parents here. And if we can still have honeymoon sex tonight."

"I think we always have honeymoon sex. You don't have to worry about that," Dallas said, reaching for the shower faucet.

"Good answer." Greer stayed close, but far enough away to keep from getting the spray of water on him. "I don't know how comfortable I am with you approaching your family. That seems very dark and unsure to me."

"I'm stronger now," Dallas said, stepping into the warm water. "They can get on board or not, but the holidays are coming. I want to spend that time with you. If we're to the point of getting married, I can't continue to lead a double life. That's not fair to you. And what happens when we have children?"

Greer studied the tiles at Dallas's feet unable to hide his concern until Dallas mentioned children. His gaze jerked up with a beaming grin. "All right. I agree to your terms."

Dallas chuckled at the way Greer thought about everything. They were always negotiating. He reached for the shampoo, listening to Greer think and talk, setting his new plan.

"Marriage license today. I'll get Kailey on a quick midday wedding here this weekend. And you're going to promise me you won't go emotionally low if your parents refuse to come."

"Because I'm the headcase?" Dallas teased halfheartedly, before ducking his head in the water to rinse away the soap.

When he came out from under the spray, Greer was closer and in his line of vision. "Don't go there, even joking. I want to bury your brother for the way he treats you." Greer's full lips pressed into a straight line, showing his sincere aggravation. "Get dressed and let's go get our marriage license. I'll wait in the living room because I really want to take care of that." Greer pointed to his plump cock, his body's natural reaction to Greer being within ten feet.

Dallas ducked his head, sucking some water into his mouth to squirt at Greer who anticipated the move and quickly hopped out of his way.

"I'll be out in a few minutes."

Greer swore he heard a pop of bubblegum on the other end of the line before his sister started to speak again. She worked best while chomping on gum. Right now, she was creating miracles. It might be a two pieces of gum kind of afternoon.

"Mac's handling the food and drink. He also knows a baker who's going to do a rush two-tier wedding cake in wedding cake flavor. I know you like that, Greer. I hope Dallas does too."

His gaze lifted to Dallas who reached for a can of water in the refrigerator. "Do you like wedding cake flavor?"

Greer had been dealing with an internal struggle over how hard he was pushing Dallas, but the sweet, doe-eyed look his mister gave him, with their marriage license lying in the center of the island between them, filled Greer with the warmth and reassurance that only Dallas could give him.

"Is that a flavor?" Dallas asked before taking a long drink.

"What flavor of wedding cake do you want?" he countered.

"I don't care at all."

"I'm going to say wedding cake flavor is fine," Greer said to Kailey.

"I've planned for me, Beau, and Olivia, Evan and Skye, Mac and his wife, and Ducky. If Marisol isn't running the restaurant, she's invited. If Ducky has a plus one, that's fine too." Kailey lowered her voice as if Dallas might hear. "Should I plan for the rest of Dallas's family to attend?"

Despite everything Dallas had said, Greer wasn't a hundred percent sure Dallas could hold strong against his hateful family. He could see a struggle coming for them. Before he considered Dallas's parents, they had Donny to contend with. If the brothers' relationship went any further south, Greer would have no choice but to become involved on behalf of the investors. Of course, he'd always side with Dallas, putting Donny on the losing side.

"I guess it won't hurt, but unlikely."

"Okay. Want me to tell mom and dad?"

Kailey knew how to ask all the suck-ass questions. Of course, he didn't want his parents there. He would rather Dallas be legally bound to him first, so he didn't go running away when he finally met them. "I'll send them an email on Sunday."

"All right, big brother. I just received an email. The justice of the peace confirmed he'll be there at ten forty-five Saturday morning. The dry cleaner will be by your house in the morning. Leave your suits at the door to be cleaned. I'm supposing Dallas has something to wear. Your credit card's been in overdrive in the men's department. I'm guessing all that was for Dallas, right?"

"Yup." His eyes remained on Dallas. Greer had styled Dallas as if he were his very own Ken doll. Luckily, Dallas seemed receptive to the idea and appreciative of Greer's efforts. "Let's get Ducky into Nieman's for a fitting."

Dallas gave him a thumbs up at the idea and said, "I'll call him this afternoon and tell him to call Kailey. He likes the way your clothes fit. He talks about it all the time."

"I heard Dallas. I'll let them know about Ducky. I've also arranged for boutonnieres and two large bouquets on pedestals. If the weather holds, I see this happening by the swimming pool because Dallas loves that part of the house. I wanted to have a backdrop of someplace pretty for the pictures. I've got to call the photographer back, and I'll be there early to guide everyone. Beau promises to be on time with Olivia. We'll see."

"Thank you for all you're doing." Greer did appreciate the seriousness with which Kailey made sure they had a special, simple day as Dallas had requested.

"Thank you, Kailey," Dallas called out. His mister hadn't heard a word of what she planned, but his appreciation came from a lifetime of gratitude. Greer was working hard to be that same man.

"You two have a good day. I love you both." Kailey disconnected the call as Dallas came toward him.

Greer put the phone on the island and turned on the barstool as Dallas slid between his parted thighs, letting Dallas know his fate. "You have seventy-two hours to change your mind."

Dallas's endearing gaze had Greer's inside doing a little flip. His man. How did he ever get so lucky?

"There's not a chance I'll change my mind," Dallas countered with a hint of a challenge, as if there even was one. Greer lifted as he started off the stool. Dallas leaned in. Their lips met and lingered. Where Greer may have wanted this kiss to lead to the bedroom, Dallas kept it short and pulled away.

"We need to move the furniture around. Have you checked the weather? Can we have the wedding outside Saturday morning?" Dallas pulled his own cell phone from his pocket, most likely checking the weather himself as he turned away and started outside. Greer's ass hit the barstool again, watching Dallas go. Boy, he loved that ass bounce.

CHAPTER 39

The traffic from downtown Dallas to Grand Prairie, Texas, was unusually light for this hour of the morning. Dallas hoped that was some sort of foreshadowing of how this might play out for him. Who was he trying to kid? No way his parents were going to be anything other than pissed off.

He nervously gripped the steering wheel of his old Camry a little tighter than necessary as he forced measured breaths from his lungs to keep from hyperventilating. He took the curve onto his parents' street and let go of a steadying exhale as he pulled to the curb in front of their house.

Dallas hadn't yet told his parents about his new car. They'd think it was flashy and unnecessary, a waste of perfectly good money. Looking for two approvals in one day might be pressing his luck. Dallas flipped down the visor, checked his hair in the tiny mirror, then stared himself in the eyes.

He was nervous.

What did he hope would happen?

Maybe that should have been his running mantra for the ride over instead so he could rein in any good karma he may have earned over the course of his life.

Honestly, he didn't know what he wanted. He wasn't the same man he used to be. The idea of putting himself last and living by everyone else's rules was no longer an option.

Those were hard lines for him. No compromise.

His confidence built, but it honestly wasn't that shaky to begin with. He no longer sought his parents' approval. Especially his father's. He wanted to be viewed as his own man. One living his own life, asking nothing from anyone.

He also wanted to be respectful and be respected in return.

The beep on his cell phone drew his attention down to the console. With a flip of the hand, he closed the visor then picked up the phone. Greer had sent a message.

"I'm sending you all my good thoughts. Call me when you're done."

Dallas pushed call in lieu of sending a return text and reached for the door handle, pushing open the car door.

"Hello." Greer sounded pleasant yet unsure which brought a smile to Dallas.

"Before I rock my parents' world, are you sure you don't have plans to leave me at the altar?" Dallas asked teasingly, putting a foot on the pavement while taking in the clear fresh morning air and almost cloudless sky. What a beautiful day. That had to mean something.

"Not on your life. I'm not sure I can be any more certain. You're the one for me," Greer drawled in that fun way he had.

"Hmm." Dallas's gaze cut back through the window toward the small house. The opposition to his complete happiness sat like a heavy cloud over his childhood home.

The insecurity was back in waves.

"Let's see. No, we're not rushing it. Of course, I really love you. Yes, you're the perfect man for me. Did I hit any of the doubts you're suddenly having?"

"Maybe," Dallas said, getting to his feet. Greer did make him stronger.

"You should have let me come with you. Or better, sent our parents a joint email on Sunday morning." Greer chuckled. "We could have done a group message so they could all get to know one another."

"I'm telling them more than we're getting married. This is my official coming out. I need to do it in person." Dallas took slow strides around the hood of the car to the curb of the sidewalk.

"There are no rules that say you need to do this face to face. Get in your car, come back home, and we'll do it together the coward's way."

Dallas lifted a foot to the curb with a smile tugging at the corner of his lips when his parents' front door burst open.

"Andy! Don't do this!"

Dallas's gaze jerked to his angry father barreling forward with a newspaper in hand. His father looked tired, but that was the third shift wearing on his face. The anger though was a surprise.

"What the fuck is this?" his father bellowed.

Dallas lowered the phone and stopped dead in his tracks. He could feel a sick calm descending over him. His normal defense mechanisms shielding him from his irate father stalking toward him.

"Dallas, just go," his mother yelled, holding her robe closed as she ran after his father. "Give us time, honey."

"Time for what?" Dallas asked, refusing to take the small step backward as his father charged at him.

"Dammit, I knew it."

Dallas braced for a slap or a punch when his father hurled the newspaper at him. It wasn't the small bundle that Dallas thought when he started to duck. Instead it was one page that fluttered in his face. Dallas caught it with his free hand but never took his eyes off his father.

"You make me a goddamn laughingstock." His father's hand flew out, missing Dallas by a few inches as he cast a menacing glare over his shoulder at his mother. "I told you he needed something stricter. We're not standing for this. I'm not standing for this."

His father stalked within half a foot of his chest, yelling his anger in Dallas's face. He was sure the entire neighborhood had to be at their front windows to see what was causing all this ruckus.

"I don't know what you're talking about, Dad."

His mother had finally made it to his side, tearing the newspaper from his hand. She turned it over, sticking it in his face, but he'd learned years ago to never look away from his father. The unexpected hits hurt the worst.

"Please, let's go inside. Andy, don't do this out here. He's our son."

"I wanna see him deny it." His father's finger pointed in his face. "Goddamn you."

"You'll embarrass him." His mother broke into tears.

"I don't care. He's fuckin' embarrassed me for the whole goddamn city to see." Only then did Dallas quickly venture a look at the newspaper. The headline read, "Thank You Grand Prairie For A Year To Remember." The advertisement was placed by the Boys & Girls Club.

The loud pounding of his heart drowned anything more being said. There was a picture of him with Greer. Greer leaned over his shoulder, whispering in Dallas's ear. The caption read, "March's highlight: the highest bid—Greer Lockhart outbid the room for a date with crowd favorite, Dallas Reigns." He hadn't even realized someone had taken their picture. The night that Greer bid on him seemed like so long ago now.

His stomach churned, his lungs seized, refusing to draw in oxygen. He was left dizzy and unsure. How had he never considered something like this happening?

Luckily, a settling of relief calmed him as he thought of a life with Greer. His lungs relaxed, allowing him to take a much-needed breath before he passed out. One step down, another to go. He no longer had to fear how his parents would take his coming out. They had done exactly as he had expected.

His father's mouth was moving, his mother stood between them, and he didn't care in the least. His foundation of strength was unshakeable. Greer had been the one to give him such a sturdy base. He spoke loudly, drawing both his mother and father's attention.

"I guess this makes the reason why I'm here a little easier to say. I'm getting married on Saturday morning. I'd like you two to attend. It's a small service at Greer's home—"

"You're what?" his father burst out, advancing on him. Dallas had no choice but to move back several steps and start for the car's door. He knew that look in his old man's eyes, fists would be flying soon. Dallas refused to lower himself to fighting with his father. Hell, this was already too much for a Thursday morning.

"I had hoped for a reasonable conversation." Dallas reached for the car door, pushing it open as a barrier between him and his father. "I found love. I love him, and he loves me. We're getting married Saturday morning. We want children and a family. If you can see past all your hatred, then we'd like you to be there. If not, that's your choice."

At this rate, if his father didn't calm down, he'd have a heart attack right there in the street. His face was as red as he'd ever seen. It was time to go. Dallas dropped down in the driver's side seat and shut the door.

He tossed his cell phone in the cubby and started the engine. His mother stood on the sidewalk openly weeping. That might have been the hardest part of it all. Dallas dropped the gear shift into reverse then the car gave an awful cracking sound and began to rock. His father's heavy fist slammed down on top of the hood.

Thank God, he hadn't driven his new baby. Within seconds, he stepped on the gas, peeling out as he shot backward down the street. His gaze stayed focused in the rearview mirror until he could back into a driveway. He quickly shifted gears and headed out of the neighborhood the same way he'd come in.

He only looked back once. His angry, tantrum throwing father was having a full-on fit in the street, stomping on the newspaper. His mother had turned away, heading back inside the house.

An earsplitting whistle had Dallas looking down at the cell phone in his cubby. He picked it up, taking the curve out onto the main road.

Oh hell. Greer was still on the phone. He had to have heard it all.

"Dallas, talk to me."

Dammit. He quickly lifted the phone to his ear. "Hey. I'm sorry you had to hear all that."

"Are you okay?" Greer asked in his hard-edged tone.

"Yeah." Weirdly, he was. He somehow felt in the midst of it all that everything was going to be okay. All his new shields had fallen easily into place, protecting him from such intense hate. There was so much adrenaline flowing through his veins, he felt almost invincible. The dread and oppressive weight he'd shouldered for most of his life had vanished.

Maybe he should pull the car over.

No. He really was okay.

"Dallas, are you there?"

"Yeah. I was assessing the truth of my *yeah*, and I'm truly good. My luck's not particularly good though or maybe it is, I don't know." Dallas was rambling, so he just clamped his mouth shut to keep from doing a verbal dump on Greer.

"What happened?" Greer's soft tone meant that Dallas sounded more manic than he realized.

He let out an exhale and turned on the next available side street, pulling his car over. He pressed on the brake and dropped his forehead to the steering wheel. "When I got there, my father must have seen me pull up. While I was talking to you, he came barreling out the door. He was angry, and my mom followed. She was upset. The local newspaper was in his hand. I guess the Boys & Girls Club did a special thank-you for the great year and..."

"Oh no," Greer said, instantly.

"Yup." The timing couldn't have been any better. His gaze lifted out the window, taking stock of his surroundings. He saw the back side of his apartment building. He'd forgotten this back way and started down the residential street. "You were the highest bidder. They highlighted your donation with the shot of you whispering in my ear."

"Your father got the paper this morning and exploded. Got it. You handled it very well, Dallas."

"I don't know if I did or not. I didn't do anything to try to de-escalate the problem. I'm sure I added insult by inviting them to the wedding, but I don't care." Dallas pulled his car up to the security box and typed in their private code. The gate opened, letting him inside. "I should warn Ducky and Skye, but her car's not here and Ducky's been riding with her to the office. I'll drive by there."

"Where are you?" Greer asked.

"I picked up my old car. I haven't told them about the new one. They'd think it was too much money," he tried to explain, parking the car in the lot. He'd kept this car hoping Ducky might want to learn to drive.

"It's your money." Dallas almost mouthed Greer's response, knowing what he'd say.

"I know." The edge had worn off and Dallas found himself smiling as he left the car to switch to the Tesla. "Let me go by the office then I'm coming home. Donny's gonna find out soon, and we don't need a meltdown at the office."

"If you want me to come get you, I can. I should have gone," Greer said, guilt in his tone.

Dallas gave a bark of a laugh. "Definitely, shouldn't have come."

After months on the decline, Greer's pacing roared back with a vengeance.

Damn this over-the-top emotion coursing through every fiber of his being. Surely to God, this level of mania would ease over time. Maybe once he and Dallas had years under their belts, he might be able to handle Dallas's abusive family. But that wasn't today.

Right now, he wanted to bury those motherfuckers for their continued abuse.

Greer looked down at his wristwatch, keeping track of the time. He was antsy as hell.

The hard knock at his front door had Greer looking toward the entry, surprised to see he'd been walking the U-shape of his home. Damn, it was a shame he didn't have X-ray vision so he could see through the walls between him and the front entry.

The dry cleaner. Right. He'd forgotten.

Greer grabbed their pre-decided wedding clothes and started for the front door as the forceful pounding started in earnest.

"Hang on," he called out, his voice as hard as his thoughts.

As he reached for the doorknob, Donny's angry voice echoed in the entryway. "I know you're in there. Open the goddamn door."

Greer's hand fisted, he paused even as his brow arched at the solid wood separating him from Donny. He never backed away from anything. Those lessons had been hard earned a long time ago, but this was Dallas's family.

What would his love want him to do? Probably not give the guy a right hook in lieu of a greeting. Everything slowed on the exhale as he forced himself to calm. It wasn't easy, and he wasn't sure he was successful as he straightened his spine and opened the door, tossing the suits aside.

"Where is he?" Donny demanded. His chest heaved, and he stood in fight stance with his hands fisted, a newspaper in one of them.

Oh hell. Greer could only shake his head and said the first thing that came to mind. "You need to calm the fuck down. Once your brother and I are married, I'm not going to allow you to continue to hurt him like this."

"What the fuck are you gonna do?" Donny hurled, mockingly. Livid laughter laced each word. "Where's my brother?"

"He's not here..." Greer started, but Donny cut him off.

"Bullshit!" Donny scanned the house behind Greer as if he were lying. "Now I get what the fuck's going on. Did my brother have to suck your dick to get you to work with us?" He advanced as he spoke, and Greer dug in his heels, determined no one was getting past him. "Is that why he's gotten away without doing jack to help run our company?" Donny jammed his finger into Greer's chest. "Mine and Duncan's company?"

"Donny, this is your last chance..." Even getting robbed on the side of the road hadn't pissed Greer off like this. And that was before fucking Donny cut him off mid-sentence again.

"I'm not having a fag brother. It's not gonna happen." The offensive words reared Greer back, and Donny took advantage, shouldering past Greer into the house. He yelled as if Dallas would hide and cower to this dumb fuck. "He knew the deal. Where the lines were drawn. And he didn't fucking care. So why should I? Dallas! Get your ass out here, you pansy ass."

Greer's restraint reached its peak. "Donny, get out of my

house…"

Donny whirled around on Greer, stalking back toward him. "You know Dallas is a fucking head case, right? This is how he's always been. He can't keep a goddamn straight thought. He'll ruin everything you have like he's ruined everything my whole life. I want out. I should have never gotten involved with him in the first place. I knew fucking better."

"Dallas is gay, Donny, and it's been the hardest fight of his life. I've spent some part of every day with him for almost the last year. I know Dallas like I know myself. Your brother is a good man. Maybe the best man I know. He's no headcase or whatever you keep calling him. The way your family has treated him has caused untold damage—"

"You don't know what the fuck you're talking about. I was there. All my parents ever did was try to help him."

And the *motherfucker* cut him off again.

He could do little more than laugh a sinister sound in Donny's face. Greer moved in closer, done with this conversation. "Help? You call that help?"

"What's going on?" Ducky asked quietly from the front door. Greer risked a glance over his shoulder to see Skye standing behind Ducky who had come to a dead stop in the middle of his doorway.

"You knew about this, didn't you?" Donny accused Ducky. His youngest brother didn't back away. He stayed calm, tucking his hands inside his front jean pockets.

"About Dallas and Greer getting married? Yeah. Why're you here?"

Donny's angry gaze clashed with Greer's. "Married? You're getting married to Dallas?" His hands flew in the air as if this whole thing wasn't worth a second more of his time. "I want out. I'm so out of this. I'll start my own goddamn company." Donny's finger shot out, pointing in Greer's face. "If you try to lowball me, I'll shut this whole goddamn deal down, and we can fight it out in court. This is bullshit and it's fucking gross." Through Donny's dramatics, he turned aggressive, staring at Ducky who took a large single step to the side, letting Skye in through the door. "I bet you're a goddamn fag too."

"I'm bi," Ducky said as he leaned against the small entryway table. Clearly, comfortable with himself and this situation. Since Dallas wasn't there, Skye hovered close to Ducky just as Dallas might do, but Ducky didn't need it. He was the solid young man Greer had gotten to know. "How y'all treated Dallas made sure that I'd never tell any of y'all about my sexuality. It wasn't right what you did to him. It fucked him up for a long time because he only ever wanted y'all's acceptance. That's not right. He's not wrong."

The pulsing vein in Donny's forehead might have actually burst with the way he drew back in outrage. Greer was ready to light a match to this guy. Let the fucker know exactly who ran this show and the provisions Greer had added to the contract for this very possibility. Donny could easily be cut loose, and would be, without a backward glance.

Fuck the guy for trying to intimidate him with his violence and threats.

"What's going on?" Dallas asked. Skye hurriedly stepped aside, letting Dallas in, but he didn't come far.

"Fuck you. You remember, you fucking did this." Donny started to leave but flexed his muscles at Ducky in a show of force. Ducky gave a small shake of his head and visually shrugged Donny off. Dallas's instincts got the best of him. He threw out an arm, protecting Ducky. At the same time, he reached for Donny who automatically reared back to throw a punch.

Greer's blood boiled, but before he could react, Dallas blocked the incoming fist and executed a maneuver that made Greer's inner wrestler sing with joy. Within three seconds, Dallas, who out-matched Donny in both size and bulk, had him pinned in some sort of physical restraining hold. A move he'd seen used before on children intent on self-harm.

Donny hadn't known what hit him and instantly freaked the fuck out, fighting to be released.

Dallas easily kept his hold and propelled his brother out the door. When he let go, he sent Donny staggering backward several feet. Remarkably, Dallas didn't immediately combust under such hatred aimed his way.

His protective man kept his big body between Donny and the three of them. Donny looked damn well ready to pounce. Several tense seconds passed where Greer wondered if there wouldn't be a full-fledged brawl in his front yard.

"This is why you did this," Donny hurled. Spit and venom flew out of his awful mouth. "You put Skye in to vote me out. Fuck you. You're all gonna pay." Donny punched the air, his angry gaze landing on Greer. "You'll be hearing from my lawyer."

"Unnecessary. Be at my office in two hours," Greer called out, coming to stand beside Dallas.

"Greer," Dallas warned quietly, never taking his eyes off the threat.

"Fuck you all. Lockhart, you're gonna be sorry, you can trust that. He's fucked up," Donny tossed out his final insult and spun around, stalking through the yard toward his truck.

The rumble of the engine echoed off the houses, quickly followed by the squeal of tires on pavement. He didn't even bother to look in the direction of all the commotion. Donny wasn't his concern. "Is everyone all right?" Greer asked, taking Dallas by the forearm and guiding him inside the house. "Are you okay, Ducky?'

"Did you see that Donny peed on himself a little bit? I bet he hates he did that," Ducky said by way of an answer. Some knowing look exchanged between the two brothers before Dallas reached out a hand and drew Ducky into a tight hug.

"My mom called me about the picture in the newspaper," Skye started, coming to the brothers. Standing inches away, she looked deeply concerned. Dallas reached out a hand and included her in their hug. "We tried to call you, but it kept going to voicemail, so we came."

Greer's hand went to Ducky's shoulder, giving him a gentle squeeze and a pat. Ducky had stood up for Dallas in a big way, even forcing his own outing. "Are you okay?"

"Yeah," Ducky said, moving out of Dallas's and Skye's hold. "Are you okay?" Ducky asked Dallas.

"Yeah, I guess," Dallas answered honestly, replacing Ducky with Greer, taking him into his arms for a tight, soul-connecting embrace. Greer should be offering this comfort to Dallas, but instead, focused on releasing the fear of Dallas recoiling back into himself and pushing Greer away. "I'm sorry. It never occurred to me that he'd come over here like that."

"Don't," Greer whispered in Dallas's ear. He forced himself out of the hold. The anger building at what Dallas had suffered this morning for the simple act of loving him vibrated throughout him. "Are we good with removing Donny from the team?" Greer knew he should give this decision a minute to settle, but Donny was a destructor in the making. Waiting even two hours could blow StreamTrainer up. Donny needed to be reminded of his non-disclosure agreement and be given his payout options as soon as possible. "Can you handle Donny's department on his departure, Ducky?"

"Yeah," Ducky said as if it were a no-brainer. "We hired a consultant a few months ago because we grew out of Donny's knowledge base." Ducky did his signature move and crossed his arms over his chest. "It's a company Tristan used to develop their WilderBooks hardware."

"Wait a second," Skye said, interrupting them. "Do you know your brother came out?"

"What?" Dallas asked, his whole focus and concern landed on Ducky.

"Yeah." Ducky turned his attention to Dallas with a big smile splitting his face. "Seemed the right time. I can't let you keep going through it alone."

"Brother." Dallas came forward, drawing Ducky to him again in a hug, crushing his youngest brother to his chest with his arms still crossed. "You never told me."

As much as Greer wanted to be in this moment, he caught Dallas's eye and nodded toward the door. "I need to go to the office. You all stay together until I can sort things out. I'll call you when I can."

Dallas let go of Ducky, his worried gaze scanning the length of Greer's body. "What're you planning to do?"

"What I need to do." Greer gathered his keys and started for the garage. He struggled to push all the emotion aside. Apparently, Dallas overrode his ability to reason.

He had to think.

CHAPTER 40

The force of Greer's trimmed fingernails digging into his palms had to be drawing blood. Almost three hours since Donny's outburst inside Greer's home and nothing had tamed Greer's frustration or Donny's hatred. Not even Donny's pretty wife, who Greer had never met before, could tamp down her husband's insulting, vicious mouth. Boy, it was hard to stomach anyone who made Greer's own family seem loving. Yet, Donny did that in spades.

"You gotta be kidding me. My low estimate of StreamTrainer's value comes in at about twenty-five million dollars," Donny said arrogantly. Of course, he had nothing to back that number up except a hastily written piece of paper with what looked like chicken scratch scribbled on top. Donny had gone so far as to laugh at the generous offer detailed by Greer's lawyer in a folder that sat untouched in front of Donny.

Even more astonishing, Donny seemed unfazed by the legal repercussions of their ironclad contract. In the case of a family disagreement, the majority party rules. If an agreement can't be reached by the family, then Greer becomes the decision maker. Donny's hard head refused to see he had no real options.

"This offer to buy StreamTrainer"—his lawyer said, reaching across the conference room table for the folder, opening it to the second page—"was made two days ago and exceeds the current value of the company by almost double."

Greer's steely gaze stayed trained on Donny as he said, "Your share is a more than generous offer that comes off the table if you walk away."

Donny's sinister sneer had Greer's eyes narrowing. Fuck this guy. They could spend the next however many years in court hashing shit out for all he cared.

Greer pushed back from the table, looking at Evan, who had volunteered to be in the meeting for moral support, then at his attorney. "He's a fool. If he walks away, withdraw the offer. We'll see him in court. Either way, his ownership of StreamTrainer has come to an end, effective yesterday."

He took long strides toward the conference room doors, refusing to waste another minute of his day or his life dealing with that stupid, arrogant fuck. He pushed through the door to see Kailey standing feet away, talking on her cell phone in a whisper. Her gaze lifted to meet his. She went silent until the door shut behind Greer.

"It's Dallas," she said in hushed tones. Her hand extended, giving him the cell phone. He took it, never stopping his long stride to his personal office. Of course, Kailey followed.

"Babe, hang on." Once inside his office, he turned with his doorknob in hand, shutting the door once Kailey made it inside. "Why're you at work? I'm paying you to be on maternity leave. Olivia needs you with her."

"She's in good hands. I wanted to be here if you need me," she said quietly, blowing off Greer's concern with a carefree wave of her hand. "Did he accept the offer?"

"Not yet." He lifted a finger to his lips to silence her. No one but the people in the conference room and Kailey knew the terms of his offer. Not even Dallas. Especially not Dallas. Greer had gathered every available dollar he had, lumped it together and wrote Donny a check for his fifth of the value of the business.

"Greer." Dallas's troubled voice drew him to their conversation. "What did you offer?"

Greer had initiated and put in place some hard rules where he and Dallas were concerned. They agreed to never lie to one another. As naïve as it sounded, Greer wanted their relationship to be based on the truth, no matter the circumstance. Now, it seemed like the dumbest idea on the planet. Why would he have ever put that commitment to voice and then had Dallas return the oath? Stupid, silly love.

"You're being too quiet," Dallas prompted.

"Babe," Greer started on a sigh, "I'm not sure I've told you, but I received an offer from Bike World a few days ago."

Kailey rolled her eyes and went for his office chair. She believed omitting facts was the same thing as lying. Greer didn't hold her same beliefs. Thankfully.

"Offer for what? StreamTrainer?"

"Yes. Biker World offered fifteen million dollars—" Greer started to explain.

"What?" Dallas exclaimed loud enough for Kailey to hear. She looked up from picking at one of her fingernails, her brows lifting at him. "They offered fifteen million to buy this company? Did you take it?"

"Of course not." Greer smiled at Dallas's excitement as he started for the window. "You guys are building a name for yourselves. The industry's watching. There'll be a magic number when we start to pay attention to the incoming offers…"

"I say fifteen million dollars. My God," Dallas said, flabbergasted. His mister was a healing balm, washing away the last traces of Greer's anxiety. He closed his eyes and turned teasing.

"I say two hundred million dollars." Greer's grin grew at Dallas's silence. Man, he was a lucky guy. "Are you still there, babe?"

"Did he go silent?" Kailey asked.

"He did." Greer looked back over his shoulder, winked, and nodded.

"I thought so." Kailey's singsong laugh made Greer chuckle too. "He'll get used to you tossing around numbers like that."

"I don't know if you're joking around or if you've lost your mind," Dallas finally said.

He turned toward Kailey, grinning like a Cheshire cat as his ass hit the windowpane. Dallas sounded good, and even under all the pressure, they felt solid. This might as well be like having one of their random chats throughout the day.

"Would you still love me if I did lose my mind?" Greer asked, teasingly.

"Greer. How much did you offer Donny? Can we afford it?" Dallas asked, his tone turning firm.

"Eventually. StreamTrainer will be able to pay me back. And if not, that's okay too. It's part of the risk," Greer explained. It was how he saw it too.

"Tell me the number," Dallas replied.

"I don't want to," Greer countered happily.

"I'm coming up there."

"*No.*" He pushed his ass off the window as if that alone had the power to stop Dallas. "Where you think you're not worth anything, Donny thinks he's worth everything. Stay away, Dallas. I'm serious. He's either going to accept my offer or we'll enact the provision I set in the contract which states we'll pay his salary through the end of next year and call it done. Either way, you guys are protected. This new offer has a tiered payout with a stronger, long-term NDA. It's generous."

After a moment of Dallas's complete silence, Greer looked down at the phone to see if they were still connected. They were, so he waited.

"Greer, our individual balances are off in our relationship. You give more—"

"Love, I feel that way about you every day. You're too good a guy for the likes of me. Please let me feel like I'm balancing out contributions to us." Greer turned back to the window. This time he saw the electrician's beginning to install the Christmas lights on the property ahead of the Thanksgiving holiday. They had more important things to discuss than money. "How are you doing with it all? I didn't stick around long enough to know."

"I was fine until you started talking about money. Two hundred million dollars? I was hoping to consistently earn a hundred thousand dollars a year."

Greer grinned again and lowered his voice, teasing when he said, "Woo. Daddy makes the big bucks. I'm gonna be living like a king."

It worked. Dallas barked out a laugh as Kailey's high heels hit the floor and she started for the door. "This is taking an unexpected turn into something I'm not going to be able to scrub from my brain."

The knock on the door had Kailey stopping in her tracks, and Greer turning to look that direction.

"Answer it, Kailey. I'll call you back, Dallas."

"Not on your life." Dallas's voice hardened.

Greer couldn't make himself hang up, no matter how badly he wished he could. He wanted Dallas to always see him as a man who could move mountains. Not one who utterly failed to protect his love when it mattered the most.

Evan stood in the doorway. Donny and Cari waited several feet away at the top of the staircase.

"We need your signature and to get copies made. Can you handle that for me, Kailey?" Evan asked, sounding serious and stern. The giant grin and thumbs-up he hid in the middle of his chest where Donny couldn't see told Greer everything he wanted to know.

Kailey rushed to take the paperwork and started for his desk. She had a pen in hand, extending it to Greer before he got there.

"Did he agree to the terms of the new NDA?" Greer asked, hopefully loud enough for Donny to hear.

"Yes. And all payments will cease if the terms are broken."

Greer scribbled his initials and name where Kailey pointed. He whispered for her ears only. "Work at lightning speed."

"Got it," she nodded, gathering the papers and starting for the door.

"Evan, will you stay with her?" Greer asked. Who knew when the ticking time bomb out there might blow.

"Of course." When the office door shut, Greer let go of a pent-up breath as his ass hit the edge of his desk.

Greer's relief was staggering. The dark cloud of worry over Dallas's family that had hung over him for months and months had fizzled into nothing. He and Dallas had weathered the storm together and had come out on the other side. His hand instinctively lifted the cell phone to his ear.

"Did you hear all that?"

"Enough to hear Donny took the deal," Dallas said. "Ducky's with me now. We promise to pay you back every dime."

"I know you will. I have no fear. Listen, Ducky's got a lot about to hit him with your family. Talk him into staying with us for the next few weeks. We'll deal with it all together."

"I'll tell him but I don't think he will. He's got a gaming tournament this weekend and into next week. I'm hearing that he's reserved a suite at Escape properties for his team. He's taking some days off. They've already got the place set up with their computer equipment. The team's name is Team StreamTrainer Extreme. Our wedding is messing with their play time. We've been instructed to be efficient with the ceremony." Dallas chuckled as he spoke that last line. He could hear Ducky talking and laughing too. Greer's gaze lowered to the floor, his smile growing along with the brothers' revelry. He loved his new family. "He's bringing his new gaming laptop. A lot's changed with him since I've been preoccupied with you."

"You two sound good," Greer murmured.

"I'm worried about what you just did, but the rest feels healthy and freeing. Ducky's nodding too. Skye's heading a class, but I think she would agree."

Greer pushed off the desk. He had work to do. "If Donny bothers you or Ducky, he forfeits the payouts. Make sure I know if he does. I love you. Check in with me in a bit."

"Thank you," Dallas said in his most sincere voice.

"It was nothing you wouldn't do for me." Greer took his seat and booted up his desktop, letting that be enough.

CHAPTER 41

The soft sounds of a slow dance tune began to play, pulling Dallas from his deep concentration. He read recipes on his cell phone and committed an ingredient list to paper for a homemade Thanksgiving dinner.

They still had a couple of weeks before the big holiday. Who knew if he and Greer had the kahunas to pull off cooking such a large meal, but it seemed to help Dallas's nervous energy to plan, and he loved turkey and dressing with cranberry sauce, so he guessed they were going to try.

"Greer, did you know that the outside packaging of butter is marked with lines to indicate individual tablespoons sizes and it's also marked by cups? The measurements are done for us," Dallas called out, amazed at such a simple, ingenious idea. "I wonder what else is packaged like that?"

Greer's proximity startled the shit out of him as a strong palm slid down his arm to lift his hand, giving a solid tug to pull him off the stool. "I did know. Come dance with me. Tomorrow's our wedding day. We need a bachelor party."

Dallas let himself be coerced into the center of the living room and into Greer's arms. "How long does this last?"

"What?" Greer came flush against his body and murmured against his ear.

"All this romance. You're really good at it."

Greer must have approved of his question and his answer. His full lips pressed against Dallas's whiskered jaw, right below his ear. "I'm only good at it because it's you. Are you doing okay? You seem to be good, but you've been through a lot in the last two days."

Their bodies fit perfectly together as if they were made to be just this way. Dallas's arms locked around Greer as they swayed to the sultry sounds. He wasn't sure what to make of his family. His parents and Donny had gone radio silent. Ducky hadn't heard from any of them either. Waiting for the other shoe to drop sucked, but he also refused to borrow problems.

Besides, Greer made it hard to think past this moment with the enticing scent of his cologne and his hard chest rubbing against Dallas's. Those perfect lips kissed a trail back to his ear.

"Let's talk about the honeymoon."

Dallas's eyelids slid closed. His head bent into Greer's kisses. "I know money's tight right now. You never let me pay for anything. I should pay for a honeymoon…" Their bodies stilled. Greer's chest rumbled before the chuckle left his lips. The laugh turned to a full body thing as Greer reared back, his bright smile in place.

"I'm not that broke. All I did was pull together the cash I could get my hands in a two-hour window. Where should we go?"

Dallas arched a brow, trying to decide if Greer was laughing at him or with him. For peace's sake, he decided on the latter.

"When can we go?" he asked, taking Greer by the hips and pulling him back into the embrace.

"Maybe over Christmas break? January will be busy for you," Greer said, sliding his arms around Dallas's neck, staying face to face this time. "Switzerland is breathtaking during the holidays. Maybe Norway or the Bavarian forest of Germany. Their holiday markets are a sight to behold. Of course, we could go to New York." Greer's brows waggled in intrigue. "Or I could take you to Seattle. It's been a long time since you've been there with me. So much has changed."

Dallas gave the slightest roll of his eyes. Of course, Greer wanted to go to Washington State any chance he got. Every week, he tried to talk Dallas into tagging along with him.

"Let's negotiate. The twenty-sixth, we'll go to Seattle for the week, but we should be here for Christmas day. Ducky might not have a place to go, and I don't want to leave him like that yet."

Greer nodded before Dallas ever finished the thought. "Agreed. Did he tell you he's coming early tomorrow morning so I can help dress him?"

"You don't understand what a big deal that is. His League of Legends tournament is an annual competition he and his team prepare for year-round. It never occurred to me that we had a conflict." Honestly, it surprised Dallas that Ducky hadn't tried to bail on the wedding. That was how important this tournament was to his brother.

Greer's cell phone rang, vibrating against Dallas's thigh. He immediately shook his head *no*. "I meant to turn my ringer off. We're in wedding mode. Ignore it."

"What if it's something about tomorrow?" Dallas asked. This time he was the reason they stopped moving.

"I don't care," Greer said boldly. But ultimately, he did care just as Dallas knew he would, and finally gave in to the ring, fishing the phone from his pocket. He looked up as he accepted the call, putting it to his ear. "It's Skye. Hello?"

Greer's jaw tightened and his eyes turned serious, staring at Dallas. "Your mom is with Skye's mother and they're on their way over. They should be here any time now."

Dallas took the phone and stepped back as all the color drained from Greer's face. Not now and not here.

"Skye, stop them. It's not the time for negativity. We're getting married tomorrow. I don't want all this hanging over us," Dallas said, his take charge attitude stiffened his resolve. His family added too much baggage, and Greer had had to shoulder the brunt of their abuse. When was too much exactly too much? He was such a burden to Greer already. "Tell her I'll meet with her next week."

"Dallas, they'll be there soon. I was in a class. I think Ducky gave them the address. He talked to her. She's left your dad and is staying with my mom. She wants to apologize. They both want to come to the wedding in the morning." Skye sounded unsure and rushed.

His mother leaving his father. *What?*

That threw him completely for a loop. "They?"

"My mom and your mom."

"Someone's here," Greer said, heading to the windows facing the front yard.

Ducky shouldn't have taken this on himself. Dallas's shoulders tensed into granite as he realized this was the other fucking shoe. *Fuck.* He went toward the front door.

"I've gotta go, Skye." Dallas ended the call and extended his hand toward Greer, handing him the phone. "Let me go talk to them."

"No, Dallas." Greer reached out to take the phone then gripped Dallas's shirt, drawing him closer. "Let them in."

His panicked thoughts raced as he shook his head. "No, it's too much. I've put us through too much." The fist holding on to Dallas, gripped tighter.

"Breathe, Dallas. It's okay. Relax. At least they care enough to come. Where are my parents?"

Dallas took a centering breath and took Greer's wrist, prying his fingers loose. "Not the same thing. Why would your parents be here? You didn't tell them about us." He had to fight the panic taking hold of his reasoning. Dallas yanked open the door, prepared to handle this before it ever could get started. His mother standing there with red-rimmed wide eyes rendered him speechless. Her tears formed instantly, spilling down her cheeks. Skye's mother stood directly behind her. She stared imploringly at Dallas.

His mother let out a shuddered breath and started shaking her head before digging a tissue from the purse hanging on her arm. "I told myself I wouldn't do this. Dallas, I'm sorry. I'm so sorry for everything."

"Mom." Everything around him faded as he stared down at his grief-stricken mother. His heart broke. Over the years of his life, he'd seen too many tears in her eyes.

"No, son, I'm sorry for everything…" she said as he reached for her, having no idea why except he didn't want her to cry.

"Dallas. Invite her in," Greer said, jarring him into action.

He extended his arm, sweeping it around her back, and stepped out of the way, encouraging her inside. "Come in, Mom."

She was barely inside when her gaze met Greer's. Mrs. Wells, Skye's mother, patted his arm, following his mom inside.

"This is Greer, Mom."

Greer stood with his hands in his slacks pockets, looking as handsome as he always did. Greer searched his face before he looked down at his mom and nodded.

"This is my mom, Vicki. And Mrs. Wells, Skye's mom."

=♥=

Desperation wafted off Vicki Reigns in waves. As much as Greer had judged her poorly was exactly how much he wanted to ease her genuine sorrow her own actions had caused. "Come in, Mrs. Reigns. Have a seat."

"I'm Sheila," Skye's mother said to Greer as she shut the door behind her.

"I don't want to intrude," Vicki started, wringing her hands. Tears spilled down her cheeks as she spoke. "You're getting married tomorrow. I didn't want to wait to tell you how sorry I am. What I allowed to happen to you breaks my heart. You've always been my world, always. I'm sorry I was never strong enough to stop your father."

Greer tried to read Dallas's expression as she held all his attention. Confusion, maybe reserve, appeared to hold Dallas's tongue.

"I watched you stand up to him and gathered my strength from you. I left him this morning. I'm done. Donny is so much like your father. Duncan's like me. But you… You're smart and reasonable. You never deserved what he did to you. I tried to help make it better, easier…"

"It's okay, Mom." Dallas finally stopped the tumble of her words and drew his mother into his arms. She reached around Dallas's back, holding him tight as she closed her eyes. Greer shoved his hands deeper into his pockets, fisting them to prevent himself from reaching out and offering comfort to both Dallas and his mother. He so badly wanted to do just that.

Dallas's face angled away from Greer as he placed a cheek against her hair and tightened his hold. His chest quivered, most likely tearing up. Dallas was too good a guy not to respond to his mother's evident pain. Vicki's eyes opened; she stared at Greer for several long seconds.

"You're very handsome." Her arms tightened around Dallas, giving him a stronger hug. Greer's love lifted his head. As suspected, tears glittered in those beautiful green eyes as his gaze met Greer's. His arms loosened, but she held on tight.

"Thank you. I love your son with all my heart," he said, trying for a reassuring smile.

His words seemed to be the catalyst for her to let Dallas go and look up at her son, her palm lifting to caress his cheek. A path Greer's hand had taken many times over. "That's what I want for Dallas. He deserves a great love and a good life. I've always known he'll only marry once."

"Mom…" Dallas started. His cheeks flushed as he looked over at Greer and shook his head. Vicki only smiled and took tissues from her purse, wiping them over her eyes.

"Is the invitation still open for me tomorrow?" she asked, pushing the wad back into her purse. It seemed to be her bag of tricks. She pulled a water bottle out next.

The pause in Dallas's answer had Greer changing the direction of his approving nod.

"It's important to me that tomorrow's special. You know I want you here, but I can't allow all the drama that follows my family around."

What a healthy, direct, self-caring thing for Dallas to say. Greer's heart swelled. Dallas's road hadn't been an easy one. Greer had feared he'd pushed them too hard and fast. He was so proud and impressed.

"I'm on your side. I'll never let your father or Donny hurt you or Duncan again."

Dallas's indecision turned to helplessness as he shrugged and sought Greer's gaze. The question was clear, but Greer shrugged, leaving the answer to Dallas.

"I understand if you don't want me here, but I'm still going to start working on showing you how serious I am. I want to be in your new life, and I want to get to know Greer."

"Dallas." Greer found himself pleading on this woman's behalf.

"I want you here, Mom. But I've worked hard to pull myself together. And I've put Greer through hell getting us to this point."

Greer could only shake his head at the ridiculousness of the idea of putting him through hell. He'd been given the world. Dallas took him for who he was, no one had ever accepted him the way Dallas had.

"I say she's welcome." Greer extended a hand to the wallflower standing right against the door, almost unnoticed. "Ms. Wells, of course you're invited too. Skye's a large part of our life."

"I'd love to come." When she smiled, he saw Skye. This whole group of people were real and genuine, and everything he'd always craved from the world. Greer's heart was so full, and his palm rested absently against his chest. Mrs. Reigns took Dallas into her arms again, lifting on her tiptoes. She whispered something in his ear, and Dallas nodded, his stare focused on the floor. When he lifted, he had tears in his eyes again.

"I love you, too, Mom. I always have."

Mrs. Reigns nodded. She looked sheepishly at Greer with her kind eyes. Dallas's eyes. When she reached for him, he had no choice but to be drawn into a tight, loving hug.

"Ducky tells me Dallas is very happy with you. Thank you."

"I'm glad to hear it. I only want to make Dallas happy." All the tears started again, including his and Sheila's. "Please come in. I won't let Dallas spend the night away from me. It's a long story that makes me sound controlling, so let's leave that there."

Dallas chuckled.

The tension swirling around them lightened and he started for the living room. "Would you like something to drink or have you had dinner?"

"We haven't eaten." Mrs. Reigns shook her head, seeming to like the offer of more time with them. She looked over her shoulder to Skye's mother still in the entryway, hopeful and eager. "Can we stay a little longer, Sheila?"

The woman finally pried herself from the door and followed them inside. "Yes. I'd like to."

"Do you want to take them out to eat?" Dallas asked, his love and hope vibrating in every word spoken.

"I'm in. Let's go to Mac's. They always make room," he said, reaching inside his back slacks pocket to see if his wallet was there. He looked over at Ms. Wells as he spoke. "You'll have to drive. We're a two-seater family."

"My car's big enough to hold us all. Skye called and is on the phone now, listening to everything." Sheila lifted her cell phone in her hand. "She had a feeling this was going to work out this way and says they have a table ready for us at Mac's, like you said. She says Kailey is almost there and Beau's on his way. Evan's with them."

Of course, they were there waiting. Greer nodded. His family was a caring, obtrusive mess. He reached out to encourage his mister out first. Dallas unexpectedly lifted his hand, taking Greer's. His guy didn't try to hide their bond, making Greer's heart swell with pride.

"You good?"

"I'm good," Greer answered honestly. And he was. Very good.

EPILOGUE

The bright blue sky and gentle breeze held little interest for Dallas today. He stood close to the trinkling waterfall. One of his favorite places in the backyard. But he was transfixed by something far more interesting this morning, the jeweled depths of Greer's sparkling stare.

Dallas couldn't help all the self-reflection he'd been doing. Over the past year, his life had fundamentally changed. He lived with his true self leading the way. At times, it stunned him how lucky he was, and today was one of those days. He stood at his matrimonial altar, surrounded by family and friends. The people who meant the most to him. He hadn't lost everyone as he had feared.

His mother, who had done her fair share of crying, and Ducky were there to witness his exchange of vows. Of course, his father hadn't shown up, nor had his brother, Donny, or Cari for that matter. Not that he'd expected them to celebrate his and Greer's big day. They'd both made their opinions and decisions clear. It hurt knowing they despised him for who he was, but he was working through that with Greer's help.

The biggest lesson he'd learned this year was the one playing like a loop in the back of his head. It didn't do any good to dwell on things he couldn't change. That was their choice and he doubted they would ever come around.

Despite their hate, Dallas had found love and his heart was overflowing.

The brief exchange of vows was etched into Dallas's heart and memory, never to be forgotten.

To have and to hold, for better or for worse, in sickness and in health.

He easily committed those things to Greer who declared his love back with such raw emotion lacing each of his words that tears came to Greer's eyes.

He'd never forget the love they shared today and tightened his hold on Greer's hands. His wedding ring was going to take a lot of getting used to. Greer had surprised him with a diamond band, something unique and beautiful, if maybe a little over the top. Of course, it fit as if it were made especially for him. Just like the man who placed it on his finger.

"I know this is the moment you've both been waiting for. It's my honor to declare you married in life, for life. You may seal your vows with a kiss."

Tears filled Greer's eyes as he came forward, taking Dallas's cheeks between his palms.

"Don't cry," Dallas whispered, stepping into Greer.

The moment might have been too much. Dallas may have broken down along with Greer except Kailey's loud wail burst the love-infused bubble and increased in both volume and theatrics. She had cried for most of the ceremony, hitting the sobbing point about the time they said *I do.*

Dallas looked over at her, concerned. Beau held her in his arms and shrugged. When he looked back, Greer had also turned. His look, though, wasn't concern, but more a shut-the-hell-up look directed at his sister.

"Keep going," she instructed with a hiccup. "I'm sorry. Post-pregnancy hormones. I'm happy for you. Stop looking at me. Kiss him." She waved her handkerchief-filled hand in their direction.

Dallas couldn't help but chuckle at the dramatics. Kailey had become the little sister he'd always wanted. Although he could have done without the weeping interruptions since he was eager to start his life with the man standing in front of him.

He had found his family. Solid and true.

Dallas reached for Greer's chin, turning him back. "You heard her. Kiss me."

"I'll love you forever." Greer's lips pressed against his then retreated. "And ever." Greer kissed him again. "And ever."

Dallas smiled. His heart filled with happiness. "I'll love you back just as long."

The End

NOTE FROM THE AUTHOR

Send a quick email to kindle@kindlealexander.com and let us know what you think of Breakaway. For more information on future works click here to sign-up for our new release newsletter or come friend us on all the major social networking sites.

ABOUT KINDLE ALEXANDER

Amazon international number one best selling and award-winning author Kindle Alexander is an innovative writer who writes contemporary male male romance and erotica. It's always a surprise to see what's coming next! Happily married with too many children and dogs, living in the suburbs of Dallas.

Usually I try for funny. Humor is an important part of my life – I love to laugh and it seems to be the thing I do in most situations – regardless of the situation, but jokes can be a tricky deal. I don't want to offend anyone and humor tends to offend. So instead, I'm going to tell you about Kindle.

I tragically lost my sixteen-year-old daughter to a drunk driver. She had just been at home, it was early in the night and I heard the accident happen. I'll never forget that moment. The sirens were immediate and something inside me just knew. I left my house, drove straight to the accident on nothing more than instinct. I got to be there when my little girl died – weirdly, I consider that a true gift from above. She didn't have to be alone.

That time in my life was terrible. It's everything you imagine times about a billion. I love that kid. I loved being her mother and I loved watching her grow into this incredibly beautiful person, both inside and out. She was such a gift to me. To have her ripped away so suddenly broke me.

Her name was Kindle. Honest to goodness – it was her name and she died a few weeks before Amazon announced their brand new ereader. She had no idea the Kindle was coming out and she would have finally gotten her name on something! Try finding a ruler with the name Kindle on it…Never happened.

Through the course of that crippling event I was lucky enough to know my writing partner. I would have never gotten through those dark days without her unwavering support and guidance. There wasn't a time she wasn't there for me. For the first time I used the hand offered. I know without question I wouldn't be here today without her. It takes a special person to stand beside someone at a time like that. I will love her forever. I could go on and on about both of them, but I won't and now you know a little more About Us.

Website

https://kindlealexander.com

New Release Email Sign Up

https://www.kindlealexander.com/contact-us/

Newsletter Sign Up

http://www.subscribepage.com/s8y4c3_copy

Amazon Author Page

http://amzn.to/2hKE4YA

Facebook Author Page

https://www.facebook.com/AuthorKindleAlexander/

Twitter

https://twitter.com/KindleAlexander

BookBub

https://www.bookbub.com/authors/kindle-alexander

BOOKS BY KINDLE ALEXANDER

If you enjoyed *Breakaway* then you won't want to miss
Kindle Alexander's bestselling novels:

Reservations
Painted On My Heart
The Current Between Us
Closet Confession
Secret
Texas Pride

Nice Guys Novels
Double Full
Full Disclosure
Full Domain

Tattoos and Ties
Havoc
Order

Better If Read Together
The Current Between Us
Secret
Painted On My Heart

Always & Forever
Always
Forever

ALWAYS

KINDLE ALEXANDER

Winner, Book Execellence Award, 2020

Book of the Year 2014 Member Choice Awards

Goodreads MM Romance

Book of the Year 2014

Sinfully Sexy Book

LGBT Book of the Year 2015 eLit Awards

Born to a prestigious political family, Avery Adams plays as hard as he works. The gorgeous, charismatic attorney is used to getting what he wants, even the frequent one-night stands that earn him his well-deserved playboy reputation. When some of the most prominent men in politics suggest he run for senate, Avery decides the time has come to follow in his grandfather's footsteps. With a strategy in place and the campaign wheels rolling, Avery is ready to jump on the legislative fast track, full steam ahead. But no amount of planning prepares him for the handsome, uptight restaurateur who might derail his political future.

Easy isn't even in the top thousand words to describe Kane Dalton's life after his father, a devout Southern Baptist minister, kicks him out of the family home for questioning his sexual orientation. Despite all the rotten tomatoes life throws his way, Kane makes something of himself. Between owning a thriving upscale Italian restaurant in the heart of downtown Minneapolis and managing his long-term boyfriend, his plate is full. He struggles to get past the teachings of his childhood to fully accept his sexuality and rid himself of the doubts brought on by his religious upbringing. The last thing he needs is the yummy, sophisticated, blond-haired distraction sitting at table thirty-four.

Best if Read Together

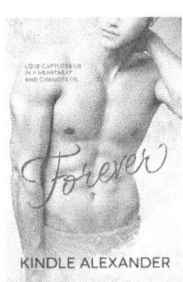

HAVOC

(Tattoos and Ties Duet Book 1)

Keyes Dixon's life is challenging enough as a full patch member of the Disciples of Havoc Motorcycle Club but being a gay biker leaves him traveling down one tough road. With an abusive past and his vow to the club cementing his future, he doesn't believe in love and steers clear of commitment. But a midnight ride leads to a chance meeting with a sexy distraction that has him going down quicker than a Harley on ice.

Cocky Assistant District Attorney Alec Pierce lives in the shadow of his politically connected family. A life of privilege doesn't equal a life of love, a fact made obvious at every family gathering. Driven yet lonely, Alec yields to his family's demands for his career path, hoping for the acceptance he craves. Until he meets a gorgeous biker who tips the scales in the favor of truth and he can no longer live a lie.

Can two men from completely different worlds…and sides of the law… find common ground, or will all their desires only wreak Havoc?

Tattoos and Ties Duet

PAINTED ON MY HEART

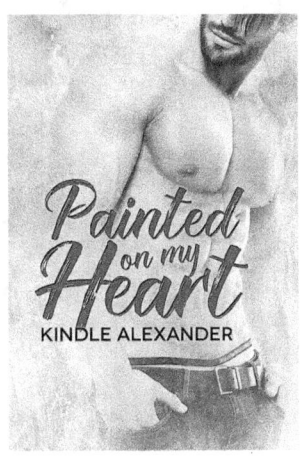

Winner of the 2017 eLit Award Romance category

Winner of the 2017 eLit Award LGBT Fiction category

Artist Kellus Hardin let love and loyalty cloud his past decisions, a mistake he definitely won't make again. Now, lost and alone, he's left to pick up the shattered pieces of his broken heart while facing the truth of his reality.

Arik Layne exudes power, confidence, and determination. But when an encounter with the guarded artist shakes him to the core and alters all his future goals, he finds more than just his heart on the line.

For Kellus, opening himself to love isn't an option.

All Arik wants is to make the artist his.

Can love create a masterpiece when it's painted on your heart?

FULL DISCLOSURE
(Nice Guys 2)

Book of the Year 2014 ~Sinfully Sexy Book

Deputy United States Marshal Mitch Knox apprehends fugitives for a living. His calm, cool, collected attitude and devastatingly handsome good looks earn him a well-deserved bad boy reputation, both in the field and out. While away on an assignment, he blows off some steam at a notorious Dallas nightclub. Solving the case that has plagued him for months takes a sudden backseat to finding out all there is to know about the gorgeous, shy blond sitting alone at the bar.

Texas State Trooper Cody Turner is moving up the ranks, well on his way to his dream of being a Texas Ranger. While on a two-week mandatory vacation, he plans to relax and help out on his family's farm. Mitch is the last distraction Cody needs, but the tatted up temptation that walks into the bar and steals his baseball cap is too hard to ignore.

As Mitch's case gains nationwide attention, how will he convince the sexy state trooper that giving him a chance won't jeopardize his life's plan...especially when the evil he's tracking brings the hate directly to his doorstep, threatening more than just their careers.

SECRET

Silver Award Book of the Year, 2015 elit Awards

Tristan Wilder, self-made millionaire and devastatingly handsome CEO of Wilder-Nation is on the verge of a very lucrative buyout. With tough negotiations ahead, he's armed with his acquisition pitch, ready to launch the deal of a lifetime. There's just one glitch. The last thing he expects is to fall for the hot business owner he's trying to sway.

Dylan Reeves, computer science engineer and founder of the very successful social media site, Secret, is faced with a life-altering decision. A devoted family man with three kids and a wife, Dylan has been living a secret for years. Fiercely loyal to his convictions, his boundaries blur after meeting the striking owner of the corporation interested in acquiring his company. For the first time in his life, reckless desire consumes him when the gorgeous computer mogul makes an offer he can't refuse.

WHAT READERS ARE SAYING ABOUT KINDLE ALEXANDER BOOKS

Secret

"INSPIRING, HONEST, BRAVE, RELEVANT—A MUST READ!!!"

~ Natasha is a Book Junkie

"This is a powerful story and truly one of Kindle Alexander's best books."

~ Beyond the Valley of the Books

"Secret tells the story of men who are mature enough to value integrity over pleasure and know that loving each other means caring about the others priorities."

~Indie Bookshelf

Full Disclosure

"In the end… OMG the end… let's just say Mitch and Cody have their happy, one that touched my heart."

~Denise, Shh Mom's Reading

"I give this story five+ perfectly delivered stars."

~Toni FGMAMTC

"Mitch and Cody are perfect and so bloody hot, it made my IPAD melt."

~Jules Swoon Worthy